CRIMSON INK

A Novel of Modern Iran

GAIL MADJZOUB

Copyright©2019Gail L. Madjzoub
All rights reserved.
ISBN:

*To the ones
whose faith
can neither be silenced
nor imprisoned.*

Your resilience evokes awe.

'O Son of man!
Write all that We have revealed unto thee
with the ink of light
upon the tablet of thy spirit.
Should this not be in thy power,
then make thine ink
of the essence of thy heart.
If this thou canst not do,
then write with that crimson ink
that hath been shed in My path.
Sweeter indeed is this to Me than all else,
that its light may endure forever.

- The Hidden Words

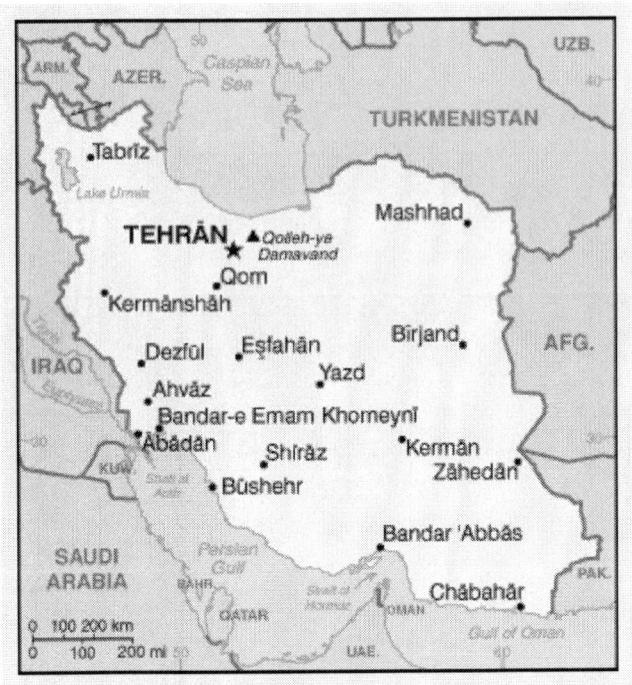

MAP OF IRAN

CRIMSON INK – a novel of modern Iran by Gail Madjzoub

CHARACTER FAMILY TREES (1)

(Major and important characters in bold face)

JALILI / AZADEH AND HASHEMI FAMILIES
(Farah and Reza are siblings)

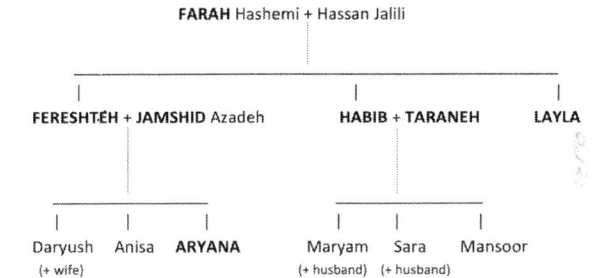

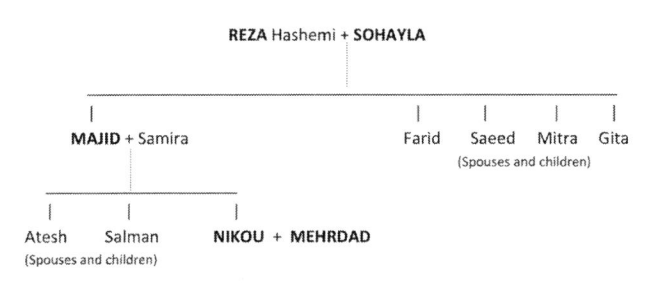

FARAH Hashemi + Hassan Jalili

FERESHTEH + JAMSHID Azadeh	**HABIB + TARANEH** **LAYLA**
Daryush Anisa **ARYANA**	Maryam Sara Mansoor
(+ wife)	(+ husband) (+ husband)

REZA Hashemi + **SOHAYLA**

MAJID + Samira   Farid   Saeed   Mitra   Gita
                          (Spouses and children)

Atesh   Salman   **NIKOU + MEHRDAD**
(Spouses and children)

2019©Gail Madjzoub

vii

CRIMSON INK – a novel of modern Iran by Gail Madjzoub

CHARACTER FAMILY TREES (2)

RAHIMI FAMILY

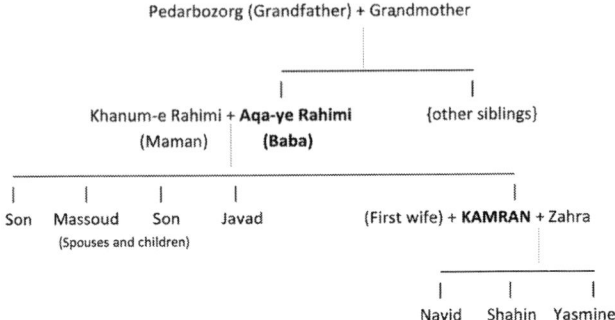

OMIDVAR FAMILY

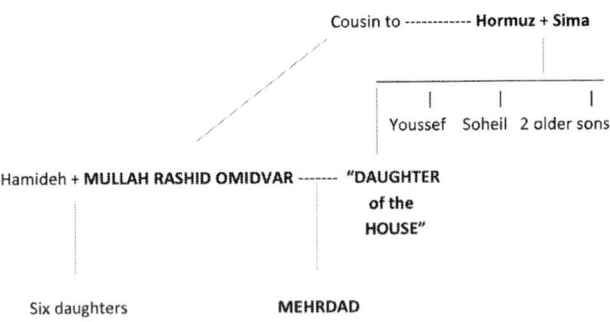

2019©Gail Madjzoub

BOOK ONE

PRE-REVOLUTION
1955 – 1978

Prologue

**Hurmuzak,
Province of Yazd, Iran
28 July, 1955**

Another drop joined the rivulets of sweat that had already saturated the collar of her plain cotton blouse. She blinked as it passed her eye, but kept her focus on the yard outside the tiny window. The hum of cicadas, a constant thrum in the noon heat, was the only sound. Not a breath of wind disturbed the dust or rustled the tall dry grass in the field outside the little compound. No cloud interrupted the perfect blue of the sun-drenched sky.

How long had she been watching? Munirih was dimly aware of the aches in her limbs and a growing gnawing in her stomach and she shifted her position. The movement brought her out of her reverie: how different it all had been last summer! The crops were maturing and they had already been making plans for the harvesting. In the cool evenings they would all gather in the tiny copse and enjoy refreshing cups of sekanjabin while sharing the day's news, telling stories and laughing together. The older children joined in and the little ones were safe in their beds.

Safe.

She shook her head to clear it and thought about eating something. *But no, better wait until Esfandiar returns.* She hoped and prayed he would return. They would eat together. *I'll plate a bite to eat he'll continue the watch.*

THEY ATE the meager meal slowly, exchanging the news in low murmurs. Both agreed it was unfortunate that Ghulam-'Ali, Hedayat and Aman had allowed Asad to go along with them to the village of Khusraw. They'd been foolish to think that they'd be allowed to use the baths - they'd been barred from them for weeks now - and Asad's presence, Muslim though he was, wasn't going to suddenly give them access. The very fact that he'd gone along with them was worrying. He was no friend. In fact, he might even be using them to get information that the rest of the agitators could use. Then, of course, there was his sister, Khavar…

"When was she ever not scheming to find new ways of making life difficult for all of us? No, Asad's involvement isn't good," she said. "And what about Reza? Was he with Asad, because if he was –"

Shrill voices stopped her mid-sentence. Loud against the stillness of the afternoon, the epithets leapt over the gate and into the yard, banging against the door like fists. Deep threatening tones joined the vulgar female chorus. The men were with them this time.

Munirih and Esfandiar sat, rigid, hardly daring to breathe, resisting the temptation to respond. What was this, the third, fourth, no, the fifth time since yesterday? On and on came the insults, the taunts, the promises that the time was at hand for a more permanent solution to the pollution of their existence. The pollution of Baha'is among Muslims.

Perhaps it was the heat that finally persuaded them to stop. Or the lack of response. The shouting and gate bashing became sporadic and finally there were only the sounds of the crowd receding down the lane.

Munirih let out a long breath and got up to clear the table.

A few minutes later came another burst of curses, a cry of pain, and a woman's rapid insistence, "Go inside, go inside… don't say anything. Let them go! Go in!" A door slammed; a gate hinge creaked, and scornful female laughter faded as the taunters moved off.

Munirih and Esfandiar fanned themselves, and sat down again to keep their watch.

IN THE LATE afternoon she suggested, "Let's go down to the pond. It's no use sitting here any longer. If they come back… well, let's just go. I need some air and the trees might brighten my mood." They opened the door cautiously and left the compound by the back gate.

Others had had the same thought and they found a few friends sitting on the grass by the water. They shared the fruit they'd brought, but the mood was somber and conversation desultory.

It wasn't long before they heard the first sounds of another round of invectives. This time the group was smaller - women only - but they were relentless and the incessant harping was more than enough to finally send them home.

Munirih paced while Esfandiar sat at the window, staring out. The still, dusty air and thick stone walls pressed in on her. "I'm going to the fields," she said finally. "Others will be there." Maybe cutting grass for hay would loosen the tightness in her chest.

"I'll keep watch. I'll come and get you if something new happens," he said.

The expanse of the fields released her from her growing panic. A breeze came up and her breath came more easily. She let herself be taken by rhythm of the work and the simple, practical thoughts of providing fodder for the animals. She refused to consider the possibility that any or all of them might not see the season's end. She refused to allow herself to brood over last evening's gathering and all the talk about the dangers they were facing. She pushed aside the story the 15-year-old had told; that awful dream and its ghastly images. *Aqa Razzaq really never should have let the girl speak. She was like a prophet of doom. Who could sleep after hearing all that? I'll have to speak to him about it tomorrow*, she thought.

Mah Manzar was bundling her grass. "...I've put them in the bread oven at Uncle Razzaq's", she was saying to Golshan.

Munirih stopped cutting & stood up straight. "What did you say?"

Mah Manzar turned to her and repeated, "The children. I've put them behind the pile of wood in Uncle's bread oven. Just in case. Khavar and Reza are sure to come back and they won't rest until they do something. They've probably already sent a message to Siyyid Vaziri in Banafat. An appeal like that will be irresistible to him. Maybe he's already preaching to the crowds, telling them to come for us. We adults can manage. The people will do whatever they want to us in any case and we've already seen that the gendarmes are only interested in what more they can take from us. So, let them have it. But not my children. Not my children!"

Her eyes blazed and her mouth was a straight line of defiance. With a swift movement, she gathered her bundle and walked quickly, back straight, towards her house.

She hadn't yet reached home when, in fact, Khavar's and Reza's taunts disturbed the stillness once again.

Nearly home now, Mah Manzar began shouting. She was running towards her brother Aman. And he was running towards her. Munirih and the rest stood still and watched. The grass swayed as the breeze strengthened. Although the light was fading, they could see a patch of dust in the air, an advance guard and a new chorus, this time masculine and more forceful, full of resolution. No need to interpret this latest harassment; the intent was clear.

They moved quickly. It was time to get home.

IN THE GROWING dark Munirih sat with Esfandiar in their upper

Crimson Ink

room, their prayers interrupted by the shattering of glass and the banging of wood and metal.. Frenzied shouts were coming from Firaydoun's place across the road. That was the starting point, then. *Who else is there? The rest of his family too?* She went to the window.

The shouting gathered volume. The banging and smashing intensified. Esfandiar went to her and held her close. A brief chorus of elation. The sky lit up. A balloon of smoke spread with the evening breeze. A few silhouettes leapt over a wall and dropped behind it. Single voices; demanding, cursing, questioning. The odor of kerosene came through their little window. Transfixed, they watched the smoke blacken. Smelled a new stench in the air; a blended reek. Kerosene. Wood. Charred flesh.

A female voice. Pleading. A male retort. Guttural. Crude. The ram of a metal gate. Figures with torches ran back and forth. The bellowing incessant. The din of battering, smashing and crashing, muffling cries and groans.

Munirih and Esfandiar barely registered the clamor coming from the other end of the lane. She had a fleeting thought about the children in Aqa Razzaq's bread oven over that way, but her eyes were riveted on the flames closer by. She was planted where she stood. When would it be their turn?

THEY MIGHT HAVE BEEN hours at that window, but they didn't notice. At some point a deep, unnatural quiet released them and they sat. Holding each other's hands, they touched foreheads and prayed through their tears.

THE MORNING DAWNED like all summer mornings in Hurmuzak, but the air was still rank with the stench of death. The early breezes failed to clear their heads, their thoughts, or their hearts from the agony of the night. Yet… that they still had heads, thoughts and hearts, that they still lived and breathed, still had a house around them and could still pray for their friends - this roused them sufficiently to get up and face the surreality of the day.

It was late morning before they dared venture outside of their small yard, slowly opening the gate to peer out into the village before walking to their neighbor next door. Gradually others joined them and they made their way to Firaydoun's place. Numb, they gathered in near-silence, connected in the collective muteness of their grief.

IT WENT on for two more days. Seven bodies lay stiff and bloodsoaked, exposed to the remorseless summer sun, their families temporarily forbidden by the latterly-arrived gendarmes to bury their dead. Investigation, after all, had to be carried out.

Permission to remove the corpses was finally granted, but there were no means to move them nor place to bury them. Denied access to their own cemetery, the bereaved found no others willing to take them.

Nor did the authorities allow friends to help. Only the relatives of the dead had permission to wash and shroud them. But they were injured or elderly.

The solution, unhappy as it was, came in the form of Husayn Hasan who, demanding conditions that ensured he would remain blameless in the eyes of his own religious community, was willing to arrange preparation of the most basic of graves. Then, for a sum of money, the gendarmes permitted the grave-diggers to transport the bodies to a barren area for burial. Ladders on the backs of donkeys bore the dead to their final rest. Attendance forbidden to loved ones and friends, strangers dropped the bodies into shallow holes in the lifeless earth.

ATTACKS BEGAN AFRESH, and the little community either hunkered down or fled to the surrounding hills. When a mob of several hundred from surrounding villages arrived, Munirih and Esfandiar made their escape. Hiding in the copse, they watched again, silent witnesses as the pack pillaged, then wrecked, smashed, and burned whatever was still whole. They spared neither foodstuffs, fruit trees, vines nor crops. All was taken or destroyed.

When nothing was left but the heat of their self-righteous rage, they turned on the donkeys and the mules, stabbing and pummeling the beasts until their mutilated bodies finally lay inert in their innocence upon the dust.

The Families Jalili and Hashemi

Chapter One

SHIRAZ

Spring is an especially lovely time in this city on the edge of Iran's southern deserts. The rains of the winter months give way to early warmth and sunshine in March and April.

Together, the water and sun have been good to this ancient city, allowing its extraordinary gardens to flourish and produce not only the roses and flowers for which the area is famous, but also the citrus and other crops that make their way to far-flung places.

Shirazis' love for their gardens also extends to their poets. Hafez and Sa'adi, their most famous, are entombed in extensive grounds covered in lush greenery and sparkling fountain pools.

As if this were not enough to delight the eyes and heart, Shiraz could also boast a host of privately owned gardens: spaces of various sizes in which flowers, shrubs and fruit trees shared the earth with ponds and lawns just perfect for picnics. And for a reasonable price, some of these could be rented for family outings.

Shirazis are not hesitant to express their love for their city.

Who would ever want to leave
such a little paradise?

SHIRAZ
March, 1955

Everything had started out as she'd hoped and expected. How could it have all gone so wrong? Rubbing her arms and still wiping her tears, Fereshteh sat on the floor behind the locked door of the bathroom. She thought it all through, trying to find the place she'd mis-stepped.

Fereshteh had known that this was going to be a special Naw-Ruz, simply because Maman had bought her a party dress in her favorite shade of blue. She'd seen the dress in a shop window and had stared at it in wonder, wishing it could be hers, but then Maman had tugged at her to move on. They'd had so many ingredients to buy to prepare for the biggest (and, in her view, best) holiday of the year. It was a thirteen-day celebration of the New Year and everyone shared in it, regardless of which place you prayed in.

"I'm helping this year, Habib," she announced to her four-year-old brother. "I get to help mix the cookie dough because now I'm six and I'm going to start school soon."

"But I wanna help too!" complained Habib.

"You can't. You're a boy. And you're little." Fereshteh declared. But she smiled at him. "You want to help just so you can nibble sweets, right?"

Habib gave her a guilty smile and said, "Ok, but you want to nibble them too!"

. . .

FERESHTEH *HAD BEEN ALLOWED* to help in many of the preparations this year. Days ahead of time they'd made pastry for rice, almond, and chickpea cookies, and for halva, all kinds of baklava, *sohan*, almond cakes and heaps of other special sweets that they'd later pile high on platters and serve to the visitors who arrived to pay respects and to wish each other a joyous New Year. Maman had also been chopping and frying vegetables, herbs and meats, and steaming the rich sauces and stews that always made Fereshteh's mouth water. Standing on a chair by the stove, she'd stirred a pot or two, feeling quite grown up.

Last evening, her parents had gathered her and Habib around the special holiday table that had been beautifully set with the *Haft Sîn* - the "seven S's" - in decorative dishes: *Sabzi* (greenery grown from sprouts), *Samanu* (a sweet pudding made from germinated wheat), *Senjed* (the dried fruit of the oleaster tree), *Sîr* (garlic), *Sîb* (apples), *Somáq* (ground sumac berries), and *Serké* (vinegar). Her mother had added beautiful candles, a bowl of water with goldfish, a book of poetry from Háfez, and a small flask of *Gol-áb* (rose water). It was then that they exchanged small gifts.

TODAY WAS the first of the thirteen days of visits and outings, picnics and parties and foods in amounts that would make you burst.

Twirling in her new dress, she'd exclaimed, "Look, Habib, look!" Her brother's bright eyes sparkled at her. "Isn't this the best time of the whole year, Habib?" Habib, in his turn, twirled in his new jacket and well-pressed slacks, setting both of them into peals of laughter.

"Come on, little ones," called Maman, "into the car. It's time to go."

AFTER THE FIRST visits had finished, they'd gone as usual to the house of Uncle Reza and Aunt Sohayla. She'd been looking forward to playing with her cousins and to the traditional meal of *sabzi polo* - steamed rice with green herbs - and fresh fish that her aunt would serve them. Aunt Sohayla's food was always so yummy!

Habib skipped ahead up the walk and hadn't yet reached the door when their cousins Majid and Farid ran out to meet them, and off they all went.

AFTER THEIR MEAL the men sat down in the large living room to drink their tea and Aunt Sohayla and Maman brought in the trays of sweets. When the children had taken their portions, they ran off to play again.

Their games had been so much fun - chasing each other, jumping and laughing, running in and out of the house.

She was the oldest, so of course she was their ringleader! They always followed her games with all the energy they had...

BUT NOW, sitting on the cool bathroom tiles, she couldn't understand why any of this would make her uncle so angry at her.

For sure, he was never nice to her. When he looked at her he always seemed to have a sour look on his face; but that was just how Uncle Reza was. She didn't like him, really, but her parents told her she must, because he was Maman's brother. So she tried to be extra careful not to get him upset. She tried hard to be "good". And Habib tried too, although he didn't seem to have to try as hard as she did.

So, what did I do wrong? She went over it again in her mind, her eyes shut so she could concentrate better.

We were all having so much fun. What was wrong with that?

She thought harder. *He never gets angry at the boys, not even when Majid tried to be our leader... Maybe he doesn't like it when I'm doing that?*

What did he say when he grabbed me? Something about girls not doing such things? No. Girls should let the boys lead? No. Majid should be leading the games - this was his house, not hers? Something like that.

The words weren't clear but her uncle's actions had been. During a pause while they were catching their breaths and the boys ran into the kitchen for more lemonade, Uncle Reza left the adults - who all seemed to be having their own fun time talking - and found her in the dining room taking another honey cookie. He stared down at her, his square face hard. She stopped chewing and stared back up at him. His broad shoulders seemed to widen.

With a sudden movement his thick hand grabbed her arm and he pulled her hard down the hall into his office. He closed the door quietly, she remembered, thinking it odd somehow. Then he started talking in that low, angry voice he sometimes had, his dark eyes and frowning bushy brows uncomfortably close to her face. But she couldn't really follow what he was saying because he'd started squeezing both her arms and it'd hurt. When she hadn't answered a question - what had he asked? - he'd shaken her and said a lot of mean things, but now she just couldn't remember what they were. *Why can't I remember? It must have been important, otherwise, why would he shake me so hard?*

She'd been so focused on that, that she hadn't been able to say a word. His mouth became a straight thin line in the black frame of his large mustache. Then came the slap on her face.

"Are you even listening to me, you silly little girl?"

Stunned, she'd simply burst into tears. He stopped then and with a look of disgust pulled her out of the room, and farther down the hall to the bathroom, ordering her to go in and wash her face.

"You will say nothing about any of this to anyone. Do you understand? Do you?"

"Yes, Uncle."

His eyes boring into hers, he turned and closed the door firmly.

FERESHTEH DIDN'T KNOW what to do with all this. No one had ever hit her before. Or held her arms so tightly. Or spoken to her like that. She let fresh hot tears flow. The blue chiffon of her dress was speckled with them, but she didn't care. She never wanted to wear it again.

FARAH GOT up from the sofa to get another cup of tea from the samovar in the dining room. The water had gone down so she filled it and waited for it to boil again, trying to calm herself.

She'd refreshed the others' tea already in an attempt to distract the men from what had become another uncomfortable conversation, but it hadn't helped much. Why did Reza have to say such things to Hassan? Her husband was a decent, kind man. He always looked for the good in everyone. Asked about them. Didn't talk much about himself. Never boasted about his education or his position at the bank. Even when others got cocky, Hassan was always patient. He listened and never had a bad word to say to them. So what was the problem with Reza? He had every reason to be content. No need to lord it over Hassan yet again. So what if Hassan was successful? Reza was also successful. Goodness!

Reza had built up their father's construction business so well that he now had two branches! He had trusted managers in both Tehran and Shiraz and could now concentrate on further improvements. He was intelligent, her brother, so what irked him so much about Hassan?

And why, just now on Naw-Ruz? He seemed fine at the table. Quite light-hearted even. He complimented Sohayla several times on her cooking and told stories that even made the children laugh. What had happened? He just wasn't the same after he'd stepped out of the room a while ago. When he came back in after "checking on the children - they're too quiet!" his smile had seemed a bit, well, put-on, she thought.

She checked the little tea pot on top of the samovar. It was running low so she spooned in more of Sohayla's special blend of leaves, still waiting for the water to boil. Her stomach was uneasy as her thoughts went back to how difficult Reza had been through her whole engagement with Hassan. He'd kept trying to persuade her to break it off. It wasn't right, he'd kept insisting, for her to marry a non-Muslim man. It just wasn't acceptable, even if the Shah had established a "modern" state. The monarch could forbid the veil and establish new civil laws, but he couldn't just allow people to bend Sharia law, Reza would argue. Oh did he argue!

Farah picked up the teapot and held it under the little spout of the samovar, filling it. She returned it to its place on top to let it steep and looked out the window into the large garden. Why couldn't Reza just accept Hassan? The rest of the family did. But then, Reza often disagreed with them, certain that he was wiser. And with her, he had always been especially protective.

She stirred the tea and let it steep a little longer. Wrapping her arms around her slim waist, she winced at a stomach spasm. When it had passed she again faced the window. *No*, she thought for the umpteenth time, *he can't stand it that I changed my religion and married outside of the faith he holds so dear. For certain, he thinks something terrible will happen to me eventually, and he's just trying to protect his only sibling. Of course that's it. He gets riled sometimes*... But it really was too bad today had to be one of those times.

She poured a small measure of the strong, dark brew into her tea glass and added water. Holding the glass in its tiny saucer, she breathed in the fragrant steam. No, she couldn't let the joy of the day disappear because of a few unfortunate remarks from her well-meaning brother; she would go back into the living room with a smile on her face and an amusing anecdote to add to the conversation.

THE FAMILY WAS TOO full to have an evening meal, so Farah served a little of the traditional *ásh-e-rishte* - noodle soup - and the four of them sat at the little kitchen table instead of in the dining room. She would save the *kuku sabzie* - herb and vegetable omelet - until the next day. Perhaps it was sheer fatigue from the excitement of the day, but Fereshteh was unusually subdued and thick strands of her long dark hair hung on her cheeks as she stared down at her plate. Habib occasionally piped up with yet another report about the games he'd played and the new toys his cousins had received as presents, but otherwise the meal was quiet.

When the children were ready for bed, Farah and Hassan sat with them on the wide living room sofa and they all chanted an evening prayer. Both children chanted one they'd just learned.

"Beautifully done, my little ones, beautifully done." Hassan was smiling at them. He hugged them in turn and then said, "Just before you go to have your stories, Maman and I would like to give you a little present."

Habib's dark eyes lit up and Fereshteh's thin face seemed to come alive again. "What is it, Baba?! What is it?! Show us! Show us - please, Baba!"

From behind the sofa their father pulled out a flat green box tied with a light green ribbon and he placed it on the sofa between them. Habib kept asking what it was but Fereshteh was certain it was a book. "Open it - together", Baba told them.

Still too young to read it, they nevertheless knew what it was. The color illustrations depicted royal horses, royal guards and retainers, and hunts through fantastic landscapes. There were richly adorned ladies and their maids, bright tents, cushions and flowers. "Is this really our book?" asked Fereshteh, her eyes wide and hopeful.

"Yes, *janam*, it's for the two of you - your own *Shahnameh*. In time you will read it yourselves, but for now, you have the pictures to look at. Since you know some of the stories already, you'll remember them just by looking at these. And we will read more of the stories for you. And did you know that the famous Jamshid of this book is said to have been the one who established the festival of Naw Ruz?"

The children's eyes lit up at this and they eagerly begged their father to read them that story.

Baba moved in between them and put the book on his lap. The children scooted in close to see while he read. They turned the glossy pages carefully, looking in wonder at the great heroes of ancient Persia.

Tucked under her covers an hour later, Fereshteh looked up in the dark, pictures from the new book in her head. She sank into sleep, embracing visions of colorful Persian heroes coming to her rescue.

May

FARAH PARKED her car in the long driveway, looking forward to a leisurely morning with Sohayla. The children would play and she and her sister-in-law would have the time to relax.

Sohayla opened the door with a wide smile on her face and a sparkle in her eyes. An ample woman, pleasingly endowed in body and heart, she took time with her appearance, conscious of her husband's appreciation. In this relatively brief period when the Pahlavi shahs had banned the wearing of the chador — that long cloak that covered women from head to foot while outside the home — mid-20th[th] century urban women enjoyed fashionable clothing. Sohayla was certainly no exception.

She wore her long, thick black hair pulled back and twisted up, pinned neatly to the back of her head, showing to advantage her soft, kind eyes, fine cheekbones and generous mouth.

In her turn, Farah was taller and somewhat slimmer than Sohayla. Her new shorter haircut complemented her oval face and fine features. She, too, kept up with the fashion of the day and was never short of compliments on her appearance.

Seated now on the back patio, she appreciated the cool lemonade she held. Appreciated the peace and calm of the garden. Of being with her sister-in-law, this gentle, warm woman with whom she felt so at ease. Their relationship went much deeper than the differences in their religious beliefs. The two women found each other to be intelligent and entertaining conversation partners with whom they could share their personal lives' natural ups and downs. They understood one another where it counted most and together they became the bridge and the hearth that united their families.

Today was a day to really appreciate their friendship. For, although Farah would prefer not to admit it, the radio vitriol had hit her hard. Mostly she turned it off or ignored it, but once in a while she listened just to keep tabs on what was happening. Better to know what was being said so she could be prepared. You never knew where it might lead. The vicious sermons that *Hujjatu'l-Islam* Falsafi had been allowed to broadcast during Ramadan this year were upsetting enough in themselves but there was also the matter of their influence on her neighbors and acquaintances. She could feel their eyes on her when she went about her business. Most of them still smiled when she greeted them, but she knew their response was tainted with suspicion. As though Falsafi's words might just be correct, despite what they personally knew about her.

Sohayla, herself fasting, offered a tray of snacks, fruit and juice to the children. When they'd had their fill, they ran off into the lush garden to play, leaving their mothers to their conversation.

"I'm glad you came, Farah. You must be so upset by Falsafi's radio sermons. It's terrible what he's saying. Poison. That's what it is. Getting normally good people upset. Inciting them against you Baha'is. I hope you're not listening to it much."

"Not much. But some. Usually I just let it wash over me and carry on with life, but today it rattled me, I'm afraid."

"Has anything happened?"

"One of the neighbors started saying some nasty things to me as I was getting into my car. That was alright. But then she started in on the children. That was hard. We drove off to the sound of her shouting after us." She took a sip of lemonade and crossed her legs. "But you know, the children will hear these things more and more as they get older and are out in public places more. They might as well learn to deal with it now. It will make them stronger." She gave Sohayla a smile.

"That's the wonderful thing about you, Farah. You have a remarkable capacity to turn most situations around and find something positive about them." She fanned herself with a cloth napkin. "For myself, I'm fed up with it all. I like peace and quiet. Harmony around me. All this rhetoric has become a rant. And you're right - I see it in my neighbors and friends too. I've stopped seeing them so much because all they talk about are hateful things. And this is the holy month of Ramadan. I don't see anything holy about it coming out of our mosque. All our mullahs are repeating those sermons."

She patted her sister-in-law's hand.

Farah patted hers in return and gave her a big smile. "So, Sohayla. Tell me your news. Did I hear you say that Reza's gone on a business trip?"

END OF JULY

THE SHRIEKS REACHED a crescendo and bubbled over into the intermingling giggles that can only come from small children at play. Fereshteh led Habib and Majid round and round, faster and faster, pulling them along like wind-blown banners along the wide expanse of grass, until at last they tumbled down in breathless delight next to the reds, pinks, whites and blues of a flower bed in full bloom. Suddenly hungry, Habib stood up and made for the picnic cloth where his mother and *Zandayi* - Aunt - Sohayla were laying out the cold chicken, greens and *kuku* - herb omelet.

It was a large *bágh* - a garden and orchard in the traditional style. Lush and well-maintained, it was one of many private green areas around the city. Shirazis loved their trees and flowers and those who had orchards and gardens often rented them out or allowed friends and family to use them for picnics. In this one, vast rows of flower and vegetable beds extended into copses of trees. Ranks of well-developed fruit trees flanked the high hedges that formed the perimeter of the terrain. The rainbow of hues was artfully arranged in grand swathes for maximum visual effect. A pond attracted abundant birdlife and ducks congregated at one end near a gazebo. Several families had come today, Farah's and Sohayla's among them. Blankets and mats were dotted under the trees, where they had spread their picnic fare sheltered from the midsummer sun.

"I'm thirsty, I'm thirsty, I'm thirsty," insisted little Farid, as he tugged at Sohayla's dress, his little feet threatening to trample on the plates she'd just laid down.

"Be patient, my son. I'm getting you some juice." But he continued his rant as he kicked the plates across the cloth and scampered away.

"Faridjoon, don't! Come here, come here!"

"I'll get him!" called Farah. With surprising speed for a woman with a 6-month pregnant belly, she grabbed the little boy, picked him up and put a cup of juice in his hands. She held him close as he drank, then placed him back on his feet next to Habib, who had just scampered up to the picnic blanket.

Fereshteh and Majid arrived on his heels, breathless. Eyeing the serving dishes on the cloth hungrily, they asked, "Can we eat now? Can we, can we?"

"In just a few minutes," said Farah with a smile. "Here, have some juice while we finish getting everything ready. Habib, *asalam* - honey - run over there and tell Baba and Dayi to come now. There's a good boy!" She frowned slightly as she looked in the direction of her husband and brother, but her face brightened again as she urged her son to his task.

"Let's go look at the pond!" shouted Majid, and he grabbed Fereshteh's hand, pulling her into a run with him. The meal finished, he was eager for new adventures.

"Wait! Let's wait for Habib and Farid!" she protested, and tugged back.

"Habib will catch up, don't worry!"

"Yes, but what about Farid?"

"Noooh, he's too little; he's just a baby. We can't take him to the pond." And as if on cue, Farid let out another howl.

"It's okay. I'll stay and play with him. You go to the pond." Habib turned and smiled at the 2-year-old, picked up a brightly colored ball and gently took his hand, encouraging him over to a bright open space not far from the picnic. Fereshteh looked back, then followed Majid, who by now was already half-way to the pond.

Sohayla watched Farid and Habib and smiled, "What a good boy you have, Farah! He's always so good with little Farid."

Farah returned the smile and nodded her satisfaction. "I hope he's as gentle with this new baby." She patted her belly and chuckled. "So how are *you* doing, huh?", looking pointedly at Sohayla's abdomen. "Will it be in early January?"

"That's what the doctor says. Everything is fine so far. Let's hope it's another boy, for Reza's sake." She glanced over at her husband. After a few moments, she looked down, then confided, "Last year, you know, when we... when I... when I lost that baby... you know, when we found out it had been a girl... well, you know... Reza wasn't even sad..." She paused and took a breath, looked back at Farah, forcing a small smile. "He kept saying 'the next one will be a boy - don't worry; the next one will certainly be a boy'". Sohayla reached for the box of baklava, got up, and took it over to the men.

REZA HASHEMI SHIFTED his stocky frame, leaning on his elbows as he kept his eyes on Habib and Farid. *That Habib's actually quite okay*, he decided. *He seems to know what Farid needs and how to keep him satisfied. More than I can say for his sister, that all-too-free-running Fereshteh. Mouthy little girl. Too forward. Disrespectful. But okay, let her run now. Let her keep my Majid busy and laughing.*

Reza turned his attention to Sohayla's baklava and chose a large piece. He looked over at Hassan, who was also watching the boys. He'd attempted to draw him into a conversation about a current political issue, but Hassan wouldn't bite; he only made some milquetoast comment about not wanting to get involved in the intrigues.

It wasn't easy talking to his brother-in-law. Not that Hassan was a difficult man at all. In fact, he was a nice guy. But too nice. Too correct. You couldn't get him into a full-blooded conversation about anything controversial, so he was really no fun to be around. So they sat here side by side, only because of their love for Farah. They agreed to these family outings because of her. What else did they have in common?

They were both devoted to their work, of course. Hassan spent long hours at the bank and often traveled to other branches in the country for meetings, leaving Farah alone with the children, and now, with her growing belly as well. *What will Hassan do when the baby arrives? Who's going to be with Farah then? It'll have to be Sohayla*, he decided. *Well, that's what family's for.* And that was the end of that thought.

He tried a new tack with Hassan: his construction business.

"You know, Hassan, this business is growing fast. After all the years of hard work, it's paying off. I've finally got all the right people lined up and ready to help us expand - well, for wages, of course!" A small laugh. Hassan smiled an acknowledgment.

"Yes, I've got a new contract waiting for me to sign tomorrow. A major job, I can tell you."

"Go on," said Hassan.

"Yeah, it's going to change things a lot for us. We'll need to hire more laborers, and probably need more office space."

"More office space for one contract?"

"Oh no, not just one. No. I've got more meetings coming up and more proposals in the works. I tell you, Hassan, we're heading in a new direction and we've got plans. We're going places! My father's got quite a few years in him still and then it'll be me and my sons. I can already see that we're going to be *the* company to get this city's big projects. And then there's the Tehran office. Lots of new business there too. We'll have to enlarge it — of course that means I'll have to build a house there, and then —"

"Rezajoon, Hassanjoon! Please can you find Majid and Fereshteh? We keep calling them but they don't answer and we need to pack up now and go home." Farah smiled but was looking uncomfortable as she rubbed her abdomen. That smile would do it to him every time; Reza left his lofty plans floating in the warm evening air, got up and went to look for the children.

THE TWO FAMILIES inched their way through the city. The heat of the day lingered and motorists fanned themselves from open car windows. It was early evening but the traffic was heavier than usual and as they approached a mosque the cars came to a standstill. Police were directing vehicles down a side street and drivers were honking and complaining. A very annoyed Reza finally got his chance to question a sweating officer.

"Sorry, sir, we have orders to redirect all traffic. There's a big demonstration at the mosque —"

A clamor erupted and a surge of bodies, fists raised, flowed into the street ahead. Reza lost no time in turning into the side street and a quick look into his rearview mirror confirmed that his sister and family were right behind him.

He pulled into his drive and ordered Sohayla to take the children inside. Looking around, he hurried over to Hassan and Farah's car as they pulled over to the curb. The radio was on.

"You just better get home. Just go! If you stop you'll really be in for it. Go home. And bolt your doors. Anything can happen in your neighborhood. Go!"

He gestured them away, turned and strode into the house.

Hassan sat by the radio as Farah got the children ready for bed.

"But Maman, really, what's going on? Please tell us." Anxious, Fereshteh climbed into bed but sat up, looking her mother straight in the eye.

Farah looked over at Habib on the other side of the large room. He lay on his side, wide eyes inquisitive as he looked back at his sister and mother, who adjusted her position so she could look at both of them.

She seemed to think a bit and then said, "You know, my little ones, lately there have been some people saying some unkind things on the radio and also at the mosques. These are people who… because they really don't understand us and what we believe, are angry at the Baha'is. They have all kinds of opinions and all kinds of fears about what we think, how we pray, what we do and so on. It's just because they don't really understand. They're not really bad people. But somehow... somehow they think that our beliefs are not correct and they want us to become like them."

"Are they correct? I mean, is what they believe correct? Are they right?"

"Well, Fereshtehjoon, they have their way of understanding God and they have their laws and their ways and places to worship. They're not wrong. But we are not wrong either. We just have a newer understanding of these things and have different ways to pray and be together in our community. We respect their beliefs and try to be good friends to them, just as we do with the Christians, the Zoroastrians or the Jewish people who also live around us. We are a country with many faith communities and we Baha'is wish everyone to be well."

"But why don't the mullahs and Muslims want *us* to be well?"

"As I said —"

"Uncle Reza and Aunt Sohayla are Muslims. *They* talk to us. *They're* nice - well, Aunt Sohayla's nice to us."

"Yes, they are - both, Fereshteh, both - nice to us. They are our family. They understand us better."

"What's going to happen now, then, Maman?" Habib wanted to know.

"What is going to happen is…" Farah's face brightened and she gave them both a wide smile. "…Is…that… I'm going to tickle you both till you squeal!" And she made good on this, scooping them both in her arms.

IN THE DARK, Fereshteh looked up at the ceiling, still basking in the warmth of the bedtime routine that was her mother's chanting and singing. Her mother had something almost magical in the way she could allay her fears, warm her heart and kindle her imagination. Tonight she'd started reading them a new story from the Shahnameh. It was a long tale and she'd promised, as usual, to continue it tomorrow night. But tonight Fereshteh was impatient to know what was going to happen next. She turned onto her side. "What do think, Habib? How's that story going to end?" she whispered. But her brother had fallen asleep and she was left to her own speculations as she, too, eventually drifted off.

August

THEY THOUGHT SHE WAS ASLEEP. But how could she be? Too many questions still needed answers and Maman had said, "Enough, now, my little ones. Let me hear you chant a prayer and then you should go to sleep."

Fereshteh complied with some reluctance. Why should they go to sleep? It was summer and there were no special plans for the next morning.

It was true that Maman had answered some of her questions - and some of Habib's, but why not all of them? And the more answers she got, the more questions she had.

Fereshteh sat up in the darkness and tried to make sense of the things she'd been told or the things she'd heard on the radio. She tried to piece together the stories. If she could make them into something whole, then maybe she could understand it all. She knew that her family and other Baha'is had to be extra careful. Radio sermons were stirring up trouble and making people upset. Sometimes big groups of men marched through the streets shouting things she didn't understand at all. Some people had been robbed and their houses ruined. Some people her family knew had left Shiraz suddenly and others had arrived in the city from villages

Maman's little shout of alarm distracted her from her reflections. She went to the door and peeped out.

"Ssshh, Farah! The children!", whispered Baba.

This is interesting, thought the child, as she crept out into the dark corridor. She crouched in the shadows near the doorway to the living room.

"Okay, okay. But Hassan, that can't be true! Tell me again. I must have misheard something."

"Okay," he agreed, "but please, let's speak more softly. We cannot wake the children."

As he told Maman about some people who'd been badly hurt, Fereshteh's young mind picked up the main events. It was different from hearing the stories from the *Shahnameh* and other tales. These were things that were happening now.

Baba was saying that in a place called Hurmuzak Baha'is had gotten hurt. Their neighbors had been bothering them for a while and saying they'd do bad things to them because the ayatollahs said they should. The neighbors and some other people had beaten them up and killed some of them.

Fereshteh had never seen a dead person, so she really didn't even know what that meant except that no one would ever see them again because they got buried in the ground. *How terrible to lie in the ground with dirt piled on top of you!*

Maman was crying. Baba talked about a big fire and houses burning. One lady who didn't die told some Baha'i friends about what happened and that's how the news had reached them in Shiraz. But the lady said some people got burned too. The same people who got beaten up also got burned.

Maman put her face in her hands and asked more questions. Her shoulders shook and Baba put his arm around her, pulling her close.

"No, Farahjoon, I don't know any more than that. Really. That's all I know, *Azizam*. But I'm sure we'll find out more. Soon. Soon."

But Fereshteh's thoughts were stuck on the people who were beaten and burned. She knew how awful it felt when she fell or bumped herself. Then there was the time she accidentally knocked a hot glass of tea onto her arm. She'd shrieked and cried. It took a long time for that burn to heal. It was even worse thinking about being burned by fire. *Imagine touching a burning candle!* She sat down on the floor and hugged her knees, resting her chin on them.

But the story she'd just heard was not about accidents. It was about people hurting other people on purpose. She fixated on this. Up until now, even after hearing all the other news about people shouting in the streets, wrecking houses and shouting bad things at the Baha'is in her community, she hadn't thought about people getting hurt and about how other people hurt them.

Maman and Baba had told her that some people were unaware and uneducated. So she'd asked if they hadn't gone to school and hadn't heard about good manners and being kind to others. Asked how they could think it was good to hurt anyone. Even she knew that that wasn't okay. And she was only six. Why, even four-year-old Habib knew that! Her parents were always telling them to be polite and kind. 'Didn't all parents do that?' she'd asked.

When Maman had said that not all parents did, she thought about her cousins Majid and Farid. Well, she thought, Farid was only two, a baby, really, so he didn't know anything yet, but Majid sometimes was mean. Sometimes he pushed her and other children too hard. That hurt. And then he'd laugh and tease them. But his maman surely told him that wasn't nice to do - she'd heard her aunt say that to him sometimes. But she couldn't remember her uncle saying anything like that. She thought a bit about this. No, Uncle Reza always said something like, 'Oh that's okay; Majid's just playing. He's just being a boy'.

Baba was getting up from his chair. Fereshteh slipped back into her room and ducked under her sheet. She squeezed her eyes shut in case Baba or Maman came to check on them. They didn't. The little girl lay awake, her thoughts circling in her head. When she finally drifted into sleep her dreams were plagued with shouting strangers and flames.

Chapter Two

Autumn, 1955

Fereshteh's heart was racing with excitement as Maman led her by the hand into the schoolyard. Her first day of school! "Oh Maman, I can't wait to start." She smiled up at her mother, who beamed at her in return.

They joined a group of mothers with their first year daughters, some looking shy and some eager. All of them looked at the groups of older girls talking and playing and Fereshteh's wide eyes took in every detail: she was pleased to see that, just like her, the other girls wore well-pressed cotton uniforms, and their hair, like hers, was firmly braided.

Looking around some more, she took in the tarmac paving, the wide concrete steps, and the heavy wooden double doors, open and waiting.

When a woman came out and told everyone to line up according to their grade level, Fereshteh jiggled up and down and squeezed her mother's hand.

"It's time for me to go now, Fereshteh. You'll join this group of first years. Just do as this lady tells you."

Crimson Ink

"Yes, Maman," she smiled. Letting go of Farah's hand, Fereshteh walked quickly to the designated area. As she lined up with the others, she flashed her mother another wide smile as Farah slipped out through the gate.

Unfortunately, Fereshteh was not prepared for the cold water splash that awaited her.

A FEW DAYS LATER, after having settled the class into the rhythm of the new school year, Fereshteh's teacher, Khanum Soltanpour, made an unexpected announcement to her new charges. "In this class," she told them, "is a little girl who comes from the hated Baha'i sect. Of course, she is young - like all of you - and that means we can try to help her, in spite of her family's religion. Let's see what we can do." The teacher proposed that, from now on, after their morning reading of verses from the Holy Book, they should question "poor Fereshteh" about what she'd understood.

Fereshteh told her mother about this, and each evening Farah explained the verses and how they could be understood from the Baha'i Writings. Fereshteh would go back the following day with her new understanding and if she was given a chance to speak, which, admittedly wasn't often, she would say a few words. These were met with disapproval or were simply dismissed.

Although her situation was difficult, it wasn't terrible. Fereshteh was learning to cope with it. But one day a new figure came into the classroom. Khanum Soltanpour receded into the background as Mullah Marandi took command of the class. He wore a long dark robe and a discreet white turban. Standing in front of them, his gaze passed over the rows of small bodies sitting stock-still at their desks in front of him. He seemed to take in the room with intent, his eyes resting briefly on each little face.

The Mullah finally nodded with a curt "hm", as if he'd come to some kind of conclusion about the quality of the class, then graced them with a benevolent smile as he introduced the purpose of his visit. He was here to speak to them about the duties and obligations of good Muslim girls. He would be coming to their school to assist the teachers in guiding their pupils. Their aim was to cleanse their young hearts from any misguided notions that might be present among them. Surely they were aware of the exalted speeches of the renowned *Hujjat'ul-Islam* Falsafi.

"If you have not yet grasped these things, then I myself will enlighten you." And he did.

"Unfortunately for good and righteous Muslims," he said, "there are those among us who are misguided. They are unable to live proper lives because they have not accepted the True Faith and Law of God. They are like wolves in sheep's clothing, ready to devour the unsuspecting faithful."

He paused for effect and was not disappointed. Fereshteh noted the wide eyes and open mouths confirming the class's general shock and dismay. "The God-fearing," he said, "need to be on their guard, need to protect themselves. It is an act of faith to shun — no, even to persecute — such people."

Fereshteh wondered where such people could be found and felt a tiny frisson run through her, trying to imagine what sorts of terrible things such people did and how she could avoid them. As the Mullah continued speaking, her mind drifted, creating visions of menacing creatures lurking behind doors, ready to pounce out at small children.

A long pause in his deep voice pulled her back to attention and she saw him directing his stern gaze straight at her. Startled, she turned her eyes away, looking this way and that, but found the entire class, the two Zoroastrian and the one Christian girl included, now focused on her. As the cleric resumed his speech and the girls' eyes returned to him, Fereshteh saw that her teacher Khanum's had not. She stared hard at Fereshteh, her mouth a tight, knowing smile.

The Mullah went on to declare Baha'is "apostates". Fereshteh went cold as she struggled to understand what this meant. She was aware that she was in serious trouble. She began scratching her forearms, unable to take her eyes off the cleric.

The word stuck in her mind long after the Mullah had left and she wondered if the other children understood what an apostate actually was. During the lunch break, she found out.

First in whispers among themselves, and then in taunts directed at her, she realized her classmates had learned the morning lesson well. One girl who dared to whisper to her admitted that even though she didn't know what that word meant, if the teacher and the Mullah said it was something bad, it must be true. So Fereshteh must be bad. The girl drew away from her and ran to a cluster of friends on the other side of the asphalt yard. They swallowed her in their embrace, casting dagger-glances back at the object of the esteemed cleric's contempt.

Mullah Marandi's visit had sealed her fate in that class. Fereshteh, was a strange, suspect creature; an oddity from a family and community of people with deviant beliefs and ungodly practices. Clearly, Khanum's efforts had been insufficient to cure or save her. It remained to be seen whether the Mullah's could.

FARAH HELD little Habib's hand and waited at the school gate as usual as the children emerged after their day of lessons. She saw her daughter at last, coming slowly down the steps, looking uncharacteristically unsure of herself. Other girls were laughing and talking in small groups. Some rushed past Fereshteh, jostling her to the side as they came down the walk to the gate. She stopped for a moment and stared blankly at the asphalt.

Three little girls of her size came up from behind and gave her a shove. "Dirty little apostate! Dirty little apostate! Dirty little apostate!" they chorused, laughing as they passed her.

"Fereshteh! *Joonam!* Come, we're here." The child looked up, eyes searching. She walked quickly to the gate. Farah bent down and embraced her daughter, ignoring the sniggers from the departing pupils and the surprised faces of their mothers. She took her by the hand and began the walk home.

They were silent as they negotiated their route through the traffic, walked several blocks until they turned off into a series of side streets, and wound their way into the quiet neighborhood where they lived. Under the shade of the tree-lined cul-de-sac, they passed three two-storey dwellings before they reached their home. Farah gave her daughter's hand a warm squeeze and then opened the grilled gate to the little brick courtyard, its vines, creepers and potted plants lush and green under the early autumn sun. She opened the front door and sent the children to the kitchen with the promise of a favorite snack.

It was not until Fereshteh and Habib had finished their treat that their mother addressed the issue. Sitting across from them at the kitchen table, Farah gazed at her daughter and said gently, "Tell me, *Joonam*; what happened today?"

Habib immediately looked at his sister beside him. The little girl squirmed as she looked down at the empty plate in front of her but said nothing. Her brother started to speak but Farah looked at him, putting a finger of silence to her lips. His large brown eyes looked questioningly at his mother but he obeyed.

Farah placed a gentle hand on her little girl's and held it there. Fereshteh, her head still lowered, lifted her eyes to her mother's. A tear rolled down her cheek. Gentle pressure from Farah's hand brought another tear and then another until Fereshteh wept unapologetically. Farah and Habib waited.

Finally, Fereshteh spoke. Tentatively at first, she recounted the unexpected classroom visit of Mullah Marandi. Her lips trembled and she rubbed her forearms. Her mother and brother waited for her to continue and, finally, it all came out in a rush.

"What does it all mean? What's an apostate, Maman? I know it's something terrible. The other girls started whispering and then made fun of me. Then they all kept away from me. What's wrong with me? What's wrong with us Baha'is? I know what you said last summer about those bad things that happened, but I don't understand. Why don't people like us? And why do they want to hurt us? They say all kinds of things to us, and we just let them! Why don't we fight back? It's not fair!" She sobbed, wiping fresh tears on the sleeve of her school uniform.

"Fereshteh, my sweet girl, it's —"

Crimson Ink

"No, Maman! Those girls are calling me names; they pushed me whenever we had break time today. That Mullah was scary; he kept staring at me like I was the only one in the class. Khanum Soltanpour was really mean, and mean to only me! Why? I just wanted to run out of the class. I hate it there! I hate it! I never want to go back there again!" Fresh wails accompanied her pounding fists, bringing Habib to tears too.

It was all Farah could do to calm her children. By that time, she had to prepare dinner, so she promised them they'd all talk once Baba was home and dinner finished.

Leading the children to the cozy armchair in what the family called the living room's 'reading corner', she suggested: "How about if the two of you look at your favorite books until dinner is ready? Here, how about these?" She scooped up several books stacked on top of a little bookcase there and sat with them a few minutes until they had immersed themselves. She walked back to the kitchen, turning around to look at them again before starting her cooking.

As she sautéed the vegetables she asked herself: How do I explain fanaticism to these little children? How can I explain it to myself, even? She knew that this issue was never going to go away. Schools were not kind to Baha'i children. Hassan had told her about his own dread of the classroom throughout his time at school, despite the fact that he'd had a few Baha'i friends there.

Farah had had a totally different experience: she'd been on the "right side." A Muslim by upbringing, she'd been steeped in the rhetoric of the local Mullahs, heard at home the opinions and judgments of her family, and observed her teachers', classmates' and friends' slurs, insults and abuse of the Baha'i girls at school. At first she'd gone along with it all. As a child, what else did she know? She'd joined the little cliques who'd taunted, pushed around or ostracized the "dirty nonbelievers" among them.

Then one day she'd found herself on the other side of the fence. She was thirteen. It had begun with a comment from a classmate about Farah's mother being a dirty, good-for-nothing who'd abandoned her family. Farah couldn't fathom this, but her questions had elicited an unpleasant look from the girl as she'd walked off. Over the days that had followed, Farah's friends had distanced themselves and dropped away. Most of them had said nothing; they'd simply ignored her and walked or looked the other way when she approached. She'd had one last ally and decided to question her directly, asking her for the plain, full truth.

"Shadi, tell me, what's going on? Why is everyone ignoring me or whispering about me? Why?!"

Her friend had looked at her with a mixture of pity and coolness. "Okay, if no one else will, I'll tell you. I heard it from Mahvash, and she said she'd heard it from Toulou, who said her brother told her. I don't really know how he found this out but I think somebody overheard something from one of the boys' fathers. Anyway, the story's gone around really fast and everyone believes it. Here it is: They're saying that your mother abandoned your family. That she just up and left your father. They say she was unfaithful to him. I won't say the words they're using to describe your mother, but I think you get the idea and you certainly know what it means when a woman does that."

A pause, a deep breath, a look around her. Shadi continued: "Anyway, they say your father found out about her going to secret meetings where she learned all kinds of crazy Western ideas. They say that the meetings were mixed — you know, men as well as women. So of course she must have met a man there. Of course she must have had some kind of relationship."

Looking around again, checking to see if anyone was watching them, Shadi had rushed through the rest of it: "So, yes, it seems your father found out about it all and got very upset. Really, I don't know how they could know this, but anyway, they say he was going to take her to one of the mullahs at their mosque and denounce her and that she was so scared that she ran away. They say your father used to go around cursing her, cursing the West, cursing any ideas that were different from "the old ways."

"But when was this? My father told me our mother had died!"

"How should I know? But think about it: you must have been really young. Maybe he said that to you so you wouldn't be ashamed. Good thing you have your grandma." She'd looked around nervously.

"Look, I can't talk to you anymore. I'm going to get into trouble just for this conversation. I like you Farah, but I can't be your friend any more. I'm gonna tell everyone that I just gave you the what for and warned you to stay away from the rest of us. I have to say that or they'll start in on me." Shadi had turned and walked away.

Farah had gone to her brother later that evening. "Reza, do you know anything about this?" she'd asked after relating her conversation with Shadi.

Reza's face had darkened briefly but with the cockiness of the 15-year-old big brother he was, he'd told her, that, sure, he knew all about it. He'd done his share of eavesdropping: on his parents' arguments when he was five, on his father and grandparents, and on other relatives all through the years. He'd developed a kind of radar for these things and meant to know anything he could, he'd said.

"No shameless woman's ever going to do that to me." His look had been far away but the touch of Farah's hand on his had brought him back. His face had softened and he'd said gently, "I know you'd never do anything like that. And don't you worry about anything, Farahjoon, I'll always look out for you."

AFTER DINNER FARAH and Hassan gathered Fereshteh and Habib between them on the sofa to begin a conversation that they knew they'd have to have many times if their children were going to cope with the inevitable prejudices against people of their religion.

Farah took the lead. "Today, Fereshteh, you had a hard time at school, didn't you?"

"Yes, Maman." Her lower lip quivered as she looked at her hands in her lap. Habib looked at her, then snuggled in close, leaning his head on her arm.

"I'm so sorry for that, Fereshtehjoon, so, so, sorry. I would like to say it won't happen again, but I can't. But Joonam, let's see if we can make it easier for you to be there."

"But how, Maman?"

"You know, most people mean well, but sometimes they say and do things because they don't know any better."

"But I tried to tell them that what they were saying wasn't true about me - that I'm not a bad person. That we're not bad people. But they wouldn't listen!"

"I know, my sweet girl. I know. And you're right: if people don't listen, there's not much you can say except that they're wrong. Once they're ready to listen you can explain things to them."

"Like what, Maman?"

"Well, you can tell them that we believe in God, just as they do; that our religion tells us to be loving, kind, and helpful to everyone; and that even though we pray differently, and have different holidays and things like that, we do respect other people's religions. Of course, there's much more we can say, but this is a very simple way to start."

Hassan said, "I know, Fereshtehjoon, that today was very difficult for you. I can well imagine that the Mullah frightened you. Then to have the rest of the class stare at you. It wasn't your fault." He took a deep breath. "And then to have your own teacher behave that way…"

Farah hugged her child tightly and planted a kiss on her forehead.

"Will they ever be nice to me again, Maman? Baba?"

Hassan sighed. "My sweet girl, I don't know. Perhaps. People do some strange things, but one thing I do know is that if we behave badly when others are mean to us, all we'll have is bad behavior all around. Two bad things coming together lead only to more bad things." He paused, patting his daughter's hand. "Sometimes people are afraid of things they don't understand. Sometimes that's why they say mean things."

"But what about my teacher, Baba?"

"I'm sure your teacher's doing what she thinks is right according to what she believes. Mullah Marandi too. But they don't really understand our Baha'i beliefs. Until they -- or anyone else, for that matter -- until they learn that there's nothing to worry about, you'll just have to be patient. We can't make them understand. We can't force them to change their opinions of us. This is why," he said as he looked intently at both his children, "we teach you to always search for the truth. Find things out for yourself. Don't just listen and believe everything you hear from others."

He looked into his daughter's wide eyes, where questions still lingered. "Fereshtehjoon, you need to know that there are also many people who do want to understand us and what we believe. Most people have good intentions. God-willing you'll meet many such people."

"But what can I do at school? What can I do now?" Her small face looked desperate.

"*Azizam*," said Farah, "You remember how one time we made those little boats with sails and put them in the garden pond? And how if we blew hard on the sails we could move the boats any which way we wanted?"

Fereshteh's eyes narrowed. She nodded.

"It's the wind that controls those boats, right?," her mother continued, "Someone might be blowing and blowing at our sails, but if we move our boat away from the wind they're making, our boat won't be affected by it any more. Their wind is there but our sail is out of their wind. Can you understand that?"

"So that means I should just move away from all the bad things they say at school? Not listen to those things?"

"As much as you can, yes. Then, inside yourself, wish these people well. Do this especially at times when you can't physically move away from them. Just think good thoughts." They all sat still for a minute.

"But Maman, how should I answer them if they ask me questions? What if they say things that aren't true? What if they tell me I should not be a Baha'i?"

"Just let them speak. When people get angry or upset, they just need to get it all out. Wait for that before saying anything because they won't be listening anyway."

Hassan said, "If they ask you something, answer them. Or if they say things that aren't true, correct them if you can. If you don't know the answers, come home and ask us and we'll explain them to you, don't worry. If they want to know why you don't give up your faith, remind them that the first Muslims did the same thing. They kept their beliefs even when the idol-worshipers tried to force them to change. Tell your classmates to ask their parents about their own history."

Fereshteh and Habib sat very quietly. Very seriously.

"Now", said their father, at length, "I think that's plenty for this evening. Tomorrow is the weekend. We can talk more about this if you want. A little bit at a time. But right now, let's plan what fun things we can do together tomorrow!" He smiled broadly and tickled them both.

Farah, to the extent her huge belly allowed, joined in. "Oh!" she cried. "Feel this! Your baby sister or brother is kicking up a storm! Here, put your hands right here!" All hands went to Farah's middle and all eyes filled with the wonder of the burgeoning life within her.

THE WEEKS PASSED and the Mullah's visits finally ceased. The taunting gradually lost its shine for her classmates, but Fereshteh had numbed herself to it anyway. A few of the children started to talk to her again, tentatively at first, approaching her as one might approach a strange animal. Testing her in conversation and finding her tame, some of them decided she could play with them in the schoolyard. But only in the schoolyard, because they knew from others that it wasn't allowed to have such children as real friends.

Fereshteh learned more than she'd expected from school. Within weeks she mastered the rules of survival: Keep your head down, lie low, speak when spoken to, play when you're invited to, and do your lessons diligently.

Learning became her refuge and source of enjoyment. It didn't matter that Khanum Soltanpour (not to mention her classmates) became annoyed at having to give her the highest marks in the class. Or that her teacher often found a way to punish her for this —- a sarcastic remark, a trumped-up error, a spill or a dark smudge on a returned paper. It didn't matter to young Fereshteh that despite her excellent work it was others who received the accolades, awards and prizes. Love of learning became the warm coat she put on in that cold classroom. She wrapped herself in it and got on with her lessons.

At home Fereshteh devoured books. Her parents were well-educated and their house was full of them. When her mother or her aunt wasn't reading or telling stories to her, they would sing or recite poetry from the Persian classics. She fell in love with the rhythm, the rhyme, and the melodies of Ferdowsi, Hafez, Sa'adi and others. She caught the spirit even if she didn't understand their esoteric meaning. Her heart became full when she listened, eyes closed and arms crossed over her chest, to the sweet chanting of the prayers and readings at Baha'i meetings and holy day celebrations. Her mother's prayers at her bedside every night sent her off to a sleep and when she woke early in the morning, the muted chanting from her mother's room wrapped her once more in its peace.

AT THE END OF OCTOBER, Layla was born. Family and friends visited from near and far. Fereshteh and Habib proudly showed their cousins and friends their tiny new sibling.

After school she'd play with Habib and their baby sister until dinner, and then Maman or Baba would read to them. Whether it was a story from the *Shahnameh* or from Baha'i history, Fereshteh lost herself in the action, the joys, and the sorrows of past ages. She dreamed she'd grow up strong, bravely facing arrows and swords and the wicked plots of enemies. She and Habib improvised costumes, weapons and horses, taking turns as the evil foe and the righteous hero. These stories filled their sleep. They braced Fereshteh on her way to school every morning.

JANUARY BROUGHT with it the birth of a new cousin, Saeed. Aunt

Sohayla looked relieved and Uncle Reza beamed. He was so busy strutting around showing off his new son to everyone that, for a short while, he forgot about Fereshteh.

On weekends there'd often be a visit with them. For Fereshteh, these get-togethers gradually became as uncomfortable as school. It wasn't as if she didn't play and have fun with her cousins. It wasn't as if Aunt Sohayla wasn't kind and sweet to her. It was the fluttering in her stomach, that plagued her, and the way she always felt that she had to watch and listen and be careful of what she did, because of her uncle.

He always found her, and caught her doing something he didn't like. Did he look for things to get angry about? Did he make up things to get angry about? She could never be sure, but no matter how much she thought about it afterwards, she just couldn't see what she'd done wrong.

Mostly she was afraid of being caught in a corner where others couldn't see her. When that happened, he'd take her by the hand to somewhere private in the house, whether their house or hers, and give her another dressing down. She was trying to learn how to hold back her tears, but couldn't. Lately, he'd hit her more often, as if he wanted to slap her into not crying.

Her uncle was adept at choosing his moments carefully so no one else noticed what was happening. But Fereshteh herself became an expert in hiding these incidents, as well. She was determined to protect not only herself but her parents from what she intuitively knew would be an ugly revelation. She was, however, less successful at hiding the incidents from her brother.

"I saw," Habib was standing outside the bathroom when she opened the door. Fereshteh, eyes wide, jumped when she saw him.

"I saw it," he repeated. She grabbed him by the shoulders, shifting her stare to the hallway on her right, alert to any sign of approach.

"Sshhhhh!" Looking her brother straight in the eye, she warned him, "Don't say anything. Never, ever say anything to anybody!"

"Why not?"

"Because. Because that will make it all worse. He told me so. He said I'll get into huge trouble if I say anything. And you will too! So, shush!"

Ignoring his complaints and questions she led him down the hall.

"Go play with Majid and Farid. Go! I'll come soon. Go!" In her heart she loved his concern for her, but there was no way she would talk about this, not to anyone. Habib obeyed, but looked back twice before disappearing around the corner.

On another occasion, Habib saw her, her face moist with tears and her nose running, coming out of their room, and on yet another, he'd walked into their room to find her sitting on her bed crying and rubbing her left arm raw. Neither said a word; she just looked him in the eye and he turned away.

Each time was an embarrassment, but worse, it frightened her. Somewhere in her 6-year-old mind were thoughts that her brother might blurt out something in front of the adults, or, much worse, in front of Uncle Reza. What would he do if her little brother embarrassed him with a question or an accusation? Fereshteh feared for Habib and she feared for herself, but still, never said a word.

In her prayers she asked God to help Habib keep quiet.

APRIL, 1956

The concrete hulk of the school stared back at her as she stood at its inner gate staring in. Fereshteh scanned the yard & entrance to see if any of her friendlier classmates were there. She couldn't see them. Taking a deep breath to steady herself, she pushed the heavy slatted portal and went in, its grating sound robbing her of courage as it slammed shut behind her. She joined her class's row among the ranks of small bodies and let herself be herded with the rest towards their respective classrooms.

Khanum Soltanpour looked cheerful. "Welcome back, children! Welcome back. I hope you have all enjoyed a joyful Naw-Ruz. Have you?"

"Yes, Khanum!" they chorused.

"Wonderful! Let's talk about this a little. I'd like a few of you to share your stories. Tell the class what you did over these holidays. Parvin! I'd love to hear what you did! Stand up and tell us."

And little Parvin did that with enthusiasm. And the occasional sneer at Fereshteh.

Then came the turn of Shamsi. Then Molook. Mitra. Fatimeh. Each one proud to tell her story. Each one happy to send Fereshteh another sneer.

Knowing that Khanum would never call on her to tell the class about her Naw-Ruz, Fereshteh silently recalled her own: How she and Habib had watered and watched the sprouted watercress seeds form a thick ball of green on a clay pot; how they'd sniffed the heady scent of the hyacinths they'd planted. On the day itself, Fereshteh and Habib woke to find new outfits laid out for them. Even Layla received a new dress.

She remembered the visits, the sweets, the large picnics in parks and excursions out to the nature reserves to see wild animals. There were visits to the cousins who lived out of town. The long drives had been rewarded with grilled lamb and huge platters of steaming rice, several kinds of khoresht - meat and vegetable stews - mmmm! And plates of sabzijat - fresh garden greens. Sliced fresh fruits so juicy that they dripped when you ate them joined the *shirini* -- sweets -- on the dessert table. Fereshteh and her many cousins — dozens, she reckoned — had run, played and laughed themselves silly. Exhausted by the time they had climbed back into the cars, they'd shouted their usual 'see-you-soons,' vigorously waving hands, looking back as they drove away.

"That's wonderful, girls. I'm so happy you had such a lovely time. Now, then, let's open our reading books…"

Naw-Ruz meant a renewal, the start of Spring, the start of a new year. It was supposed to bring new and wonderful things. But now, the cheerful wishes were over and the last of the sweets had been eaten. Fereshteh was back at school.

Mid-April, 1956

"I don't believe what they say about you."

Fereshteh, startled from her brooding, turned around. Minou, a classmate, came up beside her and stood, also staring, at the inner gate to the schoolyard. Fereshteh's lips parted but no sound came out. She looked at Minou, a girl she hardly ever noticed, perhaps because she was so quiet. She wasn't part of any of the cliques and all their gossip. She didn't subscribe to the unwritten rules and codes of conduct required to belong to those little groups.

Minou repeated her simple phrase and Fereshteh, staring straight ahead again, finally whispered, "Why not?"

"Because it can't be true. I watch and listen, you know. I see how you act and hear how you speak. But mostly, I just feel good around you, so you can't be a bad person."

Fereshteh didn't say anything, but Minou continued.

"They won't let you fit in because they're afraid of you. That's because they can't really see you." She paused. "I know this because they can't see me either. I don't fit in because I won't act like them. So they ignore me."

The outer school gate clanged as more parents dropped off their children. Girls walked by and pushed open the gate to the assembly yard while Fereshteh and Minou lingered.

"It doesn't matter, you know," said Minou. "It doesn't matter if we don't fit in. My maman says I just need to be the way I am. She doesn't like gossipy groups either."

Fereshteh found her voice. "Uh-huh. My maman says that too. She says gossip is really bad and it's best to stay away from it."

They watched the yard fill up and knew it was time to go in. Minou turned suddenly to Fereshteh, her expression now bright and cheerful. "Can we be friends?"

Surprised, Fereshteh hesitated but broke into a smile and said, "Yes!" Together they pushed open the gate and went in.

Chapter Three

Autumn, 1970

Fereshteh sat on her bed, scratching her arm. She heard the good-byes at the front door; Uncle Reza and family were leaving. Still feeling the flush on her face, it occurred to her that after all these years she should not still feel irritated by everyone else's cheerfulness when the families got together, but she did. One part of her brain also whispered to her that by now, as a young university student, she ought to have conquered her fears and been able to stand up to her uncle; her limbic brain, on the other hand, insisted on sending her immediately into a cold sweat in response to his insults, threats, and creepy touch. Limbic brain won out every time. She could never stand up to her uncle.

"Fereshteh!" Layla called out but Fereshteh didn't respond. Her sister called again, nearly passing her door. Fereshteh cursed herself for leaving it ajar.

"Here you are!" said Layla, coming in. "We wondered where you were. As they were leaving Aunt Sohayla invited us over next week for dinner. Maman said she'd have to check with you about your schedule, but no one knew where you'd gone.

Fereshteh sat and scratched, her face turned towards the window.

"Hey, what's the matter?"

Fereshteh carried on scratching.

"Is something wrong?" Layla looked at Fereshteh's arm and made a move to touch her sister. "Wow, that's looking nasty, what happened? Can I see it? Maybe --"

"Don't!"

"Wha--"

"Don't! Leave me alone. Just go!"

"Whoa, slow down there, Fereshteh! I'm just concerned ab--"

"Concerned? You're concerned about what? Me? What do you know anyway? As Fereshteh flashed a dagger stare at Layla, Habib came in.

"Hey, what's going on? What's the matter, you two?" he asked.

Fereshteh turned to both of them. "What's the matter? She's the matter! 'Little Miss Sunshine's' the matter!"

"Fereshtehjoon, I just don't understand why you're upset at me. I --"

"That's right, Layla. You just don't understand. Everything in life is good, rosy, beautiful. People are always wonderful to you. You've got friends all over the place – even at school, for goodness sake! The world is a happy place, isn't it?"

"I – but – I mean --"

"Yeah, the world's great, as far as you're concerned. You can excuse anybody, can't you? You always find a way of defending even nasty people – 'Oh, poor her, maybe she's like that because her mommy doesn't love her enough'; or 'poor him, maybe he didn't mean to say or do that nasty thing'; or 'oh Fereshteh, don't feel bad, you'll find some nice friends at university; these school girls are just blind to how beautiful you are… don't worry' and on and on. Right, Layla? Seeing sunshine where there isn't any!"

"But --"

"Layla, you are the most naïve, clueless girl! You can't see how bad the world really is --"

"Fereshtehjoon," began Habib.

"No, you just don't understand anything, Layla. Maybe one day you'll see. But for now, just get out! Get out of my room!"

Habib looked at Layla's stunned face, gave her a nod to comply, and she backed out of the room shaking her head.

He closed the door and said softly, "Again?"

Fereshteh nodded, stared again out the window and rubbed her arm more gently now.

Habib sat on her reading chair and waited.

When tears began to flow, Fereshteh said, "I'm sorry, Habib. I'm sorry. You weren't meant to get into this again." She wiped her cheeks.

"And I know I shouldn't have lashed out at Layla. That was unfair. But she infuriates me, Habib." She looked at her brother. "She just has no idea about how bad people can be and listening to her bringing her big-eyed cheerfulness into every damn situation is sometimes more than I can stand." She pulled out a tissue and blew her nose. "Habib, I know I'm wrong. I know I just envy her. She's always had friends at school, she's got a cheerful heart, and – let's face it – she's never had any real problems in her life. So, how can I expect her to understand?"

"And she doesn't know what I know," said Habib quietly. "And even I still don't know much." He sat back and looked at the ceiling then back at his sister.

"Fereshteh, don't you think it's time I said something about this? I'm not a kid anymore; I think it's time for me to talk to Uncle Reza and tell him to leave you alone. I always wanted to tell Baba and have him tell Uncle to back off, but you never let me. And now it's too late. If he were still with us, I would, Fereshteh, I would."

"No, Habib. No. Even if Baba were alive I still wouldn't let you. This is my problem, my secret, not yours." She blew her nose again. "And as you said, you don't know enough about it. And I'm not going to tell you. Not even you. It's too hard to explain."

"But--"

"No, Habib. Just don't think about it. If you say anything to Uncle it'll make it all worse for me. And if Maman found out anything, it would crush her. She loves him; and she depends on him more now that Baba's gone." She saw the skepticism in her brother's face, and went on, "Look, Habib, you and Layla are okay. Uncle likes you two and you need to keep it that way. For the sake of the family. For my sake, Habibjoon." She took his hand and held his eyes in her own.

T*HE NEXT DAY*

S*EVERAL BOOKS IN HAND*, Fereshteh came out of the study. Her father's office when he was alive, it now served the family as library, den and study space. Pleased with the books she'd found on the high shelves, she was about to pass the kitchen on her way back to her bedroom when Layla's and Farah's voices, low and urgent, trailed into the hallway. Fereshteh stopped. She moved silently to the wall.

"But I've told you, Maman, I don't know why. She seemed to get upset over nothing. Nothing, Maman!"

"Did you say – "

"I told you, all I said was that Aunt Sohayla'd invited us for next week. And then I asked her what was wrong. She was scratching again."

"Scratching?"

"Yeah, you know that nervous thing she does sometimes. But it looked worse and I thought maybe it was something else. Anyway, she was scratching and it looked nasty and I was concerned. Then she just started yelling at me! Maman, what did I do wrong? I didn't mean –"

"Of course you didn't mean anything bad, Joonam. I know that. And I think your sister knows that too."

"But Maman, she's been acting like this towards me for so long and it seems to be getting worse. Well, maybe it's just because I'm reacting to it more… I don't know." She sighed. "I've tried to talk to her – many times. But she – well, she doesn't seem to want to talk to me. Keeps calling me "Little Miss Sunshine" or some dumb thing like that. Says I'm naïve. She keeps saying that the world's a bad place. That kind of stuff. Maman, I just don't know what to say or do anymore. She's my sister for goodness sake! Why doesn't she like to talk to me?"

Fereshteh heard a chair move and fingers drumming on the table. A sniff. One of them blew her nose. Then, a sigh and her mother said, "Laylajoon, sit for a minute." A chair moved.

"Layla, you are, in a sense – the best sense – an innocent. You have a rare ability to see good in most everyone and everything. You overlook the faults of others; you're the soul of patience. Most people can't do that. Your sister has an especially hard time with that, so she can't understand your cheerfulness."

"But –"

"Please let me finish. Fereshteh has had a hard time at school all her life. From the first weeks of school she was targeted by her teacher and classmates and – well, she's never gotten over it, no matter what we've done to support her. She finds it hard to trust other people. She's not extroverted like you are. She doesn't make friends easily, not even now at university. The only exception is her friend Minou. Even with the other Baha'i girls she's – well, she isn't close with them. She gets along with them all right, but she's not ever been close friends with them."

"Sorry, Maman, but why are you telling me this? I know it already."

"I'm reminding you. I'm encouraging you to see how differently she sees the world from the way that you do. So you can understand her better and be even more patient with her."

Fereshteh stiffened. She closed her eyes for a few seconds, took a deep breath and tip-toed back to the study. After closing the door, she grabbed a small blanket from the armchair and curled up with it against the cushions on the little sofa. Hugging herself beneath the blanket, she let the sting of her mother's and sister's conversation spread through her chest; felt the familiar collapse of something vital there, like she was falling down through an abyss. Felt her self-confidence shrivel like dried fruit.

Dammit, she thought, how can they patronize me like that? Especially Maman? Maman who's been through plenty of heartache herself? So, that's what they think of me? Am I now a charity case for them? So now it's Layla who's wise? A saint maybe? Ha! A saint! Saint Layla? And what am I? The fallen angel?

Spring, *1971*

Reza liked his sister's place. He liked the flowers and shrubs she fussed over as if they were babies. She seemed to have more of them now that the children were mostly grown. Always that maternal side to her. He liked that a lot.

He walked up the front path in this frame of mind. But as he approached the door his thoughts turned to his mission for this visit. He'd deliberately chosen a weekday morning, taking time away from his office, just to be here when he knew Layla was at school and the others at university classes. He wanted no interruptions, no comments from those who didn't know any better.

Farah welcomed him with her usual warmth and sent him out to the patio, assuring him she'd be out in just a minute with their tea.

The chairs under the pergola were comfortable and had a good view of her flower beds. The blooms were well advanced, he noted.

As Farah sat down, Reza looked appreciatively at his sister's still slim figure. Her shoulder length hair was beginning to gray, he noted, but the style still suited her oval face — the face that looked at him now with the easy, gentle love she'd always shown him.

Conversation at first centered on the usual pleasantries, weather and garden included, and when the inevitable lull arrived, he made his move.

"So, what's happening now with Fereshteh and Habib?"

"You mean —"

"I mean their studies. You know, you were talking about universities."

"Oh yes, of course. Well, we're going ahead with that. They'll be transferring from the university here to England, as I've said."

"But they're doing well here. What's this mad idea of sending them somewhere else?"

But of course she had her answers.

She told him, "Hassan made arrangements for this a long time ago. On one of his trips to his cousins in Manchester they discussed accommodations and agreed that the kids could stay there. No need for a flat or anything. I've been talking to them recently and they've got everything prepared, they said. I know the kids will be safe and well taken care of, Rezajoon." She smiled at her brother.

"And his cousin helped them fill out all the applications for the University of Manchester and things like that. We just got word that they've been accepted there. Both of them. They'll be leaving at the end of the summer."

Reza was not convinced. "I just can't understand this ridiculous need to go elsewhere for an education when we've got perfectly good universities here in Iran - even in Shiraz, for goodness sake. Look at my own sons! Don't I want the best for them? I'm sending Majid and Farid to the university right here. And when it's Saeed's turn, he'll go there too.

"What about Mitra and Gita," she asked, though she already knew.

"My girls don't need to go. I'll see to it that they find suitable husbands when the time comes. Plenty of time to think about that. By the way, what are you going to do with Layla?" he countered.

"Hassan and I consulted a lot about the whole question of university studies for the kids. All of them. I will send Layla to England too - provided, of course, that's what she wants to do. If not, she can study here. And she's got another couple of years at school before we need to think about that. I'm not forcing them, Reza. We just thought that an education in England - in English - would give them advantages here later on.

"Hmmph. What are they going to study, anyway?"

"Fereshteh is transferring to medicine and Habib will continue with physics and engineering. They both want advance degrees --"

Reza lost his patience. "Why is she getting into a man's profession? God help us! Women don't need university in the first place, never mind getting into work they're not suited for! She should get married and be a good wife and mother - just like you! Look what a wonderful person you are, Farah! You never needed to study. You never wanted to study!"

Farah looked down and then far out into the garden, her face somber. She let his words hang in the air. For the longest time, he thought.

"Okay, if that's the way you want it, at least she should study something more appropriate for a woman. Like art, poetry, maybe even history or something like that. But really, why should she even study Western literature and history when there is such a rich Persian tradition?"

Her tone even, Farah said, "Yes, that's true. But Fereshteh - all three of the children, in fact, spent years at school studying these wonderful subjects. And at home Hassan and I read Persian poetry to them all the time. You know that. Fereshteh loved it so much that she even studied the poets on her own." Farah paused and took a sip of tea and a rice cookie.

"Now it's time for new things," she continued. "Fereshteh and Habib have done very well in all their studies, including English. They are ready for Manchester."

Reza had no answer. She was so firm, so emphatic, that he thought it best to leave it, at least for now. He regarded his tea glass intently.

It was a few minutes before Farah passed him some fruit and began to speak again. Her tone was more gentle now, more like herself.

"Hassan went to Manchester a couple of times, Rezajoon. He stayed with his cousins and saw how they lived. He toured the University. He asked a lot of questions and got answers that he, and I, were happy with.

"But how are you going to pay for that? The costs to study must be very high. And even if they stay with family, they have to pay at least for their food. And what about transportation?"

"Transportation is the least of the expenses," she laughed. "Yes, the other costs are there. It's not cheap for foreign students, that's for sure. But Hassan wasn't sitting and doing nothing all those years, my dear brother." She chuckled. "You may never have liked him much, but you always knew he was smart. He made investments there. Those will pay for everything."

Reza indulged her with a small smile, but he was not so sure about foreign investments. Anything could happen.

June, 1978

"So, my son, today is your day!" Reza clapped Saeed on the back as they looked out the young man's bedroom window onto the garden, where family and friends were gathering. "All these people are here to celebrate you! Congratulations once again! You've done a fine job at university." He smiled and pulled Saeed into his shoulder, noting his son's strong build with appreciation.

"Thank you, Baba. Thanks for all your help and for encouraging me." He released himself and wiped the sweat from his thick black brows. The summer heat had set in in earnest.

"Have you thought about what I've said, Saeed?"

"I have. It's a relief to finally be done with exams." He glanced over at the stack of books sitting on the blotter of the large desk. "I've had enough of books; I want to get out now and do something. Join one of the activist groups I've been watching closely. Political Science is worthless unless it's backed up with action."

Reza smiled at him. "As I've said, you've earned some time off. Take the summer and maybe the fall and do that. They need men like you. Smart men who know how to work against the Shah without getting arrested in the process. They need more leaders and you'll be one of them. They'll see that soon enough. Get involved and get recognized."

"That should be easy. The number of dissidents is growing but a lot of them don't know much. A lot of them are like sheep. Angry sheep, for sure. Too many lost parents to the Shah's torture prisons. But they don't know how to organize. And really, Baba, too many of them just don't understand the system and the role of the super powers in our country. They don't see how complex it all is and so don't have a clue about how to work against the regime."

"That's where your Political Science degree will serve you well. And your grasp of history. You know — hell, we all know — that change is coming, whether the Shah likes it or not. He can't hold onto power much longer."

Reza turned to his son, looked at him full in the face, took hold of his broad shoulders and said, "You, Saeedjoon, will be in the forefront helping the rest of us create a new Iran." They locked eyes and smiled.

"It's been great having you guys visit. We've been missing you so much!" Posing for her husband, Jamshid's camera, Fereshteh pulled her brother, Habib, and his wife, Taraneh, in close and gave them a squeeze. Jamshid, his tall frame bending and leaning to get just the right angle, looked every inch a dashing pro photographer as he took several shots before changing places with Fereshteh so she could take a few more.

Laughing, they returned to the shade of Sohayla and Reza's patio. Most of the party crowd was out enjoying the huge garden and its fine lawn dotted with clusters of chairs and tables . Sohayla had outdone herself on this celebration for Saeed. They watched her now, moving among her guests, her eyes smiling, her laughter warm, as she offered yet another dish she'd brought out from the kitchen.

Helping herself to a glass of juice, Fereshteh turned to her sister-in-law. "*Taranehjoon*, I bet your parents pampered you silly while you were in Tehran! I bet you soaked up every bit of it and then some!" Then leaning in she whispered, "You look gorgeous! And I love your sundress, by the way. Bet you got that in London, didn't you?" She smiled conspiratorially at her petite, attractive sister-in-law.

Taraneh gave her a quick wink and an elbow nudge, then looked at the others. The smile on her heart-shaped face was infectious.

"Yup! My parents made our stay so wonderful. But of course Farah-*khanum* is stiff competition for my mom and we're being impossibly spoiled here too." She chuckled.

"And loving every minute," chimed in Habib, wrapping an arm around his wife.

"Gotta stock up on all of it, right? No moms in Manchester!" Jamshid's dark eyes twinkled as he laughed.

"Oh that's for sure," said Taraneh. "With our work schedules there, we're lucky if I have time to cook a *khoresh* or two on a weekend."

"We've become regular patrons of our local fish and chip shop. And it's beginning to show," grinned Habib, pointing to his little paunch. "Can't be healthy. But that's our hectic life in the UK at the moment. It'll change." He winked at Taraneh, who returned his smile.

"We'll be sad to see you go, you know. When's your next visit — let's set it up now!" Jamshid, eyes wide and mischievous, suddenly produced a small calendar out of his back pocket.

They enjoyed a warm laugh.

It had been their doctoral work that had brought Habib and Taraneh together. On slightly different tracks in physics and engineering, they'd nevertheless had program overlaps and, as sometimes happens, one thing had led to another until in 1977 they'd married. In some ways it had made the stresses of their final year easier to bear.

At the end of their studies new jobs had awaited them, even before they'd received their certificates. Companies were eager for high achievers.

They were working hard, saving money, and building their contact network. Their teaching stints during and between terms led to some serious thoughts about academic work as a direction once they'd had some industry experience. Life in the U.K. was treating them well and they planned to stay.

"So it seems Majid's only here for another few days as well?" Jamshid asked, taking a sip of his drink.

"Yes," said Habib. "Uncle Reza told me he's sending him back to the Tehran office. Seems they're in the middle of some major security upgrades there. With all the unrest going on you never know if things will get nasty. There's been property damage in places. We saw some of it while we were there. Uncle will follow him in a few days. He's helping Farid with the same things at their office here first." He poured himself another glass of juice.

"Do you really think that all these protests are going to continue?" Taraneh wondered. "I mean, the Shah might put the army on the streets and if that happens, this will all blow over, don't you think? We've seen protests before, after all."

"I don't know," said Habib, rubbing his chin. "This time it all seems much more serious. From what I've seen and heard, I think it may take hold. People are sick and tired. And angry. It's not just students any more. Or the communists. The most unlikely groups are on the streets together. Now it's activists of all kinds: journalists, religious groups, the clerics of course, and lots of professional types. Much more mainstream. They're all singing the same song, so to speak."

"So," a deep voice interrupted, "are you enjoying our little party?" They turned to see Reza stepping out from the dining room.

"*Baleh, baleh, Dayi* — yes, yes Uncle," Habib greeted him with a small smile, but noticed that Fereshteh's face had gone pale. As Reza came towards them, she quietly excused herself as she began to head for the house. In that little dance that sometimes occurs when two people try to pass each other but only succeed in getting themselves more in each other's way, Reza managed to bump squarely into his niece before she was able to make her way around him.

"What's your hurry, little niece, eh?" He looked at her retreating form and laughed.

"I'm going to get a sweater; I suddenly feel cold."

Taraneh followed.

TEHRAN, SEPTEMBER 8TH

SAEED WAS in Tehran on Black Friday. Joining a select group of his political activist friends that day, he blended in among the thousands of students and sympathizers that continued their protests against the Shah.

The hatred against the regime had been building up for the past 25 years. Rather than forgetting, Iranians nursed their anger against the American-installed autocracy that had cut off at the knees the beginnings of democracy under Prime Minister Mossadegh.

Reza Hashemi hadn't forgotten. No, he'd often talked about it. And when Saeed had started university, Reza encouraged him to study political science. He urged his third son to challenge the corruption and heavy-handedness of the Shah's regime. He urged him to take a stand against what he called the pernicious influence of the West. He wasn't disappointed. Saeed moved from theory into action.

Political activism was rampant and universities were seething with dissidents. But no matter how great the opposition became, the Shah's reprisals were greater still. The government's tactics had become brutal in the extreme and Saeed had lost more than one friend to the torture chambers of SAVAK, the Shah's secret police.

Yesterday the Shah had declared martial law. Thrown down the gauntlet. Today the protesters took it up.

Carrying one side of a huge banner demanding an Islamic government, he marched with his fellows in the streets of Tehran to stage their protest in Jaleh Square.

Thousands lined the wide boulevards and shouted slogans. Peaceful but insistent, their voices were heard. Especially by the military.

The protesters rejected the soldiers' orders to disperse, thus upping the ante. Escalation was inevitable. In response to the protesters' pushback, the soldiers opened fire into the crowd.

From where he stood, Saeed couldn't see what was happening, but he felt the backward wave of the mass in front of him in response to the shots that continued to ring out.

Much of the crowd began to turn around. The press of people took on momentum and Saeed almost lost his balance. The other end of his banner dropped and he realized that his friend had disappeared. Saeed dropped his own end and the slogan was lost under trampling feet.

Unable to do otherwise, he turned and moved with the crowd around him. Gradually, though, he navigated himself to the side of the disintegrating column and broke free. He got his bearings and found an apartment building to duck into. At the end of a hallway he found the emergency stairwell and climbed up until he reached the roof. Giving the door a shove, he stepped out onto the flat concrete and walked to the boulevard side from which he'd come. Leaning on the parapet, he surveyed the situation below.

It was chaos now. Gunshots precipitated uproar, shrieks, and howls for help. Curses blended with cries of panic. Bodies ran and bodies collapsed. Some stood in shock. Soldiers fanned out and military vehicles moved towards the retreating swarms. Blood was on the pavement. Lots of it.

This is it, he thought. *This is it. There's no going back now. There will be no talks, no diplomacy, no compromises. The Shah himself has set the revolution in motion!*

The Family Rahimi

Chapter One

YAZD

The hamlet of Hurmuzak and its neighboring villages depended on the city of Yazd for supplies and trade but in 1955 the way there was a long one. Depending on which of the two roads you took, you drove 80 miles through the parched foothills between the mountains on your immediate north and the endless dusty open plains to your south, circling around and up the milder slopes of the range's eastern edges, then through the empty expanse of the flatland that finally acquired shape in the form of the mud brick structures that were Yazd City.

Or, you drove 50 miles on the newer "hill road" that took you north, east and then northeast over the unforgiving raw rock peaks through a series of hamlets, villages and a town or two until you emerged onto the same flatland that would eventually reveal the same mud brick city.

There were few trucks and fewer cars that made that regular

journey. Villagers knew how to stock up and manage. They lived a simple rural life, content in their traditions and their ways.

A few of them lived in relative comfort. They had city relatives and connections and had established understandings and business dealings that suited both parties.

They enjoyed the safety, security and order afforded by the local authorities: political appointees and clergy whose well-oiled relationships with the gendarmes constituted the local law enforcement.

Yazd City was a more complicated place.

Lying dead-center in the inhospitable desert of central Iran, 3000-year-old Yazd was not the most likely spot for human development. Nevertheless, it eventually became a major trading center — praised even by Marco Polo for its silks, no less.

Except for the minarets and domes of mosques, the roofs of Yazd are flat, a vast network of adobe buildings and courtyards resembling a collection of monochrome boxes.

Summer heat regularly exceeds body temperature and winter brings the sting of bitter cold. There is an absence of surface rivers and a traveler there might well wonder how life can be sustained without rainfall or lakes.

It is thanks to a surprising feat of ancient engineering, that even today is respected and studied, that Yazdis have fresh water and a natural basement cooling system: *qanats* — underground water canals dug by hand and linked into networks that run beneath and between houses.

Within the mud walls and in the covered dim alleyways and bazaars, shops offer colorful arrays of high quality silks, textiles and glassware. Traditional coppersmiths hand-hammer intricate designs on vessels or polish them to a brilliant sheen. Pastry shops offer delectable, heavy-laden trays of sweets infused with sugar, milk, honey, nuts, fats and fragrant spices.

The mud brick and clay plaster are occasionally relieved by the brilliant polychrome of elaborately designed mosaic tiles in places like the Jameh mosque and the Amir Chakhmaq complex.

Pools, fountains and trees might be the biggest surprises in this city of clay.

Historically, Yazd has escaped battles and invasions. Surrounded by the unremitting harshness of its desert and the jagged peaks of mountain ranges, its citizens have remained secure from the outside.

This city that has clung to life over millennia has also clung to its traditions and religious orthodoxy.

> When it has come to new beliefs, its citizens have not been known for tolerance.

1955

May

The Rahimi family occupied a piece of land on the outskirts of the city. There were few houses in this area in 1955 and they counted themselves fortunate to have acquired the sizable plot on which they'd built a modern concrete home some years before. A new and reliable water source made the area attractive for future development and ensured added property value.

While *Khanum* Rahimi tended her children, her house and her vegetable garden, *Aqa-ye* Rahimi tended his burgeoning business. He had built up his father's smaller trading company, still enjoying the benefit of the older man's canny knack for attracting customers, and was now fully bringing on board his eldest son. He knew they were a formidable trio and lately he often found himself smiling. If good fortune prevailed, his eldest son would carry on in the family tradition and add his own measure to their success.

Aqa-ye Rahimi was a proud man and like his father, very firm in his opinions. His life was well-ordered. His home was well-ordered. His wife and his children were obedient.

He kept good relations with the merchants at the bazaar, where he conducted his worldly business and with the several clerics at his mosque, where he conducted his spiritual business.

It was with the recent help of these two that he had extended his reach into many of the surrounding villages. He knew the villagers' needs and understood their ways. And he helped them.

May 1955; The holy month of Ramadan – the Muslim fasting period

Shortly before sunset a car pulled up in front of the Rahimi house. A tall, well-built man of around thirty got out and stretched. The drive had been very long and very dusty. Fingering his parched lips and calculating the time left until nightfall, he thought, *Really, Ramadan is not the time for such journeys*.

But his father had insisted, "This is a new business opportunity, my son! These people are well-connected merchants. Who knows what this could mean for future business? It's sure to help us expand our company. No, there is no putting it off, you have to go."

Because it was the month of Fasting, the invitation was to come for prayers and dinner and then stay the night. They would talk business the following day.

And so it happened.

The Rahimis were excellent hosts and provided every comfort. Their home reflected prosperity and good taste. The food was excellent, the children polite and the conversation over tea and fruit after dinner was stimulating enough to keep even the tired traveler alert and interested.

They had much in common, as it turned out. They exchanged views on the traditional topics of faith and family and understood from this that they shared the same values. Reminded and regenerated by the Ramadan sermons both in the mosques and on the radio, they all knew their purpose in life. When conversation moved on to the politics of the day, they again found themselves in perfect agreement.

After an excellent night's sleep in the comfort of fresh linen, the traveler performed his prayers and then shared the plentiful pre-dawn breakfast with *Aqa-ye*-Rahimi and his father in the dining room while the rest of the family ate in the kitchen.

The threads of trust were skillfully woven last evening, the traveler thought. What was said, what was not said, what was implied, what was questioned, what was answered; a look, a gesture, an attitude — all were part of the delicate dance that disclosed who you were and what you stood for.

Yes, he thought, *I can easily work with these people. I like them.*

This morning they would lay out the construction remit and he would propose his solutions.

For the next several hours the men worked on the details, making the arrangements for extensions and renovations in both the Rahimi house and business facilities. The traveler would be supervising his construction crew and foreman personally. He grinned, "It seems I'll be driving this road often!" Returning a warm smile, his new client replied, "And we will have the pleasure of your company as our honored guest."

Before noon they had viewed the Rahimi residential property and the traveler had taken the necessary photographs. They had looked at the existing floor plans. Then they drove into the city and viewed the Rahimi business facilities to do the same. By mid-afternoon, the heat now oppressive, they were on their way home. It was time for a nap until dinner time.

Their second evening together solidified not only the business relationship, but also a friendship. It was in a mood of considerable satisfaction that Reza Hashemi departed the next morning, right after breakfast, with the intention of getting a good start on the long, long, dusty drive back home to Shiraz.

End of July

Eight-year-old Kamran Rahimi peeked around the doorframe,

his large brown eyes barely extending beyond the smooth wood. There in the evening shadows he took in the tableau of *Pedarbozorg* - Grandfather, *Babajoon* - Dad, Masoud, and their guest from Shiraz. It was a mark of his recent coming of age that his oldest brother was now permitted to join their grandfather, father and the Shirazi businessman while they smoked and sipped their after dinner tea.

"...went really as planned. *Aqa-ye* Mortazi was very satisfied."

"So, all the houses were burned down?"

"No, only the one, but we got the worst of them. Praise be to God there are seven fewer of those *najjess* - unclean ones - in that village now," said Baba with a certain pride.

"And a new flock of sheep for *Aqa-ye* Mortazi," Pedarbozorg laughed heartily.

Massoud took his cue and did the same. "So what will happen now?"

"Now the villagers will offer prayers of thanks at the mosque and Mortazi, Mahmoudi and the gendarmes will distribute the property that they confiscated. And perhaps… Who knows, they may have more plans. You know, for the others that remain." Baba took a long drag on his cigarette, his look speculative as he blew out the smoke.

"If they have any sense, the others will leave," said Grandfather dismissively. "That will save *Aqa-ye* Mortazi a lot of trouble and the village will profit from the harvest and the properties. It's only fitting." He took an appreciative sip of his tea, then asked, "So, Masoudjoon, how was your first experience out there?"

The young man sat up straight and puffed out his chest. "I felt so proud to be following Mullah Mohsenzadeh's directives. It was inspiring to be a part of that group, knowing how we were helping those villagers. Knowing that we were really in battle for the true faith."

"You should always remember our glorious history," his grandfather said. "Think of how the Prophet - peace be upon Him - and his followers struggled to cleanse the cities from the infidels, and use that as your example. Carry the love of the Prophet in your heart and you cannot go wrong." He stood up, Baba, Masoud, and their

Crimson Ink

guest doing likewise, and embraced his grandson. "Goodnight," he said and started for the door.

Kamran quickly pulled his head back and slipped soundlessly down the hall and into the kitchen, where his mother had put together a bowl of raw meat and bones.

"There you are," she said. "Here, you can take these out to the dog."

"Yes, Maman." But he hesitated and quietly asked, "Maman, what did Baba and Masoud do in that village?"

She looked at her son curiously, then turned and busied herself with some vegetables she was preparing for the next day's meal.

"They were helping those people to... They were helping them."

"What do you mean, Maman? I don't understand."

She scrubbed some carrots. After a moment she said, "There were some other people in that village who do not follow the true faith. Those people have lived there a long time and benefitted from the land that should really only belong to Muslims. Baba, Masoud, and our Shirazi friend were helping to cleanse the village."

"But Maman, Baba said seven of them are gone now. Pedarbozorg was saying something about a battle. What happened to them?"

She scrubbed harder. "You know, my son, some things are like these vegetables. You see, some parts are rotten and we don't eat those. Sometimes the only way to get rid of what is not good is to cut it out and throw it away." She took a sharp paring knife and began trimming the carrots.

Kamran looked at the floor as he contemplated this. Then tentatively he asked, "But Maman, if those people were bad, why didn't the gendarmes just put them in prison?"

She stopped for a minute and sighed, looking up at the ceiling. "It is not for us to say, Kamranjoon. Have you not heard what Mullah Mohsenzadeh has said in his sermons lately? Have you not heard *Hujjat'ul-Islam* Falsafi on the radio?"

"Sure, but what does that have to do with that village?"

"My son, the people that Falsafi and Mullah Mohsenzadeh have been talking about - those Baha'is - those are the people" - a deep breath - "those are the people in that village, the ones who needed to go - ouch!"

She dropped the carrot and the knife and clutched her finger. Kamran went to her. "Maman, what happened?", concern widening his eyes.

Putting her finger under cold water she forced a smile and said, "Nothing, just a little cut. Now go and feed that dog. Go!"

For a few seconds he watched the pink-stained water run down the drain, then retrieved the bowl of meat and bones and went out the kitchen door into the dusk.

THE LARGE DOG strained against his chain as Kamran walked toward him. The heat had been merciless today, even for Yazd, and even though the dog had the shelter of a kennel and had been well-watered, he'd grown irritable. Kamran approached with caution.

"Sit," he ordered, holding the bowl back. He put the food on the ground as the dog obeyed, then went to unchain the animal. On command again, the dog went to the bowl, making short work of the chunks of meat before grabbing one of the fresh bones to sit and chew on.

Kamran sat on the ground a few feet away, watching the gleam of the animal's teeth in the fading light.

AUGUST

"I THOUGHT we Muslims were supposed to be kind to others, even people who have a different religion." Kamran was sitting across from his father in the well-appointed room he used as his study and library. His father sometimes indulged his youngest son. No one else dared to disturb *Aqa-ye* Rahimi if he was in there with the door closed.

"Yes, my son, that is true." Pausing, he put his palms together

Crimson Ink

and inclined his head, his fingertips touching his mouth. Then, lowering his hands to his thighs he looked up and continued.

"Yes. However, this refers to People of the Book. That means Jews and Christians. But we also make exceptions for the *Zardushti* - Zoroastrians. Our mullahs are clear about this; it does not include Baha'is. They are, well, misguided. They say they believe in all the prophets and all the religions, but they also say that there is a prophet after Muhammad - may peace be upon His blessed person. And these infidels actually believe that the Promised One has returned; that is the foundation of their belief. We do not accept this. The Prophet was the last. There is no one after Him. Except the return of the Promised Mehdi that we pray will bless us soon with His coming. You know this about the Mehdi from your lessons, don't you?"

Kamran, anxious to please, said, "Yes Baba!"

"Good. Also, their beliefs about the roles of men, women and the family, about education and about the organization of society are different from ours. We know, to name but one example, that, for all that women have their important roles, they are not equal to men and need to obey their husbands. Those Baha'is think that women are the equal of men!" He laughed.

"We also have our particular ways of worship, our clergy, our holy days, our marriage laws — all these things that the Baha'is do differently. Why, they don't even have priests, for goodness sake! Instead, they have elected assemblies that are supposed to take care of their communities. How can that possibly work in a religion?" He laughed, incredulous at such a notion.

"Ahh, no, my son, they have what they think are 'advanced' ideas but we don't agree with any of those."

His father paused for a minute, taking a sip of water from his glass. Although the thick walls of the house spared them from the worst of the heat, it was an exceptionally hot day,

"I tell you, my son, we who live here in and around Yazd at least, do not tolerate such nonsense."

A satisfied little smile on his face, he raised his hand in an expansive gesture as he continued: "We have eliminated Baha'is in the past

— many times, many times in the last one hundred years — and we're certainly not going to let them take hold and spread their heretical ideas here among us now. Or ever!" He took a long drink from his water glass, emptying it.

Kamran watched his father and said nothing. He had no idea what to make of these things, so he waited for more.

"I know you are young, my son, but since you have asked, I will tell you one other thing. These Baha'is are only one of the problems that we true believers have. A big problem to be sure, but not the only one. Western countries - you know, Europe and America - are mixing themselves up in our affairs here, trying to take advantage of us. They don't care about our beliefs and our values. They want our oil and they want to tell us what to do for their own advantage. The Shah is working hand in glove with them. He's sold out our country, sold out our religious values!"

His voice had risen in volume. Kamran fixed his eyes on his father's face.

"This is our country, our religion, not something that can be bargained at the bazaar! It's the Mullahs' job to bring the faithful together and preserve our values and they do it any way they can. To be sure, they are always focusing on the Baha'is, but you will learn as you grow up that there are also many other enemies of Iran and many are right here amongst us. Radical groups, Communists, and others, pretending to be loyal citizens – even loyal Muslims." He poured another glass of water from the pitcher on his desk and drank.

Kamran tried to imagine who these enemies could be. He began to worry about their neighbors and the men in the bazaar stalls. Were the enemies hiding there in plain sight?

"If the Mullahs say 'do something' we do it." His father raised a pointed finger, punctuating every phrase.

"We do not question it. They are the learned ones and they know what is required to keep our Faith strong." He paused and looked at his son, letting him take this in.

"Look, Kamran, there are even Sunnis amongst us. Do you know what they are?"

Kamran shook his head, his eyes still riveted on his father. Somehow, this seemed even more ominous.

"I'll tell you then. They call themselves the faithful but they are not. They believe in Muhammed - may peace be upon Him - but they don't believe in the Holy Imams. They do not accept them as the true and only legitimate leaders of the Faith. They used treachery right from the death of the Prophet to take power - worldly power - in their hands and they used that power to control the Faithful. There were many bloody battles. As you well know, we mourn the deaths of the Imams every year on special occasions. You've been to these."

Kamran spoke up at last, his small voice earnest. "Yes, Baba, I know, but how could anyone want to kill the Holy Imams? They were the Prophet's own family!"

"Who?" Baba sounded surprised. "Why, their own brothers in the Faith killed them! For personal power, Kamran, for personal power!" He banged his fist on his desk and Kamran jumped in his chair. Continuing at a near shout, his father said, "These were the Sunnis. And they still live amongst us!"

He leaned towards his son, pressing his point. "And then there were the early enemies of the Faith who were Jews. Your classes at the mosque will tell you about this, too. Then later came the Christians, who tried to wipe out our Faith through their Crusades, trying to take control of Jerusalem, then take back southern Spain where the Faith had been securely established. Their purpose, Kamran, was to wipe out the civilization that Islam had developed."

"What do you mean, Baba? I don't understand."

"You don't yet know where the first real hospitals and doctors and libraries and science and mathematics came from? Now there's a history lesson for you! Hopefully you will have a good lesson on it in school one day." He smiled. "It was Islam that gave all of these to the West. Islam! Those stupid, dirty Europeans lived in ignorance. Their conditions were primitive when they came storming against our educated culture! My son, you will read about these things."

He stood up and selected several books from the shelves behind him and showed them to his son, who eyed the thick tomes with great respect.

"When you are able to understand these, I will let you read them. Meantime, I will speak to Mullah Mohsenzadeh about giving some extra classes to your group so that you can learn more about these topics. That will help you to understand who our enemies are and why they are our enemies." He leaned forward, his face close and earnest.

"Kamran, listen to me and listen well. The only way – the only path – in this life is to obey our learned Shia clerics. They are our rock. They are our protection. We do as they command. Do you hear? We do it."

"But what about the Shah?"

His father sighed. "Well, my son, we live under his rule and we must also obey his government. And right now, he's doing the right thing by allowing – even encouraging – the sermons on the radio. He's supporting the true Faith. We should be happy about that. But sometimes he goes too far in his cooperation with foreign countries. He wants to modernize our nation and make it like many others. You can see in the newspapers and magazines the kind of frivolous Western lifestyle he has." He paused, staring at a small tapestry on the wall opposite. Its fine threads in rich colors depicted a scene from Persia's ancient history.

Returning his gaze to his young son he said, "Still, we love our country and we show our patriotism by obeying its laws. We get jobs, do our work and do whatever we can to get ahead. We who are truly loyal to God should get ahead and we can do this by whatever means there are. We use our networks and friends. We always help each other to get ahead; do you understand?"

Kamran wasn't exactly sure what this meant, but he nodded. His father straightened his back and stretched, then took another long drink.

"Now, my son," he said, smiling and clapping both hands on his thighs, "I have things to do. Go play."

Kamran went to his room to think about what his father had said. The space was small and he shared it with the youngest of his three older brothers, Javad. He wished the construction were finished, as he was looking forward to having a room of his own.

Sitting in the dim corner on his bed, he brooded over his father's words. Javad came in. Ignoring Kamran, he rummaged in his drawers.

"Javad, I have a question." Javad paused for a moment.

Kamran told him about his conversation with their father, and asked him what he thought. Javad had a chance to slide into his wise-big-brother role.

"Kami", he said, "there's nothing to be confused about. When Baba says 'obey whatever they say', that's what he means."

Javad had heard about the village massacre. "Massoud told me," he said proudly.

"They were following the instructions of our mullahs. Without question. Of course they were doing the right thing. The mullahs said it was necessary and they know. His Honor Falsafi and many other mullahs had been preaching against the Baha'is for weeks. Why are you so worried about that? Would you feel sorry for exterminating vermin? Haven't you ever killed cockroaches in the pantry? What is it you don't understand?"

"What counts in life is loyalty," he explained to his younger brother. "Loyalty -- to the clergy, to your family, to friends. To your community. And Baba and Grandfather know how important this is in business."

He continued: "Loyalty is rewarded. You have to know people and show them that you'll help them and then they'll also help you. It's simple, little brother. Don't make it so complicated."

His speech completed, Javad took his book and left the room, leaving Kamran to his ruminations.

His brother's explanation seemed convincing. Of course obedience was important. All the adults he knew expected that. Still, he kept thinking about burning and extermination, his imagination conjuring images of mutilated carrots and squashed cockroaches. He was trying to grasp what these looked like when applied to people.

These thoughts left him queasy. No one else seemed to feel that way. Why couldn't he be more like his brothers?

Unable to reconcile his thoughts, Kamran went to the window and looked out into the yard. The hens were quiet in the afternoon heat, having retreated to the little shed in their enclosure. The vegetables drooped under the relentless sun and the dog lay panting, tongue lolling, in a small circle of shade afforded by a neglected bush.

He's thirsty, the poor animal, thought Kamran, and so am I. The boy went to the silent kitchen and after taking a long drink of the lemonade his mother had left on the table, filled a pitcher with water and went out into the yard.

The dog, chained as usual during the day, sat up. The water hardly had time to reach the bowl before the animal began to slurp it down. Kamran refilled the pitcher and poured more water until the dog lay down again. The boy sat on the dirt next to it, giving it an affectionate rub on the head, and the grateful animal laid its head in the boy's lap.

Chapter Two

ISFAHAN

The vast flat expanse of Iran's third most populous city sits at a north-south / east-west crossroads that has connected people for thousands of years. Open to the northern winds that cool it during hot, dry summers, Isfahan is flanked on the west by the foothills of the Zagros Mountains that run from Turkey in the north to the Persian Gulf in the south, dividing Iran from its neighbor, Iraq.

"*Isfahan, nesf-e jahan ast*", the saying goes. Isfahan is half the world. The capital of ancient Persia twice, it was the seat of advancement in culture, and the arts and sciences over many centuries and that heritage is still honored and carried forward in modern times.

Its past glory is still visible in the graceful architecture of its covered bridges, palaces and mosques. High arches characterize the supporting structure of the many bridges crossing the Zayandeh River that runs through the city. Enormous palace and mosque complexes, their tiled facades a display of intricate designs in brilliant hues of blues, attract Isfahanis and visitors, the pious, the inspired, and the curious.

Yet for all its ancient grandeur, Isfahan is a growing, modern city.

> A place where the new interfaces with the old, where
> secularism, commerce and technology squeeze in between
> and beyond ancient edifices, gardens,
> and traditional ways of life.

1978

Spring

Leaning his chair back against the dingy gray wall, Kamran Rahimi flicked the ashes from his cigarette just as a puff of wind blew through the window beside him. The ash blew onto his suit trouser leg, its color barely distinguishable from the cloth. He swore under his breath, stood up and tried dusting it off. Only minimally successful, he stubbed out the remaining butt and grabbed his suit jacket. He'd had a succession of days like this over the past couple of weeks and he felt plagued by a universe that seemed determine to grind him into the dirt.

Without telling his co-workers where he was going, he left their drab shared office and walked down the hall, noting the worn gray linoleum, dingy paint and unwashed windows. *Why was it,* he thought, *that government buildings were all like this? Dismal environments to house dismal jobs. A matched set.*

It was Thursday afternoon. His officemates would guess he'd gone for the weekend. What did it matter if he left early? Pushing a few more papers around that afternoon wouldn't make anyone else's day better or easier. It could wait until after the weekend.

He climbed into his second-hand beige Peykan sedan and pulled out another cigarette. Noting that the ashtray was full, he pulled it out and emptied it on the tarmac of the parking lot, then lit up and pulled out into the street. He headed for home.

The traffic was no better than expected and he inched forward, surrounded by other hopeful early leavers. *On their way home too*, he mused, and wondered about what that meant for them. A nice roomy apartment? A beautiful smiling wife? Sweet, cheerful kids? A fun weekend ahead of them? Bitter thoughts chafed at him. Suddenly swinging off course, he leaned on his horn, blasting at the cars in his way, and headed west out of the city towards the Zagros Mountains.

Pushing the engine hard, he climbed a section of the foothills, taking every turn tight and fast. He rolled down the front windows completely, gulping the cool air, letting the wind clear his head.

He found a place to pull over and got out. A breeze lifted his hair and rippled his loosened necktie. He pulled the tie off and tossed it into the front seat, then walked to the edge of the road to look down the steep slope at the valley below. Neither the splash of color there nor the warmth of the sun on his face could save him from the sadness that welled up and spilled over into tears.

Kamran stared at the bright blossoms. New foliage in that delicate shade of green peculiar to early Spring, its newness offering a sense of promise after a cold barren winter. Before summer's relentless heat darkened the leaves, parched the plants and abandoned them to layers of dust.

He kicked the loose dirt on the roadside, and looked down at his dusty shoes. When had he last bothered to polish them? He couldn't remember. There was so much he couldn't remember – possibly because there was little of consequence to remember. What was his life, after all? A perpetual motion machine of unremarkable civil service – "service"! Is that what it was, "service"? — an unremarkable civil service job relieved only by an unremarkable and barren wife, her unremarkable cooking and housekeeping, and sporadic visits with their few unremarkable friends in their unremarkable neighborhood. They left their unremarkable little apartment and drove in their unremarkable car to attend unremarkable sermons at an unremarkable suburban mosque on unremarkable Fridays.

Looking up at the sky, he held out his hands in supplication, asking out loud for something, anything that would take him out of this fruitlessness.

He'd tried his father's advice: finish school with good marks, get into public service with all its opportunities, strive hard, obey your betters and your superiors. And marry a good, traditional woman and raise a good family. That would bring you happiness.

But perhaps he'd missed one small detail. No, he hadn't missed it; he'd intentionally ignored it. It was the one piece of himself that he'd tried to be loyal to; the one thing he'd promised himself: he was not going to ask for favors or take advantage of what his father called "strategic connections". *I've been the obedient, loyal and devoted son my parents — and my brothers, for that matter — expected. Done everything according to their playbook. Except this last thing. And look at me. Look at me, dammit! Look at where this got you, Kami! You are a no one, a nothing, a mediocre little paper pusher with nothing, nothing, nothing to show for more than 10 years in a crappy little job in a crappier little office.*

He'd married the girl their parents had "suggested", been the dutiful husband and son-in-law and the whole story. But even his in-laws had lost their optimism for his potential "high prospects". With no grandchildren after all this time, both sets of parents were now hard put to keep up the welcoming smiles and visits that had been so much a routine in the early years of the marriage. Family get-togethers on either side had become awkward. Even his brothers couldn't hide their disapproval. "When are you going to get a real job, Kami?" they'd snigger, "Or a wife who'll give you kids?"

Running his hands through his hair again, he felt the gall in his gut and the heaviness in his chest. He looked up and around and shook his fists at the sky in a fit of anguish and anger. Was everything stacked against him? Did he have to give up this last piece of himself to change it all?

Answered by silence, he shouted back, "Ok. Is that it? I've been wrong all along? Play the game, obey every single rule, is that it? Am

I seeing it all from the wrong angle? Am I the only one here who's too stubborn to see reality?" He wiped an eye. Only silence.

He sniffed and looked up again, fists raised and shaking once more. "Alright! Alright! Alright!" He emphasized each syllable, "I will do that. If that is what it takes. The whole quid pro quo stuff; become a boot-licker if I have to. And whatever else it takes - ok? Just, just... ahh..." and he looked down, eyes closed, shaking his head, arms by his side, fists still clenched.

Mouth open, he pulled in a long breath then opened his eyes and looked out over the valley again. He took another breath, and another, and another, sucking in the fresh breeze until he felt calm again. He got into the car and turned back to the city. He needed to call his father.

The Family Omidvar

TEHRAN

There was a side to Tehran that belied the opulence of the Shah's show-city. Composed of complex interlocking of streets, alleys and urban trails, it resembled a rabbit warren created for and by a multitude. The disenfranchised, dissolute and despairing resided in its nooks and crannies. Far from the palaces, monuments and tree-lined boulevards, the boutiques, hotels and fine dining establishments, the city's underbelly churned with the manpower that fueled the engine of the monarch's modern state.

> Like any metropolis, Tehran never slept. Its people worked and traded, dealt and colluded, in the legal and illegal, and fought for their bread every day and every night.

1970 – 1971

SPRING, 1970

A potholed cul-de-sac, hardly more than an alley, led to a ramshackle little house. Set next to similar dwellings, its corrugated iron gate opened into a crumbling courtyard. A battered truck pulled in beside a motorbike that had been resurrected from spare parts, and parked within inches of a cracked kitchen window. A single wire strung between the building and the breeze-block wall that enclosed the property served as a clothes line. The house had a partial upper storey, an afterthought added to expand the original structure to accommodate – inadequately, it turned out – for seven people.

Traces of its past, its brickwork formed pointed arches and encased diamond-shaped wooden panes that had once framed colored glass. All but two of these windows were now bricked up. One of the remaining openings had been converted to a glass window, and the other to a rickety door giving onto a small section of roof from the house beneath. It was possible to stand out there, but most people would know better than to lean on the rusted wrought iron railing.

This tiny outdoor space offered a view into the neighboring courtyard with its single tree on the right, and the peeling facade of the building opposite.

Sima looked through the dirty kitchen window, eyeing her husband as he locked the truck, walked the few paces to the house and pushed open the battered wooden door. He grunted as he dropped his tool bag onto the floor of the main room. His son Soheil sat on a large faded cushion in front of a tiny TV set. Horizontal lines hovered uncertainly just short of the center of the screen, interrupting the picture.

"Why isn't Youssef home yet?" Hormuz's voice was gruff as he took off his shoes.

"I don't keep track of my brothers." Soheil kept his eyes on the screen.

"I need to talk to him." Hormuz walked to the kitchen.

"I'm hungry," he barked, then turned and went to the table. He held his head in both hands briefly, then ran them through his greying hair. Addressing no one in particular, he complained: "What's wrong with this family? Where is everyone? Why isn't the food on the table?"

He went to the kitchen again and stood in the doorway. "Come on, woman! Bring me some food!"

Turning, he kicked the shoes at the door. "Where is that daughter of mine? Why isn't she helping you? She should be doing the meals anyway. What else does she do around here except eat, sleep and sulk?"

"She went to get your other shoes from the shoe repair. He said they wouldn't be ready until the end of today." Sima brought in four melamine plates and bent spoons, then a platter of steaming rice. Last came a bowl of a watery vegetable and bean *khoresh*. She served her men and sat down.

"What do you need to talk to Youssef about?" she asked, but she thought she already knew. She saw it in her husband's eyes, but dared not say it herself.

"I need to find out how his little business is going and when he expects to get his money. This job is taking too long."

Sima raised her eyes but kept her head down as she chewed. They were short of money again. Hormuz's work wasn't getting any better, and she was lucky she had her job at all. Soheil and his younger sister were still at school. The two oldest boys had moved away to try their luck in the oil fields, but the occasional money they sent back didn't take the family far. Youssef and his business seemed their best chance, but it wasn't regular enough. And he was getting restless. He might follow his brothers, she thought. Well, if he did, she wouldn't have his mouth to feed, at least.

Hormuz moped all evening. Youssef didn't come home. Soheil went to his room and Sima sat under a dim lamp sewing. She watched Hormuz as he stared at their daughter shuffling around in the kitchen. He watched her a long while and Sima knew his thoughts. They'd talked about these things again and again. Their daughter wasn't bad looking. She was strong for a girl. But she was still at school and jobs for girls were scarce.

She watched her husband long after they went to bed, as he lay flat on his back, staring up into the blackness of the tiny room.

"Sima! Sima come here and listen." After days of brooding Hormuz had come up with an idea. Two weeks had passed and today he relaxed his frown.

"Listen," he said as she sat with him at the table, "My cousin Rashid's coming in a week's time. You remember him? Long time ago. Came to my father's funeral. Remember? The skinny guy who was studying at that seminary in Qom. I never really liked him, but you know, I get in touch sometimes. Pompous ass, thinks he's so much better than the rest of us. Swans around that swanky mosque up in Elahiyeh and rubs elbows with those posh Tehranis up there."

"I saw his picture in a newspaper a couple of weeks ago and I got to thinking. He's doing ok for himself, really ok, and he's been talking a lot about charity and helping some of the poor and stuff like that. His sermons got a lot of interest and the papers interviewed him. So anyway, I wrote him a letter and asked him to come here to talk. He knows where we live. He couldn't refuse. After all his talk he's gotta show people he's doing what he says. So he's coming and I've got a deal for him." He smiled, rubbing his hands together. "We're gonna get some money!"

Mullah Rashid looked down at the wrinkled envelope with distaste. It was not often he heard from his cousin Hormuz and when he did, it was never good news. An unfortunate one, he was. One on whom the stars never bestowed their luck.

Well, it was too bad about the two older boys leaving them. No doubt the other two would follow. Then all they'd have is the girl. What did they expect? Young men don't want to stay tied to poverty if they can seek their own fortune elsewhere. Was his wife complaining again, too? It was understandable that his cousin was an unhappy man. But what could he do? How was he supposed to help? For that was what this letter implied. Hormuz was certainly not inviting him to that dilapidated little house for a social visit.

Rashid mused about his own family, a familiar path of regret and resentment. What has my own wife produced for me? A succession of girl children who were now growing up with empty heads and all the silliness of female vanities. And costing me too much.

Not that money was a problem, but it could not buy the respect he deserved, and that he'd have if he had sons. It could not give him the satisfaction and pleasure of meaningful male conversation on matters of importance. It could not ensure him a legacy.

He'd married Hediyeh with great hopes for a family of sons. When she'd failed him in that and grown fat and irritating, he'd taken to finding comfort and entertainment elsewhere.

He fingered the envelope again and sighed, indulging in the personal pity and fatigue of spirit that set in when one knows there's an unpleasant obligation at hand.

Mullah Rashid avoided the southern part of the city as much as he could. For all his preaching about helping the poor, he preferred to do so from the comfort of his own elite suburb, sending his minions to check on the grass-roots in need. Today was an exception.

Rashid parked his car on one of the more respectable streets in front of a shop and arranged for the owner to keep an eye on it. After compensating the merchant for his trouble, he left the shop and turned down the first of the side streets that diminished in width and quality as they fed into each other and led him deeper into the labyrinth that was his cousin's neighborhood. He strode along, his goal to get off the streets as fast as possible without twisting an ankle in a pothole or soiling his cleric's robe in the ubiquitous muck or garbage.

The tiny house was cleaner than anyone could remember. The rice was fragrant and the *khoresh* thick and rich. The Daughter of the

House was wearing a decent new dress from a second-hand shop run by a local tailor, and Sima and Hormuz, well-scrubbed, had dressed themselves in the best they had. After having cleaned up the courtyard, Soheil and Youssef had left, banished for the day.

After having observed the normal courtesies and appreciating a tasty meal together, Rashid, Sima and Hormuz sat in the main room sipping strong tea. Before the serious talk began, the parents sent the girl to the kitchen to clean up behind the closed door.

It took several glasses of tea and not a little verbal maneuvering to clarify the proposal. Even humble folk understand the need for the indirect approach in matters of delicacy.

"So what do you say, Rashid?" Hormuz spoke with some confidence as he enumerated the advantages of his proposal. "You can have the contract for as long as you want – minimum of 6 months, of course – but you decide. She's pretty, isn't she? And you see she can cook and everything. She's 16 and fresh as a rosebud. She can bring some smiles into your leisure hours. We can send her to you or you can come here. We have a little room upstairs that is very private."

Rashid fingered his graying beard slowly, almost a caress. He considered the proposition carefully. It was not entirely unexpected. His eyes narrowed to black slits as he calculated his advantage in the transaction.

"It's a good deal, Rashid. Others could cost you much more. Come on, what do you say?"

The creases in the mullah's rough cheeks deepened as he weighed his options. He could refuse, politely of course. He could find some reasonable excuse that Hormuz would accept even if he didn't believe it. There were ways to save face in such situations.

But then, what could go wrong? There would be a contract, drawn up by his helpful colleague, as usual, and the terms would be clear to everyone right from the start. He could accept 6 months, 8 even, and see how things were. Over the long winter, nights would be cold.

His gaze returned to the room and his cousin as his decision was made. "Yes. Yes, fine. I'll draw up a contract – let's start with 8 months – and bring it to you in say, two weeks? I have some affairs to attend to in the meantime."

A few minutes later he made ready to leave, expressing his thanks for their hospitality. He stood up and gave them a tea-stained smile as he allowed Hormuz to open the door for him.

"How am I supposed to fix up that room? You want a new bed there? New everything? We don't have money for decent food, and you want new furniture?"

Sima was beside herself. She knew Hormuz was right, and she also was anxious to make this deal work out, but what was she supposed to do? She was took out her worries on her husband yet again and he was getting irritated.

"Youssef's got some money coming in. Soon, he says. This week. He knows this is important. We'll get the money and you can get what you need to make the room nice."

Hormuz's reply was sharp. He must be worried, no matter what he's saying, she thought.

She frowned but held her tongue. This was all so difficult.

"Okay. Look, I'll go to Salavati and get him to give us credit for the stuff you need. I'll go now, okay? Give me a list and I'll talk to him."

The following afternoon Sima left Salavati's shop, her shopping bags full of linens. The furniture would be delivered the following day.

Not one to take time with the finer points of homemaking, Sima nevertheless found herself agonizing over the placement of not only the new bed and nightstand, but also of the arrangement of some soft furnishings designed to add some style and attractiveness to the little upstairs room. This didn't come from any kind of sentimentality; she had none. It was for purely practical reasons: create an attractive setting for his new temporary marriage and Rashid would be satisfied with their end of the bargain. A satisfied Rashid meant a continuation of the *sigheh* contract and an important extra source of income.

It was true that *sigheh* relationships were not as common now as they had been in the past, and it was also true that an initial contract was not automatically extended or renewed. Some such contracts were even known to be valid for a matter of hours. Sima thought about a distant cousin in Kashan and shivered as she recalled the shame that incident had brought on her family. Still, that girl's poverty had left no other option.

She went onto the tiny balcony and shook out a blanket. Sima was determined that her own daughter would be in this relationship for a long time. A young girl like her and that old Rashid – he should be happy that anyone would even take him! For a cleric interviewed by a newspaper, he was no prize. Ah, but his money would do nicely for them. Why, considering their age difference, this marriage could go on and on. Sima had heard of some *sigheh* contracts going on for decades, and that was her plan for her daughter. Decades.

With time, she thought, Rashid would want a finer place for spending time with her. Maybe he'd help them get a better house in a better neighborhood. More rooms, better furnishings. Nicer streets for him to park his fancy car on. Maybe a little garden to sit out in during the warm weather?

A crow landed on the power line leading to the house and immediately set to squawking. She shook the blanket with force and hurled an insult at the bird. Taking flight, it dropped a dollop of excrement in the center of their courtyard.

The Daughter of the House had never been consulted. Her parents had made the decision. The three oldest brothers had been enlisted to provide the cash advance for the new furnishings of the bedroom upstairs as well as new clothes for her. They'd get their money back once the contract was signed and a cash gift received from Mullah Rashid. For once the arguments had been short, initial objections and complaints subsiding once they'd heard the contract terms. Although not off the hook for providing some cash, they'd have more of their earnings to keep for themselves for a change.

"And sure, Baba," they'd said. "We can make ourselves scarce when cousin Rashid comes."

Today Sima had paid Salavati for his goods. The room was ready. The house was clean. The rice was steaming. Maman was humming to herself in the kitchen. Baba was watching the news on the television. The Daughter of the House was sitting prettily in the main room watching it all play out.

Cousin Rashid complimented Maman again for the delicious meal as the men sat down in the main room. Maman brought in the tea and sweets and served everyone over polite conversation.

The Daughter of the House observed that her parents were on their best behavior. She hadn't seen Maman smile like this in years. Baba's language was the most courteous she could ever remember; she wondered if he'd rehearsed it. As he and Rashid shook hands in agreement of the contract terms, the Daughter of the House noticed that her father's fingers no longer bore their perpetual grease stains. He really wanted to impress his fine, educated cousin.

The official contract was now on the table, ready to sign. Cousin Rashid's colleague had prepared three signature-ready copies. Now it was up to Rashid and herself.

He produced a fine pen, signed and gave it to her, brushing her hand as he passed it. She felt a light shock at this and gave a start. Maman's eyes flashed large and full of warning at her, willing her to stay calm, graceful and accommodating. Right. She could do this. Had to do this. Everyone counted on her. She gently took the pen and put her signature on the pages as instructed.

More tea and sweets followed the congratulations, and the men began their own conversation. Maman led the Daughter of the House upstairs.

Her parents had explained that she and Rashid would have the use of their bedroom, the upstairs room, whenever he visited. For the first visit, Maman had prepared the room, showing her daughter what to do. After that it would be up to her to prepare it and then when Rashid left, clean it and wash the linen herself. Except for Rashid's visits, she would continue to use her usual sleeping space, an alcove separated by a screen from the main room.

Leaving her now in the bedroom, Maman descended the worn wooden stairs, ducking her head under the low lintel, and closed the downstairs door. They would have some more tea, but soon Rashid would be coming up. Maman and Baba had arranged to go out for the evening.

The Daughter of the House closed the upper door then stood still and stiff in the little room. The little play she'd been watching took a new turn. Now she was centre stage. The closing of the door was her cue. Time was slipping by but she didn't move, couldn't remember her role. Tick, tick. Was something wrong with the old clock? It was too loud, wasn't it? Tick, tick, tick. She saw Maman's exaggerated smile. Heard Baba's rehearsed courtesies. Tick, tick. A pen. Tick. A brush of flesh on her hand. Tick. The scratching of nib on paper.

Baba's loud laughter broke through and sent her into fast forward. She knew all too well what his wrath would be like if she didn't comply with the "marriage," as they all referred to it.

With agile movements, she prepared herself as her mother had told her and put on the new robe. She freshened the make-up she now was encouraged to wear. She sat down on the wide bed, covered in new linen. How white it was! She'd gone through all the correct steps. Now she sat and waited.

Her thoughts raced. Her heart quickened. Her breath shallowed. Her palms sweated. The clock ticked. She heard good-byes and the click of the front door. She heard footsteps approach the downstairs door. The steps were on the stairs now. Her heart pounded, demanding an exit from her chest. The door handle began to turn. Her lips quivered. The door opened.

1970 - 1971
Autumn, Winter, Spring and Beyond

The little room at the top of the stairs served its purpose well for a few months. The Mullah was pleased and the girl dissimulated quite well, playing her role according to expectations. The *mahr* — a sort of dowry — had been duly paid to her parents, who smiled broadly whenever Rashid arrived. Her brothers stayed out of the house more than ever, and Youssef was talking about leaving to the oil fields. Maybe she could move into his small room. It was closer to the bathroom and that would make it easier for her. She wasn't feeling well lately, especially in the mornings.

But the new routine began to unravel. Youssef did leave for the oil money and at first Baba didn't act as if he was too concerned. He assured Maman that their son would send some money home, after all. But he didn't. He didn't write, didn't call, didn't come visit, didn't explain.

Angry at this betrayal, Baba told Soheil to get part-time work while he finished his last year at school. He'd have to earn his keep.

But he didn't. "There's no more work for boys my age. Other guys got those jobs. If I want to work, it's got to be full time. But I'm not quitting school. Not for work that pays like that. And I'm not going to the oil fields." When Baba argued with him, Soheil shot back, "I'm not doing it. I won't! Look at all of you! And look at Rashid! He's the only one who had the sense to finish school, and then some. I'm going to finish school no matter what!" And he'd stormed out.

Baba was angry a lot; that is, when he wasn't sitting in a sulk. Maman didn't smile any more either. When Rashid paid his visits there would be tea, but no meal. If Baba was home when Rashid came, they'd sit down for a while to talk but increasingly their discussions would get heated. It gradually became clear to the Daughter of the House that Baba was asking Rashid for more and more money. At first he was willing to assist a bit, knowing that Youssef had up and left. Rashid could understand his cousin's pain and worry, so, sure, a little assistance was fine. He even used his contacts in the south of the country to try to locate Youssef and get a message to him; but it didn't work.

Baba's behavior took a turn for the worse one evening. His whining and complaining to Rashid reached a new level.

"Why don't you ever help me, huh? You can help all your fancy friends, but not me? Huh? You can give all your charity to everyone else, but not your own cousin, huh? What's the matter with you? You're a cheapskate, is what you are! You don't love anybody but yourself, you snob! We're not good enough for you, is that it?" His eyes burning and his lips dripping spittle, he went up to Rashid and gave his chest a push.

The mullah's steps did not approach the stairs that evening, but his voice penetrated both closed doors, stinging the ears of the Daughter of the House, who'd run upstairs in terror.

Maman tried to calm them. To no avail. Rashid slammed the door on Baba's shouts and Maman's pleas, and from the upper window the Daughter of the House saw her future stride away.

How could she have known that she'd have to carry all the blame? In the mornings Maman's expression soured when she saw her daughter at breakfast. In the evenings Baba's accusatory look followed her as she cleaned up after dinner. Soheil got his share of grunts for sure, but he stood his ground, then put his head down to his school books and ignored their father's irritation. Her other brothers stayed away. Occasionally some money came from the two oldest ones, but Youssef's disappearance was complete and Baba just couldn't get over it. He muttered things like "My faithless son; he sold me down the river!" and pounded his fist. When he looked at his daughter, he glowered. "Good-for-nothing", he'd say, or "useless waste of space," as he wiped the snot from his nose.

About three months after Rashid's departure, Baba finally figured it out. There would be a new mouth to feed. He was furious. Nothing and no one in the house was safe from him that evening. He circled the main room hitting his fist on anything available. The walls shook, tables teetered, cushions flew. No one attempted to calm his rant. Soheil left the house and Maman took refuge in the kitchen. Left alone, the Daughter of the House tried to run out into the courtyard to hide but Baba caught up with her and he yanked her to him, hurling his garlic-breath abuse directly in her face.

"What kind of a good-for-nothing are you that you couldn't even hold onto your husband? You're so young – Why didn't you charm him into staying? In fact, you should have been able to charm all kinds of presents out of him, all kinds of gifts, all kinds of help for me, your poor father, who is, after all, his cousin! That was your job! I set it all up for you, made all the arrangements, paid all the money to make a comfortable place for that miserable Rashid! I - your father, damn it! - I did everything - everything! To set you up; to set up all of us so that we could have *just* a little more comfort, *just* a little bit better food. But no, *you*, you ungrateful, useless piece of garbage who eats my food and lives in my house! You couldn't keep him here, could you? Did you plan this, you little whore? Did you plan to get us another mouth to feed, huh? Give us another mouth and let that cheapskate cousin of mine run away. Finally, her cheeks wet and swollen, she wrenched herself away, ran to the bathroom and locked the door. But her sobs brought nothing but complaints from her mother and threats from her father. So, she forced herself to stop. She sat on the cold cement floor for a long time.

Weeks of this passed, and when nothing changed, she stopped trying to figure it all out. There was no point in looking at this logically; no point in putting the blame where it truly belonged, because no one in the house would ever accept that. It was all on her.

At school she got curious looks. It was clear that she wasn't going to be able to hide her condition any longer. She stayed until she was called to the head mistress's office. She was told to leave.

After an earful of shaming from both the school and her parents, her mother saddled her with all the household chores. "Since you're having all this leisure while your father and I work ourselves to the bone providing for you, you can take care of this house and earn your keep that way, at least."

She did her best, even if it would never be good enough for them.

Her time came and she delivered a healthy boy-child. Her father contacted Rashid to tell him. The mullah came once, a couple of weeks after the birth. Confirming she'd be alone, he came to verify what Hormuz had told him. He had to be sure that his cousin wasn't trying another tactic to get money from him. He told the Daughter of the House that the boy was to be named Mehrdad. He said that he would provide money for the child to be fed and clothed and he wrote to Hormuz to confirm this. He told them, too, that he would see to the boy's education, although what that meant, she couldn't begin to think about.

If she thought that the baby's birth would improve life in the little hovel, she was gravely disappointed. The money came regularly as promised, but Hormuz took it and spent it as he liked. After all, a nursing baby doesn't eat food and doesn't need much clothing.

No one cooed or oohed the little one. No one looked at the wrinkled little face with anything but disdain. Maman complained all the time. Baba cast his insults liberally and gave The Daughter of the House a slap whenever he considered it necessary. She fed the child. She changed his soiled diapers. She tried to stop his crying when her parents were home, but only then. The rest of the day she just let him cry unless he was feeding.

Something in her had died. Her glassy stare barely registered the world around her. She knew her chores and she did them mindlessly. When there were moments of calm she closed her eyes in search of oblivion.

. . .

The boy grew. He learned how to survive in that heartless household. His grandmother barely tolerated him. His uncles remained absent. No one talked much about them anymore. Soheil was there for a while, but he was pre-occupied with his studies. He talked about university. He was biding his time until he, too, could get away. When he finally left, Grandfather's mood swings intensified. Some days the old man seemed almost thankful that there was more space in the tiny house and fewer mouths to feed; but on other days he flung his irritation everywhere he walked, until it seemed to bounce off the walls and ricochet off every surface. The atmosphere was full of his self-pity and righteous indignation. He'd slam his fist on the table; he'd kick and shove most movable objects. A small person could get hurt in the fallout.

BOOK TWO

**REVOLUTION
1979-1980**

The Families Jalili and Hashemi

Chapter One

SHIRAZ
AUGUST, 1979

"Welcome, *Aziz-am, al ahn miyam* — I'll be right there." Farah called out from the living room as Fereshteh entered the front hall of her mother's home. She was putting down her bags and tending to the baby carrier as her uncle came through, followed by her mother. He stopped and looked again at Farah, saying, "You just think about what I said. You just think about it." With a dark look on his face, he brushed by Fereshteh, muttered a perfunctory 'Salaam', and walked out, slamming the door behind him.

Putting on a smile, Farah gave her daughter a hug, then stepped back to look at her. "You know, my dear, motherhood suits you! You've kept your elegant figure and you look more beautiful than ever!" Before Fereshteh could refuse the compliment, Farah turned to coo at the little bundle in the baby carrier. Then she led them into the kitchen, where she'd laid out the tea glasses, plates and sweets.

"Put little Daryush on that chair, *Joonam*", she said, already busy at the samovar. "The tea is ready and —"

"Why do you still let Dayi Reza talk to you that way, Mamanjoon? I'm sick of it. Every time he comes there's something else for him to complain about or criticize."

Seating herself, Farah said, "No, *Joonam*, he was just talking about something that he had heard and he was worried about me... sit down, *Azizam*. Sit. Sit. *Befarma'id* "please, help yourself". She slid the plate of almond cookies over to Fereshteh.

"What do you mean, 'worried'? When has he ever been worried? He's just mean to you — mean to all of us."

"*Na, asalam*, he's really not..."

"He is, Mamanjoon. He's a mean, nasty person who never thinks of anyone but himself and his own opinions. You know this, Maman; he's been talking to you like that ever since I can remember and I bet he did it before I was born. He certainly never missed a chance to criticize you for marrying Baba, or for pretty much anything else you did or didn't do. How can you stand it? And why, why, why do you still put up with it? You're your own person. Okay, Baba's no longer with us, but you're doing fine. You have a good house. Friends all over the place. You have all of us and now you even have your first grandchild. We all love you, Maman, and we'll take care of you. You don't need to listen to Dayi Reza's ranting, so why do you?"

Farah sighed, then looked squarely at her daughter and said earnestly, "First of all, he's my brother, my only sibling. Secondly, we are indebted to him, Fereshteh; can't you see? He has helped us for years and years. How else could I have managed after Baba died? How else could I have sent you all to England for university?"

"What do you mean?" Fereshteh sat up and stared at her mother. "Baba left us money, right? And you were doing all that sewing for everyone; they paid you, right? You worked so hard!"

Farah held her tea glass between her hands and stared at the clock on the wall. Finally she said, "No, *Azizam*, that money was never enough." She looked down at her plate. "I used what I made from the sewing to send you all your pocket money — just so you wouldn't have to ask the relatives there for anything more than they were already giving you. The money that Baba left — well, there were some problems with the investments that he'd made overseas… We didn't lose it all, though, so with care, I was able to keep us living day to day, and all of you in university all those years. That's all. And now…" She toyed with an almond cookie. "Well… it just takes care of me." She looked at her daughter, then dropped her eyes. Her voice low, she said, "Your Uncle Reza bought this house from me so that I can manage."

The confusion on Fereshteh's face quickly gave way to outrage. Her mouth hung open but no sound found its way out.

"*Asalam*, try, to understand. Please. He did that only to help me. He didn't have to. So if he's sometimes a little gruff, it's okay. He's looking out for me."

"But -- I -- ," Fereshteh closed her mouth abruptly and sat back in her chair, staring blankly in front of her.

Lost in their own thoughts, they sipped their tea, now gone too cool, though they didn't really notice. A few more minutes passed and Farah got up, took their empty *estekan* — tiny tea glasses — and went to the samovar. She added more water and changed the tea in the little pot atop it. The automatic ritual always calmed her and helped her to organize her thoughts.

When the fresh tea was ready, she poured the steaming amber liquid into the little glasses, adding a little of the hot water to dilute strong brew. She put these on their tiny saucers and brought them back to the table. Pushing the bowl of cubed sugar and a plate of fresh halva over to Fereshteh, she smiled.

"Dayi Reza is not a bad man, *Azizam*. He can be difficult, yes, but he is not a bad man. Think about how well he takes care of his family. Think about how he always – always – asks how things are with us. And now he is also concerned about all these protests in the streets. He is concerned. He's thinking about his children and grandchildren but he's also thinking about us and he's worried because he knows that Baha'is are getting hurt. Even today he said to me that he's worried about our houses. He said he heard people talking about finding out where Baha'is live so they can burn down their houses. . He was warning us to be careful. That's what he was upset about just now. He wants us to stay home, stay inside and not do anything that will attract attention. He even suggested that I go stay with him and Sohayla."

Fereshteh looked at her mother and nodded. "Alright. You have a point."

"Please be careful, *Joonam*. Please be careful when you and Jamshid go out. Maybe you shouldn't go out so much. Think of Daryush *koocheloo* — little Daryush."

Fereshteh looked over at the tiny form sleeping in the baby carrier and then stared again at her tea. She took a bite of halva and chewed for a moment.

"I worry about you," Farah continued, "I worry and pray for you all the time. Dayi Reza thinks that you and Jamshid should leave Shiraz. That you can easily get jobs somewhere else. Doctors are always needed. You could go to Tehran, maybe. He has important friends there; he has a house –"

"I'm not going to ask Dayi for anything, Mamanjoon. We'll be all right. We don't need to go anywhere. Jamshid is doing fine here; the clinic is calm and everyone is just working as usual. His colleagues really appreciate his work and no one is bothering him. Our apartment building is safe enough and we don't stand out. And once Daryush gets a bit older I'll go back to work at the hospital for a few hours a week and do what I've always done. I have wonderful colleagues and they like me. They really do. Why would I want to leave that?'

Her mother leaned forward and lowered her voice and said, "*Ghorbanet beram* — may my life be sacrificed for you — because you are *Baha'i* doctors, Dayi says." She held her daughter's gaze. "Wait and watch. Khanum Zava'i told me last week that at her mosque Mullah Marandi has been giving speeches against the Baha'is again. He's telling them that good Muslims will go to heaven for righteous deeds. He's encouraging them to go after the Baha'is, telling them it's good to burn down their houses and shops and things like that. And some people are listening, she told me. She is my friend and I believe her." She put two sugar cubes in her mouth and took a long sip of her tea.

Fereshteh inhaled sharply and squeezed her eyes shut.

"What is it, Fereshtehjoon? What's the matter?" Farah leaned across the table towards her.

"Nothing, Maman."

"Fereshteh… don't tell me such nonsense! What's wrong?"

Fereshteh opened her eyes and blinked. "Oh, just memories of Mullah Marandi, Maman, that's all." She looked at her mother. "It's all right. I'm okay. So, what do you think we should do – besides leave Shiraz, that is? We can't leave, Maman. Our lives are here. You are here, Layla is here, our friends are here. You don't want to leave, do you? Does Layla? I doubt it."

Farah considered the questions. She'd been fretting about it since Khanum Zava'i had spoken to her. She'd lain awake thinking about it. And now Reza had added to her worries. Was there truth to what they were saying?

She said, "No, I don't want to leave Shiraz, and Layla certainly does not. She sees all this uproar as new opportunities to help people." She paused again, staring into her tea glass. "But I agree with Dayi that it might be better for you and Jamshid to stay in your apartment as much as possible, since no one will attack a building where many Muslims are living. Still, I worry about your neighbors. Maybe you should just stay out of their sight as much as you can; you know, do your errands while most of them are at work and don't invite any guests. Keep Daryush quiet so he doesn't bother anyone."

"Yeees… Maybe. But I can't just stop living my life, Maman. You know, I finally have a few friends here. Finally! And even our neighbors are nice to us. A couple of the women have been so kind to me and really helpful, especially since Daryush was born. I want to be with these people, Maman!"

Farah took in the earnestness of her daughter's face. For some reason that Farah could never understand, Fereshteh had never had more than a couple of friends during her entire childhood. In England it had been better, of course; Baha'is weren't persecuted there and she seemed to blossom. But when she'd returned home after her studies, she shrank back into old attitudes and Farah had begun to worry anew. That Fereshteh was finally making friends was a great relief.

"Sure, sure. Of course. Just try to be as inconspicuous as you can." She offered her daughter more cookies. "But I think I'll ask Layla to come home here to stay with me. That neighborhood where she's living now isn't safe anymore. I've heard that there are groups roaming the streets around there, just looking for trouble. They've harassed some of the shopkeepers – you know, like that Armenian baker and the Jewish jeweler. What does that tell you? A few of the shops had their windows smashed one night. Khanum Ruholamini said she'd heard that some ruffians went to that restaurant on Abbas Street - you know the one where those two new university students are working? Anyway, the tough guys told the owner that if he didn't get rid of those 'scum', they'd burn his place down. He let them go immediately. Those boys finally had to leave Shiraz, it seems, since the thugs started following them around all the time, cursing and threatening them. I tell you, Fereshtehjoon, I am really worried about Layla."

Both women had good reason to worry. Not just about Layla, but for all of them. They knew well that the Islamic Republic authorities, under the auspices of the newly formed local *komitehs*, as they were called, were assuming absolute control over virtually every aspect of daily life. As they fortified their resources — enhanced almost daily by new volunteers and recruits — they'd begun to enforce the new leader Khomeini's edicts and interpretations of religious law.

Every day, between Islamic music intended to inspire patriotism and religious fervor, the radio blasted the Revolution's propaganda and warnings to those who dared defy the new order.

The Revolutionary Guard was instrumental in consolidating the autocratic rule of the regime. On some level, most people knew it was here to stay. It wouldn't be a surprise to hear, a few months later, that Ayatollah Khomeini had ordered the creation of a paramilitary volunteer militia — to be called "the Basij" — to extend the work of the Guard, so great was its scope and burden of work.

"I hadn't realized that it was that dangerous over there."

Crimson Ink

Fereshteh rubbed her forehead. "I guess Layla would be safer here. I'd take her, but we don't have the space. Still, though, she does have to go out to work every day, and there are all the committee meetings she goes to."

"I'm nervous about all the work she used to do at the Baha'i Center. Now that the ayatollahs have taken it over, they might be looking for people who helped out there."

"You're right. She needs to come here. Well, talk to her, Maman, and see what she says. Jamshid and I can talk with her too, if you want."

"Come for dinner this weekend. I'll invite Layla. We can talk about all this then, *khub* — okay?"

"*Chashm*, Mamanjoon — of course. Just let us know when to be here."

Fereshteh smiled but Farah was not fooled. Her daughter was worried.

REZA HADN'T MEANT to slam his sister's door behind him, but right now he didn't care. If that would wake her up to what he'd been trying to get into her head, then he'd slam every door in her house.

What the hell was wrong with her? Couldn't she see what was right in front of her and her whole misguided family? Since Hassan died she'd lost all perspective. At least her husband had had some sense! He'd never have just sat here in the midst of a Revolution and done nothing! Didn't she see that it was only a matter of time before the ayatollahs would finally close in? They'd been tightening the net around anyone who wasn't 100% committed to their ideology. With a major Baha'i holy place in their city they wouldn't — couldn't — allow that building or its community to continue standing.

He got into his car, screeched away from the curb, and headed back to his office. For the love of God, he thought, wasn't it enough to know that all their documents had been confiscated, their Center closed and so many arrested? What did she think they were going to do with all that information? Didn't she realize that they'd interrogate as many as they needed to get every last name and every last piece of evidence they could use to arrest them all, or maybe even kill them?

He knew the bigwigs in the mosques. He and his father had cultivated useful relationships and business with them for decades. He knew they'd just been waiting to make their move. He knew how they'd seethed every time that useless Shah had put the brakes on their designs. What a weakling! So sensitive to foreign opinion, so scared to lose his corrupt backers, that he wouldn't let his own people do what they needed for the good of their own country. Back and forth, back and forth, always vacillating. Letting the clerics do their job for a while and then ordering them to shut up if any of his Western friends got upset about it. Of course there'd been a revolution! It was long overdue, for the love of God!

Reza turned into the parking lot outside his office and turned off the engine. Most of his sister's assets had been confiscated already. She'd been reluctant to tell him, but in the end, she'd had to — she needed his help. Hassan had invested a considerable amount in the Iranian Nonahalan Company, as so many of the Baha'is had done. And now the investments of all of them — tens of thousands of them — were gone, confiscated by The Revolution. *Poof! Just that fast.* That was the income that was supposed to sustain her into old age. She had almost nothing left from the overseas investments.

He leaned his head back and closed his eyes and sighed. He'd bought her house so she'd have the funds she needed. And to protect her. She was ok for the moment, but he couldn't protect her much longer. *She'll have to leave Shiraz.* He saw that even if she didn't. *Maybe not just yet, but soon. I'll have to buy her a place in Tehran. When she moves there, I can rent out the house here. But how to convince her? She's so bloody stubborn! And so attached to those kids. If they moved, then she'd go. But getting those daughters of hers to do anything?* He grunted his disgust.

No, he decided, *I'll have to talk to Habib. He's reasonable and smart enough to see where things are headed. Once I convince Habib, he can talk to his mother and sisters and get them to leave.* Tehran, he knew, was going to be the only place any of them could possibly be safe now. They could blend into the millions and millions there and if they were just a little smart, they might go unnoticed.

He opened his eyes, banged his hands on the steering wheel, then got out. In his office he placed a call to his nephew in Manchester.

Chapter Two

Late August

The family had gathered at Farah's again. It was a summer so full of uncertainty and unrest that many Shirazis took refuge in the security of family togetherness. For those who had the means, their lush gardens served as substitutes for the picnic outings to their usual destinations. Farah's garden was a happy alternative for her extended family. Its broad expanse of lawn, trees and flower beds allowed space for the little groups that would inevitably congregate together. She'd arranged tables and chairs in several spots and conveniently placed refreshments on serving tables near each.

Improbably, Reza found Layla sitting alone. He figured she was probably waiting for Fereshteh and Jamshid to join her, but Farah had told him they'd phoned to say they'd been delayed. Layla looked relaxed in her chair, apparently happy just to enjoy the shade and the view. *Just the chance I've been looking for*, he thought, and went over to her. She invited him to sit and he accepted with a smile.

For a while they exchanged the usual banal pleasantries and theoretically, they could have left it at that. Layla could have courteously excused herself to get a drink or to talk to someone else. But that wasn't what happened.

Reza embarked on a new topic. It was easy for him to bring up the subject because it was on everyone's mind in some way or another. Change was the only thing people could count on as the Islamic Republic impressed itself ever more assertively and insistently on both infrastructure and populace, on opponents real or perceived.

So Reza had his pick of subjects to bring up. His youngest niece was, after all, in danger. He'd tried to warn her and tried to get Farah to rein her in. In vain.

It was – what? Not even a month ago now? – when he'd asked her, "Don't you know that you could be arrested and executed on the spot?"

"Oh, Uncle, surely —"

"'Surely' nothing! The Supreme Leader has a mobile judge whose job is to confront the arrested. He reads out his judgment and has them executed within minutes!"

"You exaggerate, Uncle…"

"I do not exaggerate. You remember how SAVAK operated under the Shah? That was nothing compared to what's going on now!"

But she hadn't take him seriously and had refused to curtail her Baha'i activities.

He couldn't understand it. Layla had always been a sweet, easygoing and cheerful child. Her laughter was contagious. It had been easy to like her. But over these last months, while she had kept that cheerful spark, she'd grown intense, almost driven. For the past year or so she'd had a tiny apartment in a rough neighborhood, saying that there was so much work to be done to help the people there, especially the youth.

Reza decided to challenge her now about the chances she was taking in her so-called service.

"I see you're still at it, Layla."

"At what, Uncle?"

"Staying out late, meeting up with those teenagers. The parents."

"If you're talking about my trying to help families whose lives have been torn apart by getting attacked, arrested and killed, yes, I'm still at it, as you say."

"Laudable, Layla, but risky. Surely you can see that by now."

"Uncle, I know it's risky, but these are people who are in real need. And before you say anything else, I'm being careful about it."

"You may think you're being careful, but if I've found out about it, you can be sure that the local *Komiteh* has too. Their spies are everywhere."

"That's as may be, Uncle, but I can't just stop serving the community. I'm actually helping people. And they're not just Baha'is, Uncle. They're Muslims too. The authorities can see that, I'm sure."

His patience waning, he decided to try a different tack.

"Layla, haven't you heard about what happens to members of any organization not sanctioned by the State?"

"Well, yes, but which ones do you mean?"

"Any that are radical and non-Islamic. You know them: communists, Mujahedin-e-Khalq, social activists. Even non-Shia Muslims. And of course, you people."

"So, what do you want to say, Uncle?" She sounded so composed. Almost indulgent. Infuriatingly imperturbable, he thought.

Taking a deep breath, he said, "What I'm saying is that they will use any excuse to take prisoners and any method to get a confession out of them."

When she didn't respond, he went on, "And even if they don't confess, the judges don't need any evidence."

"But there must be lawyers to give that evidence."

He laughed. "Lawyers? Are you joking? There *are* no lawyers! Or if there are, they're useless. Defense attorneys have no access to documents or information and almost no time with their so-called clients. It's hardly possible to prepare a case like that! No, Layla, there's a prosecutor. He has all the evidence needed. And the judge.

They do it quickly, you know. A Revolutionary Court trial — remember, Layla, these are *Revolutionary* Courts and have thousands of cases on their dockets — might take only a couple of hours."

He grimaced. "I've heard of trials of even just a few minutes, so think about that! Think about what you're doing, girl!"

"You're trying to scare me, Uncle!" she laughed. "But I won't back down from helping people in need. It's *because* it's a revolution, *because* life's very challenging now, that I'm doing this!"

"Don't you see that it's not just about you, you silly girl? It's also about the rest of the family. We're all in danger of being judged. *Your* family's going to be more exposed because of *you*. And *my* family's going to be judged simply because we're related to you. You Baha'is are enemies of the Republic! You're too headstrong, young lady. Too involved in matters you should leave alone; too open in your religious activities."

"No, Uncle, I'm not! We're not! We obey all the laws, we follow the rules. We're trying to help our country!" Her surprise was clear.

Perhaps it was the heat. Perhaps the stresses of running his business in the midst of the Revolution. Or perhaps it was the fact that she could be so calm in her situation while he could not be in his. Whatever it was, he finally snapped.

"You don't know what you're playing with, young lady! You have no idea! Your childish idealism is going to get you into trouble, and us with it! You think you understand the things that are going on around you now, huh? You think you can just go out there with your own ideas and break the rules? You think that what you do is going to make a difference to those people or to anyone? You are so mistaken, girl, so mistaken! You really think — don't you? — that your sweet little words and cute little smile are going to help you when the Revolutionary Guards show up — that they'll just back off at your request when they come for you?"

His voice was still low, but he could see that his sarcasm bit. Her smile had disappeared, though her posture made it clear that she was still undeterred in her intentions.

He challenged her. "How can you just sit there like that?" he hissed. "What's the matter with you?

"Are you crazy or are you just so full of yourself that you think you're untouchable, eh? Is that it? Are you like your sister after all? Huh? You, another upstart in the family, eh?"

Layla stared at him.

"I'll teach you about arrogance! So full of herself, hah! but I've dealt with her. She knows better than to pull that nonsense with me! Oh, I've knocked *her* down and I can do the same to *you*! You'll see where your self-important attitude gets you, little niece, you'll see. Nowhere! Except dead!" He laughed.

"Yeah, you want to play the hero like some of your friends? Like that stupid woman back then in Hurmuzak? A lot of good that did her or her stupid family! You know, little niece, I've a mind to set the mob on you just like we did it back then! Idiots, the lot of you!"

With the back of his hand he wiped a bit of spittle from the corner of his mouth. "If it weren't for Farah, do you think I wouldn't hesitate to turn you lot in? Do you think —"

"What?" Layla's astonished voice brought him out of his rant and he stared at her, his mouth open.

Trying, but failing to compose herself, she asked: "Uncle, what are you saying? What do you mean, you 'knocked Fereshteh down'? And… and… what did you mean about that 'hero'? Did… d-d-did you mean — what do *you* know about Hurmuzak? Were *you* a part of that? What did you do? Were you with those mobs? Did you kill someone?" Her eyes were huge under the furrowed brows.

Everything was in slow motion. His niece's voice was far away. Blood-drenched faces and burnt bodies appeared, translucent against Layla's. He stared at her, mute.

"Please, Uncle, speak! Please tell me that you were not capable of doing those ghastly things!"

He couldn't.

And the look on her face, the posture of her body – everything about her in that single moment told him that she knew the truth.

Layla's azure eyes looked him straight in the face, and with infinite sadness she murmured, "I wonder what your beloved sister would say if she knew this."

A raw fear gripped him, its iciness cutting through his heart and

Crimson Ink

stopping his breath. He stared at her and saw not her but only his ruin through betrayal. His mind reengaged and scavenged its resources, trying to find a way to fix this. It found its way at last to clarity and began to calculate. He was still staring at his niece.

She turned her gaze from him and looked across the garden, her eyes somewhere far distant. She was not afraid of him, he saw, but making her own calculations.

Neither of them moved. Neither of them spoke.

Without looking again at him, Layla got up, muttering something. Whatever it was, he couldn't hear her because she turned on her heel and went back into the house, sliding the door shut behind her.

LAYLA STAYED over at her mother's again that night. She knew that Farah liked having her there; she thought her daughter would be safer with her than in her own apartment, so sometimes she obliged her. She'd brought a stack of committee files with her, planning to sort and cull what she could here at her mother's since it really wasn't safe anymore to keep such things in her own apartment. Too many places had been raided lately.

She closed the bedroom door, sat down at the small desk and took the top folder from the stack in front of her. She opened it and started to read but her heart was too heavy. She returned it to the stack and got ready for bed.

She had no intention of telling her mother. In the barest whisper, she'd said to her uncle, "I won't tell her." And she'd walked away weighed down by his revelations.

So no, Maman would never know. Such a piece of information would crush her. Uncle Reza knew this, too. And he really did love his sister. In spite of every difference they had, Layla knew that he loved her and she loved him. No, Layla would not go down that road. The question for her now was, what was she going to do with her feelings? How was she going to come to terms with what she now knew?

The little lamp on the bedside table gave her old room a warm glow. Her childhood's sense of home, comfort and safety that had always soothed her to sleep.

Sitting up against her pillows, Layla opened her journal. She sat still for a few moments, staring past the objects in her room and into her own thoughts. Then she began to write.

Chapter Three

Early September

Layla was ready when they came three days later. After her uncle's tirade she figured something would happen. It was only a matter of time. And time, well, what *was* it anyway? Time and space were just a stage where we all played out our roles and did what we liked to think was our best. Truly, though, no one actually knew what their best was - or *could* be. Layla simply hoped that her best was worthy.

She put on her chador and opened her apartment door before they knocked; their voices in the stairwell had been enough to alert her.

"Layla Jalili! We have orders to question you." She stepped aside and in they came: two tough young men with their grim older leader, all bearded, all carrying automatic rifles.

"Search everything! And make sure you find something!" On the older Guardsman's orders, the other two began the ransacking that was standard for such visitations. Layla stood near a wall and answered the leader's questions calmly and politely.

"So, you're a filthy subversive Baha'i? Show me your I.D."

Layla took her documents from a desk drawer and handed them to him with a polite "*Befarma'id* — here you are."

He looked at her papers and photographs, then pocketed them with a grunt.

"You live here alone? Or do you have a boyfriend, huh?"

"I live here alone."

"No young woman lives alone. Only whores. You run your whore business from here? Answer me you cheap little tramp!"

"As I said, I live alone. I live here because it's close to my job."

"Your job. Ha! Your job! You hear that, guys? She lives here because of her job! Plenty of cheap tricks in this neighborhood, right boys?" A chorus of laughter.

"But you don't come from here, do you, little tramp? Did your family throw you out because of your whoring?" Another round of laughter.

Then another tack. "Where is your family" was followed by "Where are your books, documents, committee papers…" and on and on. He was clearly not listening to her answers, but seemed instead to enjoy assaulting her with questions and the muzzle of his rifle, hopeful, perhaps, to see her cower.

But he failed. Layla stood before him, her eyes lowered, her face impassive and her hands held together loosely in front of her.

It didn't take long for the young roughnecks to finish their job. Her two-roomed place was simply furnished and contained very few personal items. They'd pulled out the books and leafed through them, hoping something incriminating might fall out. They'd emptied her closet and small chest of drawers, searching in vain for hidden treasures of some kind. They'd continued with the cupboards in the small kitchenette, even digging into her little fridge-freezer, no doubt hoping for a sealed packet of some sort.

"Sir, there's nothing. The bitch must have tossed it all or maybe she gave her stuff to friends."

"Yeah, filthy scum, where'd you stash your stuff, huh?"

The three men pointed their rifles at her. The leader pushed the muzzle of his weapon into her throat. This, at last, got a rise out of

Crimson Ink

her: for a few seconds her eyes produced the flash of fear they all wanted to see. With a grunt the leader moved his rifle from her throat to her arm, forcing her to turn.

"Cuff her!" He ordered and his minions obeyed.

"Now move! Down the stairs — move it!"

It had all been too easy. She'd disappointed them and they let her know it by manhandling her down the stairs and finally shoving her into a waiting van. There, another Guardsman put a blindfold over her eyes, uttered a few imprecations and slammed the door.

They drove a long time, making stops along the way. Each stop seemed to be just like the previous one, and the "passengers" now numbered at least seven, she guessed. To still the pounding in her chest she focused on whatever her senses could pick up, trying to create a logical picture of what was happening. If she could just assemble facts and focus on those... *Had she been the first of that night's roundup? These always took place after 11 o'clock at night. What time was it now? Who were the people sitting with her?*

Most of the others were silent, probably from shock, she guessed. Many had probably been asleep when the Guards had come for them. She felt them around her, heard their sighs, felt their shifting and sensed their fear. Occasionally there was a sniffle, a *sotto voce* appeal to the Divine or a whispered comment. It was certain that at least one of the Guards was sitting with them and no one wanted to aggravate the situation.

At the next stop the van doors remained closed. The exchange of voices was followed by the sound of moving metal. A gate opening, perhaps. The van moved on, turning sharply, then braking and starting forward again. A final stop and the engine cut. They'd arrived. The door opened, releasing the stuffiness, and one by one, Layla and her companions were yanked out into the freshness of the night air. Layla savored it by inhaling deeply.

Propelled along by rifle butts, they shuffled away from the vehicle, finally reaching what must have been an assembly point. There was a roll of metal wheels and they were pushed forward.

Layla tilted her blindfolded head towards the heavens and took her last deep breaths of the free night air before the new walls closed them in.

SHIRAZ
SEPPAH PRISON
EARLY SEPTEMBER

THE INTAKE PROCESS separated the men and women and led them off into opposite corridors. A woman commanded Layla to hold onto the rolled-up newspaper she pushed into her hand and towed her along beside her. Layla had heard of this: the prison guards, considering the Baha'is *najjess* - unclean, did not want to touch them, so they used the rolled papers to tow them instead.

There were formalities, of course; the inevitable paperwork to register the prisoners and begin their dossier of charges, as well as to document the course of their incarceration. But after that had been done, a guard pushed Layla towards a crowded holding cell and removed her blindfold.

The hands and fingers clinging to the cell bars were old, young, be-ringed, bare, clean, dirty, smooth, rough, and wrinkled – hands that told whole stories about Layla's new companions. The chadors and scarves, the shoes and stockings belonged to women of every stripe.

One guard unlocked the cell while another held her rifle ready. The guard with the keys shouted at the women to move back and the other pushed Layla in.

Among the pockets of odors that circulated slowly through the stifling air shared among the fifty or so bodies, Layla found her tiny space. She gazed at them all, taking in each face, each frame. A microcosm of her city was crammed in here and she considered what the stories might be that had brought them to prison. People who would never have crossed each other's paths, never have had a conversation were now sitting cheek-by-jowl.

She spoke to some and above all, she listened. Her companions were housewives, students, drug-users and prostitutes; even a murderer or two. Some held menial jobs, some were academics. Some were ideologues, some were protesters. Some were atheists and some were devout adherents of Iran's multiplicity of religions: Christians, Zoroastrians, Jews, Sunni and Shia Muslims. For tonight, at least, Layla was the only Baha'i. All suspected of some crime of action or belief and considered threats to the new order of life in the land, they would pass through the filter of official interrogation that would decide their fate.

Interrogation was by now a well-oiled machine and it wasn't long until even the newest of the detainees began to grasp the process.

SHIRAZ
ADELABAD PRISON
MID-SEPTEMBER TO LATE OCTOBER

TO BETTER ACCOMPLISH THEIR GOALS, the authorities transferred the prisoners from Seppah to Adelabad Prison.

From the holding cell that served to house the newly arrived, Layla's group was taken to a smaller unit. The Baha'is, who were becoming numerous, were ordered to keep to themselves and to one side of the 4 x 6 meter cell that housed them. Apparently even other criminals were given the courtesy of remaining unsoiled by the *najjess*. There was a filthy, threadbare carpet on the cement floor and each prisoner had one dirty blanket to lie on and a second one for cover. Except when the cell became too full. Then they had to share blankets. Although it was early autumn and the weather still warm, the prison's thick concrete walls kept the inside cool. As the weeks went on, cool turned to cold and no heat or extra blankets were offered.

All prisoners received food two, maybe three times a day, but the Baha'is had to share their meals: three or four to a bowl or plate and told to eat with their hands. This worked in the case of the scrap of hard cheese that was their breakfast and of the meager rice portion that sometimes served as dinner. It was harder to do when it came to the watery soup they got for lunch. But they managed. They were a tight-knit group and most of them knew each other anyway.

Everyone was wakened before dawn with the Call to Prayer, but the Baha'is were not allowed to chant their prayers aloud.

Interrogations started at 8 a.m. There seemed to be no special order as to who or when; only that several were hauled out then. You could be called at any moment and be kept there for any length of time, Layla soon learned. You might be interrogated in several different sessions, returning to your cell in between. Or not. If they wanted to keep the prisoners uncertain and off-balance this often did the trick. But you could count on interrogations on most days.

Layla's first encounter with this was in a group. They were led blindfolded down a few flights of stairs. Well before they reached the stairway she heard the shouts, the cries and the screams. As they descended, the pitch rose, piercing. On those first days the animal-like sounds from below gave her gooseflesh. Not that she ever got used to them, but somehow she found a way to wrap herself in a bubble that allowed her to just keep walking.

From the outset the interrogators' tactic was to ask questions that they already had answers for. The same basic questions were put to her over and over, no matter what she answered either verbally or in writing. The badgering seemed designed to hammer her into submission. Layla kept her answers truthful and consistent.

"What's your name? What do you do for a living? How long have you been a Baha'i? What kinds of things do you teach those children and youth in the classes you give? What are the names of the other teachers? Where do they live?" They knew the answers already.

They knew everything about the Baha'is. For decades there had been organizations dedicated to discovering every detail about Baha'i history, principles and teachings. They had secretly infiltrated Baha'i communities, attended Baha'i activities and monitored the community's structure and finances. So, no, they didn't need this information. What they wanted was to get the prisoners to incriminate themselves and others. And they wanted the Baha'is to recant.

Among many, and certainly the new regime, there was a belief that Baha'is were enemies of Islam.

Layla sat blindfolded on the floor. There were never enough chairs when there was a group. They kept trying to pit the Baha'is against each other, trying to convince them that they'd already betrayed each other in separate, individual interrogations. This didn't work. The interrogators didn't understand the level of trust that these people seemed to have with each other. But there were other tactics.

For about a week or so - she'd lost count of the days, actually - they brought her to the same room, each day increasing the number of hours she spent there. Finally, one day, they hammered Layla for fourteen and a half hours with accusations, insults, demands, threats, questions, twisting her responses and using them against her; refusing her food, water, and even the toilet. The wretched room still stank from the vomit of a previous prisoner. But she'd hold out, she told herself. After all, what could she say or write that she'd not already given them?

On the verge of collapse, she was forced to stand up, blindfolded and dizzy, thirsty and weak from hunger.

"Walk", came the command.

"Where?" she'd asked. "I can't see anything."

"Just walk as I tell you. Walk straight ahead."

She obeyed and in three steps bumped into a concrete wall, the impact sending her to the floor. Moaning, she held her head in her hands.

"Get up and walk! I didn't tell you to rest. Get up!"

With one hand Layla felt the cold floor beneath her and with the other reached out, trying to find the wall in front of her. Breathing heavily, she maneuvered herself into a standing position and turned, taking tentative steps.

"Put your arms by your sides! Now turn right!" She obeyed and after a few steps again hit a wall and cried out. While her interrogator laughed she steadied herself, then complied with his new command. Wary now, she shortened her steps and slowed her pace.

Somehow she remained on her feet. He played this game again and again, laughing every time she hit the wall.

When he finally tired of this he called the guard and ordered her back to her cell.

She collapsed into the arms of her cellmates and fell asleep almost before they laid her down. But it seemed she'd hardly closed her eyes when the guard shook her awake and ordered her to get up and go with her. Two of Layla's cellmates whispered to her in the dark and helped her up. The iron door clanged shut. Blindfolded again, Layla was soon descending the stairs. It was strangely quiet. Only a low moaning. She wondered vaguely what time it was.

The guard pushed her into a new room, pulled off the blindfold and left. The space had a few wooden tables and on the far side she identified the source of the moaning. Lying still on one of the tables was a woman in a fetal position, her back toward the door. The walls and floor were splattered with dark stains, large and small. Among the usual odors of such rooms she detected a fresh stink that her exhausted brain couldn't quite place.

"Get onto the table. This one." The person speaking seemed to appear from nowhere, but he must have been standing in the corner when she was brought in. He wore a mask over the lower half of his face.

Impatient with her hesitation as she tried to take in what was happening, he shouted the command again, adding a few expletives.

She climbed wearily up onto the table indicated, forcing herself to sit, and pulled her chador more closely around her.

"You won't need that. Take it off."

She did.

"You filthy, piece of vermin, are you finally going to recant your misguided beliefs and return to the true Faith?"

Layla shook her head. She couldn't find her voice.

Again and again he repeated his phrase, then said, "I'm giving you one last chance. You see this?" Layla saw that he was holding what looked like a thick electrical cable. She barely nodded.

"Just make this easy on both of us. Recant and then I won't need to use this. You can go back home." She shook her head again and closed her eyes.

The man ordered the guard, still standing by the closed door, to push Layla onto her stomach and tie her to the table. This accomplished, the guard stepped back and went out of the room to wait. As the door clicked shut the man raised his arm and began to swing his cable over the back of Layla's tensed body.

LAYLA WOKE TO EXCRUCIATING PAIN. Even though she was now lying on her side, even though her shredded clothing had been removed and replaced by a sheet, her skin was on fire. It seemed that something wet and cold was moving across her lower back. She opened her eyes and saw her right arm outstretched and taped to a board. A needle and a tube were attached. A voice behind her was telling her not to move and she felt the cold wet pressure shift from her back to her legs.

"I'm almost finished cleaning you up. Don't move." She couldn't have done so anyway.

After some minutes the person behind her came around to face her. "I'm a doctor," she said. "I'm also a prisoner. They ordered me to patch you up a bit. I'm giving you some intravenous fluid. You'll be in this treatment room for a little while before they send you back to your cell.

"I know you're in pain, but I can't give you anything for it. Just lie on your side. You'll be ok. It seems you weren't in there that long because you passed out. So he stopped. For now." The doctor called in an assistant and told her to tell "him" that Layla was conscious. "Ask him what else we should do with her."

IT WAS PROBABLY a week before Layla was able to walk again. After the prisoner-doctor had been ordered to release her, she'd been returned to her cellmates on a gurney and they were told to carry her into the cell. They'd been exceptionally kind, taking it in turns to add some of their meager rations to hers "to help build up your strength, *Azizjoon*" they all told her.

One day the guard arrived for her. She knew enough not to ask where they were going. She braced herself as she hobbled, dreading a return to the "dungeon", as she thought of it. But the guard led her in a different direction and Layla was astonished to find herself in the visitors' hall. She hadn't been allowed to have visitors since she'd been arrested and had resigned herself to possibly never seeing her family again.

The guard led her to a flimsy metal chair on the inmates' side of a long partition. It was sectioned into small semi-cubicles, each with a surface to lean on. Thick plexiglass above revealed an identical setup on the visitors' side. Small microphones provided for communication.

Layla sat as best she could; her back, buttocks and thighs still smarted under the scabs. She waited, her heart light and hopeful.

Out of a sea of chadored figures emerged the beloved faces of her mother and sister. Every emotion played on their features as they took in the sight of the sister they'd no doubt feared was lost to them. Layla felt it all — every expression of theirs was hers. The words they spoke, the gestures they made, the tears of joy and pain, anxiety and relief, — all released a flood of tension, worry and heartbreak.

Torrents of questions and answers rushed back and forth and when they finally paused for breath, Layla said, "Please pray for me." She interrupted their assurances that that's all they'd been doing.

She continued, her voice soft but earnest, "Please continue to pray. Pray that I may have a good end —"

"*Joon-e-delam* - my darling, don't speak that way! They'll release you! You've done nothing wrong!"

"Mamanjoon," she persisted, "my dearest Maman, and you, Fereshteh, my beloved sister, please listen. Please pray for me and if I pass from this life —" More protests.

"If I pass from this life, please pray for my executioners. If you should find that you're called to collect my body, please offer sweets

Crimson Ink

to those who give you my remains. Please. I ask this of you. Just this one tiny thing. Bring the sweets because you should be happy for my soul. I will be free of all this and I will be happy. Bring the sweets and share in my happiness."

Farah looked deep into Layla's eyes. Layla saw the searching, the sadness, the shadows of worry, the moisture that gave voice to her mother's breaking heart; then, finally, the acceptance. It was reluctant, but it was acceptance, Layla understood.

She whispered, "Thank you, Maman, thank you."

She turned her gaze to Fereshteh, but her sister's eyes were closed. "Fereshtehjoon?" She repeated it twice before her sister lifted her lids.

"Will you do this for me, my sweet sister?" Layla asked softly.

"I...," but her voice caught in her throat. Her face was deathly pale. "I... Laylajoon... Layla, you... I..." But her words were cut off by a disembodied voice that filled the room. *"Visiting time has ended. Visiting time has ended. All visitors are requested to leave."*

A guard came up behind Layla and ordered her down the corridor through which she'd come.

She turned to wave. Farah's hands were flapping and blowing kisses. Fereshteh held up a still, tired hand and stared, her eyes dark against her chalk face.

Two days later the guard led her a fair distance from the cells along a labyrinth of unfamiliar corridors. Although handcuffed, Layla wore no blindfold. They stopped in front of a heavy door and the guard ushered her in. The room was large and clean and its frosted window was partly open, so the air was fresher here. Bright sunshine poured through, uninhibited by the heavy bars.

The guard stood her before a high desk. Seated at it was a judge. A snowy turban sat neatly above the creased forehead and bushy gray brows. The trim full beard did nothing to mask the fatigue and distaste in the stern face.

"I'm giving you one last chance to give me the names of your teacher friends and to recant. One last chance, do you hear?"

Layla nodded.

"So?"

"I've told you again and again…" She was so tired.

"Speak up! I can't hear you!"

"I have no names to give. I won't recant my faith." Her voice was clearer now.

Silence.

"I can have you put on that table again, you know." She recognized that voice. She turned and saw the face of her interrogator for the first time.

"Yes," she replied, facing the judge again. Her voice was measured. "I do know. I know that you will do whatever it is you feel you have to. For me it's the same. I am doing what I have to."

The judge spoke. "Because these Baha'is - your people - are making you do this. Aren't they? Isn't that what you people do? Pressure you from the time you can walk?"

"No, your honor. We choose our beliefs and our loyalty to them. No one forces us. Not even our parents. We choose." Then she added, "I have chosen."

She looked respectfully but intently into his eyes. "Now, your honor, which will you choose: your table, your hangman's rope, your rifles?"

He saw the set of her mouth. He'd seen this expression before. When it got to this stage, there was nothing more to do. *Stupid people; they went like lambs to the slaughter. A waste of my time when there are so many others to deal with just now.* He exchanged some words with his colleague, then pronounced her unrepentant of her crimes: being a Baha'i, being a spy for Zionism, and spreading corruption to children and youth. The sentencing was quick. She would be hanged the following day.

LAYLA STILL WASN'T sure if she was the best she could be, but whatever she was, she felt a great peacefulness spreading through her.

She had spent the rest of the day in quiet conversations with those of her cellmates who had not been taken downstairs. After the others had gone to sleep she had lain awake, considering her short life and all the joys it had given her. She spent some hours in meditation and silent prayer, only moving her lips, feeling the motion of the syllables and hearing in her mind her own special melody. Her pain temporarily forgotten, she sat and imagined herself inhaling the fresh clean air of the countryside, and lost herself in a cinematic landscape of exquisite beauty. Finally she lay on her side and slept lightly until the guard came for her.

It was still night and when she walked past them, most of the women simply shifted position and dozed off again. But three of her friends rose and gently embraced her. They kissed her on both cheeks, mingling their tears with hers, and whispered their love and encouragement. She left them and followed the guard.

The dismal network of corridors eventually opened to a courtyard enclosed by high walls topped with razor-wire.

The first thing Layla looked for was the sky. In the pre-dawn, the stars were bright. Her blue eyes wide, she smiled up at them and inhaled the cool air deeply before stepping up onto the platform. Three other women stood on adjacent platforms. They wore blindfolds. Layla refused the one offered her. Her heart was calm and she felt serene.

A guard stood in front of her, ready to put the rope over her head. But Layla took it from her and placed it over her head herself.

From the row of guards facing the four women came an order. The platform hatches dropped.

When the last of the bodies had ceased to twitch, the guards went over to take them down and put them on a flatbed cart. Layla's was the last one. As they laid her with the others, they noticed it.

Layla's face bore the trace of a smile.

SHIRAZ
LATE OCTOBER

Two days after the execution, Jamshid phoned Habib and Taraneh. His heart and mind heavy, he relayed the news about Layla. Without waiting for them to respond, he continued his story.

"Farah and Fereshteh are too exhausted to talk, I'm afraid. We got an unofficial report that Layla had been hanged but when we went to the prison, no one seemed to know anything, let alone if there was a body to collect.

"That was two days ago. But this morning Farah got a call to go to the prison to pick up Layla's remains. You know," he continued with a tired, aching laugh, "she was lucky in that. It seems that some families have waited a long time to hear anything. Sometimes weeks. Some never hear anything at all and go every day to the prison, only to be told to go home; they don't know anything. That's the way things are. Things here are complicated," Jamshid sighed.

Habib began a string of questions, but Jamshid begged their indulgence: "*Bebakhshid* — I'm so sorry, but right now I — I just can't talk any more. I'll call you again soon. Soon. *Khoda hafez* — good-bye."

Jamshid called them three days later to inform them about Layla's burial. "It was a very quiet affair. We couldn't invite anyone. It's too dangerous to get together in groups now. Everybody's being watched. The Komitehs are suspicious of any kind of opposition or what might look like opposition."

Habib said, "Jamshidjoon, listen. We're coming back."

"No, no, no – don't! There's no need. Please don't. Farah and Fereshteh know how you feel. And they're okay. We're all okay. Well, you know what I mean."

"Yes, but we've made our decision. We need to be there."

"Why? What can you do? You can't bring Layla back. You can't change anything. You –"

"We're coming, Jamshid. We need to be with our families. And don't say that nothing can change. It may. And we need to be part of that. To do whatever we can."

"Like what?" Jamshid felt his control slipping. "You have no idea what things are like here –"

"We're watching the news and we can see –"

"News? What does that show you? It's –"

"We've seen the marching, the huge crowds, the –"

"Yes, yes, yes, sure. The crowds and all that, yes. But that doesn't show you what's really happening to ordinary people, Habib. You really have no idea what it's like here. Stay where you are."

"Thank you for your concern, Jamshidjoon, but tell Farah and Fereshteh that we're coming home."

Chapter Four

Late October

Fereshteh put Daryush down for his nap and walked into the kitchen. Jamshid had taken Farah to see a few close friends, and Fereshteh had promised a midday meal for the three of them at her mother's home. She applied herself to her task and turned on the rice cooker, determined to stay focused only on the meal. But failed.

All she could see was Layla. The last image she would ever have of her sister seemed burned into her brain. The emaciated face, pale as the death that awaited her. The bruised forearms briefly revealed as she lifted – stiffly – her hands to the glass dividing them in the visitors' cubicle. The delicate fingers that pressed on that glass, reaching in vain for theirs. The bony form waving good-bye as they were forced to retreat from the dismal hall.

With a shudder she dumped a kilo of diced lamb into a large frying pan and sautéed it with short, quick strokes.

Images intruded. Identifying Layla's body. Friends helping to move it with what dignity they could into a van. Waiting in an anteroom while her mother and two women friends washed and shrouded Layla's corpse. Barely taking in the brief interment service at the cemetery. Lost in loss during the private prayer service held just afterwards at her mother's home.

She reached for the salt and pepper, shaking them with some force into the pan, mixing them thoroughly with the meat cubes.

"Oh, dammit! The onions!" Turning down the heat to a simmer, she grabbed the chopping board, knife and onions, and diced them, feeling the sting and tears in her eyes. She sniffed back the moisture gathering in her nose and pulled out a small frying pan, then added the onions to it with some oil.

As she swirled the onions around with the wooden spoon, older images came to mind: Layla on a hundred different occasions, laughing, joking, smiling. Layla thoughtful. Layla kind and considerate. Layla compassionate and wise.

Layla, who understood so much, yet, strangely, so little. Who had no idea what Fereshteh had suffered through; not at school; certainly not with Uncle Reza. 'Saint Layla' – "Ha!" she looked up from the pan and laughed. "Yeah, 'Saint Layla'!" And Fereshteh's tears trickled down to the corners of her twisted mouth. Layla, whose perfection infuriated Fereshteh even as she admired it. Layla, whose clear blue eyes lit up a room but could not light up Fereshteh's heart; that only seemed to shine a spotlight on every shortcoming, every weakness in Fereshteh's soul.

She took the onions off the burner and stared at them. "Every shortcoming, every weakness," she whispered. "She was everything I cannot be." And she saw how, in Layla's shadow, she'd retreated, kept to herself, left it to her sister to volunteer for any number of 'good will' projects, left it to her sister to take the lead in social situations. Let her sister take the limelight while she, Fereshteh, cowered in the wings. Hid like a mouse while Layla languished in prison. Hardly showed herself in public since the funeral.

She added the onions to the meat and stirred, remembering her heroes: the gallant soldiers of the *Shahnameh*, defending their king; the thousands of early Baha'is who gave their lives defending their beliefs. Willing to give up everything rather than recant. Her heroes. Her inspiration. She'd always hoped she be like them. If they could see her now, they would surely find her wanting. No, she was not made of the stuff of martyrs.

Fereshteh grabbed the heavy wooden spoon again and stirred the pot of simmering vegetables. "Yes, wanting!" She sniffed. "I'm weak! I'm not a martyr, so stop asking me to be one!" She spat out the words to unseen souls.

Adding the meat the large pot of vegetables, she stirred vigorously, and plunked on the lid.

Her fists pressed onto the countertop, and she cried up at the ceiling, "Maybe I'm too much like Layla's executioners. Maybe I'm judgmental and critical and maybe my soul is doomed. But I cannot forgive those vile, ignorant people who tortured my sister. Who are torturing and killing innocent people all the time in that hell-hole prison! And no! I couldn't hand them sweets and be happy for my sister or what they did to her! No! Vile people! Vile! Vile! Vile!"

She squeezed her eyelids and let the teardrops fall, seeing again the indelible last image of her sister's rawboned frame.

"No. I'm not like Layla. I could never face the insanity of interrogation and prison, never accept that kind of death, never forgive my executioners. No! No! No! And I don't care! I don't want to be like my sister! I don't want any of it!"

She shook her head vigorously and walked over to the sink. Looking out the window at the slate sky and the thinning trees rocking in the wind, she shivered.

MANCHESTER, ENGLAND
NOVEMBER

IT WAS surprising how quickly they were able to set things in motion. Employers understood, of course — family ties and all that. "Right, then. We'll see you back in a few weeks — well, once you've sorted all this dreadful business out. Dreadful, dreadful. So sorry."

The young couple smiled and thanked them, knowing all the while that things were not going to be that simple.

They decided to rent their flat furnished and had no difficulty in finding good tenants willing to pay premium price for the prize location.

On the 4th[th] of November 1979 Habib and Taraneh landed in Tehran and entered Khomeini's world.

TEHRAN and SHIRAZ
Early November

THE FOURTH OF November 1979 was chaos in Tehran. As soon as they arrived they heard the news. The buzz was on everyone's lips: *Students have taken over the U.S. Embassy! They're holding the Americans hostage!*

The taxi took a long time to reach Taraneh's parents' apartment. The driver had to zigzag his way in order to avoid the demonstrations.

Even the welcome home was disturbed; the TV broadcast played continually in the background. Mobs were everywhere and their shouting and chanting filled the neighborhoods. Speculation was wild all day. Some said that the Embassy occupation was just temporary. Just the students' way of protesting against American imperialism, as they called it. Others weren't so sure.

It was evening before the Supreme Leader's pronouncement came. When it did, the entire event acquired a new meaning and a new purpose. Khomeini sanctioned the takeover. The radio reported that the Ayatollah had called the seizure "the second revolution" and the Embassy itself an "American spy den in Tehran". The hostages' fate was thus sealed and the supporters of the Revolution had a new symbol.

Over breakfast the next morning the family discussed the situation and during the day they monitored the news. The demonstrations continued unabated and the media broadcasted its support. Taraneh's parents advocated for them to settle in Tehran, insisting that despite the current unrest it would be safer than Shiraz.

"And get your family to move here, too, Habibjoon," encouraged his mother-in-law. In Tehran, she stressed, they stood a better chance of escaping the eyes of the authorities. In Shiraz, by contrast, the Baha'is were a priority target for arrest, imprisonment and torture. She continued, "They've arrested and killed so many and they're burning houses and attacking people in their homes. If it's not the authorities, it's gangs of vigilantes."

"There's nothing to be gained by having more martyrs in the family, so would you please — please! — think about what we've said while you're visiting the family in Shiraz?" Taraneh's father held her hands and looked her straight in the eyes.

Habib could see the merits of what they were saying but wasn't completely convinced. He was anxious about the unrest in the capital and wanted to get home to his own family. But when two Muslim friends came to see them the following morning, the news they shared finally got through to him.

"Khomeini's going to use this for all it's worth," said one. "I don't like him, but he's clever. He knows that this will bring people together. He knows that this will consolidate support for him from all the different factions. The Commies and all the rest of the leftists will be only too happy to help him humiliate America. So will ordinary people. They haven't forgotten the coup against Mossadegh. Oh no. They're all going to be behind him, you'll see."

His other friend agreed and added, "Yeah, and you know, he wants to hold a referendum on the new constitution. This is just what he needs. I bet he'll even make sure that the presidential and parliamentary elections take place soon too. He'll have the whole population behind him now. You wait. It'll happen."

"So, Habib, it's not going to get better any time soon," said the first. "You better get to Shiraz, take care of your family there and get out. Make sure your family leaves because down there, the authorities are already tearing you guys apart. With all this new stuff going on — you know what people will be like. This will be like heaven for those ayatollahs. They'll be all over you Baha'is there. Even worse than here."

"Yeah, Habib, believe it. Get your family out. Here it's easier to keep yourselves under the radar."

"Or better yet," said the first again, "get them out of the country altogether. While it still might be possible."

"'Might'?"

"Yeah, 'might'. The way things are going and from what I hear, that's looking dicey. But at least get them out of Shiraz."

"Okay, I hear you. I get it. We'll go. We'll be careful." He took a moment to compose himself, wiping his cheek with a flick of his hand.

He looked off to the far side of the room. "But I know my mom and I know Fereshteh. It won't be easy to get them to go anywhere."

Everyone understood. No one pressed him further. But on the way to the airport later that day, Habib asked his father-in-law to make some enquiries about apartments in Tehran.

SHIRAZ
Early November

FERESHTEH BROUGHT three mugs of steaming tea to Farah's living room and handed one each to her husband and her brother. Sitting down next to Jamshid, she let her head drop onto the back of the high sofa and sighed.

"So, Habib, what's the news from Tehran?" Jamshid asked.

Farah had broken down in sobs of relief when Habib and Taraneh had arrived the evening before. They planned to stay for a few weeks.

"It's not good, The city's full of marchers – all supporting Khomeini and shouting 'Death to America'. This seems to be spilling over from the student protests. Now the general population's involved. Lots of people out. It's not safe right now, but I imagine it'll settle down. People need to go to work and get on with life, so this can't last too long."

"You know, these people are stupid, Habib. If they had any real idea of what this new regime is doing, they'd back off quickly. I mean, I don't know what they'd do about those American hostages, but if decent, educated people really knew what Khomeini's henchmen are doing to ordinary people, they couldn't support him." He sat forward, looking at Habib. "On the phone I couldn't tell you what it's been like here." He looked briefly at Fereshteh and faced his brother-in-law again. "I couldn't describe to you how much violence Shiraz has seen. How much vandalism and looting; people being attacked. All it takes is for one of those new fanatics to point their finger at someone – anyone – and then this new militia comes tearing over and beats them up."

"Or comes for them quietly late at night and carries them off to prison," said Fereshteh, her eyes closed.

"Right. Or comes for them late at night. And we've seen what that means." Jamshid took a big sip of his tea. He tapped his foot rapidly.

"Which is why," Habib said, "now would be a good time to leave here."

"Leave? Are you joking?" Jamshid stood up and started pacing the room. "And go where?"

"To Tehran. Or leave the country." said Habib.

"Tehran? Tehran? You just told us how bad things are there! Why would we go there? And leave the country? Are you serious? We have nothing outside of Iran. Forget that! At least here we have our homes and workplaces. We have friends, we have –"

"Yes. But that's now. Things here are going to get worse. And because people know you, they can point fingers at you, like you said. It –"

"But we have friends. They'll stand up for us because they know us. They know we're ok. We're not a threat."

"Just like Layla, you mean?" Fereshteh asked, "Like Layla who wouldn't – couldn't hurt anyone if she'd tried? Her voice began to rise and she sat forward. "Like Layla, who got arrested for helping kids, for God's sake? Who got killed for helping kids in a poor neighborhood? Who was she threatening, Jamshid, huh? And who stood up to defend her, huh?"

Crimson Ink

"Fereshtehjoon, I di—"

She put down her tea and glared at both men. "What are you two even saying? The whole country's a mess. There's chaos in Tehran and violence in Shiraz. Where are we supposed to go? Another big city? It's the same there. A village somewhere? That'd be like carrying a sign saying 'here we are, come get us'. Oh no. No thank you. I am not going to put myself in harm's way. And I'm not going to depend on friends. I'm going to make myself very, very small and unobtrusive right here where I am."

"Fereshteh," Habib stood up and started towards her.

She got up and faced him squarely. "What? What are you going to say to me? What do you know about what's happened here and what happened to Layla? You didn't see her, Habib. You didn't see what they'd done to her. You didn't see the smirks on the faces of those prison guards who handed over her body. You didn't bury her. You —"

Jamshid put his arm around her shoulder but she shook it off. "Stop! Stop it, both of you. You can say what you want, but it won't matter!" She was shouting through her tears as Taraneh came through from the front hall, Farah behind her. Taraneh approached Fereshteh, but Habib warned her off. "Just let her be."

"Let me be? Don't patronize me, Habib! Or you either, Jamshid! You can talk all day about this, but it's not going to help!" She turned and sat on the sofa again, arms crossed. Taraneh took the easy chair next to her and sat very still.

"What on earth is going on here?" asked Farah, shrugging off her coat and dropping it on a chair.

"Maman, I was just telling them that it would be good to start thinking about leaving Shiraz; to move to Tehran where we'll attract less attention."

"And I'm saying that at least here we know people and that might be safest for us," said Jamshid.

Farah's face went dark and she looked at each one of them in turn.

"Do not," she enunciated, "do not stand here and argue in my house. Do not, Fereshteh, speak of Layla that way. She's hardly cold in the ground and you're all carrying on like this? How dare you?" Her eyes accused each of them in turn. "Layla was my daughter. You will not stand here and argue about her or what happened or what we're going to do. We are going to mourn her decently. Respectfully. We are going to go about our business quietly. I will tell you when I'm ready to talk about anything else." Then Farah turned and left the room.

Chapter Five

SHIRAZ
FEBRUARY, 1980

The dark, stern eyes seemed to bore into hers as Fereshteh stood eating next to the kebab kiosk where she'd just bought a quick meal in between errands. Khomeini's gaze seemed to monitor the street traffic below the facade where his giant portrait had been painted. *Wherever you look,* she thought, *there he is. The Shah's gone now — another country's burden. But the Supreme Leader is here, front and center everywhere you walk.*

For some people, he was a holy, God-sent liberator from the Shah's decadent rule, for others, the powerful commander, lawgiver and guide of a Revolution in full progress. There were some who were having misgivings about the direction the regime was taking. Still others had reason to fear what he'd brought upon them as a society. But for Fereshteh in that single moment he was the eyes and expression of her Uncle Reza.

Scenes from her younger years invaded her mind. Although she was considered tall for a woman, her uncle still seemed to tower over her. Standing there nibbling her grilled tomato, she might as well have been eight years old again. His hulking figure and quick sharp eyes followed her, accused her, and willed her into submission.

The decades had mitigated nothing in her reaction to his malignant scrutiny.

She sprinkled some more *somagh* - powdered sumac - onto her kebab and looked around at the busy street. Small storefronts - in various degrees of sophistication and cleanliness - competed with the ubiquitous sidewalk kiosks selling everything from fast foods to clothing to electronics. An abundance of entrepreneurial creativity and determination catering to the endless appetites and various wallets of Shirazis.

After all these years, she thought, he still can't get over that my parents helped me to get my medical degree in England. It still irks him to no end that a daughter of Iran could have been purposely exposed to the corruption of the West. Although, come to think of it, he still can't seem to decide whether my so-called corruption comes from the West or from my religion. The notion of equality with men, and that she was in a man's profession seemed to give Uncle Reza a constant dyspepsia. Now that the Revolution validated his beliefs about the place of women in the new society, Uncle Reza was entitling himself to an increase in his usual diatribes against her.

She could hear him: "Doing the same work, having the same education and freedoms as men - what nonsense! What blasphemy! If nothing else, it's dangerous for the family! Women fraternizing with men in the workplace, coming and going as they please without their husbands' knowledge - how can Farah allow it?"

He'd fed her parents no end of dire predictions for the fate of their children and their "Western ways". He had no respect for their spouses because they represented more of the same. They were Baha'is after all. And then there was Layla. The "I-told-you-so's" never seemed to end.

She chewed her last piece of kebab and thought about her cousins. According to her uncle, "the boys know their responsibilities, rights and privileges and the girls, now suitably married, know their place and duties."

Wiping her mouth with the rough paper napkin, she looked up

once more at the mural of the severe cleric, threw the packaging into the rubbish bin and walked away to finish her errands.

March

UNDER THE COVER of Naw-Ruz preparations Farah, Fereshteh and Jamshid moved. While everyone else was busy with buying new clothes and fresh groceries, cleaning out their closets, polishing the silver and rolling pastry dough, Farah's family was acting on the decision they'd postponed for months. They packed up their households and ferried them away to the capital.

Not that it had been that simple. For months Habib and Taraneh had been trying to convince them to move to Tehran, citing the increasing clamp down on all manner of dissent. "The reactionary right is growing in influence," they told them. "Those people are choking out any views differing from their own. You need to get out of Shiraz."

But for Farah, Fereshteh and Jamshid it had been possible for a while to delude themselves that they were safer in their own city. They even began thinking that as the Revolution celebrated its first anniversary, life would soon return to normal. Governments did change, after all, and once in place, life went on. Didn't it?

And although many of their friends were leaving Shiraz, many were not. So, it couldn't be all that bad.

"We'll just keep ourselves below the radar and let this all blow over," Farah had said. They'd lived through pogroms before. "We'll get through this one too," was her attitude.

In an effort to disabuse them of this naive notion, Reza had spelled out in clear language what was happening and how this was going to affect them all very directly — soon, he'd emphasized. In February he'd warned them about the recent proclamation banning Baha'is from government and teaching jobs, and suspending their students and children from the universities and schools.

For good measure he'd added, his look ominous, "Oh, and by

the way, I've just heard from friends in Tehran that there've been raids on some of your prominent Baha'i friends there. And arrests. If they did it there, think about what they'll do here. They're coming for you."

A family conference over dinner at Farah's had eventually led them to the conclusion that a move was the best option they had. It was true that their own professions as such weren't under threat, but, since Baha'is weren't going to be allowed to work in any public facility, Fereshteh would soon lose her position at the city's main hospital. And Jamshid had admitted that his colleagues had begun to look askance at him under the unmitigating anti-Baha'i propaganda.

"Guilt by association" and all that, Jamshid said. "Clinic positions will be off-limits soon too."

Of course, for all of them, there were the memories of what had happened to Layla.

What followed were endless telephone exchanges with Habib and Taraneh, who worked the plan from the Tehran end while a few Shirazi friends helped them to work it locally.

Fereshteh and Jamshid had managed their own packing. But Farah, against their protests, had insisted that she'd tackle hers by organizing some younger women friends to fill her boxes.

"You two have enough to do," she'd said. "I can manage. These friends are looking for ways to be helpful. No *ta'arof* this time. I'm letting them help. It makes us all happy."

It was done quickly.

"Farahjoon, what do you want to do with these books and personal items?" Shayda stood in the middle of Layla's old room. Although she had made headway, there was still a great deal lying around. "Do you want me to sort through them so you can throw some things away and have less to take with you?" She looked at Farah, knowing how painful it still was for her to decide on her daughter's things.

Farah stood in the doorway and looked around the room. At last she said, "No, Shaydajoon, please just pack everything. I can't decide on these things now. We have only a couple of days until we go. Please, just put it all in the boxes and I'll look at it after we get settled in Tehran."

Wiping a tear, she looked down and added, "Thank you, Shaydajoon. *Dastet dard na-koneh,* — thank you so very much for all the trouble you've taken to help me."

When Farah left the room, Shayda resumed her quick, methodical pace, filling one box after another. She started on a new box for Layla's books. Noticing a volume on the floor by the wall where the bed had stood, Shayda picked it up. Its plain cover bore no title, just Layla's name, but she had no time to be curious about it. She needed to finish this room. She placed it in the new box and piled the remaining books on top of it, and, folding the top flaps closed, sealed it with packing tape.

MARCH - APRIL

WHILE FARAH, Fereshteh and Jamshid negotiated the challenges of their move to the capital, Reza was meticulously planning his own relocation. He'd decided that his business interests would best be served by making Tehran his main base of operations. He would leave Farid in Shiraz to manage the smooth-running enterprise that Reza's father had created decades earlier. Farid had proven himself capable and Reza was proud of him. This allowed him the peace of mind needed to beef up his Tehran branch. He had to be ready for the emerging opportunities there and was determined that his eldest, Majid, should learn the business of expansion and development. After all, Majid would take over one day and he needed all the experience his father could put in his path.

Then, of course, there was the matter of acquiring a larger, more befitting house in the capital.

Properties were now unbelievably cheap and easy to come by. The Revolution had confiscated many, of course. Those who'd fled the country and the ones who'd stayed and gotten themselves executed for their opposition to the Grand Ayatollah had left behind an astonishing array of real estate. The State was happy to distribute it according to their own new set of rules and priorities. Khomeini appreciated the loyalty of clerics such as Rashid, and, by extension, their loyal friends. Case in point: Reza, one such friend, whose only dilemma was choosing which property he wanted.

Meanwhile, he had to tidy up things locally. Although he left his niece and her family to fend for themselves, he felt responsible for his sister. She made it clear that she didn't want to live with him and Sohayla, so he made a temporary arrangement for Farah to rent an apartment in Tehran until he had time to find a more permanent place for her. He had one major task left: renting the Shiraz house Farah was living in to good Muslims of means. Highly recommended for their integrity. He needed the assurance that the property would be well looked after until he could sell it. At a handsome profit, of course.

TEHRAN

In 1980, the capital city of the Islamic Republic of Iran had a population of about 4.5 million — about half of what it would become some 30 years into the Revolution. Thanks to the Pahlavi shahs, it was a modern city. It boasted impressive architecture, museums, art galleries, shopping districts, wide, tree-lined boulevards, and literally hundreds and hundreds of parks and green spaces.

Transportation was decent and industry capable. Universities and educational institutions were abundant.

So it was good, then, that Tehran had room to expand. The war with Iraq and the general instability within a country simultaneously still working its way through the throes of revolution meant that an inflow of the jobless, homeless, and war-maimed would join the inevitable influx of those who would always leave the provinces for the promise of "making it" in the big city.

May

Reza was extremely pleased. His acquisition of the spacious villa had taken very little time. The Elahiyeh property had been empty. Taken in hand by the government in the absence of its businessman owner. Poor sod, thought Reza, just up and left, scared his connections with the old regime would get him into trouble. Well, he'd been right, of course, and Reza didn't mind. The classic design of the 2-storey mansion with its large garden suited both Sohayla and himself. It was an older property and solid as could be. And if anything should need repair, well, Reza was, after all, the owner of a construction business. No job was too large or too small for him.

Farah's children had had a different experience. Reza had heard that they were staying temporarily with friends until they could find something for themselves. Some middle-class neighborhood. Some of those were okay, of course, but others? Well, he thought, they'll never get far. They'll be lucky to just stay there. They'll be lucky enough if they can pay rent.

For his sister, though, Reza had leased a nice little apartment in the upscale area of Pasdaran. When they'd settled a bit and had the time, he'd buy her something permanent.

The Family Rahimi

ISFAHAN
May, 1980

Staff Sergeant Kamran Rahimi of the Army of the Guardians of the Islamic Revolution — otherwise known as Revolutionary Guard — walked into the training room where the new recruits stood waiting. He looked them up and down, his eyes hard as he mentally assessed the potential caliber of this particular group. Some of them were really young; some were past their prime.

He knew from experience that they joined up for all kinds of reasons, not all them the right ones. Every intake group required weeding.

He could already see the ones who could be intimidated easily and checked them against his roster, making a mark to remind him which ones to single out for his special treatment. Keeping them a little off center, as he liked to think of it. They shouldn't count on anything. That was the only thing that would teach them constant vigilance and obedience. If they couldn't manage that, they didn't belong here.

As soon as their basic training was over and they could be

trusted to hold a weapon without shooting themselves in the foot, he and his instructor team took them out in the vans. Their practical training began in the field on real runs.

Shortly after 11:00 p.m. they pulled up in front of a well-kept home in one of the better neighborhoods. His driver, an experienced and reliable junior officer, let the three new recruits out of the van and stood guard by the vehicle while Rahimi led the others to the front door. This was the standard simple direct approach they learned first. Putting on the sternest faces they knew how to make, they followed Rahimi into the house. They'd only had to pound the door a couple of times. Maybe they'd been expected.

In many of the raids this was so. The guilty knew who they were and knew it was just a matter of time until they were arrested. Some, of course, tried to flee and even succeeded in disappearing. They'd be on the run for months. Many were doing that right now. But in the end, they usually got caught. Basij informers were everywhere and growing in number.

Some of the guilty escaped through Turkey or Pakistan, but those routes were not for the timid. Getting through Baluchistan's terrain, for example, required off-road vehicles, donkeys and a reliable network of smugglers who were well paid for the risks they took on both sides of the border. And once across the border into Pakistan — well, all bets were off there. The runaways deserved whatever they got, and what they got was sometimes no better than what they'd get right here at home. They could just as well save all of us the trouble, was Rahimi's opinion.

Tonight's first targets were typical of the average activists. These were the ones who'd believed that in helping the Revolution they'd get into power themselves. Or at least be part of the government.

"We want our voices to be heard," they all insisted. "We have important agendas and we can help the Ayatollah with his plans," they maintained.

Well, their help in overthrowing the Shah they'd all hated was much appreciated, thank you very much. But that was where their shared goals ended. If the Communists, the radical fringe groups like the Mujahedin-e-Khalq and the plethora of other activist and rights groups thought that they could all fit into Khomeini's plans, then they were more naive than their brains and fancy education should have allowed.

Rahimi began with the husband, who had made an admirable attempt at bravado and resistance, insisting on the innocence of their position. His wife had emerged from the back of the house and hadn't had the presence of mind to put on a headscarf. Perhaps this was part of her defiance when she spoke up to defend their cause.

"Put on your head scarf, woman! Show some decency!" he barked.

She didn't flinch, nor did she make a move to rectify her error. Her husband moved to her side, as if defending her lack of respect for both decency and authority. Rahimi knew this tactic too well and decided to use the situation to maximum advantage to show his recruits how it was done and done thoroughly.

"You cheap tramp, get your scarf now!" On his order one of the recruits gave her a push with his rifle and the woman finally obeyed.

Returning, she stood next to her husband and jutted out her chin and bored her angry eyes into Rahimi's.

"Defiant whore! What's your game, eh? What kind of female acts like that? And you," he said, approaching the husband, "what kind of man marries a tramp? Or... maybe you're not married. Maybe you're just two degenerates, huh? Is that it? Both immoral scum!"

He pushed the woman with the end of his automatic rifle, forcing her to fall backwards onto the sofa, knowing that her husband, thinking he was defending her, would follow. Rahimi guessed it was simply instinctive; he was rarely wrong when he did this.

He ordered his men to blindfold and handcuff the couple and then he squeezed off several pistol shots into the air. This elicited a short shriek from the woman, followed by the inevitable limb-stiffening of both of them. The verbal exchanges intensified, alternating with rifle discharges.

They cowed but remained obstinate: "We don't have any documents to give you. We have nothing. We've done nothing wrong!"

Another couple of shots into the air produced the children. Two terrified young boys, crying for their mama, came out of the darkness of the hallway, holding each other. From somewhere in the back of the house came a continuous wail.

The older boy, perhaps nine or ten years old, took in the scene first. His brother, perhaps two or three years younger, was rubbing his wet eyes with one hand and holding firmly to his brother's hand with the other. The older boy made an admirable effort to pull himself together. Looking warily at the Guardsmen then at his parents, he announced his presence.

"My name is 'Ali, sir. This is my brother Ahmad." He licked his dry lips and shifted his weight from one foot to the other, keeping his younger brother close.

Rahimi looked at him but said nothing.

"Please, sir, what's happening?" He glanced quickly at his blindfolded parents, then stared directly at Rahimi, who still said nothing. He was waiting to see how this played out. It amused him.

"Sir, we have done nothing wrong." The boy cleared his throat, then continued, "Perhaps we could sit down, sir, and talk, sir." Rahimi still said nothing.

Another glance at his parents. "My parents, sir, they're good people." Silence.

He looked down at his feet, then lifted his face again to address all four men. Clearing his throat again he said, "Please, gentlemen, could we sit and talk?" Silence.

He looked again at his parents. Their faces were proud, even beneath their blindfolds. "Please, gentlemen, may we offer you some tea — so we can all talk? Perhaps... perhaps you could put down your guns?"

Well-rehearsed, Rahimi thought. He was impressed and he smiled at the boy, then told him, "Go bring that other crying child into the living room. Your brother can come over here and wait with your parents."

A model of obedience, 'Ali soon brought in a screaming baby, trying all the while to comfort it.

"Are there any more people in the house?" Rahimi wanted to know.

"No, that's all. This is my little sister, Haleh," he added.

"Give her to your mother so she can make her be quiet," Rahimi told the boy, and he ordered one of his men to uncuff the woman and remove her blindfold for the time being.

While he interrogated the couple further, he sent his men to ransack the house in search of incriminating material and in surprisingly short order the most promising of them turned up a few folders that had been tucked away under floorboards and a heavy carpet. The others had thrown dozens of books into sacks. Probably not important, but let the guys just get some practice with standard procedure, thought Rahimi. And the new recruits grabbed whatever was still lying in the drawers of the two desks in the study.

He then stationed two of the men in front of the family, while he and the one remaining took a final look in the rest of the house. He had one ear open to monitor the living room and smiled to himself as he heard his recruits persist in the bullying. Not bad, he thought, not bad.

Considering his work here done, Rahimi ordered everyone out. But when the two boys followed, he stopped them. Against the protesting of their parents he told them, "'Ali. Ahmad. You're big boys. You don't need to come. Go back to bed. You'll see your mama, papa and sister soon."

With rifle points nudging them forward, the recruits barked "*Saket*" - quiet! - at the pleading parents and led them out the door, leaving the barefooted boys standing in their pajamas under the small pool of light illuminating the front door.

Reaching the van, Rahimi thought about the next stop on their list for tonight. They still had four more places before driving to the detention center. He hoped that baby would shut up.

The driver opened the back and scanned their surroundings, his heavy weapon ready. Rahimi monitored the novices as they secured the new detainees in the back. He was pleased. At the end of this shift he'd hold a small debriefing with them and tomorrow do a class debrief after he'd talked with his junior officers about their groups. Then they'd get back into the field.

September

Rahimi pushed open the door to the locker room, headed straight for the water dispenser and took a long drink. It didn't matter that the water was warm and stale. It had been a long day shift, the weather had been unseasonably hot, and he was thirsty. As he walked to his locker he exchanged a few words with guys coming and going but didn't join the little group of young new recruits talking and smoking in the corner. He knew them, of course. They were somewhat naive and idealistic, but still, they were fervent supporters of the Revolution. But he was too tired now to talk. He just wanted to go home. He opened the metal door, hung up his uniform jacket and sat down on the bench in front of the locker to pull off his boots.

"Yeah, well the way I heard it from my cousin, they deserved it... good riddance", one of the guys in the corner was saying.

"That's what they get –", started another.

"Well, Yazd has seven fewer of those najjess Baha'is now. From what I heard there were some nice pickings", put in a third.

"Yeah, but that's the Ministry's job to take that stuff", said the first. "Still, when they distribute the property..."

"That may be, but there's nothing stopping the Guards who arrested them from helping themselves to a few things," a snigger from a fourth and the others joined in, everyone knowing what that meant.

Rahimi sat still, one hand holding a boot, the other leaning on the locker frame. He stared into the black space, his ears buzzing; old images coming to mind.

"You know, if those people had any sense, they'd just convert. What's wrong with them? You know, they'd save everyone a lot of trouble."

"But they don't. Mostly never, that I've heard. We've got a big job to do."

The smells of cigarette smoke and strong tea drifted under Rahimi's nose.

"I'm up for it!"

"Yeah, so am I. When I think about what we do, I'm really proud. We're cleaning out our country from all these, these —"

It was 1955 again and Kamran was peeking around the door jamb, staring once again at Pedarbozorg, Baba, Massoud and the Shirazi guest.

"Infidels, you mean? Or traitors? Enemies to the Revolution in any case, whether they're the Communists, the MEK, the journalists who're in bed with the West, or those filthy Baha'is. It's all the same. They're all enemies. So, yeah, I guess I'm proud too."

Kamran didn't hear his teammate come up behind him to open his own locker. Finally he felt a tap on the shoulder and was vaguely aware that he still held a boot in his hand.

"Hey Rahimi, *tu kodom mamlikat boudi? Zoud bash; bayad berim*! – Hey, earth to Rahimi! Come on, hurry up, time to go!"

"*Chi*? – What?" Kamran Rahimi blinked himself slowly out of his transfixed state.

"*Koja budi*, Rahimi? Where were you just now? You looked like you were very, very far away, my friend! Must have been nice there, huh?" he joked. "But hurry up, it's time to go!"

"Yeah, yeah… I was just… uhh, I had something on my mind." He pulled his street shoes out of his locker and fumbled with getting the heavy boots in.

"Hey, you are coming aren't you?"

Rahimi remembered then that he and his buddies were supposed to go to a dinner.

"Sure, I'm coming. Just one minute." His voice was low.

"Hurry up then, we're going to be late!" His friend had already changed his clothes and was finishing up with his shoes.

Rahimi snapped out of his reverie, leaving Yazd and its latest acts of retributive justice behind as he transformed himself into civilian respectability.

He slammed the locker, clapped his friend on the back & hurried off with him through the door.

The Family Omidvar

Sᴏᴜᴛʜ *TEHRAN*
Lᴀᴛᴇ *Nᴏᴠᴇᴍʙᴇʀ, 1980*

Mehrdad couldn't recall exactly when he'd started making the notches. Maybe it was just one day when the constant pain in his belly had simply gotten the better of him and he'd lashed out, targeting a floorboard, in some ill-conceived retaliation.

He'd taken the little knife from the back of the cutlery drawer in the kitchen. He'd needed it, he felt. Its sharp point and small firm handle had fit his hand well. Somehow it had lent him its power, its steeliness, its protection. In time he'd befriended it fully, carrying it with him always, trusting it as an ally.

It had simply become natural to carve the notches with it: one for every accusation against him; one for every punishment; one for every blow from his grandfather's rough belt; one for every slap from his grandmother's calloused hand; one for – well, none for anything from his mother. What was the point? Her grey, drawn face with its furrowed brow never altered. It was the only feature that gave an identity to the shapeless form that engaged him only when it had to: to bring him his meals, lay out his clothes and send him off to school. It offered nothing. At least in that there was consistency.

So no, there could be no notches for someone who was so absent in her presence.

As he sat in his usual nook, this singular tiny upstairs bolt hole away from the rants and recriminations below, the boy turned his gaze from the crisscrossed pattern of notches on the floorboard under the thin rug to the rat out on the balcony. Its alert beady eyes fascinated him as they scanned the balcony's gritty surface. Its nose twitched and the boy watched as the rodent moved towards the edible scraps ahead, unaware of the trap. Mehrdad smiled.

The small creature inched forward, still scanning, still wary. The boy held the scene firmly in his gaze. His heart accelerated and he could feel the tingle of anticipation run through him as the rodent stepped up to the morsel he'd left for it. It tugged at it. The sound of the snap dampened by the soft fur and flesh beneath the metal bar produced in the boy a kind of climactic excitement he would have been hard put to describe. His eyes danced.

He went out onto the little balcony and retrieved the rodent, loosening it from its trap. Holding its limp form by the tail, he observed it for a moment. This one was a bit smaller than usual but it would still do. He pushed it down on its stomach, its head even with the floor, and took out his knife. How tiny this one's eyes are, he thought; and he wedged the slim point of the blade into one miniature socket.

BOOK THREE

**POST-REVOLUTION
1989 - 1993**

The Families Jalili and Hashemi

Chapter One

TEHRAN
JANUARY, 1989

The only mitigating factor in the fierce wind and rain of that dark and frigid January afternoon was that it succeeded in clearing the air. City smog levels were at their lowest, but there were probably not many who wanted to be outside that day to enjoy it.

Fereshteh and Jamshid had thought twice before wrapping up themselves, 10-year-old Daryush, 6-year-old Anisa and 18-month old Aryana for even the short journey to Habib and Taraneh's apartment.

In this part of Tehran, one apartment block looked much like all the others. During the last several decades the city had all it could do to keep up with the steady influx of people to the capital. Looking for work and life opportunities unavailable in the provinces, or looking for anonymity among the masses, Iranians were growing their largest city exponentially. Old gardened villa properties and open land were bought up and thoroughly exploited. Gray or beige concrete blocks of four to ten storeys were everywhere. Many apartments had balconies, but otherwise nothing much to distinguish them from their neighbors. The newer buildings were often taller, offering city-scape views. If you were lucky, you might have a glimpse of one of the hundreds of parks or green spaces around the city or your street might be lined with trees.

This area was built for affordability. No frills. But Habib and Taraneh's building, like Jamshid and Fereshteh's, did have a working elevator and underground parking for its residents.

Taking a long detour to the north to pick up Farah from her more upscale neighborhood there, the family arrived shivering at the Jalili's sixth floor apartment. Taraneh, her eyes bright and smile wide, ushered them in quickly and got them settled into the welcoming warmth of the modest but comfortable living room. Hot tea was waiting for the adults and *shir-neshasteh* flavored with a little cinnamon was poured for all the children. The thickened hot milk drink was appreciated for its ability to warm the body quickly.

Taraneh gathered the youngsters and served them while Habib saw to the rest. Then he took little Aryana onto his lap and fed her a warm bowl of the thickened drink while Maryam, Sara and Mansoor took their other two cousins off to play in their room.

The family relaxed, just happy to be together for a long afternoon. City and work life being what they were, it had been a while since they'd all had a chance to be together.

Aryana giggled as she hopped up and down on Habib's knee, reveling in her uncle's indulgence and warm smile.

"What a cheerful little girl she is! So adorable and so smart! Listening to her chatter, you'd think she was much older," Taraneh smiled as she watched her husband and niece.

"Mansoor loves her," Farah added. "You should see the two of them together. I think he's the one teaching her her words. He chatters the whole time they're playing."

Farah was just happy to be with her whole "brood", although it wasn't as often as she'd like. Still, she was glad that they actually all had work and she was happy to look after Mansoor and Aryana; she had a purpose.

Fereshteh and Jamshid were the only ones of the four allowed to work in their profession, provided they only worked in private practice, that is.

Taraneh and Habib had had several jobs over the last 10 years. Banned in 1980 from teaching at any level, Taraneh had resorted to an assortment of odd jobs and Habib had started driving a taxi. But when the authorities discovered how many Baha'is were cab drivers, they issued additional decrees to forbid them this as well. Habib had eventually found other jobs that suited his talents if not his wallet. The community was struggling and had had to become more creative in finding work. Most had to come to terms with becoming part of a cheap labor force, even those hired quietly for responsible positions. Not an insignificant number of their fellow citizens disregarded the ban on hiring Baha'is. There were several reasons: they had long had a reputation for honesty and hard work and many were very well educated. No longer able to run their own businesses, teach at universities or schools, work outright in any of the established professions in private industry or government, Baha'is constituted a high-caliber work force available now at a pittance of their worth.

It should have been simple for Jamshid to work, but with his assets confiscated, he could neither afford an office for a private practice nor find a partner brave enough to share his private practice with him during those first few years after the Revolution. He worked odd jobs like his brother-in-law during those years, then eventually found a sympathetic Muslim colleague who had a space, and this allowed him to finally see patients again.

It had been a struggle, squeezing all of them together in the Jalili's then much smaller apartment until Jamshid had found someone who would rent to them without asking questions about their religious affiliation.

In 1985, Taraneh finally had found a position as a bookkeeper for a small company who appreciated her mathematical skills, if not her doctoral degree and she was still working there. The arrangement suited everyone and there was a growing mutual respect between her and her employers. Fereshteh hadn't started work until a year later. As a woman doctor who, under the Islamic regime, was allowed to treat only women patients, demand for her skills was high and she had ultimately found a small group of tolerant Muslim women physicians who had offered her a space at their private practice. At the moment, Habib had a job supervising a small technical team at yet another firm. He kept a low profile. These were still uncertain and dangerous times.

The 1980's had been harsh to many, not only the Baha'is. As the Revolution settled into the country, "enemies of the state" had been rounded up, interrogated and imprisoned. In an effort to cleanse the nation from non-Islamic influences and bring the population together under the banner of Khomeini's rule, the government had executed large numbers of ordinary citizens for their politics and ideologies, and in the case for some Christians, Jews and Sunnis, for being outspoken or too visible in their religious beliefs. As if this culling were not painful enough, Iran's war with neighboring Iraq brought with it massive casualties. It was hardly surprising that the '80s were known as The Bloody Decade.

Now, over the meal, the Jalili families' conversation was light and cheerful, as much for the children's sake as for their own. The older four quickly learned, as their parents had, how to deal with the bigotry of school classmates and the injustices of many of the teachers. Daily life was so complicated even for the young that the adults tried to make family time as sunny as possible.

The meal finished, Taraneh stood up, inviting the others to move to the living room. She went over to the living room slider and opened it a crack to check the weather. The rain continued but the wind had stilled and the air become thick once again with the city's usual acridity. She closed it, wrapping her sweater more tightly around her slim frame, and stared a moment at the dwindling light before joining the others.

With the children off again playing in their rooms and Aryana napping, the adults settled comfortably into the well-worn sofas to share their thoughts and concerns, their experiences and their worries within the little fortress of trust and harmony that they were to each other.

"So, Fereshteh, how's it going in your office? How many physi-

Crimson Ink

cians are you now — you'd said something about a new one joining you?" Doing the honors, Habib brought fresh glasses of tea and set them on small wood tables in front of each of them before taking a seat in his favorite armchair.

"Yes. She seems very nice. But really, I've hardly had a chance to get to know her because we've been so busy moving the office to a larger space. We now have our own small lab and a second x-ray room."

"Wow - I had no idea. Are you competing with the local hospital or something?!" Taraneh chuckled.

"Hardly. But we'd all been discussing some of the challenges we've been having, like getting diagnostic work done more quickly with this steady increase in our patient load. So, through some contacts that one of the other doctors has, we were able to get the space and the equipment and we moved in a couple of weeks ago." She picked up her tea glass.

"Oh, that's right, I haven't seen either of you since before all that and it all happened rather quickly. Actually, most of us doubted we'd get it off the ground but all of a sudden it came together and we were able to move." She sipped her brew and leaned towards the large coffee table to take an almond cookie.

"Why is your patient load expanding so much?" Habib wanted to know. He helped himself to a piece of baklava.

Fereshteh reached for a sugar cube and took another sip as she considered her answer. "We've been getting a steady stream of new, younger patients." She looked down at the glass in her hand. The others waited for her to continue. Next to her, Jamshid looked at her and took her hand briefly. "Are you sure you want to hear this? It's not a happy story."

Murmurs of assent and encouragement.

She looked at Jamshid again and gave him a sad smile, then continued. "These are women who've recently been released from prison. You know, journalists, leftists, various social or religious activists and so on. These are the ones who've supposedly been 're-educated'. You know what I mean."

They did. She looked out the window at the downpour, still visible despite the encroaching darkness.

When no one spoke she continued. "Although I'm not sure that they've actually changed their opinions or beliefs. From what they hint at, they know they're being watched constantly and they're afraid, so they can't say much. But every now and then I hear some small thing that convinces me that their time in prison may have silenced them but it hasn't succeeded in any 're-education'."

"Kind of like the Soviets and their Gulags or Mao and his re-education camps, maybe?" offered Taraneh.

Habib sighed, "History's full of that, isn't it?"

"That's my guess. So, these are a lot of the patients we're seeing at our practice, and yours, too, Jamshid, right?" She looked at her husband and he nodded. "Yes, so, we're seeing a lot of trauma, both physical and psychological." She paused, reflecting. "Isn't it strange? None of us at our practice comments on these patients in terms of where they're coming from or why they've got the issues they have. No one dares say a word. But we have a kind of unspoken solidarity, and we depend on each other when we provide whatever treatment we can for these poor women."

She took another sip of tea and looked at Jamshid, who nodded again.

She looked at the others. Their solemn faces were all riveted on her.

"Some of them are just plain acutely ill, but most of them have chronic problems because they became sick in prison and never got the treatment they needed. Unless, as a couple of the patients have told us, they'd been on the verge of dying. It seems the interrogators believed they could get still more information out of them. Then, apparently, the prisoners got just enough emergency treatment to keep them alive and conscious for more questioning." Another sip of tea. "And of course I'm talking only about the ones who survived. Some stories I've heard say that many have just disappeared."

Taraneh got up and quietly brought her a fresh glass of tea and placed a sugar cube on the tiny saucer. Farah, her hand over her mouth, shifted on the sofa. Habib was staring out at the darkness.

"I had a new patient this week." Fereshteh looked at the window again but her gaze was much farther away than the lights in the distant apartment blocks.

"This patient — let's call her Fatemeh — had been in Gohar-Dasht prison for over a year. She never told me what her crime was, but I suspect she may have been a journalist of some kind. She came to me because she couldn't sleep. She kept having nightmares and generally was so anxious she had trouble doing most everything. On top of that, she had severe stomach problems and couldn't eat. I believe she has an ulcer and other related problems and so last week I sent her for extensive tests at the hospital. I've seen her twice this past week, and late yesterday she came in again and stayed after hours. Turns out, she needed to talk about what happened to her. I told her I'd listen to it all. That she could talk as long as she needed to." Fereshteh took a deep breath. No one said a word.

As if replaying the conversation for herself to convince herself that this was indeed what she'd heard, Fereshteh continued.

"Fatemeh told me about her experience in 'The Box'; some called it 'The Grave'. She said that they were forced to sit — no, live — for months in tiny little boxes that were exactly the size of graves. There were many of them — all lined up in rows, she said. They were blindfolded and had to wear both chador and headscarf. Aside from being allowed to go to the toilet three times a day, they were not permitted to sleep during the day, nor walk, nor even move their hands or feet. When they were allowed to sleep, it was a struggle. All day long they were forced to listen to verses from the Qur'an blaring from loudspeakers at such a volume that it hurt their ears. They also had to listen to recorded forced confessions played over and over and over. She said they'd hear friends' voices over the loudspeakers — friends in interrogation. They'd confess to anything, so it became impossible to trust anyone else."

She paused for a minute to slow her breathing. "Fatemeh said that before she was put into The Box, she and her cellmates were visited by a woman who'd finally been let out of it. She'd been in it for six months. When she entered their cell she told them all to keep their distance, that she was dirty. She said she was a changed person and that they shouldn't tell her anything because she'd report it." Fereshteh put the tea glass to her dry lips and drained it.

Farah, her face paler now than before, moved her lips in whispered entreaties to the Divine. Habib had assumed a posture of unnatural stillness. Taraneh's hands fidgeted and her mouth became a line.

Jamshid leaned towards his wife, took her hand again and held it gently, his warm presence a bulwark against the monstrous tale she narrated. "Finish it, Fereshtehjoon. Finish the story. Get it out of you."

She looked at her husband, still unsure whether to continue. His hand squeezed hers and he nodded as he looked into her eyes.

With a sigh she continued.

"Right after she was arrested, they had put Fatemeh into solitary confinement — horrendous enough — but she said that The Box was much, much worse because there, you lost yourself. She said that the constant pounding from the loudspeakers, all the verses, the confessions, the messages — all of it took away their senses and feelings to the extent that they couldn't accept themselves any more as human beings. Gradually they felt as though the pressure of the extra thick blindfolds was spreading over their entire bodies and since they had no normal movement or activity for so long, it felt like a slow death. Fatemeh said she'd rather have been buried alive, since that would have been a quicker end to her misery."

Another pause. Fereshteh looked at her family again. They sat mute, taking in every word.

"The whole concept of this Box, Fatemeh found out much later — and she didn't tell me how she found out — came from a man who called himself Haji Davood. Of course, these people never go by their real names, but, anyway, she said that he'd tell them — tell them — that this was their cemetery." Another pause. "It seems that Haji Davood's strategy has been very successful."

Fereshteh put her tea glass on the coffee table and then leaned back against the sofa cushions and closed her eyes.

On the way home, Fereshteh was silent but restless. Her hands fidgeted in her lap. Her breaths were shallow. She stared ahead through the continuing rain, unseeing, as Jamshid negotiated the traffic. She barely registered his curses at inconsiderate drivers.

Once home, she sent Daryush and Anisa to bed and handed Aryana to Jamshid; she went into her bedroom and closed the door, disregarding her husband's annoyed face. She changed quickly into her pajamas and climbed into bed, pulling the quilt halfway over her head. Lying on her side, she curled up tightly into a ball to stop her trembling. But her teeth chattered and soon she felt the sting in her eyes build up and then release in tears. Her nose filled. The trembling increased and soon she was powerless to hold back the heavy sobs. Reaching one arm out, she grabbed a tissue from her bedside table and blew her nose, then buried her face in her pillow to muffle her weeping.

When Jamshid came in he was quiet. He slid under the covers and lay there for a few minutes before saying, "Fereshteh?" She ignored him at first.

"Fereshteh, I know you're awake. How about if you talk?" His tone was edgy.

Still, she held out.

"Fereshteh, come on, don't do this again."

She persisted in her silence. Words refused to come, but tears flowed in the stillness.

She felt Jamshid turn on his side and sensed his indecision, but could not find her voice.

"Fereshtehjoon, please talk." He slid closer and carefully put his arm around her. Her body shrank away, but he held her. She began to shake again and he pulled her into him, his hold firm but gentle. She let go, releasing herself into a paroxysm of sobbing.

When she was still again, Jamshid gently turned her towards him, still holding her. At length she said, "I'm sorry, Jamshid. I – I –"

"Sshh. It's ok. It's ok."

She blew her nose again and Jamshid reached for more tissues. He dried her face.

"Jamshid, I don't know if I can go back to work. These patients are too much. I don't want to hear all these things. This – this – 'Fatemeh', I – she – I – it was way more than I wanted to hear. And now I know I shouldn't have listened. Oh Jamshid it was even worse than how I told the story tonight! I can't – I don't want – I –" She began to weep again; Jamshid held her securely.

When she'd dried her tears again, he said, "Fereshtehjoon, I know. It reminds you of Layla. Doesn't it?"

She nodded. Jamshid continued, "And none of us knows exactly what happened to her, so when we hear this kind of thing – this 'Fatemeh' story – it's easy to think that this kind of stuff may have been Layla's experience... Even though they probably hadn't thought of something so horrendously sophisticated yet back then. But that's where our imaginations can go." He stroked her head. "But listen, Fereshtehjoon, as bad as hearing this stuff is, and as bad as it is seeing the kinds of patients we're seeing, we can tell ourselves one really important thing: we are helping them –"

"Jamshid, these people are almost beyond help after what they've been through. Some of them have been in prison for years! They –"

"Sshh, sshh, Joonam." He stroked her hair and planted a kiss on her forehead. "Yes, that's true, but think about it: they're looking for help. They're sick. They're injured. They're still suffering. Physically and mentally. Let's remember that we are doctors and this is what we do. We help whoever comes to us. We can't be selective and say we'll only treat certain kinds of patients. That's not right. Is it?" He pulled back his head and looked her in the eyes. She shook her head and whispered, "No."

He put his forehead to hers and said, "We treat them. Physically. But let's consider that for some of them we might be among the few people that they feel they can trust with their 'story'. My guess is that not many – not even family, maybe – really know what they've endured. But we –" He drew a breath. "We see quite literally what's happened to their bodies. They know we understand that they didn't get these problems under ordinary circumstances. Maybe this allows them – well, some of them – the chance to talk." He closed his eyes and stroked the strands of hair that fell around her shoulder. "Fereshteh, for people like this woman 'Fatemeh', that is the beginning of healing. They need someone to validate their experience. After all the judgment they've had in prison, they need to speak and be heard by someone."

"But I didn't – I can't – it's –"

He pulled back and looked her full in the face again. "It's what? Fereshteh, that woman trusted you. Can you imagine what that means to her? She trusted you. You. Fereshteh. Her doctor. After what she's been through, do you think that came easily? She must be terrified of landing back there again, so she's not going to give the authorities any reason to arrest her again. And for sure she – all of these prisoners – and remember, I'm seeing these things too –" He inhaled deeply. "For sure these people are all being watched closely. There are informers everywhere and there are probably all kinds of ways they're tapping phones and watching them on camera."

Fereshteh shuddered but he went on, his voice louder and more forceful, tinged with a cynicism she rarely heard from him, "These ex-prisoners will never be free. They can confess to anything, true or not, can agree on paper to cease the activities that got them arrested in the first place, be released and then be hauled in again if they step out of line in any way the intelligence services decide is dissent."

"But Jamshid –"

"Don't you see, Fereshtehjoon, we have the chance to help them. At least as much as they let us. And we can assume that at least some of our colleagues are doing the same, even if none of us are talking about it. So, please, please, please, Fereshteh, try to look at this from a humanitarian perspective." He squeezed shut his eyes and pressed his head harder against hers.

She felt the tears well up again and let them run. "But I'm collapsing under this, so how can I go on helping these patients?"

Jamshid was silent for a minute, holding her trembling shoulders, then sighed. "Joonam, I can understand, but I know you have it in you. You're stronger than you think."

"I'm not! I'm a complete basket case at times. You've seen me. The anxiety attacks. You know too well how little it takes for me to run and hide." She buried her head into his chest.

"Ok. Sure. I know. I've seen it. Especially lately." Another sigh. "And you're worse after our visits with your uncle's family. Although why he upsets you so much I'll never understand. He's just all bluster, that man. Annoying, but harmless." He shifted onto his back and they lay in silence for a while.

Turning to her again he said, "Ok, Fereshtehjoon. How about this? To keep our sanity we'll have regular debriefs. After we put the kids to bed every night, we'll talk. Not just after something particularly bad as we've been doing. Let's have a daily debrief about what we've seen during our workday. Just talk it out and be done with it. We can mix it up by talking about all our cases, not just the ex-prisoners."

"But won't that risk normalizing what the ex-prisoners have gone through?"

"Maybe. Yeah. Maybe. But this is what's 'normal' in our country now."

"Yes, but it's not 'normal' in the moral sense, so how can we do that? Just act like these are simply ordinary cases?"

He shifted again to his back, keeping one arm around her shoulder. "Ok, you're right. You're right. But how else are we going to cope? I mean, Fereshteh, I know I haven't said too much, but I've listened to some sick things from quite a few of my patients and believe me, that's been tough for me. I have to keep giving myself a pep talk just to keep going. Telling myself everything I've just said to you." He exhaled forcefully.

A sudden sense of shame cascaded through Fereshteh as she took this in. It had never occurred to her that Jamshid might also be struggling. That all this talk was also a way for him to unload. This was no time for self-centeredness. She reached across his chest and pulled him towards her again.

"Jamshidjoon, I'm sorry. I am so sorry. I've been so wrapped up in myself that I never thought about how all this is affecting you. I guess I always see you as my rock, standing tall and tough against any storm."

He squeezed her to him.

"Jamshidjoon, let's do what you suggested. The debriefing. You're right, we've got to unburden ourselves if we're going to cope. And I'll really try. I want to help, but it's just – it's triggering the whole Layla thing – it's – I'll try anyway. I'll try." She held him tight. "And I'll pray."

Late Summer

It was the start of the weekend rush-hour when Fereshteh left Habib's apartment. She was still trying to digest what he'd just told her. Of course, she knew that his intentions were in the right place. That work needed to be done. It was honorable. Important. And brave. He was risking everything to do the "right thing". She was proud of him, admired him. As Layla had done, Habib was putting others' needs above his own. He was sacrificing his safety for the sake of a younger generation in need. As Layla had.

Memories assailed her: Layla's activities, the carefully planned efforts, the precautions - clandestine, really. Rather like stories of the Resistance during World War II. Except that the Hollywood glamor of those stories was tarnished in their re-creation in the here-and-now of modern Iran's Islamic Republic. And now it wasn't only politics, was it? It was religion. Inextricably enmeshed in politics. So maybe Habib and Layla were more like characters in the world of The Inquisition. Under her chador Fereshteh shivered in spite of the warmth of late afternoon sun.

At the end of the street she turned right into the tree-lined boulevard and walked another block, moving automatically with the rapid stream of men and chador-figures past the shops and kiosks and their brisk business transactions. She came to a halt at the curb and looked at the endless multi-laned flow of rush-hour vehicles separating her from the other side.

A long delivery truck revved its engine into second gear, spewing its sooty exhaust into the air in front of her. A motorcycle wove between the truck and the curb she was standing on. Two cars, one an ancient Peykan with a straining engine, jockeyed for a new opening in the far left lane, horns blaring and the drivers hurling insults at each other. A young man darted in between, leaping at the last second onto the dubious safety of the thoroughfare's middle island.

So, she thought, *Habib's joining some friends and old colleagues in their education program. But how's that going to work? Of course, it's terrible that so many Baha'i youth can't go to university in their own country. And it's brave of this group of academics who are trying to help them.* What they were doing wasn't illegal. They were unpaid volunteers, not paid teachers. They called themselves BIHE. Baha'i Institute of Higher Education. They were simply helping Baha'i students get an academic education, not teaching, preaching or influencing anyone outside their own community, after all. *But what a risk! If he or his students are discovered, what will happen to them?* Even if their activities weren't strictly speaking against the law, they ran counter to the Regime's intention of depriving the Baha'is of higher education. *The Powers That Be will do something about that and it won't be anything good.* Anyone could be detained for any reason at any time these days. Layla flashed into her mind; Layla and her devotion to the young kids she'd taught. *And how had that turned out? Humph.*

Fereshteh felt a nudge on her right side. Two little girls, their patterned headscarves securely knotted beneath their chubby chins, were tugging at the hands of the short, round chador-figure who was holding them tightly. The lady's face was wrinkled and weary, but her small eyes were alert and determined. One of the little ones was whining. "*Saket bash* – stop your whining - we're crossing the street," she was saying.

Fereshteh took in the little scene and briefly wondered about the three of them. What was their story? Everyone, after all, had a story. Others' stories were always so interesting. Any story that wasn't her own was always interesting. You could follow it but not have to take responsibility for it. Just like novels: you could read and read and read, forgetting your own life for hours and then close the book. It took you away from yourself and then you could simply put it down and not have to deal with fall-out from the dramas. Then you could get busy with cooking, cleaning, laundry, shopping... The rhythm of routine activities brought you down out of the uncertain atmosphere of thoughts; ruminations that could take you anywhere and might drop you off a precipice into a black chasm filled with your own self-destructive introspection.

What will happen to these little girls, she wondered. *For that matter, what will happen to my own kids? What's their future going to look like? What about their education? Will they even have one after secondary school?*

Several more women stopped beside her, waiting their chance to brave the street crossing. Fereshteh turned her head and faced the other side of the street. Her eyes looked up and met those of The Supreme Leader painted in gigantic proportions on the side of a building opposite her. The artist was able. The Leader's dark, intense gaze seemed to follow her across the busy boulevard, burning into her very heart, as if challenging her personally. These ubiquitous portraits always seemed to morph into images of Uncle Reza, bringing up scenes she kept trying to forget. Nothing had changed. Not even in a metropolis like Tehran.

Towering over her as she now weaved across the street, she dodged his hulking presence as real in that moment as the cars, motorcycles and buses surrounding her.

The crowds were thicker now. She walked rapidly along the rest of her route home, trying to ignore the occasional jostling. She turned into a smaller side street. The sound of car horns and shouting drivers was amplified between the close, high buildings. Exhaust fumes mixed with the aromas from kebab stands and tea shops. The smells of frying vegetables and meat escaped from open apartment windows. She passed two men arguing loudly. Above her a child was crying. Somewhere a couple were shouting. Young voices were complaining. Ahead, a beggar was pleading with a well-dressed middle-aged man.

Her thoughts returned to her children and their chances in life. But she found no answers.

September

The apartment windows were open to catch the breeze of the mild September afternoon. In her small kitchen Fereshteh took a moment to stand by the window and take it in, welcoming a little relief from the smog that had been sitting over the city for months. This older building, standing as it did only a side street's width from its neighbors, generally offered meager air circulation and only a minimal view of any greenery; and that, only if you lived on the fifth floor or above. Fereshteh and family counted their blessings, therefore, that they occupied a modest three-bedroom end apartment on the seventh floor. Some cross-breeze ventilation was thus possible and their small balcony afforded them at least a cityscape view of treetops in distant green spaces.

She returned to the dining room and her lunch guests, neighbors living in the same building. No need for headscarves today; they'd all left their husbands to their own devices and were enjoying their monthly get-together to share news and intelligent female conversation.

Setting the tray of fruit on the long dining table, she took her seat among her friends. She appreciated the unexpected humor that popped up in their stories of every-day circumstances. It was a relief to join their laughter. She'd had a difficult week at her practice.

A heavy thump on the ceiling, followed by a loud cry stopped the flow of talk briefly, but, as nothing followed, the women picked up their topic and carried on. A second and third thump and then a loud shriek interrupted them a few minutes later. As they exchanged looks, they heard a man's voice shouting over a woman's protests. Another thump and the sound of shattering. Muffled now, the voices continued then stopped.

Mouths open with wordless questions, the women turned to Fereshteh. She collected her thoughts before speaking.

"Unfortunately, this isn't new. We've heard these… outbursts before."

"I think I know who that family is," said Firouzeh. "I'm pretty sure I've seen the man. He passes our door on his way out and I've seen him by the elevator. He always looks angry, somehow. Never says hello. Rather rude, really."

"What about the wife?" asked Bita.

"Isn't she the one with that little green shopping cart? She always pulls her chador so close around her face that all you can ever see is one eye, even when it's only women around," added Golshan.

"Yes, she's the one. And you're right about the chador. She's a bit extreme about it. I saw her last week on my way home from work. She was limping and I offered to help her with her shopping cart, but she kept insisting that she could do it herself. Then when I asked if she needed some medical help - said I was a doctor - she got upset and just pulled her cart away. She wouldn't even get into the elevator with me," said Fereshteh.

The little group became silent, each woman off somewhere in her own thoughts.

"Fereshteh! Didn't you say you'd baked an almond cake for us? Let's have it!" Niloufar's face was bright and enthusiastic. She got up and pulled Fereshteh into the kitchen. When they returned to the table with the cake and fresh tea, Soussan was in full swing with another humorous story.

Chapter Two

TEHRAN
SUMMER, 1993

Their three children in tow, Habib and Taraneh walked the wide paved path into the park. They passed through the tree-lined entrance and emerged into the brilliance of late April's sun drenching a wide expanse of lawns, paths, picnic and play areas. The young ones ran ahead, shouting as they made for the nearest climbing frames.

"No, no, no, not here! We're meeting the others further into the park. Come on back now! You can play later," Habib shouted.

"Oh, Habib, come on," said Taraneh. "Let them play a bit."

"No, we'll be late."

"Habib, it's a picnic, for goodness sake," she said, shifting the large tote bag with their food to her other shoulder. "It's not a formal lunch. Another few minutes won't make any difference."

"Taraneh, we've made an arrangement and need to stick to the time we all agreed on. We're already a bit late."

"But the kids are so excited to get out. They've been cooped up all week and they want to run around."

"They can do that later. There's no excuse for being late." He called again to the children. "Come on. All of you. Let's go." There was a collective protest, but he ignored it. "I said, let's go. Now!"

Her mouth screwed up, Taraneh watched them drag themselves back. She shook her head.

"Look, Taraneh, they've got to learn to be on time. Discipline is important. You indulge them too much." The children got back onto the path and with that they moved on, Habib quickening the pace.

A few minutes later, they found Fereshteh and her family occupying a group of picnic tables. A charcoal grill was smoking and kebabs were already on it, their luscious aroma wafted by the soft breeze. Jamshid was monitoring them like a mother hen, while Fereshteh and Minou, still friends after almost 40 years, were setting out plastic containers of greens, vegetables and yoghurt. The children were playing nearby and immediately called out to their arriving cousins. After a quick look at their father to be sure it was now okay, Habib's children ran to join the others.

The greetings, warm as usual, gave way to general conversation, and after a few minutes, Habib joined Jamshid at the grill. He fanned the charcoal while his brother-in-law turned the plump tomatoes. Minou checked the pot of rice that was warming on a second grill while the others finished setting out the drinks.

"You're rather quiet today, Habib," said Jamshid after a while.

"I suppose I am."

Before he could elaborate, Fereshteh called out, "Are the kebabs ready, Jamshid? Shall I call everyone to come?"

"Yes, my dear, we're ready." He brought a steaming platter of kebabs and tomatoes to the picnic table as Minou spooned out the rice and Fereshteh called the children.

WHEN THE CHILDREN had run off again, the adults poured themselves tea from thermoses and settled onto a couple of picnic blankets for conversation. Habib listened as they chatted about the usual topics of the day – the weather, work, concerns about the kids.

Minou shared her news and again apologized on behalf of her family for their absence; they'd all gone to visit her husband's parents in Isfahan.

In the lull that followed, Fereshteh observed, "Habib, you're so quiet today, what's up?"

"What?" Habib, lost in his own thoughts, gave his head a shake. "Huh? Uhh, oh! Sorry. I'm just a bit distracted, that's all." He forced a smile and looked at the four faces staring at him. No one spoke.

"What? What's the matter? I can't have a quiet day?"

"Habib, what is the matter? It's clear there's something bothering you," said Fereshteh. "Come on, out with it!"

He looked in his lap, looked out at the trees, looked over at the children. He heaved a sigh but couldn't find his voice.

"Habibjoon, come on. Look at me! What is wrong?" asked Fereshteh.

"Okay, okay," he started. "I got some news this morning. It came through various people, but its source is at the U.N. Minou, maybe you know that there's a Special Rapporteur for Iran? His job is to investigate human rights violations."

"Yeah, I'm aware of that."

"I understand he's been having a very hard time getting any cooperation from our government, said Habib."

He took a moment as the others murmured or snickered, and then continued, "But he's been able to uncover some things in spite of that. It seems that he's recently written a report and submitted it to the U.N. Commission on Human Rights. A part of the report is about our Baha'i community here."

"So… what does it say?" asked Fereshteh.

"It's not good."

"No surprise. Tell us."

"Well, it seems the rapporteur discovered a document. Just recently. But the document's actually two years old. It was written by The Supreme Revolutionary Cultural Council and signed and blessed by the Supreme Leader himself."

"And?" Fereshteh and the others leaned in.

"So, it refers to what they call 'The Baha'i Question'. What to do about the Baha'is."

"I'd say they know quite well what to do about us," murmured Taraneh.

"The document turns out to be a kind of blueprint for destroying us. Slowly. No more big splashes that draw the attention of international news media. So, no more mass arrests or major attacks like we've had in the past."

Snatches of thoughts raced through Habib's mind, a gallery of the Faith's history: clergy-incited mobs leading victims through the streets with rings and ropes through their noses, or with holes cut in their flesh and filled with lighted candles; people shod like horses and made to run before the crowds; some forced into the mouths of cannon and blasted out of them. And then there were the long sieges against masses of Baha'is who'd taken shelter in old fortifications, and who, in the end, had been slaughtered by the Shah's armies. Actual armies. Then later, the periodic pogroms as well as private lynchings around the country.

"So, Habib, what do you mean? What are they going to do?" Jamshid asked.

"They've created a plan. A formal plan. They want to undermine our existence here in Iran. And they want to destroy our cultural roots outside the country. We'll be denied employment and education. We'll be watched constantly. All our activities will be considered criminal and therefore punishable."

"But – sorry to ask this – but what's different about this?" Minou asked. "They've been doing this to you for a hundred and fifty years."

"Yes. And no," said Habib. "What they've done in the past has been periodic. A lot of it according to the whims of the clergy. There were times when the various shahs went along with it, and times when they didn't. Whatever we may think about the shahs, they actually held back the worst inclinations of the clergy. Many times. Then came the Revolution and we lost any sort of so-called protection there was."

"Again I ask," said Minou, "What's different now? You're still 'unprotected infidels'; you're still 'heretics'; you're still legal targets for anyone who wants to attack you."

"This is true. But during the '80's the attacks against us made big headlines and got the attention of quite a few governments and human rights organizations." There were nods of acknowledgement.

"Those people put a lot of pressure on the Regime here. If it hadn't been for that, we'd probably all have been massacred. What this document means is that they've learned their lesson. That making headlines means they have to back off – at least to some degree. It means that now, by systematizing what might be called lesser or less conspicuous actions against us, these things will go unnoticed. And that means that they can just forge ahead and slowly, painfully root us out. If we're denied a livelihood, how can we manage to do anything? If our kids are denied an education, they have no future. This plan aims to destroy our hope and crush our spirits. This document proves that our government has formally criminalized the Baha'i Faith."

THE ENGINE GRUMBLED when Habib turned the key to the ignition. After several attempts punctuated with muttered curses, he finally got it to turn over and pressed the accelerator hard a few times to keep it from stalling. Dust from the thick exhaust wafted in through the open windows sending the kids in the back into coughing fits.

"Bloody hell!" Habib threw the car into first gear and pulled away from the curb. He'd hardly made it into the right lane when a small truck screeched at his rear and its driver leaned on his horn. Habib looked in his rear-view mirror and grimaced as he shifted into second and almost immediately had to hit the brakes as he came up to lines of vehicles stopped at a traffic light. The truck in back shifted lanes and came up beside him, its driver cursing and gesticulating. Habib ignored him, but his heart was racing and his hands formed white fists around the steering wheel. When the light

Crimson Ink

changed, he gunned the engine and followed the column, eager to get through the light, but just as he approached the intersection it was again fully red.

"Dammit!" He hit the wheel with his fist.

"Habibjoon, it's okay. We're not in a hurry. Calm down, will you? Please?"

He stared straight ahead, clenching his teeth, then took off like a shot when the light – the endless light – finally went green.

The remainder of the drive home was no different.

"Habib, please! Take it easy! Calm down!"

"Can you be quiet? Huh? Can you?"

"Hab- "

"Just stop talking. Just stop."

After his story about the Special Rapporteur's report, the mood at the picnic had become somber. The others had tried to look at the situation philosophically, observing that over the last couple of years things hadn't been any worse for them than they'd been before. After all, they did have jobs and all the basic necessities of life. Okay, their pay wasn't great, but they were able to get by.

"You just don't want to remember the bad old days from ten years ago," he'd said.

Now, as they came into their apartment he announced, "Taraneh, I'm going out. I'm taking a walk."

"A walk? But we just got back! Where are you going?"

"Out."

"But where?"

"I said, 'out'." Without looking at her, he grabbed a light jacket from the hall closet, leaving the hanger swinging.

"When will you be back?"

"When I get here." Closing the door hard, he left.

He went straight to the elevator, but it was in use and it was slow. He turned and headed for the stairs, scuttling down the six flights and then out the main door and onto the sidewalk. He didn't have a destination; he didn't care where he walked. One city street was as good as the next right now. He put his hands in his jacket pockets and turned right at the corner. Just so that he didn't need to think about crossing a street.

His first thoughts went to his car. "Piece of junk! Just crap!" he muttered. And thought about the sleek late-model Mercedes his cousins and Uncle Reza drove. Which led his thoughts to the whole issue of affordability.

Here I am, he thought, with all kinds of academic credentials and all I can do is work for a second-rate company run by guy who knows next to nothing about the tech services he provides. I do all the work and he gets all the money. If Taraneh didn't bring in the meager income she does, I wouldn't even be able to provide for my family! What kind of man am I anyway? He sniffed and crossed straight over a side street without looking. Is this what life's always going to be like? And he thought about Jamshid's warning back in 1979. Not to come back to Iran. But how could they not have returned when the family was in such straits? And who could have known that things would have turned out like this? That this regime would still be in power? That this regime would turn into – into – "Argh! Dammit!" he said out loud, ignoring the puzzled looks from passersby.

He came to a large intersection and had to wait to cross. A dark blue Mercedes zoomed by and again he thought of his uncle. Yet another reminder of the canker in his family. Habib tried his best and usually succeeded in swallowing his impatience with the man. That's why Reza warms up to me, he thought. I never call him on his rudeness or antediluvian attitudes. Thinks I'm happy to indulge him.

Habib crossed the busy street, the cacophony of ancient, overtaxed bus engines, the shouted profanities of taxi drivers, and the come-ons of street hawkers and hookers a muted hum as he thought of his uncle. Bile rose in his throat and he felt the knot in his stomach tighten.

He couldn't think of Reza without thinking of Fereshteh. A parade of scenes passed through his mind and he saw her red, swollen eyes, her tear-stained cheeks, sometimes bright red, sometimes pale as death. He saw her scratching her arm, always scratching, scratching, scratching. Until it was raw. Her eyes again. Wide. Hollow. And he saw himself, a helpless little boy, a rattled young man, a frustrated adult brother.

What has that man done to her? Why won't she tell me? Habib shook his head as he walked on. Why won't she let me confront Reza? Why – and then it hit him. He stopped in his tracks, ignoring the expletive of the man who'd just bumped into him. Why have I always waited for Fereshteh to give me permission? Why the hell haven't I just done it? Confronted the man? Addled by this new thought, he began walking once more down the busy block.

A car screeched to a halt on Habib's right as he stepped off the curb. Ignoring the driver leaning on his horn, he walked on, still wrestling with this now-obvious possibility. The eclectic storefronts he passed morphed into shabby, gritty and graffiti-covered, but he was barely aware. At length, he saw it. He understood: It's because I'm a damned coward! An inner voice accused: You won't confront your uncle because – admit it – he intimidates you. You're afraid. And it's not just him. You're scared of what everyone would say if you did it. Maman and Fereshteh especially, but then the cousins too. You're a damned coward, Habib! He took out a handkerchief, wiped his eyes and blew his nose. And continued to walk, his head down. Ruminating.

By the time the light was fading he was miles from home and brooding once more about the implications of the "Baha'i Question" document; about the slow strangling of his religious community. He thought about his children's future. It wouldn't be long before his kids would be in high school. Then what? Would they even be allowed in school then? And even if they did finish high school, what about further education or training? He hoped, he prayed they'd qualify for acceptance into the BIHE education program. Without a decent education they wouldn't even be able to get the measly jobs their parents had! What kind of future would there be to hope for?

By now his shoulders were hunched, his muscles tense and his eyes moist with anger. He didn't see the motorbike. When it hit he felt only a second of surprise before his contact with the tarmac knocked him out.

SOMEONE WAS PATTING HIS CHEEK. "*Aqa*, can you hear me?" A bright light flashed into one eye and then the other. He groaned and tried to raise his arm to shield them, but it was fastened to a board with tape. "Good, good, *Aqa*, great! You're waking up." Habib groaned again, his body now aware of pain all over. "We'll give you some pain relievers in a bit, *Aqa*. Just need to finish checking you first. No! don't pull that. That's an IV. It has to be there for a while. Now, I'm going to ask you some questions and then…"

Habib responded as best he could and finally got to ask some questions of his own, including whether he could call his wife. "Give us the number and we'll call her and let her know what's happened. You'll have to stay overnight, but she can take you home tomorrow if our exams show you're clear. You're lucky. Just a motorbike. Otherwise you'd probably be dead. Lots of bruises but probably nothing broken from what we can see. Just concerned about your head. We're gonna watch you."

Somewhere in the dead of night Habib woke. Though dim, lights were on and there was an incessant beep-beeping all around him. He tried to turn, but it hurt too much to move. Something was wrapped around his head and he saw a hanging bag dripping fluid through a line in his arm. "Ahh," he closed his eyes. Hospital. Yes. Something happened.…

Gradually he remembered being home with his family. Then deciding to go out. Being rude. Hadn't said good-bye to any of them. Had just gone. Why? Ah… yes… being so upset. Worried about –

He jerked as he felt himself falling. A machine next to him beeped urgently and he turned his head towards its flashing panel. An accident. I've had an accident. What was I doing? What's wrong with me? What was I thinking?

His head was throbbing from the sudden movement. Taking a few deep breaths, he closed his eyes and settled down again.

My God! How fragile life is! It can take a second to snuff it out.

He'd been so angry. The future had looked so grim. So hopeless. And then – he'd almost not had a future at all.

The Family Rahimi

ISFAHAN
Late Spring, 1989

The lieutenant colonel stepped out into the sunshine and adjusted his hat. A fresh breeze brought the scent of Spring from the tree blossoms in a neighboring courtyard and he inhaled this appreciatively. The temptation to take off his uniform jacket was strong but he resisted; you never knew whom you might run into. And sure enough, a junior officer was coming up the walk. Wondering what the younger man was doing at the court building, Kamran Rahimi took note of his name badge, acknowledged his junior's salute and then walked towards the street. His driver held open the door, but before getting into the car, Rahimi took another deep breath and looked up at the clear sky, a small smile on his lips.

During the ride to his office he relaxed and allowed himself to feel the lightness, the sense of freedom that this morning's brief work had given him. Why hadn't he done this years and years ago? Why had he put himself through all the unnecessary misery?

Granted, he had been home very little in the past 10 years. Putting his new career above all else, he had worked extra shifts and taken additional responsibilities, trying to stay ahead of his peers in anticipating and meeting the expectations of his superiors. They had recognized his knack for dealing with whatever they threw at him. He just did it all. They had rewarded his loyalty and talent with increasing trust and rapid promotions, cognizant of the fact that he continued to adjust his approach and responses to the prevailing (and let's face it, changing) ideology at every turn.

His father and tough old grandfather were proud of him. Even his brothers showed him some respect now.

Stopped at a busy intersection, he looked out at the pedestrians streaming across the street. A bevy of black chadored women negotiated their way as one body through the thick crowds. Like a wave, they seemed to flow together to the other side and just kept going. Unstoppable.

He lit a cigarette and blew the first deep drag out the window, the breeze carrying it up and away as the car moved forward again.

At first his wife had encouraged him. As the Revolution had taken hold, she, too, had seen the opportunities. Staying in that dreadful government job, a remnant of the old regime, was not the right place to be. She had sensed not only the dead end that the job was, but also the danger in being involved in anything that could possibly be construed as support for the Shah. She was very relieved when he finally made the decision to join the Revolutionary Guard. So, at first, he now reflected, she'd put up with his odd, long working hours. No doubt she'd hoped that this would make him happy enough to forget that she couldn't bear him the sons he'd so wanted.

But it hadn't. With the passing of the years he'd found no relief from the dullness of his home life. More, their childlessness became a stain on his record. Remarks had been made. Suggestions had been put to him. And finally, he'd begun to take his parents' counsel seriously.

Of course it hadn't really been complicated. The law was very clear about such situations. Divorce had always been his prerogative, but he'd let his odd sense of compassion get in the way. Thinking about what a divorce would mean for his wife, a barren woman, he'd kept postponing the idea. He could have taken a second wife.

The law allowed this, too. But he didn't need the hassle of two women competing against each other. Or the jealousy that a second wife's children would ignite in the first. Or the hassles and intrigues of two sets of in-laws that would, he knew from stories he'd heard, get into each other's business. No, he'd had his own career to think of and had wanted to put his focus there.

But now, having reached this point in his career, he felt it was time. He wanted a family. A real family. Children. So today he'd divorced her. He was free.

YAZD
APRIL, *1993*

Pushing his plate away with one hand and patting his stomach with the other, Kamran Rahimi smiled the satisfaction of a man who has just enjoyed a hearty homemade meal.

"*Daste-shoma dard na-koneh, Mamanjoon. Ali bud* - thank you so much for all the trouble you went to - it was excellent, Maman." He directed a warm gaze of appreciation towards his mother across the table. This was the best part of visiting his parents and it happened so seldom. His increasing responsibilities kept him in Isfahan, and the long working hours, usually 6 days a week, made an overnight visit to his parents' home a rare event. It would become rarer still in a couple of months when he'd be transferring to Tehran.

Now he was waiting for his mother to bring up the conversation he knew was inevitable. Joining his father, he made himself comfortable on the plush velvet of the living room sofa. It wasn't long before she came in with the tea and sat down in the matching chair opposite.

Since finesse was never his strong suit, *Aqa-ye* Rahimi waited for his wife to deftly steer the conversation in her desired direction. She didn't disappoint.

The domestic nature of her subject was something she loyally and ardently pursued. Kamran didn't fault her for it, though, because he knew that it was out of love for him and concern for adding to the prestige of his current position of responsibility. And that, like most mothers, she wanted to see him happy in his home life. So, when she raised the topic of remarriage, he indulged her.

Yet there was something in his father's face and the way he shifted in his chair that told him that this was not all; that there was something more to it than just talk this time. Over the next quarter hour his parents revisited all the reasons why he should take a new wife.

"It's four years now, Kami, since your divorce! It's long enough!" His father leaned forward. "This time we have a concrete proposition. We've found a perfect wife for you. A lovely woman of excellent family. Attractive in looks, temperament and mind. Excellent reputation. Capable. Independent, but not too much so. A devout believer and supporter of the Revolution. And," he beamed, "it is certain that she can bear children." His father leaned back, his self-satisfaction plain to see.

His mother explained: "This woman — she's really lovely, Kami — is the daughter of friends of ours. You've never met them; they moved to Yazd after you left for Isfahan. One of their daughters had married and moved to a small town up north near Rasht. Her husband had a business and they were doing well there. They had two young boys. Then about three years ago this daughter came to Yazd to visit her parents for a few days. She came on her own. Her husband was busy at work and the boys were being looked after by his mother there. Then it happened. That awful earthquake. You remember it, Kami, don't you? Over 50,000 people died there in Gilan and some of those other provinces."

"Yes, Maman, who could forget that? It was awful!"

"Well, Zahra's — that's the young woman's name, by the way — Zahra's husband and both children were killed in that earthquake. She is a widow, Kamijoon, and she also wants to remarry."

His father picked up the thread. He lost no time in adding support to the proposal at hand. Both parents had spoken on several occasions with Zahra's parents and they all agreed that this was an excellent match. "Her parents have spoken with her and she has agreed to meet you. Zahra is living in Yazd now. We could visit her and her parents later today. Or tomorrow."

Kamran leaned his head back, feeling the firm support of the high-backed sofa. He stared at the ceiling but said nothing.

"Kamijoon," his mother coaxed, "we know that your time here is limited to just these few days. We told Zahra's parents that. She and her parents are happy to fit into your schedule. Wouldn't you at least be willing to meet them?"

He was. And why not? Everything his parents were concerned about was true. And when he gave himself a little free time to really unwind, he found he was lonely. He looked at his parents.

"Sure," he said. "Why not meet all of them? If I don't like her then nothing's lost. I don't have to agree to anything."

The initial meeting was late that afternoon. Zahra's parents' home was in a wealthy neighborhood and their home was decorated in classic good taste. Plenty of beautifully carved dark wood. Kamran noted the antiques as well. It all spelled money and influence.

The meeting was rather formal, as he'd known it would be, but not stuffy and no one put on airs. He certainly didn't mind money and influence but he had no tolerance for pretentiousness.

His parents had been right and the afternoon turned out very well. Zahra was attractive in many ways, even if she was, as required on such occasions, quiet and reserved. Her parents were engaging and all three seemed to have a healthy sense of humor. That's a plus, thought Kamran, remembering his former in-laws and their dour faces.

Because both parties were willing, the parents arranged for the couple to meet again the following day, this time at the Rahimi's home. Anxious to further this relationship, both sets of parents spent the afternoon indoors to allow Kamran and Zahra time to themselves in the garden. It all went so well that Kamran arranged to return the following weekend.

"Oh, how wonderful that you are going to Tehran!" enthused

Zahra's mother. I will phone my brothers and tell them about you; they will invite you to their homes, I'm sure. They can help you a great deal. You know, going to such a big city for the first time — it's always good to know some people who can help you get settled there. I will phone them. In which office will you be? I will tell them and they can find you there."

Zahra's mother was as good as her word. Within two months the couple married and they moved to Tehran.

The Family Omidvar

South *TEHRAN*
Spring, *1989*

The Daughter of the House woke that day as she always did, with the heaviness that had been hers for what seemed forever. A weight that had long since robbed her of hope.

At 35, she felt old. Spring had arrived but she'd stopped seeing the color of the leaves on the tree in the neighbors' courtyard years ago. The same routines awaited her. The same demands from her embittered father and her sour mother.

She went to the kitchen. She made the tea. She prepared the breakfast. She put together the lunches her parents and her son would take with them to work. She announced to no one in particular *"Sobhaneh sar-e-miz-e"*, that breakfast was on the table. She began to chop vegetables for the evening dinner.

Today, mercifully, her parents ate their breakfast in silence and left. Clearing their dishes, she called the boy again. Silence. Annoyed, she called him again, but there was no response. She walked to his tiny room and cautiously rapped on the door. He'd grown so tall and developed such a flinty attitude lately that she realized she was a little afraid of him. She rapped again, moderating her voice as she called his name. "What's happening? Breakfast is on the table." Hearing nothing, she said, "I'm coming in."

No Mehrdad. Confused, she scanned the room again. Inordinately tidy — as usual. But today, even more so: every one of his few personal belongings was missing.

Her mouth opened as she felt the realization creep from her chest to her limbs. She stood, hardly breathing. Not thinking, just feeling. Feeling. After so long. After years.

Turning slowly, she walked back to the kitchen and stood at the sink, gripping its edges, staring through the window. Turning again, she walked to the front door and stepped out into the courtyard. With closed eyes, she took long, deep breaths of the Spring air.

A small bird began to chirp. She opened her eyes, looking for the creature. She gazed right, then left, around the courtyard.

Then, finally, her eyes came to rest just beyond the yard's walls, on the neighbor's tree. How green its leaves were!

Northern TEHRAN
February, 1993

He parked in the circle by the main entrance and heard the electric gate click into place behind him as he mounted the finely hewn stone stairs to the entrance. A male servant opened the ornate double doors before he had a chance to knock, then ushered him into a large hall, where he took the visitor's coat and produced fine leather house slippers in exchange for his shoes.

Moments later the servant ushered the guest through another set of double doors into a large library, lavishly furnished in the French Provincial style. Two needlepointed fauteuils faced a large, ornate desk on one side of the room. By the large windows opposite, a group of armchairs and small settees encircled an exquisite table set with china plates and serving dishes loaded with Persian delicacies. Finely etched tea glasses sat on ornate silver saucers and to one side a handsome antique samovar and teapot sent fragrant breaths of steam into the air.

Rashid, his white turban and long robes impeccable, left his desk and welcomed his visitor, leading him to a settee. When he had ensured that his guest had been comfortably settled and well provided with refreshments, and had enquired whether he was in good health and had found his house without too much difficulty, Rashid came to the subject of his invitation.

"So, let's see now. About a year in the Basij, more than three now in the Guard; promotions all the way since 1989. And you're not satisfied?" Tilting his head slightly, he raised his thick eyebrows. "There are many men who would be very, very happy to have come as far as you have – especially at your age."

Mullah Rashid paused while he stroked his neatly-trimmed beard and stared at the tea glass in his hands. Looking up at his guest he said, "But I appreciate your ambition. In fact, I'm glad to see it; glad to see, in fact, that all the money I put toward your schooling has born good fruit."

Another pause as he took a sip of the hot, golden brew. "Do you know what I think? Given your obvious intelligence, ambition and hard work, and given your goals – admirable, I must say – given your goals, your straightest path to success will be through Law."

"Law." It was a statement.

"Yes. There is a great need for men like you in our legal system. Intelligent men with insight who are willing to work hard. Men who are not afraid of taking on tough, complicated cases; not afraid of making difficult decisions. You know, some of our best lawyers have gone soft. They refuse the important cases and instead take on the social cases. Quite a number have even gone over to defending those so-called human rights cases. They don't get very far, of course and I, for one, question their loyalty to the Revolution. They're closely monitored, as you can imagine.... No, we need more lawyers ready to pursue the true work of the Revolution. We need men who will dedicate themselves totally to the struggle of bringing our beloved country fully into the attitudes and practices of Islam. For men who will do this there are many opportunities, I can assure you."

He helped himself to a delicate honeyed pastry and chewed thoughtfully, sipping his tea in between little bites.

Mehrdad sipped his own tea but never took his eyes off his father.

At last the cleric said, "I have a proposal. I will arrange your acceptance to the University and you will study the appropriate courses to prepare you fully for your law degree. I will cover all your academic and living expenses if – he stared pointedly into Mehrdad's eyes – if you dedicate yourself completely to the work required. I will monitor your progress, be sure of that. And if – if – you find that you can work hard enough to finish your studies early, I am sure that I can arrange for you to get a position well ahead of normal entry level."

He wiped his hands carefully on the fine linen napkin and selected another sweetmeat.

"I have one last condition. It may not be a problem, but I must be certain." He popped the delicate sweet into his mouth and sat forward, looking intently at his son.

"You absolutely must never, ever, have any contact of any kind with your mother or with her parents. My cousin Hormuz will never profit from anything you do. Is that clear." It was not a question.

The young man's deep black eyes held the gaze. "It is very clear," Mehrdad confirmed and gave a short, firm nod.

Rashid sat back and relaxed. "Now, let us discuss the details."

LAVASAN
AUGUST

On the lower slopes of the mountains northeast of Tehran the summer heat was less oppressive and clear blue skies replaced the pollution of the city. While most Tehran residents resorted to fans and excursions to parks, wealthy families like Reza Hashemi's enjoyed the mountain breezes and abundant shade of the magnificent trees in the back gardens of their summer houses.

This was Lavasan. From its slopes there were excellent views of the huge Latyan lake and dam and there was road access to the wildlife, falls and canyons of the area's nature reserves. It was the perfect place to spend the hotter months and those who could afford it did so.

Rashid was enjoying his visit to his friends, once again grateful for Parliament's summer break. This allowed him to make the rounds to the homes of his many connections, from both of his mansions, here and in Tehran. It was important to keep his social and professional contacts alive. One never knew what subjects might be under discussion, what opinions might be expressed or what useful information might come to hand. For a man of his rank and position, both among the clergy and in the government, it was important to keep himself on top of such things. One never knew when such things might be leveraged to one's advantage.

As it happened, he actually enjoyed Reza's company. He was a man of his generation and taste and they'd spent many years growing their relationship. The added bonus was that they were also useful to each other, mutually promoting their professional and business interests. And Reza had two fine homes and sons to be admired.

Perhaps this was the only thing that he had ever envied in his friend — the sons. Looking at them now as he sat in the comfortable garden chair sipping his tall glass of freshly squeezed juice, Rashid listened as they discussed their businesses, their work, their families and their successes.

Majid and Farid had become able directors of their father's construction company's two offices. By all accounts, Farid had grown the Shiraz branch so significantly that it was nearly as huge as its twin in the capital. And Rashid felt a surge of satisfaction that he'd helped them along in getting the major contracts that had set them far above their competition. He smiled at them as an indulgent, proud uncle might.

Then there was Saeed. At 37, he had already become an outstanding official in the Guard. That young man was one to watch. He was bright. Really, his acumen was first-rate. He had done well to choose a different path from his older brothers. Smart and capable as they were, they were no match for Saeed.

Rashid had an idea that he wanted to put to the young man, but would, of course, discuss this with Reza first. Saeed had the makings of a shrewd politician. The *Majlis* — Parliament — could use him. He was still a bit young, perhaps, but give him a few more years in the Guard and he'd be ready, Rashid was sure of it. And he could smooth the path for him in that direction. Or various other ones, if it came to it. Meanwhile, he would continue to observe him to see when the time was right.

Nodding politely to Reza's youngest daughter, Gita, he accepted the refill of his glass and returned to his thoughts.

Rashid now had his own son to think about. Finally, after all these years, after all the behind-the-scenes support he had given him, his son had found his way to him just a few months ago. *Ah,* thought Rashid, *I have such plans for you, such plans for you!*

He took a long appreciative swallow of the cool drink and shifted his gaze to the swimming pool area where Reza's daughters were watching their children's water play. His friend had only two daughters. He was fortunate. Rashid's brood of six, although married off, still burdened him. Far too many women had populated his household and he had become weary of all the nagging. Setting his wife Hediyeh up in her own home had been the best thing he'd done in years. Now he had the peace and quiet of his mansion to himself.

He got up, walked across the lawn and joined the little group where Reza was proudly holding an alert infant just over a month old. His newest grandchild and Mitra's first boy. After having produced three girls she had at last succeeded in winning her father's approval on presentation of a male heir.

Rashid felt his friend's pride and happiness. He knew that the future of the Revolution and of his country lay with its devoted sons.

BOOK FOUR

2008

The Families Jalili, Hashemi, and Omidvar

TEHRAN
2008

END OF APRIL

The hotel ballroom was lavishly appointed. Some things transcend the differences in politics and ideologies and this one, this vestige from the Shah's era, was appreciatively utilized when occasions of State required a show of sumptuosity.

The banquet, complete with all the western trappings of linen cloths, well-cushioned dining chairs and sparkling china and silver, was proving to be the success its organizers had intended.

The newly elected members of the Republic's *Majlis* — Parliament — were suitably impressed and enthused about the tasks ahead of them, assured of the State's blessings. Assured, the parliamentarians knew, so long as they held themselves within the parameters, written or tacit, set for them by Regime's hierarchy.

Here, clerics' robes and turbans mixed with tailor-made three-piece suits, and parliamentarians conversed with their betters from the Councils, the Cabinet, the Judiciary, and the leadership of both the military and the ubiquitous Revolutionary Guard. The enormous room was filled to capacity and smelled every bit of privilege, influence and power.

Here, relationships were forged and strengthened, alliances created or adjusted for maximum mutual benefit, and deals, political or business in nature, arranged. Everyone knew his role, his place in the hierarchy, and what the journey through the minefields of politics required.

Here among the favored and advantaged sat Mehrdad and Rashid, and the newly minted parliamentarian Saeed. Saeed was no stranger to the powerhouses in this room, however. He'd simply switched horses, so to speak.

After 30 years in the Guard, he was himself a power to be reckoned with and had sat in his share of elite meetings. But after more than half his life in steady promotion to the highest echelons, he had few places left to go. And he was bored. His brain was longing for a new challenge, a new field for exploration and for using his considerable capacity. He didn't need the money, so the cut in salary was of no concern whatsoever. He had enough investments to secure himself and his family for several lifetimes. With its increasingly heavy involvement in the nation's economy, the Revolutionary Guard had the means to take good care of its own. So, no, Saeed's material needs were not an issue; he simply wanted to try something different.

Rashid's insights into the nooks and crannies of the Judiciary and the Councils had been helpful and had piqued his interest. The older man had encouraged him and of course he'd put in the good words necessary to his approval as a candidate. The rest had been simple.

MAY

"I really do not know how to thank you," Majid was shaking his head as he leaned forward. He looked up at both Mehrdad and Rashid, his arms resting on his knees.

Reza and Farid enthusiastically echoed the sentiments.

"No need to thank anyone, Majid," Rashid demurred. "Your family has helped me a hundred times over — for decades now. And Mehrdad? Well..." Mehrdad assured them that this was indeed true.

But Majid was still insisting that the success of this latest business deal involving their construction company was beyond his wildest expectations. "Really, this is extraordinary and you must find some way for me to repay you. "In whatever way." His head was still shaking, as if he still could not believe it.

Such a small thing, Mehrdad thought. Truly a small thing, but, if Majid thinks it's big, so much the better.

"Heech-chi, deegar, na-bud," he offered - really, it was nothing. "It is only natural to help such good friends," he said, lowering his eyes and deprecating with his hands.

A discreet signal from Majid's wife indicated that the meal was ready. Majid stood up and invited them all to the elaborate wrought-iron table on the large shaded patio.

Acknowledging the approval, the women wished them an excellent meal and left, returning later to clear the main course and bring out the dessert and tea.

It was only then that Mehrdad's attention finally drifted from the men's conversation. He hadn't wanted to miss anything that could be important to him. Now, however, satiated after the sumptuous meal, the men had relaxed into lighter topics.

Nikou brought the dishes of ice cream and plates of cookies; her mother followed with a tray of delicately etched tea glasses and a fine, beaten-silver sugar bowl. While Nikou served the ice cream and passed the cookies around, Samira poured the tea from the large samovar, asking each man to state his preference for strength, then mixing the strong tea and boiling water accordingly. Moving silently and discreetly, Nikou carefully placed each glass in front of the man to whom it belonged.

Her unpretentious modesty did not go unnoticed by Mehrdad. He sat back in his armchair, his eyes following her every move.

When the women had left, he said, "That was an excellent meal, Majid; not only delicious, but particularly pleasing in the manner in which it was served."

"Yes, Majid, it was," agreed Rashid. "Another indication of the great care you've taken in establishing an ordered and respectable household."

Steepling his fingers, Mehrdad offered, "I fear that in these modern times we must make extraordinary efforts to ensure that our women acquire and demonstrate impeccable homemaking skills."

"Thank you," said Majid. "It's been my privilege and good fortune to be able to ensure an excellent domestic education for my only daughter. And of course the very best university education for my dear sons. These are, after all, the pillars of a stable and productive society."

Reza got onto his hobby horse: "That's right! Daughters need to set up a proper home and raise the children. That's their work! Anything else is a waste of time! I'm glad to see my granddaughter Nikou helping her mother at home. There's no doubt she'll make someone a fine wife."

"No doubt whatsoever," agreed Mehrdad.

Rashid decided to chime in with his own considered opinions on this topic, but Mehrdad, having heard all this too many times, stroked his trim beard and let his thoughts return to Nikou. She was pretty. Very pretty. He could see that even with her headscarf in place. Petite. He liked that. Modestly dressed. Delicate features and demure expression. Even better. She obviously knew her place and seemed content with it.

When the afternoon grew late, Rashid got up from his seat. He reminded Mehrdad that they had another engagement in an hour and that if they were to arrive on time they would have to set off immediately.

Taking their leave, they thanked their hosts profoundly,

including the women, who had come to the door. As the others continued the ritualized good-byes, Mehrdad looked directly at Nikou, his deep dark gaze engendering an immediate blush. She lowered her eyes, readjusted her headscarf and stepped back.

Majid took this in, but no one else seemed to notice, and the men made their way out of the front door and down the drive, where Mehrdad opened the car door for his father. Gathering his fine long robes, Rashid stepped in and settled himself on the leather seat.

With a final glance up at the front door, Mehrdad thanked their hosts yet again. He smiled to himself as he slid into the driver's side of the gleaming black Porsche and started the engine.

Early August

The lamb kebabs were ready. Dripping with juices and oozing their delectable aroma, they joined the platters of rice and grilled tomatoes, the salads and plates of fresh herbs. Samira brought out bowls of *somagh*, arranging the pungent powdered spice between the platters. *"Befarma'id, befarma'id!"* she said – a call for everyone to come to the long buffet table set in the shade of the patio.

After serving themselves, all ten sat in the cushioned armchairs around the outdoor dining table. The shade of the large trees out on the lawn was their best hope for catching a breeze, and certainly afforded the best view of the extensive landscaping. The family knew that Majid had spared no expense in hiring one of the best landscape architects in Tehran, and expressed their admiration. The pool with its fountain and water plants formed a magnificent centerpiece for the rock garden on one side and the hillock of bright blooms and shrubs on the other. His friends and business connections had declared themselves suitably impressed.

When the serious work of kebab-eating had been completed and the sincere appreciation of everyone conveyed, Habib ventured into a transition conversation concerning family not present. Not only was it polite, but it was safe territory.

"It's too bad your boys and their families aren't here today, Majid. We haven't seen them in ages."

"Yeah, but you know, they decided on taking a good long break from this heat. They're enjoying their summer houses up on the Caspian. They keep in touch and they say they're all having a great time. A seaside vacation is what they seem to like best. I'm happy for them. It's not that far, either. They can easily come back if I need them here at the office. So I'm satisfied."

Reza nodded and grunted his approval.

Majid toyed with his linen napkin and continued, "Yes... so I wonder, why is it that all of your children (a nod to Habib and Fereshteh) are so far away? Overseas. It looks like they have no intention of coming back to their home. Don't they miss Iran?"

Before either Habib or Fereshteh had a chance to reply, Reza jumped in, losing no chance to criticize his niece and nephew for their choices. Ignoring Farah's appeals for calm, he launched into his well-honed rant against sending them out in the first place.

Habib was prepared but Fereshteh beat him to it, saying, "You know why, Dayijan. We've talked about this so much."

"Yes, but you never answer my question. Admit it for once! You and your kids are ashamed of your country! Say it. Say it!"

Habib knew his sister would rise to the bait, so he was quick but composed in his reply: "Dayi, you know that is absolutely not true."

"Then why send them abroad?"

"Yes, why?" asked Majid. "Did you send them just because you went? Was that so important?"

Habib looked at his mother. Above the tight smile on her lips her eyes enlarged in warning. Catching a second warning glance from Taraneh, he took a breath, smiled, and answered evenly, "First of all, not all of us went. Jamshid studied here in Tehran..." He looked at his brother-in-law, but saw that he had no intention of entering the fray.

"Second of all, you know that we have the utmost respect for Iranian universities. In fact, had it been possible, I — we, Taraneh and I — would have applied to work in the university here in Tehran when we returned. That was our intention."

"But you didn't do that, did you?" Reza accused.

"With respect, Uncle, I'm sure you remember that those were troubled times — all the universities were closed —"

"Then you should have joined the Revolution instead!"

"— All the universities were closed and when they opened again, Baha'is were no longer allowed to teach or study there."

"Why didn't you join us in the Revolution, then? Or were you still all cozy with the old regime?" Majid's sarcasm hit him hard and Habib struggled to mask his surprise. *Where's this coming from?* He took another breath and continued.

"Majidjoon, you know perfectly well that we do not, absolutely not, get involved in anything political —"

"Do we? Do we really know that? The government tells us a different story. We hear all the time about your allegiances to the West, about your spying for Israel —"

"Majid, where on earth are you getting this from? You know us! You're very well informed about our beliefs. You know this is all propaganda —"

"I still want to know why you can't bring your kids home and have them study here," said Reza, switching back to his pet theme. "They can still go to university here. Doesn't matter they're Baha'is or not. All they have to do is write on their applications that they're Muslims and they'll get in."

"But they're not."

"Doesn't matter. So they're not. So what? They can just say they're Muslims and they can be Baha'is or anything else they want in private. What's the problem? Other people do this."

Habib looked at his uncle. "Number one: it would be dishonest —"

"Why is it dishonest? You think that everyone who goes to university is completely honest? What about the students who pretend to go to study when all they want to do is stir up trouble, huh? You think they're honest?"

"But —" Fereshteh began.

Majid's face hardened. "Those students, those trouble-makers — they'll be flushed out. The government's done it before and they'll do it again."

" — Number two: it would be —"

"That's right! The government will flush them out again and again until there are none left..." And his Uncle Reza went on, forgetting completely the original point of the conversation. *Or,* thought Habib, *is this, in fact, his point? Who can say?*

Scanning his thoughts for a new topic of conversation, Habib looked over at the women. Farah and Sohayla touched hands. Samira and Nikou looked away and shifted in their seats. Fereshteh's eyes were squeezed tight. She was scratching her left arm up and down.

Suddenly, Taraneh stood up. "How about if we all stretch our legs? Dessert is on the buffet table, please come. I'll serve," she smiled. Turning to Nikou, she asked, "Nikoujoon, would you please bring out the ice cream while I get started here?" To Samira she said, "No, no, no, I insist on serving. You've done all the hard work with that excellent meal, my dear. Please, relax! I'm not making ta'arof; I'd really like to do this."

"If you're sure, Taranehjoon. But really, you're our guest –"

"I'm absolutely sure, Samirajoon. Please, no ta'arof – it's my pleasure to help."

Their dessert plates and bowls now amply filled, the family moved into smaller groups around the garden. Fereshteh and Samira pulled up chairs and joined Nikou and Taraneh near the buffet table and soon settled into conversation. Taraneh had them all laughing now, Habib noted. Feeling the knot in his stomach unwind, he made his way over to Jamshid, who was sitting on his own, his chair just off to the side of Farah's and Sohayla's. He was tucking into his ice cream with extraordinary attention.

"May I?" Habib asked, pulling a chair over to his brother-in-law.

"Please," said Jamshid, indicating with his hand.

Habib sat down and dug his spoon into his own bowl, enjoying the ice cream's freshness and subtle pistachio flavor.

"Well, that was awkward," said Jamshid, his voice low.

"What? Oh you mean that last conversation? Yeah. I bet the women would have gladly disappeared into the ether if they could have. Not even Samira has the stomach for that stuff anymore. Mind you, she'll stand by Majid through anything, but I think it's getting harder for her.

"And how about Sohayla? With Reza, I mean. Personally, I've never understood how she lives with the man."

"Having known her my entire life, I guess I've never really questioned it. They just 'are'. I've just taken that for granted. But I guess you're right. She has to be some kind of saint to have put up with him and all his rants. Although I reckon at home he doesn't do that."

"Maybe because he has her and all their kids long-since well trained? They know what he thinks and what he expects, and they just do as he says. Or else." He took another spoon of ice cream and bit into a cookie. "I'm sure they learned the consequences of non-compliance long ago."

"For sure." Habib paused. "He's pretty intimidating." He looked over at his uncle, sitting with his sons.

"How's it going with the uh, 'education project'? BIHE, I mean. Imagine if Reza knew you were involved in that!"

Habib gave a short laugh. "Right. Yeah. The work's going well. Taraneh and I are super busy. We're supposed to be having a bit of a break now during the summer, but we're each mentoring a couple of graduate students who are anxious to finish their courses. A lot of students like the math and physics courses because it gives them advantages in the job market, especially if they can manage to move overseas."

"The numbers of students are increasing, I hear. Is it true that more and more overseas universities are accepting BIHE graduates?"

"Oh yes. And our faculty numbers are increasing too. Which is good, because it spreads out the work." Looking over at his wife, he added, "Taraneh really needs to slow down a bit; she's taken on too many students. She's so good-hearted, and doesn't know when to say 'no'. Just accepts more and more work even if it means she's up all hours reading and marking papers. But we've got a new colleague also teaching our subjects now, so I think it'll help us quite a bit."

"And what about you?"

"Ah. Well. I'm uh, I'm getting more involved in the admin of our work. I mean, I'm still teaching of course. That's the joy of it all. But admin is also necessary, so I've been getting more and more into that as well." He looked sharply at Jamshid. "What?! What are you snickering about?"

"Oh, nothing," Jamshid chuckled. "Just wondering about how this is different from what you said about Taraneh not knowing when to say 'no'!"

Habib made a face at his brother-in-law and said, "Eat your ice cream!"

They settled into quiet. From a few meters away, the voices of Farah and Sohayla drifted towards them.

Farah was saying, "Yes, Aryana called me a couple of days ago and she's doing fine. Her summer job is not as demanding as she'd thought, so she's actually taking an extra course before the term begins again. She's still enjoying Cambridge."

"Oh, I'm happy to hear that. I've always had a soft spot for that girl. So cheerful. So sweet!" She waved away a pesky fly. "And the others?"

"The same. Anisa's doing well at Oxford. Almost finished, I hear, but I don't know her plans. Daryush and his wife are still working on their doctorates. They'll probably stay in Boston. Oh! And did I tell you that Habib's youngest is expecting his student visa to come so he can continue his studies – also in Boston? He'll be so happy to be near his cousins."

"Oh Farah, that's great news. You must be so very proud of all of them. What could be better than to see your grandchildren succeed? And that's because your own children did such an excellent job in raising them!"

"And what about you, Sohayla? Look at the successes in your own family! You must also be very proud. And this –" With a wave of her arm she indicated the garden, the house, the buffet, the family. "Samira and Nikou put on an excellent spread today. As always, really. You're fortunate to have a capable daughter-in-law and such a truly lovely granddaughter in Nikou."

Sohayla looked over at the other women, still chatting by the buffet table. "Samira does know how to entertain for Majid, that's for sure." Looking away, she patted the moisture from her face with her cloth napkin and fanned herself. "Oh, it's really too hot today." She began tapping her foot. "But I guess I'm just getting old and sensitive."

Farah laughed. "Aren't we all?"

"You're right about Nikou, Farah. She really is a lovely girl. I keep my eye on her. She's special. I don't see her as often as I'd like, but well, you know. They're young and we're old now. They have other things they'd rather do than to sit with us!"

"Sohayla!" Reza's booming voice hadn't altered with age. Habib looked across the garden and saw his uncle getting up from his chair.

"Sohayla! Let's go! I'm tired. It's time to go home."

Sohayla and Farah looked at each other. Raising her eyebrows and offering her sister-in-law a crooked smile, Sohayla said, "Well, I guess we're leaving." The women stood and embraced each other.

She came over and embraced Habib and Jamshid. "So lovely to see you two today. Be well. Go with God," she said, and turned. "I'm coming, Rezajoon," she called, and headed towards the patio where he stood.

Early September

Rashid stroked his generous beard as he listened to his colleagues. They sat comfortably around a large solid wood table on which stacks of documents, tea glasses and sugar cubes shared the space in front of the dozen clerics assembled for this extraordinary meeting.

"Yes," one was saying, "despite what we'd anticipated, the arrest of these Baha'i leaders hasn't really done the trick."

"Not only not done the trick, as you put it, but seems to be making things even worse! It's over three months now!" was the gruff rejoinder of another.

A third added, "My sources tell me that some of the Baha'is are becoming more active than ever in their communities. Stirring people up about 'social issues' by getting Muslim neighbors involved in projects for young people and activities for women. Unacceptable, not to mention dangerous!"

"Yes, I'd heard. And thanks to that lawyer — that Shirin Ebadi woman and her so-called 'Human Rights' friends and co-workers," spat another, "Thanks to them, these Baha'is are getting publicity in their favor. You know, we really need to silence that woman."

"Security is — has been — working on that, but she just won't stop. She's added Baha'is to her long client list and she says she has no intention of stopping any of it," another of the robed clerics put in.

"It's a question of applying sufficient pressure." Rashid sat forward. Look, the Sabet woman is in solitary confinement. We'll leave her there. Eventually she'll collapse. As for the others, let them stew in their cells. There's no hurry about their cases. We have no one to answer to. And this Ebadi —"

"Who knows the law — Sharia Law, no less! — better than nearly any judge in the country!" interrupted the spitting cleric.

"Yes, she does, that's true. She was, after all, a judge herself — once," Rashid resumed. "Nevertheless —" he looked around at his grumbling colleagues. "Nevertheless, there are ways to silence these types of people." His tone was even, but his eyes were sharp and determined. "I'm sure we will be able to handle this. We have more than one prison that can, shall we say, take care of them." He paused and smiled at the little assembly. "And very able agents to, ahem, work with them."

Rashid took a sip of his tea and suggested, "Now, shall we make a detailed plan?"

Early September

"So, what did you think? That was some wedding, huh?" Taraneh directed her smile around the table.

To accommodate their whole group, the two families had pushed together several of the simple metal sidewalk tables of the café. On a side street that boasted large leafy trees and little traffic, it served some of the best café food in the neighborhood.

"I guess," said Fereshteh. "Majid had to have the best. Again. Always out to impress everyone, and now, above all, to impress his new son-in-law. An influential guy, I've heard."

Jamshid said: "Oh, I don't know, Fereshteh, don't be so hard on Majid. Of course, he has his particular tastes and yes, he does want to impress, but that's just what he does. He's used to doing that with his customers and business contacts."

"It sure looked like a lot of them!" added Mansoor.

"Yes, it was an impressive guest list," said Habib. "His major customers and financial backers do expect that sort of thing, though. He has to keep them happy. And you may be right about the son-in-law. Judiciary, I think? When I asked Rashid, he was a bit vague."

"That's all I heard, too," said Jamshid. "But whatever he does, he's certainly well off. I suppose he benefits from his father."

"Oh yes! You got that right! Did you see that suit? And his watch? His car? Wow. Nikou told me that he's been a lawyer and judge. Oh, she was so nervous, but at the same time so excited. And just the way she looked at him! She never stopped smiling. I'm so happy for her!" Aryana beamed.

"I don't like him," said Fereshteh, focusing her gaze on the rows of trees lining street.

Everyone looked at her.

"Why ever not?" asked Taraneh. "Too much money for your tastes?" She gave Fereshteh a friendly nudge and smiled.

"What are you saying, Fereshteh?" asked Jamshid.

"Oh, I'm not saying anything, really," she said, returning her attention to the others. "I just didn't feel comfortable around him, that's all."

Everyone paused to take a sip of the strong coffee they'd all ordered.

"I think Nikou is just so beautiful," said Aryana. "She's really a sweet girl, too."

"And have you ever had a good serious conversation with her?" asked Habib. "She's smart. Too bad she's not going on to university. I've always felt bad about that."

"You think everyone should go to university," Jamshid teased, giving his brother-in-law a friendly mock-punch in the arm.

"Not everybody." Habib returned the smile. "Me, for example, brother-in-law! Look where my PhD got me! Counting beans for a company whose boss probably had to buy his way to a high school diploma!"

Laughter erupted and even Fereshteh couldn't resist the jibe at her dear brother.

OCTOBER

At the back of the dress shop, Fereshteh came out of the changing cubicle to look at herself in the full-length mirror. The dress was actually fine, she thought. She could wear it with her high black boots. Her *manteau* was certainly long enough to cover her down to their tops and not reveal the dress's rather over-bright colors. No sense in attracting any attention, she habitually reminded herself. The Basij — morality police — could be anywhere and now there were so many women spies that you had to be careful wherever you went.

She turned again for a last check on the fit and was about to return to the cubicle to change back into her street clothes when she heard a woman weeping softly. The sounds were coming from the ladies' washroom a few yards away.

None of my business, she told herself, and got dressed. The crying increased, then stopped.

As Fereshteh opened the curtain and stepped out, her new dress over her arm, she collided with a woman, also making her way back into the store. With a startled cry, the woman jumped back, a look of fear in her reddened eyes. As Fereshteh began to apologize, the flustered woman fumbled with her headscarf, now fallen onto her shoulders, and pulled it as tightly around her head and face as she could. But Fereshteh saw it. She saw the swollen bruise and the cut on the woman's cheek. It looked fresh.

Her response was automatic: a polite yet insistent offer to help the stranger. "Excuse me, *Khanum*, may I help you? You don't look well. I'm a doctor. Please, let me help you."

Although nothing direct was said about it, they both knew what the source of the woman's injury was. And they both automatically engaged in that dance of assertion / denial, insistence / refusal, concern / anxiety that accompanies the sudden revelation of a disturbing truth.

"What's your name," Fereshteh asked gently.

"Homa," was the whispered response. Her eyes searched Fereshteh's, as if looking for refuge. But when the fear that was clearly chasing her caught up, she said, "Please, just move out of my way; let me go. My... my husband is in the shop waiting. I... just came back here looking for the toilet. He'll be wondering why it's taking me so long. Please." She kept her eyes lowered as if to stanch the flow of truth.

"Then take this," Fereshteh was scribbling an address and phone number on a slip of paper. "This is my office address. I am Doctor Jalili. I see many patients. Just come — when you can." Her eyes pleaded with the woman, who at last glanced up.

She snatched the paper and stuffed it into a pocket under her *manteau*, then buttoned the coat up to her throat and hurried back into the store.

Two weeks later

Homa and her companion approached the door to the medical practice hesitantly, holding their chadors closely. Straightening their backs, they took a collective breath and went in.

Whether on the buses or on foot they'd looked furtively around them on their journey here. When they had finally reached the office block, they'd looked over their shoulders once more before going through the glass doors into the foyer. The directory on the left wall had assured them that the medical offices they sought were indeed here. Taking the elevator, they'd arrived on the third floor and followed the signs to the medical practice's offices.

The waiting room was packed. Seeing this, Homa's companion was all set to turn around. "She has no time for us. I told you this was a mistake. Let's go!" She stopped only because Homa took her firmly by the arm and led her to the front desk. Not that Homa felt any better herself. She was, in fact, fighting off regret at having come, but having arrived, having had to take three buses to get here, she was not going to lose courage now. And she had her companion to think about: a far worse situation than her own. This was their chance. They had to take it.

The receptionist, although obviously busy, greeted them with a smile. She surprised them by saying, "Yes, yes, the waiting room is full; it's always full, but I have strict instructions from Dr. Jalili to admit you immediately. I'll seat you in the ante-room just outside her office while she finishes with her current patient. Follow me, please."

It had taken Homa a good ten days to make her decision to phone the number that the stranger — the doctor — had given her. When she'd emerged from the back of that dress shop she'd been terrified. She hadn't been surprised when her husband had complained about how long it had taken her. In the grand scheme of her life this was normal. But it had been a day of complaints, an almost constant scrutiny of her every move. His habit had gotten the better of him — again. His supplier had been late and hadn't had enough to sell him. He'd been edgy, restless and belligerent —

again. When she'd wanted to go out — just to get away for a while — his paranoia had set in. They'd argued. He'd swung. She'd fallen. He'd left. She'd gotten up. She'd run out the door. But somehow, as he always seemed to, he'd found her. She'd gotten a reprieve of minutes only by pleading the need for the toilet. And afterwards, well, it was always inevitable; he'd led her home, berating her the entire way.

Two days ago she'd finally gone to a public phone to call the number the doctor had given her.

"I'll have to come on very short notice. I never know when it'll be safe to leave. I have to be sure that my husband's going to be out." Dr. Jalili, had been so understanding, so accommodating.

After the call, Homa had sat at her kitchen table for a long time. She'd made another decision. If *she* was going to get help, then she'd get help for her sister too. No one knew better than she what hell her sister lived in. Courage was something Homa had forgotten she'd ever had, but while she did have it, she'd use it.

Dr. Jalili, visibly somewhat surprised, greeted them with a warm smile. "Please, Homa, come right in. I'm glad you could come." Turning to her companion she said, "And you, *Khanum*, you are also most welcome. Come in, come in."

Homa knew immediately it had been the right thing for them to do. Still, she was afraid. *What will this lead to? Is it just a matter of getting injuries treated?* That's what she'd told herself and told her sister, just to persuade her to come.

But Homa's intuition, the only part of her still unscathed, knew more. That she had two options: stay with the status quo with all its predictable misery, or travel a new road where there might be a chance of change.

Most women, she'd come to realize, were more scared of change than maintaining their status quo; change led them into the unknown and who knew what horrors might await them there. They were frightened because of the risks, frightened because the law did not protect them, and frightened because they and their children were up against a disobliging system that favored even the most brutal of spouses. So yes, Homa was terrified of change, and of taking this step, but that little voice within her eventually had won out and she'd made her decision.

Homa didn't know how long her courage would last, but it didn't actually matter. She had stepped onto the path and she was going to walk it.

Today was the first visit to Dr. Jalili. As she began to talk, she knew in her bones that there would be many more. She knew that something bigger than herself was at stake here and that, for whatever reason, this doctor, this woman was going to be part of it.

The Family Rahimi

TEHRAN
2008

O<small>CTOBER</small>

For the average Iranian, the Ministry of Intelligence was more of a concept than a place. Indeed, if you asked anyone on the street, they probably wouldn't be able to give you directions to the Ministry's offices. What they could give you, perhaps, would be their notion of what the Ministry meant; that is, what it meant if someone from the Ministry wanted "to have a meeting with you" or "to ask you a few questions."

There would be some who weren't particularly concerned about this department of their government. Possibly because neither they nor anyone else they knew ever had to deal with it. Or possibly because they were, or believed themselves to be, beyond the Ministry's reach. The difficulty was, though, that no one except the Supreme Leader was actually beyond its reach. Even trusted clergy, politicians and any number of high-ranking officials could fall into disfavor and if that were the case, well, there was nowhere to hide. The Ministry would find you.

For ordinary citizens, being on the right side of the law was very important. For those with any tendencies to act outside of strict government parameters — journalists, bloggers, human rights activists, women's rights groups, anyone with alternative political or religious views, even Islamic ones — being on the right side meant either dissimulating or going underground. Otherwise, you'd have to leave the country. Or stand your ground until your views and activities eventually bubbled to the top of Intelligence's priority lists and they paid you a visit.

So, when people asked Kamran Rahimi where he worked, he gave a variety of vague answers, mentioning security, mostly. He found that the word "Intelligence" tended to make most people uncomfortable. And Kamran liked to have friends.

But he also liked his job and what it brought him. Since moving to Tehran he'd enjoyed a steady stream of promotions, the result of both his own considerable merit and his expanding network of connections. In this, Zahra's family had been correct and true to their promises to ensure he met the right people. His combination of likability, skill, and ambition had served him well. Even his brothers' achievements now paled in comparison. They were actually asking him for favors. His father's approval kept him buoyant and determined to go as far as he could.

Right now, there were many opportunities. He had new alliances and was firmly in the camp of the current president. When the latter came up for re-election, it was Rahimi's intention to remain on the right side of that contest. That kind of loyalty always had its rewards.

Which was why Kamran had difficulty understanding his wife's complaints. "You work too much; you work too long; you work too hard" were not things he'd expected from her. "You knew how much I'd be working even before we married; why are you complaining now?" he'd said. You know how important advancement is for us. And think about our parents, our families!" They expected him to move right up the ladder, her parents in particular. They had never been pleased with her first husband's contentment to live out in "the back of beyond," as they called it, and run a mediocre business for a bunch of rural hicks. Understandably they wanted to make sure her second chance would be a man of some substance. And they were determined to further his prospects by providing every connection they could draw on to ensure that both of them, yes, both of them, moved ahead into the right circles when they got to Tehran.

So, here they were, doing just that. Granted, the pond was much larger here than in the provinces, and Rahimi was a relatively modest fish, but that was just it, wasn't it? He had to keep going, had to get noticed. Become a bigger fish and keep the sharks at bay.

Thanks to his generous salary and Zahra's family's contributions, their roomy 17th floor apartment, one in a cluster of high-end Niyavaran high-rises, boasted richly upholstered sofas and chairs, ornate wooden tables, heavy formal drapery, chandeliers, and classic hand-woven carpets. The large balcony provided an excellent view of the well-maintained greenery below and the city beyond. "Come on, Zahra, you understand how this works. And you have your own friends, too, don't you? With your good looks, expensive clothes, and everything you could possibly need to entertain our family, friends and my important associates, what more could you want?" he'd asked. More than once. Or, "Look, Zahra, the kids are going to excellent schools, wear trendy clothes, have computers and cell phones, a huge network of the right kind of friends. What are you complaining about?"

Pushing aside these thoughts, he stubbed out his cigarette with his foot and picked up his newspaper from the bench. It was warm for October and getting out for a bit of air on his lunch break was the one small indulgence he allowed himself.

He stood up, and immediately felt dizzy. *Got up too fast*, he thought, and sat down again. When his head had cleared he stood up again, this time taking it slowly. After a few seconds, he pulled his shoulders back and stretched his back, standing as tall as he could. He took a few deep breaths.

On the other side of the courtyard two of his colleagues were just finishing their smokes as well and he walked over to join them. After exchanging a few words, the three of them went through a set of double doors and the building swallowed them up.

BOOK FIVE

REFORM

Tehran
2009 - 2011

2009

Chapter One

2009

JANUARY - EARLY JUNE

JANUARY

"So, what's happening now with this woman who's been going to see you? Your domestic abuse patient?" Taraneh sat in the passenger seat and looked at Fereshteh, who was driving.

Long blocks of cheap little shops with dirty windows, and rolled back security bars lined the busy thoroughfare. Pedestrians in dark winter coats hurried along the sidewalks, wet from the morning rain. The concrete facades reflected the grayness of the day and not even the colorful advertising offered relief from the drabness of the neighborhood.

"Well, she's come a few times. She's getting long-term treatment now. She has some medical issues directly related to chronic stress, but some are the result of internal injuries resulting from past trauma that never healed adequately. Then of course all the mental trauma from her whole situation. But she's doing better and she seems to look forward to appointments."

Fereshteh looked in her rearview mirrors, took a chance, and changed lanes. She continued: "A big part of her treatment is having someone to talk to. I'll try to get her to see a counselor. I keep encouraging her to leave her husband. I've sent her to social services and they're working with her on the abuse situation, but you know how that goes."

"She has to get all kinds of proof, doesn't she?"

"Yeah. Evidence from at least four witnesses, photos, proof of his drug use. All kinds of things that are difficult to get. I mean, who's she going to get as witnesses? As if anyone sees her getting pushed around, let alone beaten. I've taken photos of her injuries and dated them, but I'm only one person — and a *woman*, so…"

"Can't she get her neighbors or family to give testimony? Or find someone who can catch the husband getting his opium?"

"Hardly. She's too embarrassed to go to neighbors and her family's too scared. And opium?" she laughed. "It's so entrenched and so common that a lot of the police turn a blind eye. And there are always some police who are okay with it as long as a bribe can be had. I don't know what this man's situation is, but that's not something I want to go near, no matter how much I want to help this woman. Oh, and she's got a sister in a similar mess."

They came to a light and sat patiently. With over a dozen cars in front of them and the three lanes merging to two, it would be a while until they could move through the intersection.

Fereshteh looked over at her sister-in-law. "I just wish I knew how to get her case pushed forward to a civil court."

Taraneh thought about this for a bit and then said, "Well, there *are* ways, of course. There *are* people who *will* help in such cases."

"Oh no. Nothing illegal or shady. Taraneh, I'm surprised at you!"

"No, no, no, no! Nothing like that! I didn't mean that at all. I just meant that there are *some* people who are working hard for women's issues, that's all."

"You mean like human rights activists, right?"

Crimson Ink

"Well, yes. But you don't even have to go that far."

"What do you mean?"

"I mean that there are some people — professionals, right? — who have the skills and the contacts and they help people like these women you're helping. And other kinds of cases of course."

"You mean like lawyers?"

"Yeah, lawyers, of course, but there are others who know the system —"

The traffic moved and Fereshteh was quick to follow. Weaving in and out, cutting in and across, they reached the intersection and halted at the light.

"No."

"What do you mean?"

"No, Taraneh. I won't do that. Professionals who know the system and stand up for people like these women are activists, no matter what else you want to call them."

"But —"

"Nope. I'm *not* going there. I will *not* take any chances. Those people — and may God bless them! — those people are on somebody's radar; somebody who's just waiting to swoop down on them and arrest them. Look at what's been happening now for years!"

"But a lot of good work's been done!"

"They've tried. But where has it gotten most of them? The lawyers who take the tough cases get arrested. Loads of them in prison. The ones who've stood up for our Baha'i community have been silenced or constantly played or stonewalled. The only reason that folks like Shirin Ebadi haven't been thrown into Evin is because they're too well known internationally. But even with her Nobel Prize, she still couldn't help us! Look at what they've done with our seven 'Yaran' arrested last year!"

"I'm not talking about *her*. I'm not talking about *us*. We know *our* situation. We're in a different category than these women you're talking about. And you don't need the big names in human rights for them, just some —"

"Some brave someone. I know. And as soon as I, especially as a Baha'i, make contact with an activist of any kind, I am *seriously* on someone's radar. No, Taraneh, I'm not having any of it. No thank you!"

The light changed; she revved the engine, freeing her car from the pack, and escaped from the congestion of the intersection.

Late May

How much clutter can there be! Farah was astonished at the accumulation of "stuff" in her spare room. In all her 79 years she'd lived in homes that had been duly cleaned every Spring and every Autumn, practicing the good habits she'd learned as a child. So, curtains had been taken down, washed, ironed and re-hung on newly cleaned windows; carpets had been taken outside and beaten thoroughly, washed if necessary, then re-rolled and returned to floors that had meanwhile been scrubbed and polished. Cupboards and closets had been emptied, brushed clean and then restocked with their contents having been assessed, culled and re-organized. Clothes had been thoroughly aired, then returned to their places or given away to charity.

But in the 29 years since leaving Shiraz she had been unable to tackle the boxes stacked in the closet of her guest room. They stood there, untouchable memorials to Layla's short life, never having once been opened since their hurried packing. Until today.

Perhaps it had to do with the energy in the air. No matter that the days were hot and the pollution sickening. That was just summer in Tehran. But this year there was something else.

This year the city was abuzz with expectation. Truly different. A new presidential election was imminent and there had been weeks of candidate debates.

People were tired of sanctions, tired of restrictions and economic cutbacks, and the usual rhetoric. Students were engaged (*but when weren't they!*), but so were young people in general. So were women and families - all in what seemed to Farah to be a new way of thinking. There was a swell of support for the so-called "Green

Movement", and this had taken on a life of its own. As a Baha'i, Farah kept out of party politics, of course, but eagerly followed the news and debates on TV. It was hard not to feel the energy.

She opened the guest room closet. There were three tall stacks of boxes. "Ah, Laylajoon," she sighed. "Laylajoon, finally, finally." Since she couldn't lift them on her own, she decided to open the ones on top and simply start going through them until they were empty. This way she was able to look at and sort the contents into piles, then remove the empty boxes and start on the next ones. She allowed herself time for a bit of nostalgia as she fingered each item and was surprised, now with so much time gone by, how much the pain had diminished. This gave her the determination to go on.

When all this was done, she would repaint and redecorate this sadly neglected room. The last time the two-bedroom apartment had been painted was just before she'd moved in. Reza had found this little gem of a place and it was a perfect match for her downsized needs after leaving Shiraz. In a slightly upscale neighborhood, it was roomy for its size, had quality finishings and a pleasant view that included a nearby green space. Her brother had insisted on her having a respectable home and had even overseen a further interior upgrade that his construction crew carried out. *Yes,* she thought, *it was high time to set this room to rights.*

On the second day of this exercise, Farah found some of Layla's books and laid them in a pile on a small table. She looked at each title to decide who should receive it. Some might go to Fereshteh or Habib, or even to her grandchildren.

She came to a book with a plain cover and opened it. Layla's name, and *"1976 - "* was written on the inside cover opposite the flyleaf. Turning the page, she saw that it wasn't an ordinary book. The pages were filled with her daughter's handwriting.

Farah recalled the calligraphy classes Layla had taken and how her daughter had struggled in copying out verses of Sa'adi, Hafez and the other great Persian poets. Layla had never felt confident in her penmanship, but Farah now saw only beauty as she read the familiar texts written in her daughter's hand.

Turning the page, she saw more verses, and Farah thought that this must have been Layla's collection of favorite passages. She continued to turn the pages, taking pleasure in the beauty of the language and cadence of the poetry as she read aloud.

She turned yet another page but the calligraphic exercises were gone, replaced by something far more personal. It looked like a journal. These entries started in 1979. Taken aback, Farah stopped reading. This felt like prying. She had always respected her family's need for privacy and had never dreamt of invading that space in their lives.

But Layla was gone. She held the journal in her lap, and looked out the window, seeing her daughter in her mind's eye. Minutes passed. Her eyes were moist.

Farah straightened her back and blinked away the tears. Her breathing deepened. She began to read. The entries were sporadic. Layla had described the momentous events and upheavals of the Revolution only in broad strokes, concentrating instead on her inner struggles in dealing with them. Farah hung on every word.

She came to 'August'. Farah sat back in her chair, putting her hand to her heart. She took a deep breath to steady herself, then held the journal with both hands and resumed her reading.

There were two short entries in the same vein as the others. Then she came to a longer one. Much longer:

How can I bear this? Yet I have to because I cannot - I will not tell Maman. This would crush her. Nor can I tell Fereshteh. Nor Habib. I have to keep this to myself...

When I looked at Uncle Reza, when I confronted him, he said nothing. He just looked surprised. But then his look changed, and when I saw this I actually shivered. It was like he'd made a decision. His whole face looked... But, no, not even Uncle Reza would...

The sentence trailed off and below it were scribbled lines, circles and repetitive designs.

Then,

I've never really taken Uncle's harshness very seriously. It's always seemed to me that he's simply a traditional, conservative man who has difficulty accepting things outside of his world view. When he sees things he doesn't like, he says so and he's usually not very polite. But that's him. He's my mother's brother, so I just accept him for who he is. So does Habib, I think. But Fereshteh... she always complained about him. She's always seemed afraid of him...

MORE SCRIBBLES.

FARAH HAD the impression that Layla had been of two minds in writing. She seemed to be procrastinating.

Disjointed phrases, written diagonally, came next:

same look with Fereshteh; worse to her - why???; F crying in her room so often after his visits - she always got upset with me, saying you 'wouldn't understand, you have no idea' and 'go away - you don't know what you're talking about'.

<u>*What didn't I know????*</u>

The last question was underlined multiple times, the lines scoring grooves in the fine paper.

MORE SCRIBBLES. More diagonals. Strong, repetitive underscoring again.

SOMETIMES SHE HAD BRUISES. *Told me to mind my own business.*
<u>*What happened? Are these connected?????*</u>
No, they can't be. Maybe she'd just been careless & bumped herself and was too embarrassed to say that to a little sister?

NEXT CAME a little stick drawing of an unhappy little girl.

Then, further down the page:

I wonder if Maman knew how unhappy she was as a kid. How about Habib? Baba?

<u>*What did any of us know??? Poor Fereshteh!*</u>

. . .

THEN, in large letters:
Why don't we talk about these things?????!!!!!

IT WAS as if Layla had been trying to put together a puzzle but not sure she wanted to see the finished picture. But finally she said it:

I HAVE TO WRITE THIS. Have to put it down in ink to get it out of my heart. I feel like I'm bleeding. Let me bleed onto the page so that my heart can heal. So that I can let go of my distracted thoughts. So that I can pray and find strength...

Uncle expressed his deep concern this afternoon about us, his Baha'i relatives. He tried to convince me to stop my activities, told me I was putting everyone in danger. He talked a great deal. At first he was more or less reasonable and I could understand his views. But something strange happened to him after I expressed my own. I was very calm and respectful. I did not mean offense. But he clearly was upset. He was quiet - because of the others, Maman especially, I guess, but he became very angry at me, said things that were — The rest was scribbled out. Then:

He started talking about Fereshteh being arrogant. Me being arrogant, just like her, he said.

SOME CROSSED OUT WRITING. Some scribbles.

THEN, in a rush he said two things so unthinkable that it took me a few seconds to grasp what he was saying. I still wasn't sure, so I asked him outright. I begged him to tell me that what I'd heard, what I'd understood was not true. But he didn't. Couldn't??? And for a moment he looked scared. As if he'd suddenly realized that he'd said much more than he'd ever intended because he'd gotten so upset and it had all spilled out.

As I understand it, he played some awful role in the mob incitement and attacks on the Baha'is in Hurmuzak village back in the 50's. He seemed to know too much and he wouldn't deny it. He refused to answer my questions on what he did, so I don't really know. <u>But he did do something.</u> *(A triple underline of the last sentence.)*

Terrible as that was, it wasn't all. It seems he did something awful to Fereshteh. He didn't answer when I asked what he meant about 'knocking her down'. It's only now as I've been writing that I'm piecing bits together. Some things make more sense now. Things I never really looked closely at before. I feel so much sorrow. The shock of these possibilities is terrible. And when I think that my sister must have been suffering and I was oblivious about it???

HERE, some of the ink had run and there were spots and blotches that looked like parts of the page had been wet.

I TOLD *him I'd never tell Maman. Couldn't. Did he believe me? Did he even hear me???*

FARAH TURNED the page and found it blank. She turned and turned but found nothing more. She checked the date again.

It was two days before Layla had been arrested.

FARAH LOOKED up and stared at the window, unable to see the hues of the afternoon sunlight on the clouds beyond. She sat and stared for a long while, barely breathing.

Finally, with an aching in her limbs that she ignored, Farah stood up, straightened her back, and then moved methodically. She completed the emptying of the last boxes in the closet, sorting the items as before. She completed the filling of various boxes and bags with the items that would be discarded, given to friends or given to charity, and set them aside. The closet space was now, finally, clear.

In her own bedroom she took out a different box — a sturdy dark blue gift box of a generous size in which she kept some of her own treasured items, the intent being that when she finally departed this life these mementos might be appreciated by her son and daughter.

She placed the box on her bed and removed the items. From a book shelf she took out two of her favorite large-format volumes and placed them next to the box. She laid Layla's journal at the bottom of the box and stacked the other books on top. Into the space remaining, she returned as many of the mementos as would fit, carefully placing them on top of the books. Then, making sure that the cover fit snuggly over the top, she put the box back into her wardrobe closet, pushing it firmly into the back right-hand corner. In front of and to the side of the box she arranged her shoes and a few other items. She stood for a moment, looking at her work, then closed the closet door.

She went to the window for a moment, noting absently that the sun had almost set, then made her way to the kitchen and put the kettle on for a pot of tea.

The following day

In a life where so much was unpredictable, complicated and sometimes downright unpleasant, his sister Farah was a reliable haven: always there, always the same. He'd had a particularly irritating day and been glad of her invitation. He'd not bothered to tell Sohayla about it, since she was entertaining her own friends that evening. She knew he'd eat out.

The dinner Farah served suited him perfectly and the chilled melon and grapes that followed were refreshing in the heat. But hot, strong tea with cubes of sugar were their ritual after a meal and once the dining table had been cleared and the dishwasher set to run, they sat comfortably in Farah's living room sipping it as they continued their dinner conversation.

But the talk took an unexpected turn. She began asking uncomfortable questions. Where had that come from? Why was

Farah asking him questions about Fereshteh? His niece seemed to be the bane of his life. *Okay, so Farah knows that Fereshteh's never been my favorite person. She's seen us argue, even. Of course! My niece and I have always seen things from opposite ends, so that's to be expected sometimes. And Farah knows that. Everyone does. It's no secret, for goodness sake! So why the questions about bruises? And crying? What rubbish! How should I know? Did I live with them? Did I see her every waking minute of her day?* Farah seemed to be accusing him of something! How could she — his sister?!

Bad enough. One of their rare disagreements. But then she pushed him further, and — so unlike her — she kept pushing, pushing, pushing. Accusing him again and again. How could she know about that? Impossible. And that? Also impossible! But she wouldn't stop.

He stood up, defending himself stoutly.

She stood up and matched his glare.

But this was supposed to be Farah, his dear sister! Who was this new woman standing in front of him?

He moved towards her, intending first to take her hands and assure her that this was all a great misunderstanding, that he had no idea where this village of Hurmuzak was or who lived there or what had happened more than 50 years ago, that it was all a mistake, and that, really, couldn't they just drop this ridiculous story, and —

She kept at it. She was unleashing a storm of hurt and anger at him, seemingly incapable of stopping the torrent. Her clear blue eyes had never before expressed this paradox of coldness and heat. It pierced him and he reacted.

Moving closer to her he felt his hand on her shoulder. A short quick press, that was all. But she stumbled over the little footrest behind her. No, that was not supposed to happen. And though it was all over quickly, he watched it in horrifying slow motion, unable to stop it.

He knelt down beside her inert form, tugging uselessly at her short sleeve, shaking her shoulder as he called her name. Minutes. How many? But it seemed forever. He tapped her cheeks, recalling the gesture from TV films. Surely this would revive her?

Then he saw the blood. It came in a trickle from her right ear and formed a bright little crimson puddle on the wood floor.

He remembered the blood from so long ago. Bodies drenched with it, clothing, floors, and furniture painted with it.

Recoiling in terror, he pushed himself up, breathing hard and fast. He looked around the room, blinking his eyes to re-orient himself. He looked down again at Farah and saw the puddle expanding. He panicked, and, combing both hands through his thick hair again and again, he saw only one solution. He stepped over her, walked rapidly to the entrance hall, and slid into his sandals. Carefully opening the door a crack, he scanned the hallway. Seeing no one, he slipped out, closing the door quietly. Instead of going for the elevator, he made for the stairs.

THE FIVE BAHA'I women sat at a corner table in the cozy atmosphere of the new café. The round table suited them, allowing them all to see each other, and their smiles reflected the pleasure they'd had in spending this time together. Their formal meetings and administrative structures long since having been banned by government decree, individual Baha'is had found ways to come together to create a community life nevertheless. They came together in small groups to pray and worship, to study their scriptures, and to consult and address the concerns and needs of their fellow believers. Sometimes, though, Baha'is just got together to spend time in each other's company. This was one of those times.

With the presidential election less than three weeks away and public interest so high, the streets, restaurants and cafés were livelier than ever. Better to get together now, before things became even busier.

It's been too long, Fereshteh thought. She'd kept postponing social get-togethers in favor of more serious matters. But tonight she'd relented and come after work to meet her friends.

"Why don't we do this more often?" they asked each other as

they exited onto the sidewalk. "We'll do this again — soon," they vowed, kissing cheeks and smiling their good-byes.

Fereshteh walked toward the bus stop, still feeling the warmth of the little group. *Really*, she chided herself, *I need to do this more often. What stops me from just calling them up and going out?*

Her timing was good; the bus arrived before she even had an answer to her question.

As the bus pulled out from the curb she gripped the metal pole firmly and took her mobile phone out of her handbag. "Jamshid-joon, have you eaten? Everything ok? *Khub* – good. I'm on the bus but I'll stop at Maman's place first. I haven't talked to her in a couple of days so I'll just see how she's doing and then come home. What? Oh, the bus is packed. You wouldn't believe how many people are out! Ok, we'll talk when I get home. See you soon."

Although she had a key, Fereshteh preferred to knock on her mother's door. It preserved the respect she had for her and gave Farah the pleasure of opening her door, her home and her hospitality to her family and friends.

By the third unanswered knock, Fereshteh felt the cold certainty that comes when intuition tells you something is very wrong. She had to be home, so why wasn't she answering? Her mother was never out this late unless she was with her, Habib or Uncle Reza. She turned the knob. The door was unlocked. Her limbs prickled; her stomach became a knot.

"Maman? Maman, where are you? Maman? Maman!"

Stepping into the living room, she saw her mother. Her doctor's instincts and responses kicked into high gear. Running to her, she knelt down and immediately began her assessment: Pulse and breath were present even if consciousness wasn't. A sticky pool of dark blood was noted. Trunk and limbs seemed free of fractures and injuries. But a skull fracture appeared highly probable, and she couldn't rule out a spinal injury. She'd have to wait for the EMTs to move her onto a stretcher.

She made the necessary calls. Her husband, brother, and sister-in-law would meet her at the emergency department of the local hospital; her uncle's and aunt's mobiles went to voicemail.

She sat down again on the floor next to her mother to wait for the ambulance. And prayed.

Anyone who's ever had to wait in an emergency room for news of a loved one, knows the pain and boredom of it. For a medical person, it's hell. You know what should be done; you could do much of it yourself. But you're not permitted to. You also know too many stories of mistakes, neglect and incompetence. So, you agonize, wondering just who is behind those doors.

How long can you pace away your adrenaline, pray away your fears, speculate an outcome, pretend to be comforted by those who share your vigil?

The familiar gentleness of Habib's hand on her shoulder brought Fereshteh out of her agitated thoughts and she turned around with a flicker of hope in her heart. "No," he said, "I haven't seen any of the medical staff. I just wanted to tell you that Uncle Reza's finally arrived."

They'd expected he'd be worried, distraught, anxious. *Isn't that what you are under such circumstances?*, thought Fereshteh. But not Uncle Reza. He was making such a noise that the staff were cautioning him to lower his voice. "No, sir, you can't go in. No, you cannot see the doctor. All the doctors are busy saving lives in there, sir. Please sit down. No sir, I have no news for you. No, it's really not my fault, sir. I don't know what happened to your sister, sir. Please, sir, sit down."

As he walked away from them he caught sight of his niece and that set him off again. He rounded on her in such anger that others in the waiting area changed their seats. Staff came running, demanding he be quiet or go outside and wait. With apologies to them, Habib and Jamshid took him by the arms and led him outside. Fereshteh was too exhausted in mind and body to be embarrassed or even afraid. She bought a coffee from the dispenser and sat near the reception desk to wait.

It was early morning before a tired but self-assured physician emerged and called Fereshteh's name. Her eyes flew open and she pulled herself up from her awkward position and went to the desk. Taraneh and the menfolk followed and the physician led them to a small gray sterile room and closed the door. Offering them the chairs, he stood before them and like a judge, a god almost, he delivered his pronouncement.

Khanum Hashemi-Jalili had been admitted comatose after a severe blow to her head. Examinations revealed intracranial hemorrhage and clotting in the temporal, parietal and occipital lobes. Efforts to relieve the increased intracranial pressure had failed to return her to consciousness. Subsequent hemorrhage had occurred, precipitating a herniation that had culminated in her expiration. He, Dr. Sanjari, was extremely sorry for their loss. Please see the nurse at the desk for further instructions.

Looking down at the seated family — through them — he seemed oblivious to their open mouths, their stunned eyes. His polite smile might just have been his appreciation of the absence of questions. Turning quickly, he opened the door and disappeared.

Early June

The look of surprise on her face was gratifying. Exactly what he wanted. Reza had planned this carefully, showing up at his niece's door when Jamshid was out and when she had no idea her uncle was coming.

She invited him in, of course, and he stepped in quickly before she had time to change her mind. He could see how nervous she was. She'd never outgrown that, had she? Always ready to crumble, ready to break out into those ridiculous tears. And he'd give her tears this evening.

He sat opposite her on a sofa. "No, I don't want tea; I want you to just sit right there, where you are, and listen." She seemed to get smaller, pulling her elbows to her sides, holding her forearms together. Oh no, there was that stupid scratching thing she always did. A wonder she had any skin left on that arm any more.

He offered no explanation for his visit. Best to keep her off-balance. Nor did he waste time with courtesies of any kind. He'd come to accuse.

He launched into it with a direct hit: she was the reason that his sister was dead. Her mouth opened as if to protest but he didn't brook any interruption. Yes, she, Fereshteh was fully to blame for the loss of his beloved sister. He laid this down with emphasis and continued, steamrolling over her objections.

"If you'd not been out that evening doing God-knows-what – if you'd been at home with my sister, looking after her properly – for God's sake she was an old woman! – looking after her properly, then she wouldn't've fallen, wouldn't've hit her head, wouldn't've gone into a coma, wouldn't've died, for God's sake! How could you be so selfish? How? Nothing's changed since you were a kid. Nothing! Your whole life you've been selfish & too busy with books, your studying, your work – why did you need to work, eh? Why? You should've just married & stayed home and been a good wife and mother and then a good daughter to Farah."

He paused briefly as he stood up and began to pace, gesturing dramatically for effect, and sneered, "No, you had to become a doctor; had to be smart; had to be noticed... and then you had to be busy with all those" – he spat this out – "Baha'i things: meetings, meetings, meetings. Going out at night all the time to meetings. Praise be to Allah and to our wise Supreme Leader that at least you can't do that anymore! So then, where were you that night when my sister fell? Huh? What were you doing out then? Did you go out alone? Did you at least come home from your job to first check on my sister? Did you even think about her that night? Huh? Did you? Did you???"

He paced some more, muttering now, aware of Fereshteh's eyes on him. She seemed to be saying something about sitting down, having some tea to calm down, to talk about this.

Incredulous at her audacity in interrupting him, he rounded on her. "Talk about this? I'm talking. I'm telling you what's what. And if you cannot see what's happened and whose fault it is that my sister is now cold in her grave in that excuse for a cemetery, if you can't see what a tragedy this is for me and my family –"

He stopped and glared at her. "No, you cannot see, can you? Shut up! You can't see past your own nose, you selfish, self-important bitch who thinks she can wear a man's trousers!"

He resumed his pacing. Even shouting seemed insufficient to express the pain, the outrage, the disgust churning inside him. He felt like screaming. He wanted to hit her, to obliterate this woman, this stain on his family's honor.

She was talking again but he was deaf to her as he continued, "I will never forget this, never! I will never forgive you for this, Fereshteh, never, as long as I live!"

He wiped the gathering moisture from his eyes, surprised to find it there.

"As God is my witness, you will pay for your sins. Someday you'll pay! Never, never, never try to contact me or my family again, do you hear? Never! I disown you, Fereshteh. May you rot in hell!"

He turned away from her drawn face, strode out of the door and slammed it behind him.

Chapter Two

2009

June – October

RAHIMI

12 June, Election evening

It was amazing to see how many were on the streets on the election evening. Rahimi could hardly move. It was just as they'd heard from their scouts and spies. Sure, he could have just relied on his minions, but to get the most accurate picture, he'd convinced himself that he had to see it all for himself. He needed to be out in the crowd to get the true sense of what was going on, to take the temperature of these masses, hear what they were really saying behind all those slogans.

So it's true, he thought, *they really believe they can overturn the presidency and install a reform-minded candidate. This isn't just the kind of crowd incitement that later plays out differently at the polling stations. These people are serious.* And they were not just the usual student and youth. From what Rahimi was seeing, plenty of average citizens of all ages were out, their green "reform" bandanas, scarves and

Crimson Ink

banners blanketing whole boulevards in support of reform candidates.

He pulled out his cellphone and snapped a few photos, then took a video to capture the chants and refrains. In spite of himself, he felt a certain enthusiasm within him, a kind of good will and solidarity that surprised him. He was smiling.

But he also knew it was time to leave; he had his work to do, of course. *That's why I'm here*, he reminded himself.

As he began to edge his way out of the crush, a sudden surge lurched him forward and he was caught in a sea of movement as the crowd took up a new chant, its volume increasing as its strains reached further and further back along the ranks of the marchers. The look of hope and enthusiasm of a minute ago took on determination and a growing passion. The kind that propelled people toward a goal. Zeal was on their faces now, he saw. He recognized it. From the days of the Revolution.

Caught in the moving press of his fellow citizens, Rahimi found his mood shifting. He tried to squeeze himself out of the throng, but it had gained momentum, forcing him with it. Surrounded by this wave of humanity, his heart accelerated and his eyes darted left and right, seeking an opening. Soon he was gasping, desperate for a way out. Sweat coursed down his cheeks and back, and filled his armpits. He pushed. He shouted. He slithered to the right, creating a brief space for himself between bodies that moved inexorably forward. One body at a time, he told himself, still out of breath. *Focus, Kami, focus*, he told himself. *Take a deep breath, Kami, come on! Keep moving!*

His goal to reach the sidelines was hard-won: he'd moved almost two city blocks before he emerged near a side street, his breath ragged and heart palpitating. For a fraction of a second his eyes went dark and he felt himself falling. A passerby caught him and helped him to sit by the wall of a building.

"Hey, you gonna be okay?"

Rahimi looked up, a weak smile of thanks on his lips.

"Just sit for a minute. Wait a couple of minutes, mister. Catch your breath. Hey, you want some water or something?"

"No. No thanks. I'll be okay."

The young man looked doubtful, but said, "Sure. Hey, be careful. This crowd's gonna get bigger." Giving Rahimi a smile and a thumbs-up, he took up the chant and joined the marchers.

Eventually Rahimi got up and straightened his clothes. Calmer now, he got his bearings, then called a taxi which eventually got him back to his office. Joining his colleagues, he monitored the situation through the live-feed cameras they'd set up.

"Yeah," Rahimi told them, "the crowds are huge and they're certainly determined. But they're happy — look at them." He pointed at the screens. In his verbal report he had not mentioned his moments of alarm. "Let them have their fun. Let them wave their banners tonight. It makes them happy and gets rid of a lot of energy. They're fine. Everything's orderly. Our people are just 'directing traffic'. Nothing to worry about. We've got things under control."

Which was why the next day, after the election results had been announced, he and his colleagues were initially unprepared for the wave of protest that arose. And why, as the days went on, they became alarmed at the proportions the dissent took on. People were actually challenging the results. Calling for a recount. Calling for the incumbent, the official winner, to step down.

It was clear that the security forces would have to step up their emergency measures and hit back hard. There could be no outcry against the State. No dissension in the ranks of a populace who owed its life to the Supreme Leader.

So, armed with orders from the highest authorities, and with everything the State machinery had at its disposal — the riot police, the Basij, and the Revolutionary Guard — Rahimi and his colleagues at security headquarters cracked down on the thousands of demonstrators unwilling to accept the official tally and go home.

"If these crowds can't understand orders and tear gas, then they'll have to understand batons and bullets," they told each other.

They ordered dozens of vans into the streets. Basij spilled out into the crowds, and, beating anyone within reach, dragged them into the vehicles, hands cuffed behind them. Snipers dotted buildings and rode motorcycles through the boulevards and alleys, catching those who were running for cover, calling more vans to the scenes to pick up the injured and cart them off under arrest.

Rahimi gave his lieutenants and minions his favorite speech: "Catch every last one. That's what you need to do. No one should go free. They have to learn what it means to defy the Supreme Leader. Every one of them, because if we let them go they'll raise their ugly heads again, thinking they can repeat their offense. Remember, men, those lessons we learned in the '80s. "Unfortunately, we're now dealing with a generation of kids who were born after we put order in our land. They don't understand. They don't appreciate all that's been done to pave the way for them. It's a pity, but perhaps that was to be expected. So, go out there now and teach them that lesson! Teach it to them well! I'm looking forward to your reports." And he sent them off on their mission.

RAHIMI WAS ANNOYED with his wife. Zahra was complaining again: the same old harangue: Work shorter hours, be home more, on and on. She kept reminding him of his age, his health and the fact that he could retire in just a couple of years.

As if he was thinking of that right now! His head was pounding. Again. He put down his fork and looked straight at his wife across the dinner table.

"Really, Kami, why can't we just get out of the city for a while? This is insane! These crowds, the heat, the noise. Why can't we go to the summer house? Enjoy the mountain air and the peace and quiet? For just a little while?"

"It's you that needs to think! Get a grip on reality! It would take us more than half a day to get there, and then what? Stay a day and come back?"

"Of course not. We could spend a week and then —"

"A week! Do you think I have a week I can take off? Now?"

"I —"

"With all these protests, we need everyone on board. Every day. They're counting on me! I can't just walk away!"

"But it's crazy out there! You might get hurt!" she pleaded.

"Don't be so weak! Stop worrying! Everything will be fine. This is a temporary situation. It will all calm down and things will be normal again."

But weeks went by and nothing was normal again. The protests and clashes continued throughout June. Scores of journalists and officials suspected to be reform sympathizers were thrown into prison, and the demonstrators, repeatedly encouraged by the leadership of the opposition movement, and disregarding the condemnation of the Supreme Leader and the Guardian Council, kept up their defiance.

By the end of the month a prominent member of the Assembly of Experts called for the execution of leading "rioters", as he termed them. Contrary to what had been intended, this produced support for the reformers in the form of international outrage from diplomats and journalists.

Then there was that very unfortunate death. The video of that young girl's body in the street had gone viral over the Internet and had turned Neda Agha-Soltan into a rallying point for government opposition. And it hadn't helped that later, two former Iranian presidents had come to the defense of the protesters. More clashes. More arrests. Full vans. Officers on extra duty. For weeks.

Rahimi and his colleagues were on constant alert.

"Where are we going to put them, sir?"

Rahimi hardly knew what to answer his lieutenant. He wiped his brow in the stifling mid-July heat. "Just keep doing your job, Faraji. You have your orders."

"But sir, respectfully, our vans are unloading detainees into centers that can't take them. They're overflowing."

"You tell those officers from me that they *will* make room for them."

"I have, sir. Believe me, I've been forceful with them. But last night Commander Jafarzadeh laughed in my face and told me to take my prisoners somewhere else. When I refused, he gave me an

Crimson Ink

earful: what did I think I was doing, trying to stuff more bodies into a warehouse already holding four times its capacity. Where was he going to put all the shit and vomit from two thousand men, even if they hardly ate a thing." He cleared his throat. "Excuse me, sir; his words not mine."

He swallowed, then, when Rahimi said nothing, continued: "So I told him to dig trenches for the... uh... waste. I told him to get the prisoners to sleep in shifts. I said I'd ask about more food. They're already rationing the water, sir." He stood up straighter. "Are there any other facilities we could use, sir?"

"We're working on that. We're also training new recruits to deal with the guard work at the centers." He turned to look out of his office window. The trees along the street were brown with the dust and soot of the Tehran summer.

"Let's hope last night's protests will be an end to it." He looked down at the stream of pedestrians and under his breath said, "If only these stupid reform politicians, these trouble-making turncoats would just shut up..."

But they didn't.

Clashes continued sporadically and battles were conducted on the Internet.

In August prominent individuals were put on trial, charged with acting against national security, spying for Western states, and plotting to overthrow the religious establishment. Prosecutors were calling for "maximum punishment" and the detentions continued throughout the autumn. New centers had to be constructed.

"THE SUPREME LEADER has announced that it's a crime to cast doubt on the election. Be prepared. Our services are needed now more than ever." Rahimi was addressing his most senior officers yet again. It was hard to believe it was already October. Would this never end?

"We're only a few days from the anniversary of the storming of the U.S. Embassy. It is our job to maintain calm and dignity at this event, but as we've seen, our enemies are using every anniversary, every opportunity to assemble and disrupt. I think it's safe to say that until we have them all behind bars we're going to be busy out in the streets."

He looked at each of the faces around the table. His trusted men. "Now, let's look at our strategy."

THEY PERSEVERED and the weeks passed. Arrests continued. The detention centers, those stifling makeshift structures not fit for cattle, and overflowing with their fetid masses of crushed humanity, continued to trouble Kamran Rahimi.

THE DECEMBER FUNERAL of a senior Grand Ayatollah — a dissident — set off fresh demonstrations. So it was no surprise when, a few days later, most other memorial services for him were banned; or that Security Forces had attacked the home of another dissident Grand Ayatollah. Or that the State decided to sponsor pro-government rallies of tens of thousands to counter the late December clashes that coincided with the Ashura religious observances.

RAHIMI'S WIFE monitored all of this.

Her hair in disarray, her cheeks hollow, and her tired eyes wet with tears, Zahra vented her frustration.

"You see, Kami? You see? I'm not imagining it. I'm not hysterical. It just goes on and on. More and more demonstrations. And I've looked at the Internet. Those dissidents aren't planning to stop. They'll never stop! You'll be out chasing them forever! How are you going to stop them? I've been right to be concerned. Look at all the trials and executions! If you hang the leaders, their supporters will call them martyrs and they'll all go on and on and —"

"Enough!" Balling his fists, he rounded on her, his eyes blazing. "Enough, woman!" He turned, strode out the door and slammed it.

But as he rode the wood-paneled elevator down to the parking garage he knew that he had been more optimistic than he'd had a right to be. Everything that Zahra said was true. His job was becoming more, not less, demanding. Because he also knew more than his wife suspected: the "official" trials, sentencings and hangings were only a speck in the murky realm of "national security". In his world, a world unsuspected by his wife, anyone could be arrested. Everyone was fair game. All were under scrutiny. Clashes and riots added to his burden, that was true, but the real body of work took place underground. Literally. In dark hidden places.

As THE MONTHS passed Rahimi burrowed deeper into his work, keeping up the punishing pace dictated by events and expectations. His considerable abilities in dealing with "subversion" earned him a new position in an elite cadre of agents who had "special duties". The toughest cases were given to them.

Ignoring his health and his wife's pleas, he fine-tuned his skills in a live laboratory.

Chapter Three

2009

June – October

FERESHTEH

June 20th

On this rare morning alone at home, Fereshteh ignored all her intended tasks and paced. Back and forth in front of her living room windows, she retraced her steps, holding her arms in a tight embrace.

In her head she started calculating numbers, just to create some kind of order, a place to hook her runaway thoughts. A starting point to take some control over her emotions. It had been about a month — almost four weeks, she needed it to be precise — since her mother's death. Nearly three weeks since the funeral. About two since her uncle's maniacal tirade. And one week now since all hell had broken loose in the capital of her country. Four, three, two, one. She felt like she would explode. As she raised both arms towards the ceiling in a kind of supplication, a sob shot up from her pelvis. Swelling in her chest, it burst through the funnel of her throat, emerging in a sound like some animal in its death throes.

The way now paved, a lifetime of resentments surged behind it, erupting volcanically, spewing the heat and fire of her anger, her grief, her pain, and her fear. Decades of frustrations flew out like boulders and her heart's pent up sorrows gushed in a cascade of hot, stinging tears. She let it flow, spew and rumble as it would. She let the images of her pain sweep and course. There was no thought.

She shivered in the chill of years of exclusion at school. Her ears pricked at choruses of schoolgirl taunts. Her chest heaved as her teachers' insults and vindictiveness hit their mark. Her blood boiled at the incessant ridicule and increasing hostility of Majid, Farid and Saeed and their friends and at the sniggers and snide remarks of their sisters. Her blood ran cold, her mouth ran dry and her skin crawled at the lies, the hypocrisy, the look... the touch... of her Uncle Reza.

Shuddering, she collapsed in a heap, sobbing violently.

ALL WAS SILENT. Had she passed out? Had she slept? With effort she pushed herself up and rested her back against a chair. She stared at nothing, thought of nothing, felt nothing. Long moments went by.

As if on auto-pilot, she got up and went to wash her face. Taking a towel to dry it, Fereshteh looked at herself in the mirror and saw someone strange. It wasn't the redness of her swollen eyes, nor the pink blotches on her cheeks. Nor was it her disheveled graying, wavy hair. No, there was something in the quality of the look itself that she couldn't recognize. There was a different woman in front of her, accusing, almost. Challenging her. *Who are you? What are you? What are you doing? Where are you going? Why?*

She shut her eyes and grasped both arms as yet another shudder gripped her. But she stood in place; stood her ground in front of this challenger. Opening her eyes, she looked back and answered out loud, "I don't know. I don't know any of it. I have no answer for you and I don't know what to do."

The stranger held her gaze and stared her down. Fereshteh

capitulated. Hiding her face in both hands, she dropped the towel and hurried out of the bathroom.

"I need air; I need air; I need air!" It was not quite a shout.

Opening the glass door to the balcony, she went to the rail and inhaled in gulps, fixing her eyes on the skyline beyond. She didn't dare to close her eyes; behind their lids she might see more than she could handle.

The city took her mind in tow. Its endless structures, its dots of trees, parks and monuments, its dependable drone of traffic, its countless pedestrians and its perpetual summer smog led her back to rational thought.

She thought again about her mother. As crushing as her grief was, she believed that she would work through it, in time. But there was the issue of legacy. Farah had embodied her culture's ideal of what a woman should be: warm, hospitable, generous, and self-deprecating. The quintessential devoted home-maker, wife, and mother.

But more than that, she'd had a strength and will that had always taken the family through the darkest of their hours, like a torch-bearer, leading the way. Knocked down, she'd get up again and forgive whatever hit her. Then she'd move on to what she'd call "useful activity" and become an example for anyone who knew her. She'd forget herself and focus on others. Always.

How can I, Fereshteh, match that?, she wondered.

Then it occurred to her that "matching" it was not the point. She was *not* her mother. *But I have my own strengths.* And she had arenas of opportunities that her mother hadn't had. Fereshteh had a profession that allowed her possibilities. And entailed moral responsibilities.

This thought raised her spirits a notch. She followed the thread of the thought.

A chorus of chanting and shouting erupted in the distance. Another demonstration. More protests. It did not bode well.

She refocused. She knew that involvement of any kind with the protesters was extremely dangerous. But in her mind's eye she saw again the ex-prisoners she'd treated in the early '90s. The ones whom it had been legal to treat.

And now she knew without a doubt that despite the risks, she'd have to help these new people, even if they were 'enemies of the State'.

That night, the night that Neda Agha-Soltan died on the street before the eyes of a multitude of Internet viewers, Fereshteh and Jamshid discussed the situation thoroughly. They knew what it meant. From the safe distance of their apartment they'd heard the explosion of the suicide bomber near Khomeini's shrine; the chants of thousands of peaceful marchers, asking for a vote recount; the shouts and sirens as riot police unleashed themselves on the protesters. They caught the whiff of the teargas in the warm evening breeze that drifted through their windows. They saw the footage and heard the state television's reports: "rioters", they reported, threatened national security through provocation of police. The detention of some 450 and the deaths of 10 had, unfortunately, been required to restore order and safety to the city. This official narrative didn't square with what too many eye-witnesses knew.

Online unofficial footage and social media sites removed any doubt anyone might still have had that these protests and demonstrations would simply go away. And where there were crowds in the streets there would be clashes. The regime was nothing if not thorough in cracking down on dissent. The brutal and relentless round-ups, detentions and executions of enemies real and perceived were all too reminiscent of the "bloody decade" of the '80s and still a vivid memory in the minds of those who'd lived through the Revolution. Even children then knew that adults could disappear from their lives forever.

Fereshteh and Jamshid knew that there were always those who, despite having been shot with live ammunition or bludgeoned by the Basij, would elude arrest and escape being locked up and driven off to who-knows-where in the nondescript vans of the police and Revolutionary Guard. People would go into hiding rather than go to hospitals. They'd scramble, crawl or be carried to shelter and attend to their wounds there. Or they'd seek private doctors. If not immediately, then soon afterward.

But Fereshteh and Jamshid knew that these patients would be different. Helping them would be aiding and abetting 'terrorism'. For that was what the TV news had begun calling the protesters. Terrorists. A threat to the regime. A threat to national security. Anyone affiliated with them would be a co-conspirator.

Leaning on the balcony rail, they watched the city, alive with a new tension, a new urgency.

"Will your colleagues admit the casualties, Jamshid?"

"I think so. There might be one who'll refuse but he'll just plead ignorance if anyone asks whether the rest of us have seen any protesters. And yours?"

"I think they will. Actually, two of our doctors are away on vacation, so they're safe. The other three? Yeah. They'll do it. No one will ask any uncomfortable questions. They have the sense to be really careful."

They held each other close, bracing themselves for whatever would come. It was the only thing they could do.

THE INJURED STARTED ARRIVING.

"We're completely inundated," Fereshteh told Jamshid as she prepared a late supper.

"Well, it's what we'd anticipated, isn't it?"

"Yes, but…"

"But. I know. We're not used to dealing with such acute injuries. These people should be at a hospital. They need x-rays, they need — some need surgery, for goodness' sake!" He banged his fist on the counter and shook his head."

"Yes, Jamshid, yes." She put her hand on his arm and leaned her head on his tall, solid frame. "But as little as we can give them, it's better than what they'd get at the hands of the Basij. Come, my love, let's sit down. Supper's ready."

. . .

So, the next morning they began again. Fereshteh, Jamshid, their work colleagues, and no doubt other private physicians, set broken bones, treated bullet wounds, staunched hemorrhaging and monitored the semi-conscious with what resources they had.

July 14th

"Thank God it's slowed down a bit," Fereshteh said, collapsing into a chair. She gratefully accepted the cool drink Jamshid brought as he eased himself down on the sofa next to her. Leaning their heads back, they sighed in a shared relief, and closed their eyes. It was the first day in three weeks that they'd been able to come home before 10 p.m. This evening they could actually enjoy the sunset.

"How long do you think this calm will last?" she asked.

Her husband took a sip of his drink and said, "Well, my guess is that it's only quiet because of the show of force on the streets. I think people are scared. And of course the media are doing their bit to convince people that everything is getting back to normal by discrediting anyone who says otherwise."

"My guess is that the reformers are re-grouping. I'm sure they've got all kinds of social media connections. They'll plan something."

"My guess too. They won't let this go. They'll be back."

Three days later Fereshteh and Jamshid were on call again, and would be for days at a time over the next two weeks. Bleary-eyed and sleep-deprived, they showed up at their practices to find full waiting rooms and wouldn't leave until every last patient had been seen. They saw no more mid-summer sunsets from the refuge of their own sofa. Fractured heads, limbs and ribs, internal hemorrhaging, concussions, and bullet wounds all found their way to sympathetic doctors. Some of these victims were demonstrators. Others were unwitting bystanders, caught in the crossfire.

August and September brought with them new horrors. Detainees from June and July were gradually being released. None of the doctors were prepared for what they began to see.

Jamshid was the first to talk about it. Strangely enough, though they did the same work and dealt with the same crises day after day, once they got home, they just couldn't talk about it with each other. The once regular 'debriefs' they'd had in the 90s had long since been forgotten. It was as if they'd made an unspoken vow to keep their personal life, their home and their precious few hours together unsullied by the pollution of the human misery that came to their professional doors day in and day out. But now the ugliness of beatings and torture had raised its head again.

He and Fereshteh took half a day off in mid-September and drove out of the city and up into the mountains. It was cooler and the air clearer. Just the openness of the landscape felt freeing. They savored the freshness of the air as they climbed higher, eventually reaching a spot where they could pull over, get out and walk onto the hillside. They spread a cotton blanket over the tall grass and opened the little picnic basket that contained their lunch.

Looking out over the expanse of the city below them and at the rough beauty of rock and vegetation around them, they ate, immersed in a silence they hadn't enjoyed in months.

Jamshid's voice was low when he finally spoke. He wasn't sure how to begin but trusted that Fereshteh would simply listen, no matter how incoherent he might sound.

"I'm not sleeping well. But I guess you probably realize this." He paused and took Fereshteh's nod as encouragement to keep talking.

"I keep seeing images of my patients, over and over. Most of the night. The ones from the detention centers outside the city. They've told me they don't even know which ones they were in because they were blindfolded and moved from one to another at night.

"They're young — 20s and 30s — and have been healthy guys all their lives. So I couldn't understand at first why they looked so thin and pale when they came in. Their eyes. Haunted, I guess you'd

Crimson Ink

call it. Dark circles. Hollow cheeks. Shrunken shoulders and torsos. They limped."

He closed his eyes for a few seconds. "Dislocated shoulders, badly healed — if you could call it healing — fractures on wrists, hands, ankles and feet." He paused again.

"I couldn't understand at first when I saw the lab results and x-rays. One of these guys was going into renal failure. He was 28. Another guy could hardly move his arms…

"They didn't want to talk much at first, but I told them that I couldn't help them if I didn't have some idea about what'd happened. Some of the guys never talked except to say 'just fix whatever you can' or 'help me get rid of the pain.' So I did that…" He faltered. "I did that…" Jamshid took a few breaths, then continued, appreciating Fereshteh's quiet attention.

"But a couple of the guys did talk. A bit anyway. Lots of flogging all over their bodies. That's pretty standard, of course. Ha! Listen to me - saying that flogging is standard!" He shook his head, looked at the sky, then continued, "Yeah… And then the kicking, punching and beating."

"The one with the failing kidneys just kept saying he'd been bastinadoed and beaten all over with metal cables. Well, the scars on his feet confirmed that. And the swelling still hadn't gone down fully. The toenails were gone; that's typical. All that explained the kidney issues."

"He said they'd put him on some kind of dialysis. Of course he didn't say that — he didn't understand much — he'd been unconscious when they'd taken him to some clinic somewhere. But when he woke up he said he saw he was connected to some kind of machine and a nurse said something about it being for his kidneys. He wasn't there very long, he said. Well, Fereshteh, I can tell you, they must have dialyzed him just enough to keep him alive and then taken him off before he had any significant benefit. He said they tortured him again several times after that. The way he is now, he's lucky he has any kidney function at all and you know he'll never get on the list for a machine back in the city." He took a sip of water, appreciating its slow trickle down his throat.

"I'll try to arrange it, though. I'll also have to send him to an orthopedic specialist — him, along with many others. He's got some misaligned bones."

"But there are the other guys too. Seems they bound their hands *behind* them, then hung them..." he broke off and Fereshteh's whisper finished the sentence for him, "...hung them by the wrists from the ceiling. And left them there all day. I've heard these stories."

She reached for his hands and held them in both of hers.

THE AUTUMN SENT a regular flow of similar patients to both of them. By then it had become clear that they nearly always needed to get specialists involved, including psychotherapists. Post-Traumatic Stress Disorder was a constant feature with the released detainees.

BY THE END of September Fereshteh and Jamshid knew for a certainty that if they didn't take care of their own health they wouldn't be able to continue the pace they'd been keeping at work. They made a pact; they'd go for a relaxing walk together several evenings a week and enjoy whatever beauty they could find in their upturned world. Parks were everywhere and it was worth whatever effort it took to get to one.

Laleh Park served their purpose one early October evening. They enjoyed a take-out supper of rice and *ghormeh-sabzie* on a bench by the pool that held the statue of Abu Rayhan Biruni. They watched the play of fountains — the water that nearly reached the ancient astronomer's outstretched arms as he directed four spheres around his head. His long hair, beard and robes seemed to flow in the soft breeze.

Still savoring the richness of the green vegetables, plump kidney beans and lamb cubes of their meal, they got up and ambled along the well-paved avenue. It had been days since they'd had a really decent meal or much fresh air.

They gazed at the pools and sighed in appreciation of the trees that lined the broad path ahead of them. And, for a while, they spoke only in soft murmurs about their surroundings.

But Jamshid sensed that his dear wife was troubled. Well, they were both troubled to a certain degree all the time, considering what they saw and heard every day, but he sensed that this evening there was something more.

Reaching for her hand and giving it a gentle squeeze, he said, "Tell me."

She looked at him and gave a little smile, then looked back over at the pond, silent, as if gathering her thoughts. They kept walking, maintaining the leisurely pace.

"It's all the drugs," she said at last.

"And by that you mean..."

"I know you're seeing it too. You have to be. It's not one or two cases. Not even five or six. This week I've seen more than a dozen."

"Go on," he encouraged.

"I've had an influx of new patients. All young. All released from the women's detention centers several weeks ago. They have the usual problems. You know. But what I'm seeing now in addition to that and the PTSD are needle marks *and* the empty eyes, hollow cheeks, tremors and all the rest that only comes from drugs."

She paused and looked at her husband. "Jamshid, they're not only using the *taryak* —opium — that they can get almost anywhere, but they're shooting heroin, snorting cocaine and — can you believe it in a country like this? — crystal meth. I've asked them, discreetly of course, how they can get this stuff — how they can continue their habit. I tell them I'm concerned about withdrawal if their supply is cut. They laugh and say that there's no chance of that. There are meth labs everywhere! I had no idea, Jamshid. No idea. Did you?"

"I do, in fact. I got a hold of some data through a colleague who brought it to our last staff meeting so we could discuss the problem. He said that Iran now has one of the highest rates of methamphetamine use in the world. In the world!"

He looked at Fereshteh, then straight ahead and they continued their walk, their backs stiffened now, their faces somber.

"Wow. But after what they've been through..." Fereshteh's voice was almost a whisper.

"Yes. After what they've been through."

"But who can blame them?" she continued. "So many of them are totally broken. The girls, most of them raped — we've talked about this — will find it almost impossible to find husbands now. Many are pariahs in their own families, as if it's *their* fault! What do I tell them? What can I offer them? Why should they stop the drugs? It's their only escape, horrific as it is. How can I give them a reason to stop, Jamshid?"

"Well, we can emphasize more than ever the therapy sessions for the trauma. And if those start to work, we can treat the addiction withdrawal symptoms."

"Sure, but how can we convince them to actually *do* the therapy so they can get off the drugs? Some of them just laugh when I prescribe it."

"I know... I know. But what I've started to say to the ones who mock psychotherapy — just imagine some of those young guys and their attitudes to that, Fereshteh!" he gave a short laugh. "What I've started to tell them is that addicts and dealers can always be arrested and thrown into jail. Then I look them straight in the eye and ask them, 'You don't want to go back there — for *any* reason — do you?'"

Early October

The little restaurant just off Vali Asr Street did a brisk business every day from lunch until late evening. A cross between a cafeteria and a service-oriented eating house, patrons queued up to order at a counter, found a table and were then served by skinny young waiters in perpetual motion. How they always got the right dish to the right person, even remembering regulars' special preferences, was a tribute to their employer's standards. You did your job well or you didn't do it at all. Portions were generous and the quality, despite the melamine of the plates, reliably good. It was the eating and meeting place of choice for not only the work crowd, but also for other little groups who met regularly. These groups kept their profile low, their dress generic, and their members limited to no more than a half dozen; the owners never asked questions.

Fereshteh sat with three women at a corner table in the rear. The lighting was dimmer here and the ambient noise was more than adequate for covering their conversations.

Marzieh pushed her plate away and said she needed to leave, but Elham's hand on her arm reminded her that they needed to arrange their next meeting. They made sure their meetings were at irregular intervals and at varying times on varying days of the week. Just a group of friends out for women's conversation. Amineh, always efficient, had thought it out in advance and they quickly agreed on the next date and time.

Outside on the sidewalk, still crowded even at half-past-eight in the evening, they said their good-byes with cheek kisses and smiles, and Elham and Marzieh went their own ways.

Amineh turned to Fereshteh and said, "Let's walk," and they soon blended into the noisy crowd.

"I've made that arrangement we talked about."

Fereshteh listened closely to her friend as they continued. "We're still keeping names on a 'need to know' basis, of course, but I want to give you the name and contact number of one other friend of mine. She's someone you can trust and you can call her in case you can't reach me. You understand what I'm saying, don't you?"

"I do." Fereshteh had in fact considered the possibility that Amineh might be detained at some point. There was always that danger. So, it was important to have at least one other person to connect with — just in case.

"Here's the information," Amineh said, passing her a slip of paper.

"Please memorize it and get rid of the paper." She laughed.

"Sounds a bit 'James Bond', doesn't it? Well, maybe we're playing 'Jaimie Bond' here, but you know the risks."

Fereshteh chuckled, but her heart was beating just a bit faster. Helping to get someone out of the country secretly was risky enough. So many desperate people had left that way, through Turkey or through the deserts and mountains of Baluchistan into Pakistan, never knowing what awaited them on the other side.

But now Amineh had started talking about getting new passports for women who didn't have them. That was a step further than Fereshteh wanted to be involved with. Women needed their husband's or father's written permission to get one, after all, and she couldn't imagine how it would be possible to get a passport any other way and still be legal. She didn't want anything to do with that. But others would.

"All I'm willing to do is pass a telephone number to women who want to take that risk. Whatever they do with it, well, I don't want to know about it. I'm not going to be a part of anything like that, okay?"

"I understand, Fereshteh. I fully understand." Amineh gave her friend a quick hug and they parted.

Fereshteh walked toward the bus stop, thinking about the meeting. Aside from this last request from Amineh, she loved this work. She had great respect for all the women she was working with and loved that they all worked so seamlessly together, unencumbered by the differences in their religious, ideological and social backgrounds.

It gave an extra measure of meaning to her life; a part of her that had been so empty for so many years. She'd slipped into it seamlessly while helping Homa and her sister. Medical knowledge was never going to be enough to solve their problems, so Fereshteh had reached out to a psychotherapist to help with additional treatment. Then there was the social worker because of the children involved. When it had become clear that divorce was going to be the only way for the women to get relief, Fereshteh, in consultation with the other professionals, reached out to a lawyer. It wasn't long before they were having conversations about more women in distress and they began cross-referrals that had developed into an off-the-books association, pooling their areas of expertise. That made so much more possible. Even if it sometimes seemed like a bottomless pit for their time, energy and resources, they did see positive results from the changes they were able to set in motion. The lives of *some* battered women were getting better. She only hoped she'd never have to use the name and number that Amineh had given her.

MID-OCTOBER

ONE OF HABIB's and Fereshteh's favorite places to meet for a short time after work was Saiee Park. Its central location along Vali Asr Street made it easy to get to.

Like so many of Tehran's parks, it was huge and had a considerable network of paths and paved avenues that spanned nearly a quarter of a mile from north to south and about half that from east to west. Whether you wanted shady lanes, open lawns, magnificent flower beds, pools, fountains, or even unusual sculptures, Saiee offered it all.

Fereshteh and Habib tried to come here once a week to talk. Together they'd breathe out their stress and breathe in the beauty of the trees and grass.

"How's it going with your 'domestic abuse case'?" Habib wanted to know.

"Oh, it's going really well. We've got several others now, too. Women she's brought. You know, she's really so capable. She gets them organized; sort of 'rallies the troops' when the others get anxious or have doubts," Fereshteh replied.

"So, has she finally gotten the divorce?"

"Yes, finally. Nooshin took her case and she did a first-class job. She got the witnesses, proved the injuries and the drug and alcohol abuse — huge evidence, in this particular case. The husband was a slippery one but Nooshin nailed him. The judge was convinced and this woman now has custody of the children — wonder of all wonders — and a new address where he can't find her. She's now our poster child for all the others."

"But you're still being careful aren't you? Discreet?"

They stopped by the little pond and watched a family of ducks paddling past.

"Absolutely. It's a touchy area. Right now, we're working only on abuse cases of the "vanilla" variety. Ordinary women. The commonest issues of domestic abuse. Our group isn't up to the task of anything more. We don't have the people or resources to take that on. We leave that up to the human rights pros."

"They are pretty special, aren't they? They've risked everything dealing with those cases and —"

"Yes. Yes. I — actually, let's not talk about that. I got so upset hearing about those death threats against them on top of all the other things that are happening to them. Those lawyers are so brave in spite of it all. They know the law better than most of the judges, for goodness sake! It galls me to see the injustice and hypocrisy of it all! Using personal terror to make them stop their work! I just get so outraged, I —"

Habib gave his sister's hand a quick squeeze. They walked on down the path, letting the bright autumn leaves divert their attention.

"So, any news from the rest of the family?" Fereshteh asked. "Besides the kids, of course. Taraneh and I manage to cover that pretty well. But, oh, congrats to your Mansoor landing that fantastic job!"

"Thank you, thank you! Yes, we're really pleased for him. And I guess Taraneh has also told you —"

"Yes! He's got a great apartment about half way between Harvard and MIT! I'm so pleased he's going to be staying near Daryush and Nava!"

"Dayi Reza won't be happy…"

"Who cares what Dayi Reza thinks? He's not happy no matter what any of us does. So, to change the subject, I know you saw Saeed recently. What does he have to say about all the election controversy? Any hope for a more moderate stance or is this going to drag on? Please tell me they're going to find a way to reconcile everyone… and let all those poor protesters out of prison… oosh!" She shuddered, then looked at her brother full in the face. Expectant.

"Well…. No, it doesn't seem so. I'm sorry. It seems that the opposition leaders aren't planning on giving up on demanding reform and the government isn't planning on giving ground. Young people are very disillusioned, from what I've been hearing." He saw his sister's hope fade.

"When I even alluded to anything about the prisons, Saeed became dismissive, and insisted that it's only real criminals who've been detained. You know, enemies of the State, as it were. Sorry again. I know that's not what you wanted to hear." He gave her a wistful smile.

"No, it wasn't. I was just looking for some good news." She lowered her head and walked on.

After a minute, she looked at him again and said with some force, "Oh, Habib, all this is beyond us. We can't change anything at higher levels; I know that. I guess that's why this extra work with the women's group just feels so good." She lowered her voice and spoke more slowly.

"But even that has its limits and as you say, it's risky business. But then, almost anything now is risky. And for us Baha'is… well, that's life. The Yaran are still waiting for access to legal counsel; I've lost track of which prisons they've been moved to. And then all the usual stories of Baha'i businesses arbitrarily being closed, ordinary people detained on trumped up charges… "

He nodded, looking briefly into the distance. They walked in silence, finally stopping to take in the gushing fountains in a large pool.

After a few minutes, new energy in her voice, she said, "Speaking of something risky, tell me the latest about BIHE. How is *that* going? I tell you, Habib, I'm always worried about you and Taraneh and all the others. Talk about taking risks! Unofficial education can get you arrested at any time. Aren't you worried?"

"Of course. We all worry. But we have a moral responsibility.

How can we ignore that? We know what's at stake for the youth and for ourselves." He scratched his head. "We focus on what we're doing and the successes we've seen. We look at all the program graduates who've been able to go on to studies outside the country, to get advanced degrees based on the work they've done with BIHE. And the ones who've stayed here and work on making real improvements in our own country."

"If they even get jobs. Or keep them." murmured Fereshteh.

"Look, our young people have options. The "safe" option means being content with whatever work is available. Many are happy doing that. They don't want university-level education. And that's perfectly fine. They don't need BIHE. They'll find work doing something. Then there are others who'd like the higher education but who don't want to take the risks involved. That's ok too and they'll find some kind of work and provide their own kind of service."

Fereshteh agreed.

"But there are so many who are really thirsty for education. They want a different kind of life and they're brave enough to do what it takes. They know what's at stake and that makes them work incredibly hard. And rewards them with incredible results. How can we possibly neglect them? They're part of the future of this country.

"And these kids want to help. They *want* to make a difference here in their own country. Some may choose to leave — also okay — but so many want to stay here and contribute to Iran's development. These young Baha'is give and give to help our society, no matter what the regime propaganda says to the contrary. I know this. If the government won't help them — their own citizens — then we have to."

Fereshteh was silent. She knew. She understood her brother so well. He'd never stop because he knew it was right.

2010

Chapter Four

2010

February

Nikou knocked on the front door of her parents' home, shivering in the February wind. "Oh, Nikoujan! Welcome, welcome! Come in, come in before you freeze!"

As she offered to take her coat her mother said, "But what's this? Why do you have only one arm in your sleeve? No wonder you're cold! What's going on?"

Nikou shrugged off the coat, revealing a sling over her left arm. "It's just a small injury, Maman. I fell, that's all."

"But how did you drive with only one arm, my dear?"

"I took a taxi. Brrr! I'm still cold. Could we have some hot tea?" Without waiting, she walked to the kitchen.

Nikou sat at the table in the elegant breakfast nook while her mother tut-tutted around her, bearing tea, sugar, sweets and fruits to the table, all the while chattering in her usual free-flow.

"Really, Nikou, I'd thought by now you'd outgrown your teenage clumsiness. Always hurting yourself, falling down, bumping into something. I never saw anybody with so many bumps and bruises as you had."

Nikou's silence deepened. She looked out into the garden, windswept and naked. Her mother continued, "Yes, I really wonder about you, my dear. Your brothers are so strong, so robust, but you... so how did this happen? I thought by now — a lovely fortunate married woman in her own splendid home... you have such a handsome husband and you must make him so proud, my dear. Are you entertaining much?"

Her mother finally had sat down and taken a sip of her tea, but she jumped up again and went to a cupboard to bring out juice glasses, still prattling away.

"If you're going to impress your husband you must impress his guests in your home. You can't be having an arm in a sling and hope to impress anyone!"

Nikou glanced at her as she returned to the table, just letting her mother carry on.

"So really, Nikou, I thought you had nice thick carpets everywhere. Last time I was there, you had them. Well, why wouldn't you? But maybe you fell in the foyer or the bath? Yes, tile floors are very hard. Here, have some more tea. And please eat! You look so thin! Come on, now; here, have this nice big piece of almond cake. I just baked it yesterday."

She got up again to refill the teapot, still jabbering away. "Since you were a teenager. I still can't get over this. You had such coordination when you were little. What happened, I wonder? Well, I'll never understand."

She sat again and faced her daughter, patting her right hand. "That's okay, my Nikou. You'll outgrow this, I know you will. Here, have an apple. I'll cut it for you." And she hopped up again, searching for the fruit knife.

Spring

Fereshteh sat next to Bijan, the interviewer, and just across from Rana to give her encouragement, and if necessary, to intervene in case she broke down. They had arranged it so that the young woman sat with her back to the window, casting her face in shadow. To further protect her identity, she wore her headscarf and chador, and the cameraman blurred her entire head. The room could have been anywhere; the rooftops outside the window were ubiquitous in this mega-city. Nothing was visible to identify her or the venue in any way. These were Rana's conditions.

It had taken many conversations with her to get her to agree to this, and she stated on camera just how terrified she was. As if challenging the interviewer, she said, "I'm doing this on behalf of all the rest who could not find the courage to tell their stories. We're all ashamed. We're all traumatized. Few can bear to speak out loud about the nightmare we've lived. Not one of us wants to endanger herself again by speaking out." She sat up straighter, as if asserting her determination and courage.

"I have to do it. I have to do it for myself and for them, whatever it takes for me to tell our story. But — I swear — I'll take my own life before submitting to another arrest."

Of this Fereshteh had no doubt at all.

Fereshteh had been seeing Rana for months. The 22-year old former university student had chronic health problems and her mother, Shadi, had finally succeeded in getting her daughter to go to Fereshteh only because her infections would not heal with home remedies. It had been the by-now-familiar friend-of-a-friend-of-a-friend link through which Shadi had found her, and this lion of a mother had attended every medical appointment with her daughter to ensure that she got the treatment that she needed.

The previous October, Rana had entered Fereshteh's office limping. She had been out of detention for about three weeks. Fereshteh had been appalled by the extent of the bruising that covered most of her body. Because she'd been malnourished for several months and had had no access to fresh air, her body had been unable to heal itself. Despite her mother's efforts to feed her, she'd been so despondent when she'd returned home that she could barely eat. The infections had continued to suppurate and Rana would lapse into temporary blackouts.

Shadi and her husband became desperate. When they finally found Fereshteh, Ahmad drove his wife and daughter to the office, prepared to wait in the car for as long as it took them. He did this faithfully every time she had an appointment. While he waited he would pray, calling upon all that was Good and Merciful to help his daughter. His innocent girl, who'd just happened to be leaving the university one day in June when a column of demonstrators had walked past. In the ensuing chaos she'd disappeared into a white van and been carried off.

SHADI AND AHMAD had accepted their daughter's wish to speak out. They thought it might help her heal. But right now, at Rana's request, they sat outside this locked room.

Fereshteh knew the story, of course, but that didn't mean it was going to be easy to hear it again. But if this young woman could *live* it and could *tell* it, Fereshteh could certainly summon the strength to listen to it again.

Bijan switched on the camera and Rana began, giving the background. A real case of "being at the wrong place at the wrong time," she related how it was she'd been thrown into the van.

"They were policemen wearing uniforms. They all had the same uniforms, the same batons — all the same equipment. They were large men — wearing hoods. You could only see their eyes and mouths. They'd ripped off their name badges. They beat us with their batons and shoved us — there were many of us, all girls, into the van. It didn't matter how much we protested our innocence. The guards that pushed us in sat with us and insulted us. They accused us of terrible things nonstop. They pushed us and hit us so much that we didn't dare move.

"One of these guards was a boy. He wasn't even old enough to grow a mustache. The older ones let him do whatever he wanted. He leered at us and then started groping us all over. Whatever he wanted. When he groped her breast, one girl protested and he slapped her hard, insulted her and carried on, groping her all over. One guy was filming us constantly, from every direction."

Looking down at her hands, Rana took a couple of breaths, then continued.

"They took us to a place that was like a warehouse. I don't know where it was or what it was. The walls and roof were high. There were so many people, men and women, and they pushed us in groups, leading the men to one part and the women to another. It was dim. No windows. They dragged us across the floor, not even telling us to stand and walk. They dragged us like potato sacks into hallways created out of curtains. They took five of us to a locked room. It was tiny and crowded, especially since there were some other prisoners already there from before we arrived. At this point I was exhausted, bruised, my face all cut up, totally devastated. We couldn't defend ourselves because our hands were bound. After a while they gave us some typed up pages, you know, with the standard bureaucratic font. And what was written on those pages? It said that I'd committed terrible acts, things I'd absolutely never done. I was supposed to copy from these pages that I was a rioter, that I was endangering national security, that I'd done this and that, *and* I was a terrorist!" Her voice was outrage itself.

"I couldn't. I couldn't write that because I wasn't those things!

"They held us there until they supposedly clarified our statuses. After eighteen hours in that tiny place, I desperately needed to go to the bathroom. The pressure was really hurting me. I felt my bladder would burst.

"Then there was nausea. I was thirsty. But all I wanted — ha! — all I wanted was to be able to call my parents to tell them where I was and tell them not to worry!" She was crying.

"We were there for three days and not even once did they say what else they wanted from us. They kept us in limbo; we wanted to scream at them, 'Enough!'. But then they tied our hands, blindfolded us and put hoods over our heads and transferred us somewhere else. We had no idea where that was." She paused.

"What haunted me, more than the insults — what haunted me the most was the groping. Their groping was torture. As they groped us they would invoke Saint Zahra, Saint Fatima!" Her voice was incredulous.

"Can you imagine that? Could Saint Zahra believe such things? Calling on Saint Fatima they touched us and they even said they did it in the name of God! They would say, 'O God accept us'! As if it were our wedding night and the guy was performing his rituals before going to the marriage bed!"

She stopped, breathing hard, and took a sip of water from the plastic bottle.

"These were not vigilantes doing these things. The authorities kept insisting to the public that these were vigilantes but they weren't. All the papers and forms they used had seals of the Judiciary and the Intelligence Ministry.

"Anyway, they took us to another place. This was more like a proper detention center, not a warehouse. This time they took me to a solitary cell. I figured out that, before and after interrogations, they throw you into solitary confinement so when you're done you don't share your experience with others.

"After a short time, maybe twenty minutes, they took me from the cell to the interrogation room. My hands were tied behind my back. I was blindfolded and gagged. They made me sit. The door opened. I heard steps. Someone sat in front of me. 'So you are a rioter!'" she mimicked. "'So, you are undermining the State! Who do you think you are? What group are you with?' I was gagged.

"He said, 'Why aren't you talking?' I teared up. I tried to say I wasn't a part of any group.

"He shouted, 'Shut up! You speak when I tell you to!' I was trembling all over. I felt my body tense up. I was defenseless.

"He finally removed the gag and ordered, 'You talk when I ask you a question. *Then* you answer! What group are you with? You want to overthrow the State?'

"It didn't matter what I said to him. I didn't do anything like what he was accusing me of, but he mocked me, and said I was lying like all the others. He went on with his questions. He asked what I did. I said I was a student. He got furious and shouted, 'No, you are not! From now on don't say you are a student!'

"The next thing he did was lick my face. I felt the life drain out of me. I felt like my whole being was escaping out of my mouth." Her voice broke into tears.

"He started to pull my clothes off. My hands were still bound and my eyes were still covered. I started crying. He shouted, 'Shut up, whore!'"

Rana tried to dry her eyes. She leaned to her left, propping up her cheek with her left fist. Her voice became small, like that of a tearful child, accused and confessing to a terrible sin. "Then he started – he opened my bra and took my clothes off, piece by piece, stroking and hitting me at the same time."

Her breaths rapid, she was waving her arms frantically now. A deep sigh. She went on, her tone a low level of hysteria despite her efforts to compose herself.

Dropping her voice, she continued, "Afterward... afterward... he urinated on me. I felt sick from the smell. Sick, sick..."

She looked up, wretched, and said: "I was told from the time I was a little child to protect my innocence. Protect it. Now it was gone! What had happened?"

Another pause, then, in a voice very small, she added, "After a while someone else came in, and meanwhile... I had wet myself."

She hung her head and pressed her hands to her face. A minute went by, then she sat up straight, cleared her throat, looked into the camera and continued.

"When he came in... when this new person came in, he smacked me in my face and said, 'You filthy scum, you've stunk up the place!'" Rana's voice mimicked his contempt.

"Then suddenly I was screaming. He'd put out his cigarette on my left hand. It hurt! It hurt! It hurt! The burning penetrated to the bone."

Her voice rose again. "A hole in my hand!"

She was wailing now. "It burned, searing like grilled meat!"

Both arms moving again, she was looking at the back of her left hand, as if she could still see the burn. "He still wasn't done. He rolled up my pants and put out another cigarette on my knee."

She hammered her right fist into the air, then raised both arms up to her head then pushed them down as if to press away her torment. She continued, as if still in disbelief, "In the middle of all that pain, he put out another cigarette, this time on my breast..."

Both hands were waving again, then pushing down, as if tallying the indignities she was recounting.

"He put out one cigarette after the other on my body. I was burning; I felt my life drain from my veins..." She was sobbing as she spoke, her hands working in circles as if to wipe away the abuse.

"Why me? How much could I endure? How much should I suffer? I was crying." She was weeping, weeping, weeping.

After several long minutes, Rana resumed her story. "Some time went by. I don't know how much. I might have passed out. I don't remember. The next thing I remember was that I was on a cot. It was night. Quiet. There was a rough blanket under me. I heard the door and the sound of boots. Someone else came into the room. He walked towards me. He said something that I could not process.

"I'd just been raped and he said, 'I've heard you're not a virgin. Did you do it with your boyfriend?'" Her voice was again incredulous.

"He said, 'How many guys have you been with?' In my head I screamed, 'You just raped me! You took my innocence, and now you're asking me how many guys I've been with?! Before, I was a virgin!'"

She stopped again, wiping the tears, taking deep breaths, trying to keep herself from screaming as she relived it all.

"Then he said, 'So you had fun with your boyfriend? When they brought you here your hymen was broken. Which whorehouse do you come from? Are you a prostitute?'

"I couldn't talk. I wanted to say, 'It was your friends who raped me.'"

Her voice was angry now, accusatory. Her hands punctuated her rebuke.

"'It was you, you all who raped me. Before this I was a virgin!'"

A pause. Deep breaths.

Her voice hollow, she continued. "Every day it was the same routine. They would take me into the room... I never saw their faces. They would beat me, rape me. Pour their sperm and excrement on me."

She faltered but then with an edge of sarcasm she said, "And they would supposedly wash me with a bucket of water. They didn't extinguish cigarettes on me anymore; maybe they thought it would leave marks. Mostly, they just beat me." She took a sip of water.

More matter-of-factly now she said, "I got an infection because of the repeated rapes."

But at this her hands started waving again. Another sip of water. A few deep breaths. She gathered herself and forced the words out.

"My uterus got infected. It smelled, I had little ugly bumps. I thought it was syphilis. I got treated there; I was never sent to the hospital. They'd kept us in limbo for so long that we stopped asking them when they would release us.

"When they finally did release me —" She wiped her nose and lowered her gaze. "When I got back, my parents just took care of me at home. But no matter what they did to help me, I still felt tortured by pain. My uterus was polluted and sick. My spirit was crushed."

She paused but then looked up resolutely. Pointing her right index finger upward, as if making a vow, then bringing her fists together in front of her chin, she said: "But I told myself to be strong. Be calm. The worst that can happen is death. In one instant it will all be over."

Her voice rose. "Death was my wish. I wanted to die. I wanted it all to be over."

The tears returned, her voice a plea once more. "I wanted to die in my sleep. I wanted peace. I prayed that I no longer existed. I wanted to die." She was sobbing again.

"I'm only 22 but I feel old. And I feel like dying. They shattered my soul so much that I say 'Damn God', because what had I done? What had I done to deserve this? All I had done was to give one vote, a vote that was never counted. Never! Never!"

Rana shook as she sobbed. Fereshteh had offered to intervene at various points, but Rana had insisted that she would continue. She had taken time to blow her nose, wipe her eyes and take deep breaths. But she'd been adamant that she had to continue to the end. Had to finish it. Complete the story. Have it out of her and out into the world.

She'd pleaded for viewers of this YouTube video to spread the word to increase awareness, to do whatever they could so that this wouldn't continue or happen again. She'd wanted her voice, and through her the voices of so many others, to be heard beyond the confines of the country that had become her larger prison. She said that she had to do this, that she knew that this was not the end of her nightmares or her flashbacks, but knew it was a piece of her eventual healing.

The filming done, Shadi and Ahmad came in, their faces a paradox of pain and pride. Rana looked at her parents and a weak smile formed on her trembling lips. As another tear ran down her cheek, she collapsed into their embrace.

Late November

Marjan turned the key and pushed open the heavy wooden door, calling her friend's name. Disconcerted by the dead silence, she closed the door carefully behind her and went into the main living area, calling Nikou and getting no answer.

She went into the large kitchen. All was still; everything neat and orderly, with no sign of anyone having had any breakfast. A sweat broke out under her arms. She told herself that this, after all, was why Nikou had given her the gate code and house key in the first place. "Just in case." The text she'd received 20 minutes ago from her friend had simply said, "Now". Not really understanding, she'd gotten in her car and driven over, anxious and cursing the traffic.

Leaving the kitchen, Marjan moved silently through the main rooms, terrified that there might be someone else there instead of her friend.

She went into the wide corridor leading to the downstairs bedrooms and baths, treading softly and slowly. Her heart was pounding and her hands had gone icy by the time she reached her friend's bedroom door. It was slightly ajar. She pushed it carefully. When nothing happened, she peaked around it.

She couldn't take in what was in front of her eyes. It didn't make sense. This couldn't be her friend's room. Unable to move her limbs, she felt her mouth open in silent shock. Nothing that Nikou had ever confided could have prepared her for the crumpled bloodstained heap on the floor in front of her.

It took less than a minute, but seemed like forever, before Marjan's capacity for thought and action returned. Then she moved with purpose. Nikou was breathing and she had a reasonable pulse, but she was not conscious. There was blood everywhere, but Marjan couldn't find any active bleeding. Her questions would wait; right now all that mattered was to get her to medical help. But Marjan knew not to call an ambulance, despite the need.

She went to a linen closet and took out a sheet and a blanket. Placing both on the floor next to her friend, she rolled her onto her side and then pushed the linen and blanket under her, carefully adjusting her friend's head and limbs when she rolled her onto her back. After wrapping her securely, tying corners and ends together to hold her in place, Marjan fashioned a rope from another sheet, secured it under Nikou's arms, knotting it over her chest, and pulled her along the smooth Italian tiles into the large entrance hall. She went out and pulled her car up as close to the steps as she could and opened the back doors. Running back into the house, she dragged out one of the small thick Kermani carpets and used this as a slide to get Nikou down the steps and just under the open back door.

On her stomach, Marjan slid along the back seat until her upper body could reach down the opposite side to where Nikou lay on the carpet. Grabbing the sheets, she raised Nikou's head and yanked the sheets inch by inch until she had her friend's head up on the seat. Reaching under her friend's arms and grasping the makeshift rope, she continued to tug until most of Nikou was over the hump of the door frame. *Thank God she's so petite!* Marjan's strength was nearing its end as she gave the final tug that put Nikou squarely on the seat. She settled her in as well as she could, then returned the carpet to the house, ensuring that all was neat and orderly, and closed the door.

Reminding herself of the address Nikou had given her, Marjan set her GPS and drove like a woman possessed until she reached the office building 25 minutes later. She double parked in front of it and put on her hazard lights. Running into the foyer, she checked which floor she needed and ran the two flights up to the office, rushing in. Without any preamble she informed the receptionist in a no-nonsense whisper that she needed several people and a wheelchair "right now and I mean right now" to help get a "very, very sick patient" upstairs to see Dr. Fereshteh Jalili. The alarm on her face and glare in her eyes brooked no objection and within a few minutes a little group was wheeling a still unconscious Nikou out of the elevator and into the doctor's office.

Disregarding the astonished looks on the faces of the patients in the waiting room, Marjan followed.

Introductions were rapid and short as the doctor did a quick overall check.

"This is my friend Nikou. I'm Marjan —"

"I know who she is," Fereshteh interrupted, and she proceeded to besiege Marjan with questions as she continued to examine her unexpected patient. She had to cut away some of her clothes and wash off the blood to get a better idea of the extent of her injuries.

Nikou remained unconscious but the rest of the neurological exam looked promising, Fereshteh said. X-rays and blood work were done and with all the shifting, pulling and tugging, Nikou groaned but did not rouse.

The questions continued but Marjan was coming to the end of what she actually knew.

"No, I don't know who Nikou's regular doctor is or whether she has medical records at any hospital. I don't know anything about old fractures, but Nikou's mother always complains that she's been 'accident prone' since she was young."

And no, she absolutely did not know that her friend was pregnant.

"What! Four or five months?" Marjan's brain was working

quickly and she did want to help, but really, what was going on here? What had happened to her friend? And did she really want to know more?

She had no chance to focus on the icy feeling in her stomach, because the doctor was shouting for a colleague to hurry in. Marjan stood to attention, asking, "What is it? What do you need? I'll help you!"

Another doctor came in and the three of them acted quickly, Marjan substituting for the absent office nurse, and obeying every order they gave.

She bathed Nikou's pale face, her swollen eyes, her sunken cheeks, and her sweating brow with cool cloths, cooing to her, promising her she'd be okay. The two physicians worked quickly.

The intravenous fluid seemed to be pouring in, followed by one injection after the other; a pile of towels, soaked bright red, accumulated in a bin. A blood pressure cuff inflated at regular intervals as the doctors worked Nikou's limp body from arms down to splayed legs. Marjan handed them more towels and ripped open packets of thick padding, then returned to her palliative tasks, calming Nikou as she gradually returned to consciousness.

It was late afternoon by the time they had Nikou cleaned up. She was out of pain now, at least, and was sleeping. Another IV was running in her arm, but slowly. Her cuts and bruises had been disinfected, and sutured, taped or dressed.

The receptionist brought them large mugs of strong sweetened tea.

Fereshteh said, "Nikou needs to be hospitalized. You should have taken her to the hospital immediately instead of bringing her here. I told you from the start that treating her here was not appropriate."

"But Nikou was adamant. She said that I had to bring her here — never, ever to a hospital! She told me over and over. I didn't know what she was talking about. I didn't really know, I ... I didn't want to know what was going on. And she didn't want to tell me much. But I'm her only friend and she was counting on me. I had to bring her here. I'm so sorry."

"Look, I understand, Marjan. You were in a difficult situation and you did what you could to be loyal to your friend. And you did a great job, by the way, in getting her here in the first place. That took strength on all levels. And thank you for your help here. We really needed you!"

She smiled at the young woman, then said: "The next question, though, is what do we do with Nikou now? We've stabilized her, but she needs continued care. And even after she recovers from this, she's going to need follow-up. Where can I send her?"

Marjan was at a loss for a response. She knew what was at stake. Knew that a hospital was still out of the question, as was an ambulance home. As was any house call by a doctor.

She ventured, "Maybe I could drive her to her parents' house?"

Fereshteh's face darkened. "No. You can't take her there. Absolutely not."

She reflected a moment, then said, "Take this" and started writing down a telephone number. Still anxious about having taken Fereshteh's office number from Nikou, Marjan was in no mood to accept another number, and told her so.

"Please, Marjan, take this. It's my private number — my cell phone. You may need it." When the young woman refused, saying she didn't want to be involved any more, Fereshteh said it out loud, telling her, "Ok if you don't want to carry anything written on you, then just memorize it — please!" And, over Marjan's protests, Fereshteh recited the number several times.

"Please, if you or Nikou need me at any time just call me."

There was a low moan from the treatment table.

Fereshteh looked over at Nikou then back at Marjan. "I can't stress enough how important it is for her to get care and follow-up treatment. And she can't stay here; we have to send her *somewhere*. Let's think."

Their quandary was resolved unexpectedly.

Shouting came down the corridor and despite the efforts of the receptionist to prevent him, a man threw open the office door and came in, his castigations preceding him.

Marjan jumped back, wishing she could melt into a corner or

disappear beneath the floor. This was worse than Nikou had ever intimated.

For the moment, his focus was on Fereshteh. He'd barely glanced at his wife on the table, but his voice wrenched her from sleep. Her eyes proclaimed raw terror and her body tensed in an effort to — to what? Get up? Defend herself? Marjan's eyes found Nikou's and pleaded for her to be silent. Nikou's sent Marjan's the same message.

"Hello, Mehrdad," said Fereshteh. Her voice was mild.

"You."

"Yes?"

"Why is my wife here? What have you done to her?"

"Oh, you don't know? Well, I've just spent the last several hours putting her back together. She —"

"What are you talking about? What have you done? Why is she all bandaged up? Why does she have a needle in her arm? Are you trying to poison her or something?"

"I'm sure, Mehrdad, that you know that's not poison. She needs fluids —"

"What? Are you saying she doesn't get water at home? Maybe you think I don't feed her either!"

"Of course not, that's not —"

"Or you put her to sleep, made her unconscious, maybe? Why, huh? Why?" What's she doing here anyway?"

"She came in here with a lot of injuries; bleeding, broken ribs and —"

"She would never come in here. Never come to see you! I know what the family says about you, you know —"

"What do they say? Anything I don't already know? Come on, why would she be here if she didn't need to be?"

"She doesn't need to be. She doesn't need *you!* Why are you meddling in our affairs? Why are you sticking your nose into our business, huh?"

"She was brought here instead of to a hospital. The place she really needs to be. She's got a lot of inj—"

"What do you know? Stupid foreign-educated doctor? Doctor?

Ha! You're worthless! If I find out that you've hurt her, you'll pay for it, believe me!"

"Mehrdad, I'm just trying to explain —"

"What's to explain? You got your clutches on my wife, probably taking revenge on her for something her father said to you when you were kids... I don't know how you maneuvered this, but I'll find out!"

"Please be reasonable, Mehrdad, I —" But seeing something in his eyes, Fereshteh shrugged and gave him a sad smile.

Marjan, watching the entire encounter, saw his look of triumph. It was clear that he'd entirely misread Fereshteh's look. She wasn't capitulating, Marjan saw; she had recognized the man for what he was and, having given him the chance to prove himself capable of a more civilized level of interaction and finding him unequal to the task, she'd decided to leave him to his own devices. He lived on his own planet with his own rules.

He gave Fereshteh a thin, severe smile. Then, turning his head at last, he noticed Marjan in the corner.

"You? *You* brought her here?" he accused.

He held her gaze for a minute and Marjan could almost hear the wheels turning as he calculated how she could have managed that. He glanced over at his wife, whose swollen wet eyes were sending her friend apologies. Looking back at Marjan his gaze was hard. He held her eyes until she lowered them just to release herself.

Nikou opened her mouth. Her attempts at "I'm sorry" and "please forgive me," pitiful as they were, were met with her husband's emphatic *"Hafeh sho"* — "shut up" — and a promise to "deal with" her later.

"Get a wheelchair. I'm taking her home."

Before complying, Fereshteh looked at him and said evenly, "She's lost a great deal of blood. She's very weak. She actually should be in hospital. But if you don't want her to go, just be aware that she definitely needs follow-up treatment."

With Nikou now in the chair, he looked again at Fereshteh. His eyes bored into hers, conveying, *"I'm the one who decides here. Be warned: I won't forget that you saw this."*

As he pushed the wheelchair through the door and into the corridor, she said simply, "Your baby's dead."

For a second only, the man stopped but didn't look around. Fereshteh stood in the doorway, looking at his back.

"He's dead. Just so you know, it was a son."

2011

Chapter Five

2011

JANUARY – FEBRUARY

E*ND OF* J*ANUARY*

It took Nikou a couple of months to heal her injuries. For some weeks she lay in bed in a state somewhere between torpor and terror. Had she had the strength she would have given some serious thought to what had happened, but she felt only despair that she'd been found out. That her plan for the emergency she'd known to be inevitable had been quashed.

It had been no small decision to choose the family's chief object of scorn as her recourse in an emergency. But she'd felt that Fereshteh's competence, integrity, empathy and understanding outweighed any of her immediate family's opinions and concerns. Having come to that decision after much internal deliberation, though, it had been crushing to have her desperate strategy not only fail, but also compound her dire domestic life and also put both Fereshteh and Marjan in danger.

After almost total immobility during the first week, she was awake a little longer each day and began to wonder what had happened to her friend. The one friend she had actually still had. She knew that Marjan was now gone from her life, but hoped she'd be safe. Nikou did not want to think further than that.

Her husband had engaged a new woman to cook, clean, change Nikou's bandages, give her medications (where had he gotten them from, she wondered) and see to her needs. During the first few weeks she had brought Nikou nourishing meals and plenty of warm drinks on a tray to her bed. Although Nikou appreciated this, she had a vague thought that the woman must also be reporting back to Mehrdad. He was hardly ever there; the woman had to be an informer. And she must have been well paid to keep silent about whatever she saw. But Nikou didn't care. Frankly, she was also beyond caring about what Mehrdad must have been telling her parents to keep them away. The very thought of her mother fussing and babbling non-stop made her groan.

As the physical exhaustion lifted, she began to do a few things again, occasionally even making herself a small snack. She drank strong sweet tea in the hope that it would give her some energy, and she found herself absorbed in tending the samovar just to give her some occupation.

By mid-December she had the strength to grieve. Although it was best that it had happened, given the circumstances, Nikou grieved the loss of her child. As her tears flowed her grief expanded, and she found herself mourning the loss of her friend too.

Looking one morning into her mirror, she peered deeply at herself and saw her sadness, her emptiness, her weakness; and she began to mourn her life. Her shaking frame collapsed onto the bathroom floor and she laid there weeping long and hard.

In her mind, she visited a gallery of images of Mehrdad, allowing herself to tense, to shiver – to retch, even. Further along this gallery were her family. When she found the courage to acknowledge these, she began to mourn another loss: the father and the brothers who had betrayed her trust and innocence, her gentleness and obedience; the mother, who had abandoned her to them by choosing not to question the true source of her "accidents". And finally, that part of her who had abandoned herself by remaining silent and compliant.

Nikou lay wrapped in her pain the rest of that day. The next day, compelled by some inner force, she pushed past her exhaustion and repeated the exercise. She did this again and again, day after day tearing open afresh every wound, until after nearly three weeks of this she woke up one morning with a clarity she hadn't felt in a long time.

For the first time since that brutal day in November, Nikou went out. She needed to get used to driving again, so she got into her Mercedes and made a short trip on some quiet streets in her neighborhood. After a few days, she felt she could manage a drive somewhat further afield. On the fourth day, she drove to the nearest shopping district.

There she purchased a cheap mobile phone, then walked to a noisy street corner where she called the number that, in the fog of semi-consciousness, she'd somehow memorized. She spoke rapidly and finished the call quickly. Nikou then crossed the street and entered a cafe, where she ordered a coffee for a change. She went over the arrangements again in her mind and felt a strange mixture of guilt, anxiety and elation. She would be meeting her cousin in three days. Fereshteh knew just the right place, she'd said, and because Nikou didn't know that part of the city very well, she focused hard on the directions Fereshteh had given her. She didn't dare write any of it down. Her husband would certainly find the paper, wherever she put it.

She left the café and was careful to do some window shopping before going back to her car. That would give her an excuse to go out again in a few days.

THREE DAYS later and right on his usual morning schedule, her husband left the house, dressed in one of his best tailor-made three-piece suits — sans necktie, of course. Even more than thirty years after the Revolution, the hated Western accessory was still forbidden. He probably had a very important meeting. So much the better, thought Nikou as she watched him drive away.

An hour later she walked to her own car. Her clothing and coat were simple, her handbag and headscarf plain. She had told the housekeeper that she was going shopping and would have lunch at a café. Well, that was nearly true, she thought. She was unaccustomed to lying.

She felt a little like a schoolgirl planning to skip a class, and she smiled to herself as she started the engine. She drove down the long drive and waited while the electric gate opened. Putting the car in gear again she passed through and then came to an abrupt stop.

Approaching her head on was her husband's Porsche. Through his open window he ordered her to back up and as she did so he drove forward. The gate rolled shut behind him. They parked in the circle by the front entrance and both stepped out of their cars slowly.

Nikou was unable to hide her disquiet but rallied with her rehearsed answer when he asked her where she was going. There was neither any point nor any wisdom in asking him why he was home.

I'm going to ask you again." His voice was even. "Where were you going?"

She noticed the "were" and realized she had no way out of this. Yet she stood by her original answer. Twice more.

"You know, my little Nikou, lying is not your strong suit." His eyes were hard despite his polite smile. He continued, "Let me tell you where you were going. Come, let's go inside and we'll talk."

The blood drained into her feet as she stood there; she couldn't move.

He took hard hold of her arm and led her into the house. Slamming the door behind them, he pulled her around to face him and ordered the housekeeper to go home. Slowly, carefully enunciating

Crimson Ink

every syllable, he began the insults. She was a deceiving little bitch; conniving, ungrateful and selfish. He pulled her into the living room. A new wave of icy fear roiled in her stomach.

Who did she think she was, going to talk to that so-called doctor? That stupid, upstart relative of hers; the one with airs and attitude; the nosey busy-body who just couldn't stop herself from asking too many questions when she had you captive on her table.

"Don't you know what that woman does?" He gave her a push backwards. "Don't you know who she spends time with?" Another push. "I'll bet you do, you little brazen little chit!" Another push. "Is she trying to recruit you into her little band of do-gooders?"

His voice rose in sarcasm. Another push, along the corridor.

Nikou seemed incapable of moving on her own. She just stared at him, mouth slightly open, heart beating wildly, wincing at the accusations he pelted as he walked and pushed, walked and pushed.

"Have you not learned by now the danger you are courting? Have you not learned how dangerous such women are to our republic's status quo? Have you no shame in telling everyone our private business - in sharing with others the intimate details of our lives?"

He pushed her into their bedroom. The icy waves were surging through her every limb.

"You should not ever underestimate how seriously I take such matters. No one — no one", he spat the words, "no one should ever interfere in people's marriages. No one has the right to incite women against their husbands!" His eyes nearly glowed.

"You will never see that woman or any of her friends again." He slid his belt from his trousers. The merest cry emerged from Nikou's mouth; water filled her eyes. She was backed up against the bed.

"If you disobey me, I will know. I have eyes everywhere. I have connections you can't even conceive of. Never underestimate me or my resources." He wrapped the belt around his fist.

"Never believe that you can escape me," he hissed, and gave her a final shove.

WHEN NIKOU DID NOT SHOW up for their appointment, Fereshteh called her back, again and again, using a blocked number. There was no answer. Mehrdad had discovered her plan, then. Nikou simply might have changed her mind, but that didn't seem likely. Her voice had been so earnest and so full of energy and determination, that Fereshteh was sure Nikou was reaching out for the help she needed. But instead she must have been caught.

She hoped that Mehrdad wouldn't – *no! stop!* she told herself. *Don't even think about that.* But in her mind's eye she recalled the encounter with him in her office and shuddered.

She knew all too well that his type of personality could find a punishable offense in anything he saw, and that timid, gentle young Nikou, who obeyed her elders and conformed to the traditional values that her family had impressed upon her, Nikou, who would never antagonize anyone, would always be his victim.

END OF JANUARY

THEY CAME for her after midnight. The pounding on the door brought Jamshid out of sleep and to his feet quickly. He let in three burly men, knowing exactly where they were from. Fereshteh peeked out from the dark corridor.

The leader of the trio demanded Fereshteh, and while he waited, his companions spread out, and began searching the living room and kitchen. Their rifles were slung over their shoulders and they worked quickly, skillful and well-practiced at their task.

Dressing gown and headscarf in place, Fereshteh emerged from the shadows. "Ah, so you are Dr. Jalili," the leader said. "I'm here because my department has concerns related to some of your activities." He offered her a polite little smile.

"Which activities are you referring to, *Aqa?*" Fereshteh kept her tone calm and civil. They might have been having a formal professional conversation in a public office in the middle of the day.

He began his script. His department was concerned with some

"security issues" relating to certain aspects of her work. They had come to escort her to their offices, where they would "ask her a few questions". It wouldn't take long, he assured her. Then, "No, sir, you may not come with us; only your wife. We'll see that she's returned to you soon. And by the way, we also need your computers, cell phones and any other electronic devices you have. Oh, and where is your desk? We need to see your papers. And books." Fereshteh returned to the bedroom to get dressed.

It took less than 15 minutes to go through everything. Fereshteh and Jamshid had long ago simplified their household and they had been very careful not to keep anything that might arouse interest or suspicion. They, like everyone in their Baha'i community, knew that this kind of search could happen at any time.

Jamshid offered the men tea and smiled, more to keep his wife calm than for any other reason. When the men declined, Jamshid asked again where they were taking her.

The leader returned the smile and said, "Just down to one of our offices. Don't worry, you'll see her soon." And they led her out the door.

As SHE RODE in the back of the SUV, her wrists now manacled, Fereshteh tried to look straight ahead and focus on the road. She knew where they were headed.

Unimpeded by the usual traffic jams that plagued daytime driving, the heavy vehicle crossed into the northern suburbs in no time. The rhythmic hum of the drive had the unexpected effect of calming Fereshteh. She let herself ride the flow of her thoughts.

Too many had been driven away like this. Some knew the exact reason for their midnight visitation and arrest. Many did not. In Fereshteh's case, she was somewhere in between. So, to keep her mind from jumping ahead in dread, she speculated on the "why" in her case.

What had she done? She could think of two things: she'd gotten herself involved in women's issues. In the current thinking, helping women with divorce, domestic abuse or protection issues was considered radical. It posed a threat to the security of the family, the foundation of a proper Islamic Society. She had been scrupulously careful to keep the lowest profile possible, but, with government spies thick on the ground and in the most unlikely places, her work could have been noticed.

Treating the election protesters who had escaped the government's bullets, batons and white vans was another matter. Again, Fereshteh had been careful because she knew too well that aiding and abetting those with dissenting voices was considered being disloyal to the Revolution and endangering national security. Who knew what information dissidents might reveal and which government agencies they might blame for their injuries? And that was dangerous.

But then, Fereshteh, thought, she was, after all, a Baha'i. And maybe the authorities feared she was spreading her beliefs among her dissident patients. This could be construed to be *mofsed fel-arz* – spreading corruption on earth – and perhaps also waging war on God. Both were potentially punishable by death...

But her conversations with patients were always benign. She never mentioned her beliefs directly. She talked with them about their conditions. She encouraged them, gave them medical advice, and occasionally philosophized in a general way. Said what she could to strengthen them if they needed that. She had no political motive. Like so many other ordinary Iranians, she simply wanted to help those in need and she used her medical and other skills in whatever way she could for the greater good of her country. It was difficult for her to see this as a crime.

Yet she knew the drill. Policy makers moved the goal posts of allowable activities whenever it was politically expedient and would meet the approval of the Supreme Leader. Or, the Supreme Leader issued his own edicts and they were carried out. Period.

For Baha'is, it was sufficient to be arrested for your belief alone. Sure, they accused you of all kinds of seditious acts to justify what they did: "*mofsed fel-arz*" was a favorite, but "spying for the West", being a "Zionist terrorist", and "spreading seditious propaganda" were among the old standbys that had brought the death penalty to

Crimson Ink

literally hundreds of Baha'is in the last century alone. And that said nothing of the thousands of cases of unofficial beatings, pillaging, hate graffiti, arson and shop closures incited by clerics and politicians alike. In Fereshteh's country, the Baha'is were at the top of the scapegoat list.

Before the car stopped, one of the guards put a blindfold over her eyes. But she had already seen their destination from two blocks away. She heard the sliding of a gate and the exchange between the driver and the gatekeeper. They drove through and before long stopped again.

"Get out."

Someone grabbed her arm and pulled. Blindly trying to get her bearings, she took a tentative step on the tarmac beneath. A rifle point nudged her forward while two solid rough hands took charge of her arms. Hinges creaked and she was propelled forward. A metal door clanged shut behind her. Her new lodgings were in Evin Prison.

Evin Prison
End of January

THEY LED FERESHTEH DOWN A CORRIDOR. At least, that's what she assumed. The blindfold and cuffs remained. A new hand, smaller than the ones from the van, kept a tight grip on her arm as this new person hurried her along. A female guard, of course. When Fereshteh failed to instantly negotiate a sharp right turn, her guard cursed and gave her a shove. There were occasional stops. The jangling of keys, the clicking of locks, the squeak of steel hinges and the slam of metal on metal marked each leg of her passage into internment.

The initial dankness of the air gradually gave way to a staleness that in turn yielded to the stench of dysfunctional toilets and mold, and to the stink of unwashed humanity. The relative quiet that had greeted her entry into the building was now overtaken by a collection of murmurs, snores, and an occasional sharp cry.

They came to a stop and the guard yanked off the blindfold and unlocked the hand-cuffs. Fereshteh looked into the large cell in front of her as the guard turned the keys and opened the door. Without a word, the guard used her rifle muzzle to push her in, then slammed and locked the door with practiced swiftness, and disappeared.

Fereshteh stood still, forcing herself to take stock of her surroundings. She focused on details, as much to calm her nerves as to orient herself and decide on where she could place herself among the dozens of prisoners before her.

Several naked ceiling bulbs lit up the hodgepodge of bodies around her. Most were curled up on the cement, imposing themselves on each other in fitful sleep or pretense of it. Fereshteh felt eyes on her, some squinting through slits, others wide open, assessing her. A few women were sitting, leaning against the bars if they were lucky, or bending at odd angles forward if they weren't.

A voice from the back left corner called her over. Fereshteh stared at the seated figure, a woman of her generation.

She called her again, "Come on. Don't stand there all night. Besides, they might be bringing in more and you're blocking the entrance. Come here. I'll make a space for you." She pointed to a spot by her side.

Still unsure of herself, Fereshteh nevertheless put her body in gear once more and picked her way across the cell. As Fereshteh approached, the woman's hands and feet nudged the bodies around her until she'd created a small patch for Fereshteh to perch on. Lowering herself onto the dirt and stains of the chill floor, Fereshteh looked her unexpected ally in the eye, said a sincere "thank you" and compacted herself onto the tiny spot that was now her allotment.

THE CLANG of steel brought her out of a disturbed semi-sleep. A guard was shouting and the forms around her began to move. Names were called and bodies stood up. A row of guards pointed their long weapons at the women that were ordered out of the cell and led away.

Fereshteh noted resignation in the eyes of some — had they been here before? Too often perhaps? In the eyes of others were fear and confusion. There were murmurs, questions, and speculation as they looked at each other, desperate, it seemed, for — *for what,* Fereshteh wondered. *For comfort, for answers, for safety, for someone to say, 'sorry, it's all a mistake; you can go home now'?*

Fereshteh's ally sat frozen beside her, eyes still closed. The remaining women spread out, claiming new territory, knowing it was theirs only until a subsequent roll call. When it came most stood up, and once again, those whose names were called lined up in front of the guards.

"Talayeh Fathi!" No response. "Talayeh Fathi! *Pa-sho* — get up!"

By the third call one of the female guards entered the cell, her rifle at the ready. She walked to the back corner and stood in front of Fereshteh's ally.

"Eh! You think this is a game? You stupid cow, *pa-sho!*"

All eyes watched the little drama as the guard gave the seated prisoner another curse and an angry shove with her weapon. Talayeh dropped to the side with a light thud. She was dead.

Evin Prison
End of January

When the guards had finally emptied the holding cell, they handcuffed the women and separated them into smaller groups, and led them down different passageways. Fereshteh found herself in a group of three going down a flight of stairs into a wintry basement corridor. Naked bulbs lighted the filthy concrete beneath her feet. On both sides of the corridor, were long rows of doors, the solid gray metal slabs relieved by thick bolts and two sliding hatches each: one at eye level and one just above the floor. A thickset female guard was waiting, heavy keyring in hand. Between them, the two guards shoved each prisoner through a separate door and slammed it behind them. They did not reply to the cries of their erstwhile charges.

BENEATH THE BARE lightbulb high above her Fereshteh took a moment to assess her new surroundings. A dim grayness came through the ceiling-height slit of a barred basement window at the opposite end, which measured about two long strides from the door. Fereshteh's outstretched arms almost touched the two side walls. She noticed a kind of drain built into the concrete in the right corner. A threadbare rug covered the rest of the floor. Two crumpled dark gray blankets - stained - lay in the left corner by the door. The walls were soiled and splattered. The air dank and fetid. A faint trace of vomit floated in the little draft created by the opening and closing of the door.

FERESHTEH STOOD TOTALLY STILL, hardly daring to breathe. Slowly it began to creep over her: her new reality. As the creep spread, she sensed monsters approaching. Her heartbeat quickened.

The deep drum beat keeps an orderly pace as it accelerates. Thump, thump, thump, thump... It morphs. Insistent, it fills her ears, her head. Her breaths grow short and shallow. Her eyes dart everywhere — what is she looking for?

The air is heavy; she strains to breathe. Thump-thump-thump... her chest tightens... thump-thump-thump-thump-thump... it squeezes... thump-thump-thump-thump-thump...

She's panting... She starts to pace... Arms clasping, hands wringing, eyes darting, head turning, searching...... pacing, pacing, pacing...thump-thump-thump-thump-thump... Deep gasping... Who is moaning so loudly?... Head turning - no one, nothing... An anguished animal yowls... She turns again and again and again... Where is it? Where is it, where is it, where IS it? Nothing, nothing, nothing, but the cry won't stop, won't stop, won't stop... WHY? WHY, WHY, WHY? Shrieks wrench her. She doubles over...

Head turns; tears fly; body rocks; fists pound air... Standing, pacing, fists still pounding, long mournful sobs... straining lungs... air so stale, lungs so desperate... walls too close, squeezing... Eyes tight, face sticky-salty, a human ball, shivering, rocking, nails digging arm-flesh... Filthy corner pressing...

Why does that moaning not stop...STOP! STOP! STOP! Go-away-leave-me-alone-go-away-leave-me-alone-go-away-leave-me-alone.... NO!... NO, NO, NO!....HELP ME! OH GOD, OH GOD, OH GOD! H-E-L-P M-EEEE!!!!! Rivers inundating cheeks, head thumping to bursting, lungs straining, mind spiraling, the ball rocking faster and faster... Desperate thoughts... Please let me die... I'm going to die, I can't do this, I can't, I can't, I can't... I must die... Take away this pain... I hurt, I hurt, I hurt... Sobbing, wailing... Lungs gasping. Shrieking. Fingers clawing hair and scalp. Eyes wild... Heart thumping so fast, so loud...Crushing tightness... Hands and feet tingling, nails blue, face hot, arms shivering...

She stands. She paces, paces, paces, paces, nerves electric. Thumping, panting, fists pounding, arms flinging... A last howl...

Head throbs, arms flail... The pacing slows. The thumping relents. The panting subsides. Slow surrender to heaviness... It drags her to the floor. She blacks out.

BEGINNING OF FEBRUARY

"Nikoujoon, why are you looking so glum? Look, the sun is shining! And I've made your favorite dishes. They'll be ready in a few minutes... *Azizam*, please bring me that *kafgir*... I want to empty this pot of rice..."

Her daughter handed her the spatula and Samira began to scoop out the steaming rice onto the platter.

"Here, can you take this to the table... that's a good girl."

Nikou complied but the large platter felt heavy. Her most recent bruises were still tender, even if they were no longer visible. Since that nightmare visit to Fereshteh's practice, her husband had been careful to stop short of beating any part of her that might be visible to others.

From the living room came the sounds of the men's conversation. There was her grandfather again, going on and on, decibels higher than everyone else. Did he think that his being hard of hearing meant that everyone else was too?

She was turning to go back into the kitchen when she heard Fereshteh's name. Placing herself out of view, she stopped to listen further.

"Yeah, it was what, a couple of days ago, eh, Majid? Habib called to tell me Fereshteh's in Evin. As if I care." He gave a snort. "Habib knows too well that I've disowned her, but still he said, 'Uncle, I just thought you should know'. He calls from time to time, you know. Usually tells me about his kids and things. Tries to keep in touch."

Majid laughed a little and said to his son-in-law, somewhat apologetically, Nikou thought, "Yes, our cousin tries his best. But what can he do, it's not his fault his sister's the black sheep of the family."

There was a general chuckle, a mix of embarrassment and derision, and then a change of topic.

Nikou returned to the kitchen, where her mother had begun ladling out the *khoreshte-bademjoon* - the eggplant stew. "I know how much Mehrdad enjoys this and I made it extra rich just for him," she said, now emptying the pot.

"Oh, I will so enjoy it when I can make such dishes for your little ones, Nikoujoon… I wonder how soon that will be?" She looked up at her daughter, giving her a grin and a wink, then turned to ladle a second pot into the waiting casserole dish.

IT WAS ONLY after they got home that night that Nikou had time to herself. The visit to her parents had gone on all day and into the evening. The huge lunch had gradually segued into a light supper, keeping her mother puttering in the kitchen and hovering over her family to ensure they'd had enough, as she liked to think of it.

Although the conversation had covered dozens of topics, Nikou's mind had remained stuck on the snippet she'd heard from the dining room: her father's cousin Fereshteh had been arrested.

She'd thought about the timing. Fereshteh had been arrested "a couple of days ago", her grandfather had said. Mehrdad's latest threats — and her latest "punishment" — had been less than a week ago. He'd been very clear about his feelings about Fereshteh and "her ilk". *Surely he couldn't have...*

But with everyone around and with all the time she'd spent in the kitchen helping her mother, Nikou had not gone further in her speculations.

When they'd arrived home her husband had been busy with one thing or another and it was only once she'd put on her pajamas that he'd announced that he was going out. *Wants to make sure I'm settled in for the night, all safe and secure before he leaves*, she thought sarcastically.

She never asked him where he went at night — and he went out frequently — or where he went at any other time either. He'd made it clear that his comings and goings were his affair, not hers. Of course, *her* affairs were both hers *and* his.

Now that she thought of it, she knew very little about this man she'd married. The marriage had been arranged by her parents and his father, that loathsome Ayatollah Rashid. He was somewhere up there in the clouds of the clerical hierarchy; somewhere politically powerful, but she'd never bothered to ask anyone about her father-in-law. She hadn't been interested.

But now she was paying attention to these things. She began to ask herself, who, really, was her husband? All she knew was that he'd briefly been a lawyer, then a judge and had worked in different positions in the Judiciary.

Early in their marriage, before things had become confrontational, whenever she'd asked more about his work he'd been vague. Eventually he'd become evasive and finally he'd told her outright to mind her own business. *What did he have to hide?*, she wondered. Or were his replies just a part of the mind games he played to unnerve her? For that was what she had at last recognized: that everything he did was calculated to destabilize her, weaken her, undermine her, and control her. *What's wrong with me? What have I done to make him do these things?*

She sat down in the capacious armchair in the den. It was her usual spot for reading or watching TV. She curled up with a knitted blanket and a hot mug of tea and looked out the large window into the garden, its darkness starkly contrasted by the mansion's security lights. It had begun to snow. Soft fat flakes dropped gracefully onto the lawn, then vanished.

Her arm continued to ache. Well, it had only been a few days since… and of course she'd carried all those heavy platters to the table. But this was a temporary ache and was nothing compared to the pain of loss she still carried.

She lifted her mug, and returning her gaze to the mellow light of the table lamp beside her, picked up the book she'd planned to read, but set it down again. Holding the mug to her lips, she inhaled the warm sweet steam rising to her nostrils and savored it for a moment.

Her thoughts turned to Fereshteh. What was *she* drinking tonight? She closed her eyes for a few seconds. *No, don't go there. You don't know anything about such things and you don't want to know.* She shook her head and took a sip of tea.

But aren't you at least partly responsible for Fereshteh's imprisonment? If you hadn't gone there, hadn't told Marjan to get you to Fereshteh's office "in the case that", would she still have been arrested?

Still, she could have refused to treat you; could have sent you away. After the way our family has always treated her, especially since Great-aunt Farah died, why would Fereshteh consent to treat you at all?

Nikou ran through her memories: years of family get-togethers. She recalled the snide remarks, criticisms and even outright disdain that her parents, her uncles and aunts, and especially her grandfather had meted out to Fereshteh. To Jamshid, Habib, Taraneh, and all their children, too, for that matter. All the "black sheep". All the barely tolerated "misguided Baha'is" in their family. And Fereshteh, for some reason, was the blackest sheep of all.

But Great-Aunt Farah's family were always forbearing and forgiving, no matter what. Every time *Aqajoon* Reza, or *Baba* and her uncles and aunts tried to provoke them, they kept calm and remained courteous. And they had good families. She'd always enjoyed playing with her cousins when they'd come. They'd never behaved like the "second class citizens" that her family had always made them out to be.

It occurred to Nikou that she hadn't seen those cousins since Great-Aunt Farah's death. On the rare occasions that Aryana or Mansoor had come home to visit from their UK university studies, she hadn't been allowed to contact them. *Aqajoon* Reza had forbidden it and forbidden all contact with Fereshteh. When Nikou had asked why, he'd been dismissive, but eventually she'd learned that he blamed Fereshteh for Farah's death. She'd been shocked; somehow the whole thing hadn't rung true.

Nikou got up and went to the window. The snow was still falling and the flakes had begun to accumulate. Captured by the beauty of the scene, she stood there for a good long while, watching the graceful dance that animated the night.

The snow stopped and Nikou turned around. She slowly began to pace the room. Fragments of conversation came into her mind. She could hear Fereshteh talking to Marjan, concerned, asking questions; Marjan trying her best to give the information Fereshteh had needed; Marjan's voice shaking, warning Fereshteh not to ask more; Marjan worried about how they would get Nikou home without her husband finding out; Fereshteh saying something about people who help women in these kinds of situations, people who could help Nikou; Marjan insisting she didn't want to know anything, that she'd already put herself in danger; Fereshteh telling Marjan that she or Nikou could call her at any time; Marjan crying; Fereshteh repeating telephone numbers to her, insisting she memorize them and Marjan saying *no, no, no, no, don't tell me, please*; Fereshteh insisting and repeating over and over, her private number and the number of a woman they could trust and *please, please give these numbers to Nikou later*; Marjan crying even more. Then there'd been blackness, a blessed pain-free peace before waking to the hell of Mehrdad's arrival… She stopped mid-pace and shuddered, then shook herself, casting off the fear, and resumed her pacing.

It was almost unthinkable. It had been less than a week since Mehrdad had found her out in her attempt to meet with Fereshteh. Less than a week since she'd been punished for that. Less than a week since Fereshteh had been arrested. Nikou was in no doubt now that these two things were linked; in no doubt now what a dangerous game this could be. He'd warned her. He'd told her she was being watched. How else had he found her at Fereshteh's office last November?

She quickened her pacing. How naive could she have been? She'd called Fereshteh and made that follow-up arrangement but Mehrdad had intercepted her before she'd even gotten out of the gate. *He knew. He pretended he was out for the day. It was all a show! He let me incriminate myself to give him another reason to show me who's in charge - how much he's in charge! Oh, how clueless I've been! Perhaps he's right; perhaps I am as stupid as he says I am!*

She walked faster, crisscrossing the room in seconds. He must have found her new phone and bugged it. And he'd probably been checking it every night while she slept!

Still pacing, she let the flood of self-recrimination wash over her. Then she stopped dead in her tracks. She looked out the window again, taking in the beauty of the soft white blanket on the lawn. A beauty she'd never have seen without the security lights all around the house.

Of course! she thought. *There are monitors, spies, watch-dogs — whatever they were called. His "monitors" observing my every move, keeping me in their sight and hearing everything.* She thought about her phone. Then she looked up at the ceiling, at the corners of the room. She'd forgotten about the security cameras inside. They were supposed to be switched on when no one was home. But what if they were on all the time? *No! That's ridiculous!*

She resumed her pacing. There were monitors, though, that seemed certain. And her phone had to be bugged. So, how to call anyone? How to meet anyone even if she could make a call?

Determined now, she left the den and went to the kitchen. She needed another mug of tea. She needed to think. She needed to find a way to outsmart Mehrdad's watchdogs.

Evin Prison
February

FERESHTEH HAD long since lost track of time. She'd thought she could get some sense of day and night from the bit of gray that she noticed through the slit window until she realized that the dim light was constant. Now that she thought about it, the sounds she sometimes heard from what she'd thought of as the "outside" were probably from another room. Maybe a room like hers.

Even meals offered her no help. She couldn't distinguish any difference in the food that was served her through the bottom hatch in her door every so often. Nothing that indicated "breakfast" as opposed to "lunch" or "dinner". It was all a kind of mush. Her stomach gave her no clue either, since its constant pain and cramping kept hunger at bay.

Toilet visits were on an "urgently need to go" basis and required considerable shouting and banging on the door before a guard deigned to come. The guards were surly and impatient. If you couldn't "do your business" in short order they came in after you and gave you a clout or two. Or three.

Neither showers nor a change of clothes was on offer.

The lightbulb burned constantly. Sleep came only when exhaustion prevailed.

AT SOME POINT a guard dragged her out, cuffed and blindfolded her and led her through a maze of twists and turns. No stairs. That didn't bode well. They led her into a room, sat her on what must have been a table and told her to wait. The click of a door, footsteps, cigarette smoke. A man's voice. She could hear him pacing around her. She thought of Rana.

He barraged her with the questions she knew would come. The questions about her life, her work, her family, her beliefs. And she knew they knew the answers. Still, they went through the routine. *So, what's the purpose, then?* she asked herself. She assumed they wanted an admission of guilt of some sort. *If I signed a quick confession, they'd probably let me go. But a confession of what?*

Fereshteh had heard her share of stories about forced confessions and she felt ill at just the thought of them. The usual kinds of confessions, she'd heard, involved admitting to spying, agitating or plotting against the State through various means and agencies. In the case of Baha'is, it was that and more: it would mean not only recanting your faith, but also execrating it as political, seditious, and evil. It meant condemning yourself and all your fellow-believers, both in Iran and outside it. The State could use such a confession to justify and increase its persecution of thousands, holding them responsible for any number of fabricated heinous deeds.

So Fereshteh was not surprised that the interrogator persisted in trying to extract a recantation, despite her consistent refusals. She was not surprised at the long hours in that room. What did surprise her was that she learned to switch off her mind and hold her tongue. At the end of each session, she'd be shoved back into her cell, completely drained, but somehow still whole.

Time passed. He called her in again. He repeated the drill. But this time, he ended the session differently.

Fereshteh reeled from the punch to her jaw, hardly recovering before the next blow hit her full in the stomach. "Next time, give me what I want," he said. His voice was almost benign.

He hauled her in regularly over the next few days. Or were they hours? She truly didn't know. Or care. With each new session, the interrogator ramped up his assaults. It didn't take long before the blue of the bruises that covered her blended in with the black of the round little burns that dotted her arms and legs.

Mid-February

At 4:53 a.m. Rahimi sat at the kitchen table, bent over his second mug of tea. He rubbed his forehead, trying to coax the pain away. *Maybe I should have a strong coffee instead*, he thought. *Yeah, that might help.* Pushing himself up with both hands, he went to the counter to boil the kettle again and rooted around in a cabinet until he found an ancient jar of instant coffee tucked behind tins of loose tea, sugar

Crimson Ink

and a miscellany of powdered drinks and dried sauce mixes. He spooned three helpings of the crusty brown powder into a large mug, added an equal amount of sugar and stirred boiling water into it.

Taking his brew to the living room, he sat back in his armchair and stared through the glass of the balcony slider at the winter darkness, continuing the ruminations that had busied him half the night. He knew he wasn't managing his workload well, but, true to form, he just kept accepting more and more responsibility. He had to, he kept telling himself. For his family — but no, this was no longer true. He couldn't hide this even from himself any longer. He took it on because that's the person he'd become and the person the Ministry expected on the job. There could be no back-pedaling because he'd be regarded as weak, as a disappointment, as a failure. He told himself that it was just a matter of the *amount* of work he had. If he could just get a grip on how to juggle it all, everything would be fine.

He took a few gulps of the coffee and grimaced. They didn't drink coffee much, but he made a mental note to tell Zahra to buy one of those new espresso makers so he could have good fresh coffee when he needed it. Putting the mug on the side table, he struggled with his thoughts until he dozed. Half an hour later he crept into the bathroom and took a hot shower. He needed to get to work.

WHEN HE ENTERED his building at 7:40 he still had a headache. The unrelieved grayness of the concrete complex against the equally gloomy day did nothing to lift his spirits. The dismal prospect of meeting his superiors' expectations after another sleepless night added fuel to the throbbing in his brain.

Passing through security control, Rahimi walked the dingy corridor to the elevator and hit the grimy button for his floor. Emerging, he walked past the closed office doors still waiting for their occupants to arrive. "Slackers, the lot of them," he muttered.

Reaching his office, he went straight in and closed the door. From a desk drawer he pulled out a bottle, poured two brown tablets into his hand and popped them into his mouth, downing them with gulps of water from a plastic bottle on a side table. He went to the window and looked out onto the brown grounds below and the naked trees in the distance.

He knew without looking at the folders on his desk what his work for today entailed. But he needed this headache to go away first, so he left the office and went to the cafeteria. Fifteen minutes later he returned with a large paper mug of very sweet tea. He sat down at his desk and opened the first folder and began to read. The new one. He read through the charges and started looking at the background dossier. Then he picked up the phone.

"… That's right…Take her out of her cell and soften her up. I'll be down in twenty minutes." He leaned back in his chair, closed his eyes and waited for the painkillers to do their job.

FERESHTEH SAT, back straight, on the metal chair, adjusting her posture to keep her equilibrium despite the teeter of its uneven legs. Given the pressure on her bruises, it was difficult to find a position she could actually hold for long. She could already feel herself slumping, so she grasped the sides of the seat and moved her feet slightly forward.

This was a new room; she'd been led up a flight of stairs and the walk had been much longer than usual. It was warmer here and the air no longer foul.

A door opened and she heard footsteps, then the scrape of a chair, a thunk on what might be a desk or table, and then the clearing of a throat.

"Wait outside", the man's voice ordered. Footsteps, then a door opening. A click as it shut. Papers shuffling. The throat clearing again. A low curse. Some murmurs.

"Fereshteh Jalili?" he addressed her clearly.

She couldn't recognize his voice. This was someone new.

Mute beneath her blindfold Fereshteh tried to give him a face, a personality, a family, a history – anything to put flesh onto this disembodied voice, to create some kind of connection between them that resembled a human and humane relationship; to create something – anything – that would allow her to hope and, as time went on, enable her to retain her sanity in an environment that invited its opposite.

She felt madness lurking in the corners of every room of this loathsome facility. It seemed as if the very walls mocked her, the ceilings jeered down upon her, the floors leered up at her as if impatient for her to collapse upon them or even wet herself on them in her blindfolded terror.

She could smell the fear exuding from her pores as a cold sweat spread itself from her armpits and down her back; she could taste its salt as its beads formed above her upper lip; feel its rivulets trickle from her brow, along her hairline and down past her ears.

Silently she cursed these betrayals of her state and vowed that she was going to rein in her mind and heart. But she couldn't.

"Fereshteh Jalili! That's you, isn't it?"

"I... yes... mmm..." Her voice struggled with her grimace as she shifted in the chair.

"Speak up, woman! Answer me!"

And with this, her new interrogator began his day's work.

Chapter Six

2011

MARCH – APRIL

Evin Prison
Early March

It was only in March that Fereshteh was allowed visitors. Immediate family only, so she'd expected Jamshid. They'd both agreed many months ago that if either of them ever were arrested, the children could be notified but that they absolutely should not return to Iran. No, it would be only Jamshid who'd come.

Heart pounding with anticipation, she stood among the many prisoners waiting to be led into one of the meeting booths. When she was finally seated, it took her a few seconds to process that facing her were her brother and sister-in-law instead of her husband. Through tears she greeted them across the glass partition, wishing she could grasp their hands.

Time was so limited and emotion so high, there was so much to say, so much to ask, but Fereshteh found herself uttering inanities, repeating the "how-are-you" and "oh-I've-missed-you-so-much" stock phrases that replace what the heart cannot express under the constraint of a monitored visit of undetermined duration.

Habib, although himself similarly affected, finally pulled his chair closer and gave his sister a quick synopsis of news that she could digest later. He quickly got to his point. With infinite gentleness and with his own tears, he gave her the news she surely did not want to hear.

"Since you got arrested," he said, "Jamshid's been working himself extra hard. It's been his way of coping with… you know… you being in here. Not being allowed to visit you has made him sick with worry and he's tried to work out his stress somehow. He's been on endless phone calls with the children, and managed to persuade them to stay put. You know, telling them that there's absolutely nothing they can do if they come here." He paused and cleared his throat. "Apparently he hasn't been sleeping or eating well.

"We don't know for sure, of course, but we think that maybe the combination of this — maybe all this affected his concentration; maybe it's made him distracted. You know, like not paying attention to some things as he normally would. Or maybe it was simply an accident." Habib looked away.

"What? What do you mean, Habib? What's happened? Tell me!" Fereshteh sat up and leaned forward, eyes riveted on her brother.

Habib chewed his lips and, his voice low, said, "Fereshteh, Jamshid was in a car accident. About a week ago. He was taken to hospital, but… Habib stopped and looked down, collecting himself before continuing. "They couldn't save him, Fereshtehjoon."

Taraneh interjected, "They called Habib and we went to the hospital and waited. And then they told us and —. We buried him three days ago, *Joonam*." Taraneh put her tissue over her face and cried into it.

Habib took a breath. Taraneh blew her nose and looked at him, then at Fereshteh, as Habib went on. "I — we… we tried to visit you right after it happened. We've all been trying to visit since you were arrested — please, you must know that! But they've never given us permission. Yesterday they said ok, we could come today. And even today, while we were waiting outside with all the other people trying to visit, we weren't sure they'd let us in. Well. Here we are. Finally."

Fereshteh stared at them, numb. When she finally spoke, her voice sounded hollow, sterile, even to her own ears. She wanted to know more details. She wanted to know about the children's response. She wanted to know if other family and friends knew.

Habib and Taraneh took turns in filling her in. Yes, the whole family now knew — yes, even Uncle's family — and of course Daryush, Anisa and Aryana. All three of them had wanted to come, but Habib had been able to convince the older two not to; they had young families now. They would hold memorial meetings and of course keep in touch.

"But Aryana — well, we couldn't stop her." Habib's distress was clear. "She — she's arriving here tonight. We're going to —"

"Time's up! Time's up! All visitors must leave immediately!" The loudspeakers' order was simultaneously enforced by the armed guards on both sides of the partition.

It was over quickly. Families were divided once again, reluctance to leave being overcome by nudges from the muzzles of semi-automatic AR-15s.

EARLY MARCH 2011

THE SECURITY at Imam Khomeini International airport seemed even tighter than she remembered. In the sleek new terminal guards and soldiers stood with rifles in hand at regular intervals. Cameras were tracking movement, some of them swinging positions as if following certain individuals. The man checking her passport scratched his trim dark beard and glanced from the document to her face several times. *Of course*, she thought, *it's hard to distinguish one face from another under this headgear.*

Although she'd grown up with it, Aryana's last four years in the U.K. had accustomed her to the freedom of an unencumbered head

Crimson Ink

and she'd resented having to tie herself into the scarf before deplaning. She sighed.

The man looked up sharply. "What did you say?"

"Nothing. It's just been a long day. Long flight. I'm tired."

In fact, she'd hardly slept for the last week. There had been the matter of packing up her whole life and leaving. She had no illusions about returning to the U.K., not even for her education. Her Masters courses were nearly completed and her professors had told her she could complete the rest of the work remotely. She'd get her graduation certificate by mail. Her place was with her family now and nothing her aunt and uncle could say would change her course of action.

The taxi sped along the highway drawing closer to the heart of Tehran, its headlights joining the pulse that was the life-blood of the immense capital that she knew as "home". She leaned her head on the window, seeing not the city but a lifetime of family vignettes. She mourned her father and lamented her mother and would soon grieve together with Uncle Habib and Aunt Taraneh. She would visit her mother and grieve with her. No, there had been no question but that she'd return. She refused to watch events from the comfort of her privileged life in England. Refused to be paralyzed by fear of an ignorant regime. She would transform her sorrow and use it to act.

THE FIRST THING Aryana did the next morning was to visit Evin Prison to see her mother. But, Fereshteh's one allowable visit that week had been from Habib and Taraneh. The prison official standing in front of Aryana was not going to budge on that. She'd have to come next week. So be it.

She returned to her uncle and aunt's apartment, and began to think about how to tackle life back in Tehran.

The adjustment was easier than she'd expected. Perhaps in her heart she'd never really left. She loved her home and missed her city.

She still had friends of all backgrounds and once she'd settled back in, she began to visit and go out with her old crowd.

Although they said they loved having her stay with them, a couple of weeks after her return Habib and Taraneh advised her not to leave her family's apartment empty any longer. "It might just 'pass into someone else's hands', *Azizam*", her uncle had warned.

Stranger things than that had happened to prisoners' families. So, within two days, Aryana was back in her old home once again.

SHE WANDERED AROUND THE APARTMENT, familiar yet somehow now strange in its emptiness. The life had gone out of the rooms she'd grown up in. She passed her hands over the furniture, picturing her parents sitting side by side reading in their favorite armchairs; saw in her mind's eye a family meal around the old dining table; caught a flash of her mother bustling in the kitchen; recalled the laughter of her siblings teasing each other. She picked up photos and knick-knacks, and let herself slide into the past. A time when her family was whole.

In her brother's old room she saw that her mother had still not moved *Khanumjan* Farah's things. The few pieces of furniture they'd brought from her apartment stood awkwardly in the small space. *But Maman can't let go. At least not yet.* She saw the stacks of boxes, still untouched. Aryana suspected that her mother would never be able to sort through her grandmother's personal belongings without help. *Well, if Maman — did I just say "if"? — When Maman gets out — when — she gets out of prison, I'll help her go through these things. We'll sort it all out, down to the very last box.*

THE QUESTION NOW WAS, what to do with her life. She needed work, both because she had expenses and because she was not going to just sit around the house between social engagements. True, she still had some graduate work to complete, but that wouldn't take long.

Her friends turned out to have good connections. They knew she was a Baha'i, of course, but didn't agree that restrictions should apply on what she (or anyone, for that matter) did. Within ten days they'd arranged an interview for her with a small tech company. They were always looking for new talent and Aryana's abilities in software and app development were going to be an asset to them. They hired her, no questions asked about her personal background.

A WEEK AFTER HER ARRIVAL, Aryana returned to Evin. The official she spoke with this time was less helpful than his predecessor and at first she thought she'd have to wait yet another week. But Aryana always operated on the maxim that "you could catch more flies with honey than with vinegar" and persevered in her conversation with him, becoming sweeter and more creative with every sentence. Perhaps it was that or perhaps it was the large, thickly lashed eyes and bud lips of this tall, slim girl that moved him. Whatever the reason, he relented and told her she could wait in the visitors' hall. Visiting time wasn't for more than another hour, but Aryana didn't mind. It gave her a chance to prepare herself. It also gave her a tiny view into the world behind bars. "People watching" was going to be her new "go-to" information source here.

Despite everything she'd thought, however, Aryana could never have prepared herself for seeing her mother in that horrid space. As the prisoners took their seats behind the glass partitions, Aryana scanned the whole line and failed to find Fereshteh. She thought there'd been a mix-up of some kind so she asked one of the guards whether Fereshteh Jalili would indeed be coming.

The guard responded with a little laugh and then pointed to the only empty seat on the visitors' side. In response to Aryana's confused stare he gestured with his rifle and said only, "There. What's the matter, can't you see?"

Aryana moved toward the hunched veiled figure staring at her from behind the glass. It was only when the figure smiled that Aryana recognized her mother. She rushed over, tears, smiles, and mouthed endearments mingling with the shock of reunion. Their hands met on the glass between them, a meager substitute for the tight embrace they both longed for. Each wanted the other's news, thoughts, and feelings. But both saw the futility of this as their words fell together in a cacophony of simultaneous speech. Still, they finally managed, finding their way back to a coherent conversation that lifted their hearts up and far beyond the walls around them.

The debate about Aryana's intention to stay in Tehran would have to wait until the next visit, though. "Time" was called and the groups were parted. But before she left, Aryana saw a flicker of hope in her mother's kind eyes.

Work was interesting enough and the salary was actually decent. But while her job was certainly a good distraction, it couldn't take Aryana's mind away from her mother's predicament for long.

It wasn't for lack of effort, but the record of the human rights defense lawyers was dismal. Cases like Fereshteh's offered little hope for freedom. But Aryana was stubborn and determined. She intended to make every conceivable effort to change that pattern.

The infamous "blue-print" to arrest the development as well as disturb and undermine the well-being of every Baha'i in the country was alive and well. The persecution continued. There were periods when it was carried out in more subtle ways, and other periods when it was practiced blatantly. The one thing that the Baha'is could count on was that they could count on nothing. One minute you could be doing rather well, the next, you could lose everything.

Yet Aryana truly believed that anything was possible. Call them miracles or whatever you wanted, but astounding things happened in the world all the time. You just had to work at what you could and be determined.

Education was one of the things Aryana had in mind. She reflected on her own privileged situation. Her parents had had the foresight — and the means, let's be honest — to send her and her siblings abroad. They were taken care of. But there were thousands of her brethren who had no recourse to higher education. Her uncle and aunt were doing something concrete about this.

She made her decision one evening on her way home from work and called her uncle to let him know she was on her way over. The Baha'i Institute for Higher Education needed all the help they could get.

Mid-March

OVER THE WEEKS that her cousin Fereshteh had been in prison, Nikou had become an astute observer.

She watched her husband. She watched the housekeeper. And she played her role as the subservient, dutiful wife. When she went to see her parents or her brothers' families, she played her role. Nothing had changed except that she watched. And listened very carefully. At the end of each day she sat in the den and while pretending to read, went over in her mind everything that had transpired, trying to parse out any information that she could use.

It had been tragic that Jamshid had died. She couldn't imagine how Fereshteh and the children felt. And she'd never know because all contact with them continued to be completely cut. None of her family went to the funeral. No one had offered any condolences. No one seemed to know where he'd been buried. Baha'is often found themselves without a cemetery that would take them. More and more of their own cemeteries had been desecrated and then destroyed.

Nikou kept thoughts of Fereshteh at bay. She simply couldn't bear to think about what her cousin might be going through. But she kept her face in her mind's eye. She held her there like a kind of icon. Like a star in the sky, giving her direction. Nikou knew her ultimate goal was far off, but if she at least had a goal post, a grail of sorts, she'd be able to focus and act.

She'd started going out. The high-class shopping malls and pedestrian boulevards of north Tehran were the "normal" destination of the well-to-do. She explored them all again, enjoying the experience all the more for having been confined for so many months.

She'd walk the long stretches of trendy designer stores along Vali Asr Avenue's main drag and duck into little pedestrian alley-ways, where specialty boutiques shared space with older, more traditional shops. She'd pick up clothes, toys and trinkets of all kinds for her nieces and nephews, for her parents, her cousins, even her grandparents. Herself.

She visited Tajrish Square's popular Tandis Center mall, then its Old Bazaar. She even wandered the pedestrian alleys of its Ghaem shopping center. Much more modest, but Nikou loved the down-to-earthiness of it all. And she loved the people-watching.

Parks were everywhere and when she'd had enough of Vali Asr's bustle, she'd nip across to the tranquility and beauty of Saiee Park.

In Niyavaran's park further north, she spent hours in its tasteful, well-appointed public library. She sipped coffee in the park's courtyard Café Gallerie. When she wanted a classy meal, she'd go to Qeytarieh or Darband. The choices were many and the atmosphere in some would rival anything anywhere. Nikou was a regular at such places.

Whatever else her husband was, he wasn't stingy. He needed her to "look good", so she had a credit card. It bought her anything that served to project her in the image most flattering to *his* public persona.

She visited museums around the city and attended cultural events. Getting out enabled her to breathe and it picked up her spirits. It also made it easier to create her intended impression of the fortunate wife of a successful man.

Surprisingly, he even allowed her to have friends. No one close, of course. He didn't want a repeat of the Marjan incident. But he allowed her to meet up with the wives of the men he thought were important. For social events. Where she could be seen. Where she could be watched. It was clear that her husband had given her a long leash because he was completely secure in his network of spies.

She had also improved her performance on the domestic front.

She became creative in planning menus and in decorating their home so that Mehrdad's guests would be suitably impressed. She spent hours in the garden, planning new projects for the landscapers that he'd agreed to engage. Although he never thanked her for any of that, she knew he was satisfied.

In the middle of March she began a new project: redecorating some rooms. Under its guise, she had the opportunity to study their every detail. The room that received her greatest attention was the lounge he reserved for "special guests". She knew it was sound-proofed, for one thing, but she noted that its "security cameras" were more discreet in size and placement. Mehrdad permitted her to change the furniture to a more sophisticated style, but had been adamant that the wood paneling would remain.

NIKOU'S DEDICATION to her goal yielded its first payoff: she had identified two of her monitors. These were not the security guards now posted at the house, nor the ones that had recently been assigned to protect her husband. These were a couple of his "spies". She smiled at the cloak-and-dagger sound of it. But she was dead serious. Now *she* could monitor *them*.

LATE MARCH

NIKOU COULDN'T LET it rest. She was still looking for answers, but regardless of the tactics she used, she got very little. What was so hush-hush about Jamshid's death, his funeral — his whole family? Her cousin Aryana had come home for her father's funeral and, strangely enough, it looked as though she'd be staying. This information came through the grapevine of snide remarks exchanged among her brothers and uncles. They never seemed to tire of criticizing their "unpatriotic, disloyal foreign-educated" cousins.

It occurred to Nikou that this regular gripe might be her family's way of dealing with some jealousy issues. And it wasn't just the men.

Her aunts, sisters-in-law and all her women cousins were the same. They played the game, toed the line, kept to their appropriate "women's pursuits" and performed the duties expected of proper wives and mothers loyal to the ethos of the regime. That made it so much easier. Nikou knew this first hand, since she'd been doing that all her life until — . She called it "being beaten *out* of submission".

Nikou was tired of listening behind doors to get news of what was going on. She was tired of being treated like a child, especially like a dim-witted one. There was only one source she could possibly turn to in her extended family. And it was a gamble.

SOHAYLA WELCOMED her granddaughter with a huge hug and kissed her on both cheeks.

"Come in, come in, my Nikoujoon! Oh, it's so lovely to see you! Life gets so busy, you know, with this family of ours. I've lost count of all the great-grandchildren now. I'm just hoping I can continue to keep track of all the rest of you!" Her laughter lit up her still lovely face as she grasped Nikou by the shoulders, holding her there so she could gaze at her fully.

Releasing her finally, Sohayla led the way to the cozy sitting room that looked out onto her beautiful flower beds. Hyacinths, narcissi, and tulips were already blooming. They stood for a moment as Nikou exclaimed on the beauty of the blooms, genuinely amazed. Her grandmother still insisted on personally planning and overseeing all the plantings in the large grounds. Sohayla tut-tutted at the praise but Nikou knew she was pleased.

"Now *Azizam*, please sit and let me pour your tea — no, no *ta'arof*, no, I won't have any of that. You know how much I enjoy having you come. Please, indulge your old grandmother and let her feel useful!"

Nikou smiled and said, "*Chashm* — of course." And for the next little while they sipped tea, ate home-made cookies and talked about everything and nothing.

As Sohayla returned from the kitchen with a fresh pot of tea,

Nikou took her chance. "So cousin Jamshid died, I heard." Sohayla hesitated a moment in mid-pour but continued to fill Nikou's and her own glasses. Nikou forged ahead.

"I know that Grandfather doesn't like us talking about it and for sure my father won't discuss any of it either, but really, *Khanumjan*, I know they know exactly what's going on and I wonder why I don't. Why maybe my other cousins don't either. I mean, is it so bad to just have news about family members? I thought I heard that Aryana actually came back and might be staying. Is that true?"

"From where have you heard these things, *Joonam*?" Sohayla asked cautiously.

"Oh, just bits of conversation here and there. But it's like some big horrible secret. What's going on? Is it really too much to have just some facts? And while I'm on the subject, why are so many other things in this family so hush-hush? It's like the men have all the information and we women get only what they dole out. I really don't even know my own family! It's not right, *Khanumjan*!"

Sohayla considered this for a good minute. Nikou waited and sipped. Finally, with a sigh, her grandmother seemed to come to a decision. She looked at her granddaughter and asked, "What would you like to know?"

IT WAS the dinner hour by the time they finished. As Nikou had suspected, Sohayla was the keeper of the family secrets. She seemed relieved to pass these on. She'd admitted that she'd kept everything in her head and heart for a very long time, sharing nothing that wasn't considered "general knowledge".

"So why me?" Nikou wanted to know. "Why did you agree to tell me all this? I'm sure it's not just because I asked. My asking hasn't gotten me anywhere with anyone else."

"Because there is something special about you, my dear girl. I don't know what it is, just a feeling I suppose — but a strong feeling. You see, I always confided in Farah, but since she passed, I haven't felt comfortable with anyone else. Who listens to an old lady like me? My sons? Ha! Never! And my daughters? No, they're tired of their mother's concerns and advice. And they're too busy with their social lives." Glancing down at her hands, she sighed, then looked directly at her granddaughter. "You, Nikou, have no ego, no need to impress. You're never going to use gossip or information to hurt others. You're a lot like Farah in certain ways. You have a kindness and strength that I can't really describe. Farah had this." Her eyes were moist.

NIKOU GRACIOUSLY BOWED OUT of her grandmother's invitation to stay for dinner, saying that she needed to see to dinner at her own home. This was not true; Mehrdad had dinner plans elsewhere. But the girl saw that Sohayla was tired. She also recognized that both she and her grandmother had much to think about and digest after sharing such confidences.

As Nikou drove home, she basked in the warmth of the love, trust and keen insight that her grandmother had shown her. More than ever, she respected and loved this generous woman who was so unlike most of her family.

Sitting at a traffic light, Nikou considered what she'd actually learned from Sohayla: Yes, Jamshid had died after a car accident. No, Sohayla didn't know where he was buried, but she knew that the only one of the cousins who'd come back for the funeral was Aryana. Aryana was planning to stay. "She must feel so lonely and isolated," Sohayla had murmured. "Such a sweet girl and you two always got along so well."

She'd looked Nikou in the eye and continued, "Your grandfather remains firm in his opinion that Fereshteh was responsible for your Great Aunt Farah's death and that no one in his family should have any contact with anyone in Fereshteh's. So, I guess it would be wise to stay away from them, or..." Sohayla had hinted, "at least not get caught seeing them."

Nikou had asked about Fereshteh's arrest.

"She should have known better," Sohayla had sighed, "but it was what they're calling her subversive professional activities that got Fereshteh arrested. And especially since she's a Baha'i, they'll use it to justify the usual accusations against them. So it doesn't look good for her." Sohayla had paused, her look far away. "How well I remember what happened to Layla. What a tragedy! Really, we were all heartbroken. I still don't know how Farah ever coped with that. And now, how would she have coped with Fereshteh in prison? Oh God!"

Nikou had urged her grandmother to tell her what she knew about Layla.

"You know, she was always an unusual girl. She was bright and cheerful, sweet and intelligent. Exceptional. And stubborn. So stubborn. When she believed in something — no matter what it was — she stuck to it. Yet she wasn't unwilling to change her opinion if there was a good reason to.

"She was not a fanatic," she emphasized, "No, she was not a fanatic, so don't think that, Nikou! But in matters of faith and morals she was a true idealist. She wouldn't budge and it showed in the community work she did. She was a person of action. We all worried about her, of course, when the Revolution started. We all tried to get her to stop. But she wouldn't."

Sohayla had looked into the distance of her memories and paused a moment. "And this drove Fereshteh crazy. I know she loved Layla, but she could never understand the — what would you call it? — zeal? Yes, zeal, I guess. The zeal Layla had in the face of the craziness of those days. She used to say that Layla was like a candle burning at both ends and that she was going to burn herself to ashes if she didn't stop. Fereshteh was really terrified for her sister and even after all these years I don't think she's ever gotten over it. I used to watch her, you know, after Layla was executed. She'd sometimes go so silent and look like she was far, far off somewhere else. She had a kind of haunted look."

The stoplight at last turned green and Nikou surged forward. Carried along by the pulse of the early evening traffic, she let snatches of her grandmother's other anecdotes flow through her mind. A family history in one afternoon that filled in so many blanks in what Nikou had known about.

It wasn't until after a light supper of left-over soup that Nikou went into her den. A mug of hot water with lemon in her hand, she sat in her usual armchair and stared at the new painting on the opposite wall. She'd found it in a little art shop a couple of weeks earlier.

Modest in measurement, it depicted a skier's path through a birch forest. Bright, fresh snow weighed heavily on every shrub and tree. A single pair of skis had left a trail into the wood, crossing over the blue snow shadows, and disappearing over the hill. Flecks of blue sky penetrated the highest branches, but it was the light in the center of the picture that captured the eye: an orange-yellow glow emerging from the heart of the cold, crisp winter scene.

The trail of *Khanumjan's* stories traveled through her mind. Nikou followed it and latched onto the one about her grandfather and his own mother. According to Farah, Sohayla had said, Reza had never gotten over blaming his mother's "crazy Western ideas" for taking her away from them. Throughout the decades of their life together Sohayla had seen this anger burn. He tended it like some sacred fire, she'd said. "You've heard him, Nikou. How he sometimes rants about 'foreigners' and the importance of 'traditional values'. How upset he's always been about your cousins being overseas."

"So, he needs a whipping boy," Nikou had suggested. "He has to take it all out on someone else?"

"Unfortunately, yes." Sohayla had fidgeted with her rings and bracelets, her mouth set in an uncharacteristic tight line. She'd looked up but not at Nikou. "His favorite 'whipping boy', as you call it, has always been a girl. It's always been Fereshteh."

Early April

She amazed herself. Nikou never could have imagined herself stealing anything at all, let alone cash from her family. But she was doing it, and she was, quite strangely, proud.

Once she'd figured out who was watching her — she'd identified

Crimson Ink

a third man — she'd needed to make a plan. The men had a regular schedule, she'd discovered, and with that as a constant, she'd finally developed her strategy.

She needed phones. She couldn't buy any without a credit card and Mehrdad controlled the statements. If she withdrew cash, he would know and want a full accounting of where she'd spent it. So she needed another source of cash. Her family had been the only alternative. Every time she paid any one of them a visit she'd find ways of nosing out cash. Sometimes it was lying around; sometimes she had to snoop. But she usually found something. She never took noticeable amounts, but still, it was funny how a family so flush with it was also so careless.

Now she had enough to get what she needed and she knew where to go to get it.

Her plan was to exploit the weakness she'd discovered in one of her "minders". He was a pretty laid-back guy. He looked so bored, even pretending to make calls or read newspapers. She'd seen him nod off a few times. *He probably has an active nightlife*, she thought, smiling.

She left the house every day now. The warmer weather invited outings of all kinds. She was patient and waited for the right opportunity to get her phones.

THE "BORED GUY", as she'd named him, had fallen asleep in his car by the curb. He'd seen her go into the little boutique often, so he obviously figured she was doing her usual mid-week rounds.

Nikou had laid the groundwork well. Out the rear service door of the boutique and into the service door of the electronic shop two doors down. She'd done a couple of practice runs already and even when her 'minder' had been awake, he'd never seen her.

She conducted her business quickly, her face largely invisible under the cover of the full chador she'd packed into her tote to serve as disguise. *These things do have their uses*, she thought. Three cheap phones, a half dozen SIM cards. Mobile internet. All cash.

When she exited the boutique — *manteau* and headscarf still in place, but minus the chador — her monitor was still snoozing. *Must have had a very short night*, she thought, and chuckled to herself.

It was easy to set up the phones while at the café. The place was full - as usual. She went into the ladies room and made her first call. She had no idea who the person was, but she knew it as the number that Fereshteh had repeated over and over to Marjan. A woman answered. She was pleasant but cautious. It took some time for Nikou to convince her that her request was genuine. Still, the woman was taking precautions. Nikou wasn't going to leave anything to chance this time. She insisted she needed to meet today and eventually the woman on the other end agreed.

They met at Yas, a busy restaurant that Nikou often went to. She needed to keep her routine as normal as possible, no matter how sleepy her "minder" might be. Nikou emerged from the ladies room a minute later in her black chador and new headscarf. Its purple and gold pattern was visible by several inches, identifying her to the woman contact who'd promised to book their table.

The ruse was successful. During this first meeting, the two women enjoyed an "ordinary" lunch while discussing extraordinary things.

In the afternoon, Nikou went into a dress shop. It was among her frequent stops, although it was a modest establishment. She'd found the owner to be a pleasant woman and they'd had many a conversation in the old style of the bazaar, where customers enjoyed a glass of tea while discussing the weather, the gossip and the merchandise under consideration. It was easier than she'd imagined.

They sat together now at the little round table in the corner. Tea glasses and an oval silver bowl containing sugar cubes sat on the embroidered linen cloth. An ornate old silver teapot steamed above a small samovar to one side.

"Sure," the owner said, pouring another glass for each of them,

" I know that ladies sometimes have too many things weighing down their handbags. I have a place in the back where they can store such things. It's quite secure, my dear." She smiled at Nikou. "You can lock them up and come get them any time that my shop is open. No problem. I do this for a few of my regular customers." No questions. She understood that sometimes women needed some special help. "We need to stick together." The woman patted her hand and gave her a wink.

End of April

EAVESDROPPING CONTINUED to be a vital strategy. She needed information and even Sohayla couldn't know everything. Nikou's skills in listening at doors were yielding good results. And, invisible as she was to most of the family anyway, no one noticed her.

She picked up all sorts of tidbits about the family's activities and began to piece them together. She'd been surprised but not completely shocked to learn about her father's, uncles' and brothers' business dealings and how far their colluding went. Thanks to Uncle Saeed, their links with high-ranking Revolutionary Guard officers, both former and current, were solid. Every week, it seemed, someone in the family was getting a new construction contract from somewhere in the system. No wonder the business had expanded so much! Aside from the new sports cars and ever-flashier accoutrements and gadgets, there was now talk of buying new properties up in the mountains. She'd even heard that Uncle Farid had recently bought a villa in Dubai.

Once in a while she heard something about Habib calling but there was never anything of substance. No one spoke a word about Fereshteh, Taraneh or Aryana.

And that was a problem. She wanted to know how to reach her cousin. However much she watched or listened, she couldn't find out anything. She suspected that Aryana would be staying at her family's apartment, but there was no way Nikou could go there. She needed to make phone contact. If she could at least find out where her cousin worked, she could call her there. Nikou would have to ask her grandmother what she knew.

As it happened, Sohayla did *not* know where Aryana worked, nor did she have a cell phone number for her.

"But of course, Nikoujoon, I do know where Habib works. And Taraneh. Unless they have changed their jobs. Would that be helpful?"

Taking the small slip of paper in her hand, Nikou gave her grandmother a warm squeeze and smiled. "*Khanumjoon*, you have been very helpful. Thank you!"

She lost no time in finding the main number of Habib's employer. Within a few minutes, Nikou had her connection.

It was generally assumed by Fereshteh's side of the family that by now all cell phone calls were being monitored. True or not, they preferred to take the precaution of avoiding anything beyond utilitarian or banal topics on their phones, and for this reason, Habib didn't give Nikou Aryana's cell number. He discouraged Nikou from calling her landline. "No, Aryana's not home much; no sense calling her there." Fereshteh's landline. He didn't have to say that it was surely tapped.

Nikou had had to warn Habib about her own situation. But she also told him that she'd found ways to get around this. They arranged that Habib would get Aryana to meet Nikou the following week at Ghahvechi Café using the same ruse Nikou had used to meet the stranger at Yas. If anything changed, Habib would call Nikou's 'burn phone' that day, or Nikou could call him at work.

Five days later, a chadored Nikou sat opposite an equally chadored Aryana, sipping espresso and eating chocolate croissants.

Crimson Ink

When they had caught up on most of the news that both connected and divided them, Nikou asked more and more about Fereshteh. She pressed her cousin so insistently that Aryana finally sat back, looking puzzled and concerned.

"Excuse me, Nikou, but why are you suddenly so interested in my mother? I mean, sure, I understand why you'd ask some of these things, but really, it's not like you two were ever very close."

"You're right. And we both know why my family couldn't get close to your mom, don't we?"

Aryana nodded. "So tell me, though — why? What's up? You know she's in Evin. I've told you as much as I can about how she's managing there. What else can I say? I haven't been here much over the last few years and even now I only know what Uncle Habib and Aunt Taraneh have told me about how she got arrested in the first place. Your family won't talk to ours and Grandfather Hassan's and my dad's families are still living in the provinces so we never see them. And what would they know anyway? And I can't exactly go to Maman's medical practice and ask anything. What else could I possibly tell you? And again, why is it so important to you?" Her tone expressed curiosity.

"Did your mom ever tell you about the time she took care of me in her office? Last November?"

"No, why would she?"

"Because I'm a close relative. Because of what she saw. Because of what happened to me. Are you sure she never said anything?"

"Never. Maman is very careful about confidentiality. Even if on the odd occasion she said something at home about some atrocious thing she saw at work, she never told us the person's name. So, no. I don't know anything about your visit to her office."

"May I tell you about it?"

And then Nikou bared her soul.

"THAT's why I'm so interested. I owe your mother my life, Aryana. My life! And now, because she helped me —" Nikou's voice caught and her hand flew to her face.

Aryana slumped. She buried her face in both hands and sat very still.

In a whisper, Nikou said, "So I feel responsible for her. I've felt sick ever since I suspected it was because of me. It couldn't have been a coincidence, Aryana." Her slender hand whisked the moisture from her cheeks. "And her being a Baha'i just made it so easy." Grabbing a tissue from her bag, she blew her nose.

Aryana looked up and straightened her back. "But —"

"There were other reasons, too, but I'll tell you about them another time." Nikou looked at her watch and glanced out the café window. "My 'minder' is going to get suspicious, so I've got to go. Can we meet here next week, same time?"

Late April

"Come in, Minoujoon, come in!" Habib welcomed Fereshteh's friend with a huge smile.

Taraneh appeared from the kitchen and embraced their visitor. "So good to see you, Minoujoon! It's been a long time." She led their guest to the sofa, saying, "Come, sit down. I've just prepared the tea."

Habib sat down across from her and began the warm pleasantries that reconnected old friends.

When the second glass of tea had been served, Minou came to the point of her visit.

"You know, I've been calling Fereshteh for a while and she hasn't answered. Then I thought, okay, with Naw-Ruz and everything, she's probably busy and out a lot. My family and I have been busy too, of course. But after a couple of weeks I began to wonder if something was wrong. I've called and called and left so many messages on her cell phone that —"

"Her cell phone? Not her landline?" Habib exchanged a quick

glance with Taraneh then looked back at Minou. "Because Aryana is at Fereshteh's and she would have gotten your messages."

Taraneh looked at Habib, then back at their visitor and explained, "Minoujoon, we're sorry to give you this news, but Fereshteh was arrested over two months ago. She's in Evin."

THE AFTERNOON WANED and they asked Minou to stay for dinner. She accepted.

After the generous meal, the women cleared away the dishes. Habib prepared the tea and brought it to the table with fruit and sweets.

Minou helped herself to an orange and began peeling it. "You know, I really can't say that I'm surprised that Fereshteh was arrested."

She looked up and hastened to clarify herself. "No, don't get me wrong! This is not a criticism. Not at all! It's just that I've always known what a passion she has for justice and standing up for the unfortunate."

She worked on her orange. "Not that she made it obvious. We all know what she — and you" — she looked at Habib — "went through in Shiraz. And she wasn't sort of 'out there' like Layla was. You and Fereshteh were never obvious about the way you helped others. But the point is, you did it."

"Yes, what you say about Fereshteh is true. She's always been the most sensitive one in our family. I guess she's always understood the world's 'underdogs'," said Habib, slicing his pear vigorously.

"But this time it seems her 'helpfulness' came up on someone's radar," said Taraneh. "Still, though, even now, even in that horrible place with all she must be going through," Taraneh paused and shivered, "she says she regrets nothing. She's been telling Aryana that she was simply doing her job. She's a doctor and she has a duty to take care of those who need her."

Habib said, "That's right. She wouldn't call it this, but I know that she considers her work a 'sacred duty'. She feels that it's her moral responsibility to use her abilities to help other people."

Minou chewed her orange pensively, then went on, "I get that. But I guess that even though I've always understood your altruism, and even practiced it in my own small ways, I don't want to go to prison because of it." She forked another orange slice. "No, even though I can understand being true to high ideals, I just don't get how far you folks are willing to go for them."

Habib sipped his tea for a minute, then said, "I think it's a matter of being aware of the gray areas and the so-called 'slippery slope.'"

"What do you mean?"

"Well, standing up for ideals is a lot of hard work. Really hard sometimes. Especially if you get flack for it. Sometimes it's easier to dissimulate, or take short cuts or to compromise. You know, do the 'expedient' thing instead of taking the moral high road."

He put a couple of rice cookies on his plate. "Ever read Sartre?"

"As in Jean-Paul? A bit."

"Well, if you've ever read 'Les Mains Sales', that says it all. The story of an idealist who finds that to further his utopian agenda he has to compromise himself quite radically. And as the title says, he gets his hands dirty because 'the end justifies the means'. That's what I mean by the 'slippery slope'. Once you take that road… well, you know."

"And that's what we try *not* to do, said Taraneh. That's why we try to stick to principles. And it *is* hard, let me tell you. Really, if we didn't have each other's support, I don't know how we'd make it through some days." She nibbled a cookie. "But of course, the biggest help we have is prayer." She looked openly at Minou. "I'm sure you're laughing at that, Minou. But it's true. We're still at it!" She chuckled.

Minou smiled in turn. "I know. And I'm not laughing. I'm not praying either, but I respect people who do pray." She helped herself to more tea from the pot, and continued.

"You know, over the years Fereshteh and I talked a lot about these things and she went on about your vision of the future. You know, the whole thing about the 'unity of mankind' as she calls it. Justice and equality for everyone, universal education, science and religion being complementary — well!" She laughed, "Hey, why am I telling you? It's your religion and this is what you all believe, right! Anyway, what I'm trying to say is that, while I agree with these things — and I really do agree with them — and while in my own way I do my bit, I can't forget that it was for some of these very same principles that we had the Revolution. I don't mean the mullahs. We all know what they wanted. But the Revolution itself was not bad. It was necessary and everyone knew it. Look at all the different groups that helped make the Revolution possible. They were all idealists. Each group had its vision of a great society for us. Everyone wanted a change for some kind of ideal. *Then* look what happened." She put down her empty tea glass with an emphatic *clink*.

Taraneh said, "Well, sure, but have you thought about the fact that all those different groups had somewhat narrow agendas? Which one of them really embraced *all* Iranians? I mean, regardless of their religious or political affiliations or beliefs? And what about those with no affiliations? If any of those groups had gotten into power, would they have — despite their ideals and good intentions — would they have been able to accept *everyone*? Would they have made room for everyone's beliefs? Or lack of them, for that matter?"

Habib added, "I think what Taraneh is saying is that what's really needed is a very broad vision. One that includes humanity as a whole. And a broad vision is also a long-term one. It can't happen in the short or medium term. It has to be built brick by brick with enormous inputs from all kinds of people and institutions."

Minou interrupted, "But people want change now! In '78 and '79 no one had patience for any long-term or long-range vision. People were fed up. People's rights had been trampled underfoot for decades and folks had had enough. They wanted a rapid change, they saw their chance and they took it. I was among them. I was in those marches before and after the Shah imposed martial law. I knew the mood of the people, and believe me, they weren't going to back down or back up!"

"Yes, Minou, you're right," said Habib. "You're absolutely right. But you see, there's where the real problem lies. It's true that we need immediate and interim solutions for the huge problems we face. But the fact that such problems exist in the first place means that there's never been a longer, broader vision to work towards over time. We keep putting bandages on society's wounds instead. The bandages are necessary and sometimes life-saving, but they're not a cure for what causes the wounds in the first place."

"So what are you saying?"

"I'm saying that we need to get down to principles that raise our consciousness about who we are as a country. And even more, who we are as a human race. Until we realize that we're all equal members of one human race and until we recognize that when one part of humanity hurts, it affects all parts, all we'll do is keep applying bandages while the disease continues to ravage us."

"Lofty ideas, Habib. Lofty. But as I've always told Fereshteh, they're unrealistic. Look at the world we live in!"

"You're right to be skeptical," said Taraneh. "We've seen so much misery here. And the rest of the planet isn't looking much better." She leaned forward and looked earnestly at Minou. "But you see, Minou, here's where it comes down to *belief*. Intellectual knowledge is important, yes. In fact, to create the means to achieve the long-term vision that the Baha'i Writings talk about, we need lots of knowledge, both intellectual and practical. Creating a different world based on what you're calling 'lofty principles' takes a huge amount of work done by millions and millions of people. But it has to start somewhere and it has to have people who have not just an ideal vision, but also *faith* in that vision. That's the key element. Without *faith* in it, given how hard it all is to achieve, we'd eventually give up."

"So you mean *faith* as in the faith of martyrs?"

"Yes, but not everyone's a martyr. You can live a normal life and still have faith in a vision. Faith in a religion."

"So you mean like the early Shi'as? Maybe even the early Christians?"

"Certainly," said Habib. "Actually, millions of people have a faith in something and try to live by the principles of their belief. In their own ways, they're furthering good things in the world."

"So where does the concept of dying for your belief come in? And why would someone do that? I just don't get it. It's not worth it."

"You don't think it's worth it?" asked Taraneh.

"No, I don't. I can just say I don't believe, but privately still keep my beliefs anyway."

"But isn't that just capitulating? If we all did that, there'd never be any new movements and no human progress. If the early Baha'is had done that, none of us would be here now to work towards a broad vision for the whole world."

"But it's not just us," said Habib. "Think about it: history is full of examples of people who refused to bow to tyranny. Think even about people like the philosopher-scientists – Galileo, for example – who stood up to the religious authorities. They stood by their beliefs and some paid the ultimate price. Even now, even today, just look at the political prisoners, the activists and the journalists in our own country who refuse to give up what they stand for. How much of *their* blood has been spilled? Do you think they've wasted it?"

Minou, elbows on the table, stared at her clasped hands. "I hope not," she murmured, "I hope not."

Chapter Seven

2011

MAY – JUNE

MAY

They had let Aryana visit her mother only sporadically since her return to Tehran. The reunions had been emotional; the tears had been a sweet and salty mix of joy and grief, buoyancy and anxiety. Sometimes they had a full half hour, sometimes they were separated after fifteen minutes. They learned to talk quickly and speak volumes with their eyes and hands.

Microphones in the meeting booths recorded whatever was said, so the visits were never really private. Aryana could not tell her mother about her work, professional or personal. Neither could Fereshteh tell her daughter about the horrors of her incarceration; she would pay for such a revelation instantly on return to her cell. But Aryana could see on her mother's face the signs of malnourishment, sleeplessness, stress and constant anxiety. While in the U.K. she'd heard and read too many stories and seen too many online videos of "the bloody decade" of the 1980s not to know how inhumanely prisoners could be treated.

Yet this galvanized her. *My mother is not in prison in vain. My father did not die in vain.* She repeated this over and again every day. She repurposed her anxieties, transforming the energy and infusing it into her work for the education of others.

Her aunt and uncle had mentored her closely and she was quick to understand. She followed the "rules" of working with BIHE to the letter. No taking chances, no running risks.

She'd done a bit of student teaching while at university, but she'd never seen anything like the thirst for knowledge and the diligence that characterized the work of these students. She soon learned that she could push them hard and they'd respond eagerly. Invigorated, she barely felt the load of her long working hours.

DURING THE THIRD week in May she went to see her uncle. Outside the apartment door she was surprised to hear her aunt's voice. It was too early for her to be home yet from her day job. Aryana knocked a few times before her aunt heard her. Taraneh was still talking on her cell phone when she opened the door and motioned her in. Clearly, something was very wrong.

"... No, I don't know. Who else can I call? Give me the number, please! Okay, I've got it. Anyone else? What? Right. Okay, I understand. Thank you." Taraneh ended the call and turned to Aryana, who stood stock still as she tried to absorb the situation.

Giving her a quick, tense hug, Taraneh said, "They've arrested him. And several others. Nobody seems to know where they are. I've called everyone I can think of. They're all upset and no one knows where they've taken them!" She paced the floor rapidly, talking to her niece but apparently still thinking of her next move.

"Tell me what I can do," said her niece, moving further into the room.

"Aryana, I have to make some more calls. Maybe you could see to this? With a sweep of her hand she indicated the living and dining room, then pointed to the study.

Everything had been ransacked. Papers lay on floors and furniture, drawers lay overturned, closets emptied, and computer components were missing. Aryana got to work. She made notes of what was there and what was obviously missing.

It was hours later that Taraneh finally had enough information to piece together some basics, but it would be days before the story would become clear. During that time Aryana stayed at her aunt's.

They finally learned that the homes of about forty BIHE staff around the country had been raided that day. Estimates were that nearly twenty people had been arrested but it seemed that more than half had been released after extensive questioning. At this point, numbers were still inaccurate. The only thing that Taraneh and Aryana knew for certain was that Habib was still missing.

Aryana bore the sad news when she next visited Fereshteh. Never knowing how long they might have together, she made her point quickly.

"Aunt Taraneh wanted to come visit you as well, Maman," she said, "but Dayi Habib suddenly had to travel and she's dealing with that." This was how she had begun. She had to couch her tale in their own style of coded language.

Fereshteh, though stunned, kept up appearances. Who knew what repercussions could come out of a conversation as loaded as this one? *Maman's becoming very savvy at survival*, thought Aryana, who was truly impressed by her mother's fortitude.

"Yes, his 'hosts' are insisting he should stay with them for a while," Aryana said. "We don't know how long he's likely to be away, but since Aunt Taraneh is still at home, I'm sure she'll visit you when she can."

Fereshteh nodded slowly. Her face was paler than ever now and she was rubbing her arm.

Aryana, her eyes wide and over-bright, went on, "She'll keep busy, though. So will I. We'll miss him but we have plenty to do. And you know how much we enjoy each other's company." She smiled at her mother. "Really, Maman, I'll give her a hand, don't worry."

With little else they dared say on the subject, they spent the rest of their time covering their wounded hearts with the veneer of banal chit-chat.

LATE MAY
FERESHTEH'S CELL

IN EARLY MAY her interrogations had suddenly abated and they'd moved Fereshteh to a new cell, which, although larger, offered little external relief and certainly no distractions.

Previously, after long hours of being harangued and beaten, she'd welcomed the relief that her cell in "Solitary" had provided. But now, in her new one, her jailers were, apparently, applying the torture of boredom.

At first, all she did was ruminate. She relived her horrors in order to process them. Relived her despair, her anger, her grief.

At some point, she found room to expand her thoughts, and every day ventured further afield. She tapped into memories and felt their comfort. And pain. She began to ask herself questions about those memories. About herself. About her life. About her actions. About her relationships.

But as she explored, she became aware of a pit. A special space within her subconscious that contained something dark and appalling. At first she ignored it. After a while, however, she had a clear sense that although she'd tried to seal it off through the artifice of self-deceit, a crack had formed. And it was widening.

A growing sense of dread began to slither within her like the presence of a living creature. It hissed and its cold stale breath whispered a warning of things that she would rather not see or hear or know.

ONE NIGHT the pit blew open and the monster emerged. As she lay on her blanket, it clawed away all the scar tissue that had bound up her grief, and set her heart's wounds' bleeding once again. As this ran its course and finally reduced to a trickle, a heavy, nameless sorrow descended. She sat in the darkness of it with only the monster as companion.

No Maman. No Jamshid. And now no Habib. Taken to a fate as uncertain as her own, he was disappearing from her too. His face blurring and fading as she watched the void claim him. All her understanding, her coping mechanisms, her plans and strategies lay in shards before her, demolished by the hissing beast.

It claimed her and pushed her over the edge. She was in free-fall into an abyss of insecurity and anxiety. Into an unknown place where all she could feel was small and vulnerable, as if she were plummeting into her earliest schooldays when the ways of the world and of adults had been frightening because they'd been a mystery to her.

But now, infinitely smaller, infinitely more vulnerable than in those long-ago days, she quaked as a figure emerged from the blackness and walked toward her.

She saw a failed woman. A selfish woman. A woman whose only desire was self-preservation. This woman wanted only to hide. To escape. To not 'have to'. Not 'have to' live up to high standards, not 'have to' be 'best' at what she did, not 'have to' do her duty to family, friends, job, or community. Not 'have to' keep up the fiction that she'd created so that others wouldn't see the hollow core of the shell that she knew she really was. A fake. A coward who wanted nothing more than to evaporate and be done with the demands of life.

Out of control and subject to forces she failed to fathom, she plunged further down: into something like a black space with no markers, no parameters of any kind from which to gather a sense of where or how or why. With neither handle nor anchor, she seemed to float.

This looseness terrified her.

AT LENGTH, she became still. There was nothing now to struggle against. Nothing to push. Nothing to rail against. She let her

Crimson Ink

muscles relax. She let herself float in the darkness behind her eyelids.

Then, from her core, her heart of hearts, something welled up. On its own it emerged: a longing, a yearning. Threads of prayers and sacred verses, long ago memorized, floated up, circled, and wove themselves around her, embracing her, hiding her from the terror.

Her mother's voice, a whisper, floated by: "*Me-gozareh, janam, me-gozareh.* It will pass, my dear one, it will pass. Just trust in God. Just trust."

Her inner voice, a silent breath, echoed, "I'm trying, Maman, I'm trying, I'm trying."

SHE WALKED A LONG BEACH, disoriented in her widowhood, in the absence of loved ones and all that was familiar. The sea and sand and sky gave her a sense of grounding. But, she knew, even in her dream, that that was only temporary.

She continued to walk. The shore seemed endless, the sand unchanging, the gentle waves somehow reassuring in their regularity. The sun was at its zenith in a cloudless sky. She had no shadow behind or before her. There was no past or future. There was only a now. Placing one foot in front of the other, she moved forward. Her footsteps were light and her rhythm soft and easy.

SHE OPENED HER EYES. Calm. The woven strands of prayer and verse still circled; still floated with her in the nothingness surrounding her.

At length, fragments of thoughts began to drift through her mind. How was she going to get through this imprisonment? Desperate for security, desperate for hope, she clung for a moment to analytical thought. *There must be a way out of this. There must!*

The heroes of the *Shahnameh* drifted in, but, answerless, they disintegrated. She scanned her memories. Was there anything there to cling to? Her children. Yes. But the older two and their families were so far away. In a country she'd never get to. Yet Aryana was here. Aryana, precious, feisty Aryana was here. Taraneh was here. But she worried for them, terrified lest they be next. Like the others she'd lost.

Her mind returned to the years of the Revolution. Homes and living arrangements had been caught in the upheaval. Trust had been betrayed. A sister had been executed. As had so many others she'd known. So many others. *Something. I must find something to hold onto!*

She closed her eyes again and, focusing on her breathing, slowed it. The gentle whispers returned. They brought fragments from other stories. She began to see other heroes and heroines. The ones who'd fought the greatest battles of all: the battles of the spirit. She saw their devotion, their detachment, and their reliance on their Maker. But still she wavered, feeling herself swing on an invisible pendulum between Letting Go and Holding On. She wanted to be – but she knew she wasn't – like those heroes.

She slipped into and out of sleep, her thoughts and dreams intersecting in their travels.

She was floating again, surrendered now to the gentle whispers. As her heart and soul sought her Maker, she wondered, *Has He loosened me from everything to let me float in this nothingness? Float here so I can begin to let go and truly rely only on Him? Finally?*

Waking again, she sat up, still held in the embrace of the whispers. Aloud, she murmured to herself, "This is the message, is it? Accept whatever comes? Embrace it? Is this really my lesson? Am I able?"

Fatigue overtook her again. Maybe that was good. She laid back down on her blanket, closed her eyes, and slept deeply.

Late May

For the third time that week Kamran Rahimi woke up in a cold sweat and sat up in bed. He ran his hands through his thick, curly hair and blinked his eyes. The sleepless city outside cast a dim light through the bedroom curtains, and he slowly took in the familiar shapes of the heavy furniture. Zahra's gentle breathing beside him reassured him all was well around him.

But all was not well within him. He got up and went to the bathroom, closing its door quietly behind him. In its bright light he looked at himself in the mirror then splashed water on his face until he was fully awake. He looked up again and saw the reflection of a man's long thin haggard face. The dark circles below the eyes seemed larger, the cheeks hollower, the forehead creases more pronounced than he remembered.

Leaving the bathroom, he padded through the hall and over the lush living room carpets to the huge windows. He opened the sliding glass door and stepped out onto the large balcony. The warm breeze brought the distant drone of the earliest commuter traffic. Staring out over the panorama of city lights, he breathed deeply to slow the thumping in his chest.

The dreams. The recurring dreams. His father, his grandfather, his brother Mahmoud. Yazd, parched and unforgiving. Visions of hapless, screaming villagers. His father pointing his finger at him, stressing the need to conform, not to be weak, not to give in to emotions. Then "Get ahead, get ahead, get ahead!!!" His grandfather looking on sagely, confirming every point of the finger, his eyes boring into Kamran's, deeper, deeper, deeper. Their faces becoming large and distorted, their eyes and mouths becoming monstrous and commanding. Kamran himself becoming smaller and smaller as the two men grew into giants in front of him. Mahmoud standing on one side, laughing; mocking. His other brothers joining the chorus, pointing their fingers.

He blinked hard and shook his head again. The distant lights became a blur. As tears streamed, he sank into the cushions of a deck chair and dropped his head into his hands, finally allowing his torso to convulse with sobs.

AT HIS DESK later that morning Rahimi sat and stared at the three stacks of folders in front of him. The stack of new cases was short. The cases in the final stages: another small stack. Both of those were easily dealt with.

It was the stack in the middle that brought on the headache. Too many of these cases where he was in the middle of the process. Too many tough ones lately. Could it be he was losing his touch? He used to push these people through the system in a matter of weeks. This lot was taking…

Then he noticed the memo. On top of everything else, a meeting with his superior in the Prosecutor General's offices later that morning.

IT WAS two hours later when he walked out of that meeting. His superior, although in general pleased with his work, was "somewhat concerned" about how long it was taking with some of his cases. He was particularly concerned about the woman doctor's case.

"I need a confession from this woman and I need it soon." His look was neutral and his voice its usual professional tone. He paused and cocked his head to the right. Rahimi, busy in his thoughts, opened his mouth a second too late.

"Is there a problem? Are you up to it, Rahimi?" Another pause. Mehrdad Omidvar straightened his head and steepled his fingers. "You don't look well."

As Rahimi struggled with his response, his superior continued, "Look. I need results and if you can't give them to me on this case, I'll give it to someone else." Another pause as he examined his manicured nails.

When his subordinate failed to respond, he looked up sharply and caught Rahimi in the crosshairs of his stare. "Tell you what. If you're sick, go to a doctor and get treated. I need you healthy so you can work. If you can't…"

It took Rahimi every ounce of willpower to look down the bore of that gaze. Every bit of deception to convey a sense of capability he did not feel. "Of course, sir. I understand fully. You will get the result you require."

When he got to his car Rahimi pulled out his phone and called his physician.

MEHRDAD GOT up from the enormous desk in his commodious office, his cell phone to his ear as he went to the small wardrobe where his suit jacket hung.

"It doesn't matter whether she breaks or not, although breaking her would be no less than she deserves, but if not, she'll simply be executed and out of everyone's way, causing no more trouble. I want this as much as you do." He took his jacket off the solid wooden hanger and slipped it on as he listened.

"That's right. I've just met with the special agent that I have on her case... Right... Not a problem. If we break her and let her go, she still won't be free — *you* know that. I assure you, our people will continue to monitor her and restrict her movements. Periodically we'll bring her in for 'a little chat', you know, just so she remembers where she stands. In short, she'll behave or else."

He smiled and ended the call half a minute later. Pocketing his phone, he walked over to the small wall mirror, where he checked his reflection. He smoothed a stray hair and adjusted his jacket, then left the office.

THE DOCTOR TOLD Rahimi to get dressed again and sat down at his desk to write up his notes. When Rahimi had finished, he sat opposite his physician and waited.

Looking up from his prescription pad, the doctor offered his patient a sympathetic smile. "*Aqa*, you should think of retiring. You're 64 years old. These kinds of headaches are usually stress-related, so getting out of stressful work – what kind of work do you do, by the way?"

Rahimi prevaricated.

"So, government work, you say? Well, maybe you'll have a nice pension and you can retire or you could open a small business of your own and hire a couple of people to help you so that you can take things a bit easier."

As he handed Rahimi two slips of paper he continued, "Tell me, are you sure you don't have any symptoms you haven't told me about?"

Rahimi sighed and admitted to the dizziness and increasing tightening in his chest.

The doctor fingered his trim beard. "You know, *Aqa*, you need some additional testing." He scanned the medical record again. Looking up at Rahimi he said with some concern, "Your last full checkup was a very long time ago. Why have you waited *so* long?" He stared at his patient a moment longer but got no answer.

"Well," he said. "I'll arrange for you to have an extensive work-up. And I'm going to order tests for your heart."

Mid-June

OVER THEIR NOW RITUAL cafe food of espresso and chocolate croissants Nikou and Aryana enjoyed the easy ambience of friendship and trust. Although it was only once every week or so, it was enough and it helped the two young women cope with their exceptional personal circumstances.

"I've read in the newspaper that some more Baha'is have been arrested for their so-called subversive academic work. I'm assuming these are from the same group your Uncle Habib was involved with?" Nikou toyed with her napkin.

"That's right. We're not sure why they're doing this in separate raids, but hey, this isn't the first time they've done such things." Aryana's nonchalance surprised her cousin.

"Really? If it's happened before, I guess I just wasn't paying attention," said Nikou.

"Oh yes. There was a much bigger raid in 1998. Five hundred homes across the country. Three dozen arrests, I think it was. And then a couple of other raids. 2001 and 2003, I think. Then all this time without anything. But that's just this group, of course. This doesn't include all the other persecution, pogroms, mass arrests and executions over the course of our history."

"What's going on? I mean, if they want to get rid of all of you, why not launch a really big raid and arrest everyone?"

Aryana chewed thoughtfully on her croissant. "In the past they hit hard with big campaigns against us. Now they're quieter. By "quiet" I mean that there's always something nasty happening to Baha'is somewhere in the country, but they're keeping things low key so they won't attract too much international attention. There's been a lot of U.N. and NGO reporting about the government's human rights abuses. And that's included the Baha'is. But it makes them look bad, so they changed their tactics." She took another bite and pondered a bit. "One thing's for sure, though: they're trying to keep us off-balance. Maybe they hope we'll get careless and do something really worth taking notice of. Who can say?" She sipped her espresso.

"So how is your Uncle Habib? Taraneh*khanum* must be visiting him."

"She's seen him only a couple of times in the three weeks since they took him. And, of course, he says he's fine. Tells her to be calm, that he'll be out soon. You know, all the stuff we'd all like to believe but really can't. I think it's their way — Dayi and Maman, I mean — it's their way of trying to help *us*. They know how we worry and all they want is to shower us with love and protect us from what they think of as the grim reality of what we can only guess at." She finished her espresso, pushed the little cup away, and took a sip from her water glass.

Nikou stared out the window, chin in hand.

"You know, Aryana, I cannot imagine what it's like for you to see your mom under those conditions. I don't even want to imagine what life is like in that place."

Aryana placed both sets of fingers around the glass, holding it lightly. Staring at it, she took a deep breath. "I have to say a lot of prayers before I go and after I get back. And those are just the prayers for myself so that I don't break down and make Maman feel even worse than she does already. She actually never says anything about what happens to her in there."

"She says nothing?"

"No. Not a thing. First of all, they listen in on every conversation. If she says anything, they'll make her life in there harder. And I can see on her face and body that it's terrible. Lately it's been a little easier, I think, but for a few weeks after I came back she could hardly stand straight and she was limping. She tried to cover them, but I could see the bruises and cuts. She's lost a lot of weight. And her face... But she wouldn't want me to know what they do to her or anyone else in there even if she could tell me. Years ago, I remember, she told us about some of her ex-prison patients." She looked up quickly at her cousin. "I've told you, Nikou, they were anonymous! Anyway, what they'd told her was really unspeakable. So, I guess I really don't want to know any more than I do."

"But how does *she* cope? I mean that's more than anyone should be able to deal with."

"She prays, Nikou, she prays."

"In Evin?"

"Look. My mom never advertised it, but I remember that every morning she got up around 5:00 and spent an hour in her room having her private devotions. She never missed it and we learned at a very young age never to disturb her. So, even in that prison, she will find a way."

"But still. I should think she'd lose her faith in God after all this."

"Well, I suppose that happens to some. I don't see it happening to her yet, though. When I visit her she tells me — *me!*— to be strong. To pray. To study our Writings. To meditate on them."

"But why? I mean you know what your religion teaches. You had classes and everything."

"Because faith isn't something to take for granted. When we were little and sometimes complained about having to read or even say our prayers, she and Baba would tell us to think of our soul as a plant that needs daily nourishment. She'd ask us if we'd go for days and days without food or water and of course we'd shout 'No!' Then

Crimson Ink

she'd say, well, it's the same with the soul. It's just that it might take a bit longer to feel hungry than our stomach does."

"She told you that?"

"She did. And if that wasn't enough, *Khanumjan* Farah would tell us the same thing. So would Dayi Habib."

"Wow, you got it from all sides!"

"Yes! And what you may not know is that even your grandmother Sohayla would remind us of the same thing."

"*My* grandmother?"

"Yes. A very special lady. But I guess you know that."

Nikou looked out the window again. "I do. If it weren't for her I wouldn't even be here with you."

They ordered another espresso.

"But Aryana, even if I understand what you're saying about praying, how's that enough? I mean, it's all fine for someone to say they believe in something, but when you're put under pressure, what keeps you from just breaking down?"

"Maybe it's a matter of really understanding why you believe in what you do. You can't defend what you don't really understand."

"So, no 'lip-service'."

"No. That won't get you beyond Day One in prison."

"But weren't there some kids in your religious classes that didn't really take it all so seriously? I mean, you know how so many kids are."

"Yeah. I guess there were a couple. They'd clown around in class and make fun of things sometimes. That happens... But those were really dangerous times for our community. Even you knew that. So most of us took our lessons seriously. We saw a lot of family friends get taken away. My aunt Layla had been taken. Executed." She paused. "Think about it, Nikou. I'm sure you'll remember hearing that some people simply disappeared. It wasn't only Baha'is. You probably heard a few nasty stories yourself. There were plenty of people at risk. Still are."

Their coffee arrived and they took a few more bites of croissant.

"But what about resisting, Aryana?"

"Resisting?"

"Yeah. What do you think about the social activists or the journalists that are always trying to make a statement, or sabotage something? Don't you think that's one way to fight injustice?"

"No, not really. The whole idea of 'fighting fire with fire' is flawed. Even the protesters after the last election knew that. They marched peacefully. But even that didn't work."

"Who can forget that?" Nikou put her hands to her mouth and closed her eyes. "But look what happened to them!" Her eyes flashed open, looking straight at Aryana. "They should have fought!"

"That would have made it all even worse, Nikou. You know that.

"Yeah but –"

"Fighting assumes you have a chance at beating your oppressor. We know that no one in this country has the resources to match what the State can muster. That's number One. Number Two, it assumes a level playing field in terms of world view. That's not the case so people who resist are wasting their breath. They can never win an argument with people whose world view and ground rules are completely different. And if you actually have a conscience, you can't win that way against someone who doesn't. You can never be as ruthless as they can. And Number Three, force will be met with force and that brings us back to Square One. We're not going to get what we want by force."

"What do you want, exactly?"

"You mean the Baha'is?"

"Yes. I mean, I get that you want to be able to practice your religion freely, but that's not all, is it? What else do you want?"

"To see the unity of the whole human race."

"Ha! Is that all?"

Nikou smiled. "Yeah, we get that reaction a lot." She circled her thumb around the edge of her espresso cup. "The world will eventually figure out that there's no other way for us to survive as a human race. And it's clear that it's going to take a while yet to get to that point. It's only going to happen in small steps. It can't happen overnight. And for it to happen we have to have a vision for it, believe in that vision and then act in whatever ways we can."

"What?"

"Look. How do you get to unity? You have to believe that we're all created equal and noble. If that's how we humans are created then we need structures in society that treat people that way."

"Like what?"

"Oh, education systems, social services…"

"But we have those."

"Sure, but look at the inequality and lack of access."

"Okay but –"

"Just look around our own country. Look around the world. Look at the plight of women, Nikou. We're not equal. Are we?"

Nikou looked at the small cup she held between her fingers.

"Nikou, fighting our government isn't going to get us our rights as women. It's not going to get higher education for us Baha'is…"

"But what are we supposed to do, Aryana? How are we supposed to get those things?" She thumped the table with her hand. "And don't you Baha'is ever just get sick and tired of… of… of being marginalized? Of being treated like vermin?" She looked out the large window to the park beyond, her mouth pinched.

"Sure we do, Nikou. Sure we do." Her voice was soft. "But we're not going to get anywhere by fighting."

"So what are you doing? I mean, you can't just roll over and play dead. You can't just not get educated or get jobs or have access to services you need. So what are you doing, for God's sake?"

"A lot. And quietly." Aryana lowered her voice. "We're not allowed by the government to have our normal community services, but we've been able to put small, informal structures in place to help each other with all sorts of resources."

"Such as?"

"Health, jobs, education."

"And how do you do that?"

"We work in small groups and use the talents of people who have the expertise or experience needed. And we do it not only for ourselves, we also include neighbors and friends in need. People who are not Baha'is. It's not just about us, Nikou. It's what my mom was doing. The official social structures were failing many, so individuals jumped in to help."

"And look where that got her..." Nikou caught herself. "Oh, Aryana, I'm sorry! I didn't mean –"

"It's okay, Nikou. She knew that it was risky. But how could she have not done it? Both my parents and many others took risks treating all those people who'd gotten injured in the election protests. How could they not have done that?"

"Your parents are brave people."

"I don't think they consider themselves brave at all. Especially my mom. They'd seen so much during and after the Revolution that they were very careful not to get noticed for a long, long while."

"Really? But how do you know that?"

"Oh I heard lots. Every time there was news about friends getting arrested or beaten up or stuff like that, Mom would go into a tailspin. I think it brought back all those memories of her sister. No, my mom would never think of herself as brave."

"And yet."

"And yet. I guess there's a time when you just do something because you know you have to. And I think that's what a lot of Baha'is have done. Are doing. As I said, small steps."

Late June

RAHIMI TRUDGED out of the elevator and down the carpeted hall. Reaching his apartment, he turned his key, stepped wearily in and slammed the door behind him. He gave the barest of *Salaams* to Zahra. She returned to the dinner on the stove, but he followed her to the kitchen and opened the fridge. He wanted something cold to drink.

"Kami, can I get you —"

"Not now!" He grabbed a juice jug and tumbler and strode out of the room.

He took his glass out onto the balcony and dropped into a reclining chair in the shade. Leaning back, he closed his eyes and rolled his head from side to side. He simply could not comprehend these people who just wouldn't listen to common sense and take the easy way out. It was only a matter of signing a piece of paper, for God's sake! Of course once they did that there was all the follow-up work of checking up on them, but that was the job of other agents. It was no longer his problem — at least not until they landed in Evin again.

If he could just get these people off his books and hand over his files for the others to follow up… It's a matter of moving these people through the system more efficiently… *Why won't they just do as I say and make it easier for all of us?*

He took a long gulp of the cold liquid.

He thought about the matter of getting a staged confession from this doctor woman. In this case he needed it: a show; an example. Weeks had gone by since his meeting over at the Prosecutor General's offices. His superior there had said nothing more about it, but Rahimi knew he was being watched. He knew that one or the other of his own subordinates was reporting back on his progress — or lack of it.

His chest tightened. Instead of his pills, he took a few deep breaths, then stood up and stared out over the cityscape, losing himself in the endless stretch of buildings below.

A few minutes later, he returned to the living room. His son sat in front of the large screen TV, absorbed in a soccer game.

"Turn it off!" Rahimi glowered at him.

Startled, Navid stared at his father.

"I said, turn it off!" Seeing his son slow to comply, Rahimi strode over to him, grabbed the remote and shut off the set. He was deaf to Navid's protests and responded with a shove, knocking his son onto the floor. When Yasmine ran in to see what was going on, Rahimi chased his daughter out and returned, fists clenched, to face the teenager.

"Why don't you just do as I say?" he screamed, and began to pound the boy. On the carpet, Navid held his arms up in defense of his head and he kicked as he shouted back. Zahra rushed in, shouting, followed by Yasmine.

On his knees now, Rahimi continued his senseless pounding. Zahra was pulling at him. Yasmine's crying added to the din. In a desperate effort to drown them all out, Rahimi kept yelling.

Then his chest tightened. His breath — he could hardly get his breath. He grabbed his chest and rolled to the side, releasing his grip on his son's arm. He was gasping.

With a grunt, the boy scrambled up and stood over his father. Between ragged breaths, he shouted, "Stop beating me like a street dog. This is not your prison!"

Chapter Eight

2011

JULY

EVIN PRISON
EARLY JULY

July. The stickiness of summer was her only companion in this new cell. The wretchedness of its walls leaned in on Fereshteh. Their painted surfaces had faded to the bleakest of grays. Years of accumulated grime from unwashed heads, sweaty backs, and desperate palms had given them a sickening sheen. Grim evidence of a desolate pain.

Perhaps the only thing that could be said for them is that they invited a morbid curiosity: who'd been here before her? What were their stories? Not 'what was their crime', but 'what were their thoughts, their hopes, their dreams'. Maybe she could forget herself in a few moments of pity for the plight of her predecessors. But what comfort, what refuge was there in that?

Refuge was an odd word here in Evin. Where could you be and what could you do in private when a camera, a light, or a guard had you in their sights? The postage-stamp "courtyard" where inmates were allowed a daily half-hour of *hava khori* – the prison administration's idea of fresh air and exercise — was a bad joke, but of course here you took what you could, camera supervision and all. Not even the toilet offered a place to hide. The guards had little patience with dawdlers and gave you a whack for their inconvenience.

A wry smile came to Fereshteh's lips as she remembered herself decades ago, the young mother of three small children. In times of overwhelm, she'd run to the bathroom, closing the door against the little ones clamoring for her, just to have a bit of space and time to herself. Running away from her children. The irony of her present situation stung her.

What would it be like to have my life back? What she had now was just marking time. "Life" was on "hold". All she had now were memories.

The grisly existence of Evin life over the past five months pelted her mind, a jumble of intertwined images and voices. Her nerves were raw. Her head ached. She was exhausted and dizzy from walking in circles in this unforgiving cubicle. She sat down and closed her eyes.

Focusing her mind's eye on an image of a candle, she tried to slow her breath, her heart, and her thoughts. She mentally counted each breath and forced a long exhale, knowing that this would help to relax her muscles and ease her throbbing pulse. One, two, three, four…Two, two, three, four, Three, two, three, four, five, six…Four, two, three, four, five, six, seven…

SHE MUST HAVE DOZED BRIEFLY, she thought, becoming conscious of a fading image of… who was it?… ah… Homa. The lady who actually got the divorce.

Fereshteh shook herself and stood up. She looked up at the tiny barred window, open now during the summer. The afternoon sun and a breath of hot air streamed in.

"Homa," she said aloud, and wondered about her. "Where are you now? Where are any of those women now? The ones I helped. And where are my friends and colleagues?" The ones she'd worked with to help free those abused women. She pictured all their faces, remembering their smiles, their laughter, their frowns, the earnest concern written in their furrowed brows. With all her heart she wished them well. Wished them safe.

How did I ever get involved in that? Me, of all people? She thought of the road that had taken her to help Homa, Rana and all the rest. The road that she and Jamshid had taken to help the injured protesters. She thought of Nikou and her friend. She wondered about them and was uneasy.

Leaning against the wall, Fereshteh slid down until she was sitting again. She felt sleepy but fought it. She knew she was in danger of losing herself to depression and had vowed not to let that happen.

She stood up again and began to jog around the cell. She stretched. She jumped. She swung her arms. Only after reaching her self-imposed exercise target did she sit down again. She reached for the stale warm water in the plastic cup and took a few sips, then leaned her head back and exercised her mind.

She traced her life, wondering where she'd started to change from the timid little girl to the confident physician. Was there a definable path there somewhere? And how had the briefly confident young physician so succumbed to fear as to make herself nearly invisible for almost three decades?

As Fereshteh thought about the 1980s, '90s, and more than a decade in the new millennium, she realized that it had gone by in a blur. With effort, she slowed her thoughts and focused on each year, remembering her children and the milestones in their lives, the earnest consultations with Jamshid, Farah, Habib and Taraneh about the children's health, education and protection in all those years of uncertainty and outright danger. She recalled the times of the bitterest persecution and the greatest anxieties. There were the moves and job changes necessary to lying low enough not to be singled out for arrest. And how could she forget the dire events that had sent thousands, Baha'is included, to prison and to their deaths? But an afternoon of reflecting yielded only pain. What about the good times? Why were they so hard to recall?

Supper came. A bowl of watery, tasteless stew. A handful of cheap rice. Overcooked. But it really didn't matter. She was glad to have three meals a day now, whatever they were. And there was the tea. It was cheap too, but it came with two sugar cubes!

When she finished, her mind returned to its reflections. She realized that for almost three decades, nearly half her life, she'd been watching her world go by, hiding in the shadows like the coward she was. Doing what she'd absolutely had to, yes; caring for her family and friends, yes; attending Baha'i community events when they'd been allowed, yes. But nothing more. Nothing of substance, nothing — ever! — that would put her at risk. Nothing that could lead her to her sister's fate.

Yet here she was.

IN THE MIDDLE of the night, the guard opened the door and dragged Fereshteh out her uneasy sleep. "*Pa-sho! Y'allah!* — come on, get up!"

In a daze she felt the warden apply the handcuffs and then the blindfold. Felt the poke from behind that pushed her where she was supposed to go, winding this way and that. Down a final corridor. She knew where she was. She could smell it: the stench of sweat and blood, pungent in the midsummer humidity. A metal door clanged open and she was pushed in.

"You're back again, eh?" The disembodied voice sounded vaguely familiar. "I hear you didn't want to answer any questions today. Maybe I can help you."

The first blow was to her back. The second was a punch in her stomach. "Sit down!" He pushed her onto a chair and swung a table of some sort in front of her. "Write!" he ordered, lifting her blindfold just high enough for her to look down onto a piece of paper. And his boots.

He kept talking and ordering, prodding her hand with the pen, but all Fereshteh could do was look at the boots. Dirty, scuffed. Stained. Dark dried stinking stains. He was saying something but she couldn't understand. What was the pen doing in her hand?

A whack with a stick. Her left arm throbbed. The boots. What size could they be? Another whack. And another. "Write!" Her left arm gravitated inward and she leaned over it. As she leaned, the boots looked larger. The stains were not just one color as she'd originally thought.

Whomp! "Write, you idiot!" She was bent in half, face almost in her lap, but she kept seeing those boots. Thick, heavy soles. Whomp! Laces that ran up.

Whomp! What was all the shouting about? She was only looking at the boots.

Whack! Her ears were ringing. "Arrrggghhh!" she heard as she was dragged to the floor, face down. She could see a boot up close now. Nicks in the blackened leather. Then, oblivion.

When she woke, she was back in her cell.

Evin Prison
Administrative offices
Early July

"What the hell were you thinking, you idiot?" Rahimi uncrossed his arms and stood up. He walked around the guard standing in front of his desk and clipped him hard on the back of the head. The guard stood at attention and stared at the wall in front of him.

"I told you to *threaten* her, not incapacitate her! I told you I needed her to write —"

"Yes, sir, I gave her a pen and —"

"Idiot! Giving her a pen and then beating her senseless? How was that supposed to work? I wanted her pulled out of sleep, threatened and told to write. Get her when she was weak and foggy enough to sign the damned papers, you fool!"

"But I meant —"

"Shut up or I'll have *you* flogged! If you can't follow simple orders I'll have you demoted. Or maybe I'll have you clean up the 'enhanced interrogation' rooms." Rahimi looked straight into the guard's eyes. "Get out! Get back to your post and wait for your new orders!" Rahimi went to the window, ignoring the guard's salute, and stood there until the door had closed behind the man.

His chest tightened and he opened the window wider to gulp some air.

If Rahimi had thought that his morning encounter with the guard was going to be the worst of his day, he was mistaken. The July heat was merciless and the air quality over the city should have been enough to shut it down, but this was Tehran and life went on no matter what. The traffic continued unabated and the factories unloaded their smoke stacks into the mix of exhaust and Freon. Not a breeze moved the thick blanket that baked the city in its poison.

At the dinner table that evening, the only sound came from the whirring of the fans that strained to relieve the oppressive heat. Sweat still clung to every brow.

Zahra looked pointedly at her brood, flashing them warnings to keep quiet. She shot looks at her husband then quickly averted her eyes. The children threw furtive glances at each other. There were muffled movements of hands and feet under the table, the suppressed agitation of children trying hard to be obedient.

Rahimi saw all this but said nothing. He picked at his food for a while, then pushed it away with a sound of disgust. Zahra offered to make him something else, but he threw his napkin onto the table and pushed his chair back, muttering under his breath.

"Really, Kamranjoon, I'll make you something else. Would you like some cold —"

"I said no! I'm not hungry! I don't want your food!"

"But —"

"Are you deaf? What's wrong with you? Shut up! I don't want your lousy food!"

As Rahimi got up Navid started to speak. Zahra looked at her son and shook her head in alarm. Yasmine and Shahin, mouths open, braced themselves.

Rahimi looked sharply at his son, as if daring him to say another word.

The boy spoke anyway.

"What kind of job turns a man from being a kind father into a tyrant at home? You come home and don't talk to us, you sit at dinner with a grim face, you complain about Maman's good food, about how she spends her time, about every small thing that happens in the house. You never take us anywhere anymore; you just go off by yourself to sit in the dark & smoke endless cigarettes or sit for hours in front of the TV. When we try to talk to you or ask you something important, you shout at us or send us away. And many evenings you don't even come home until midnight! We hear you shouting at Mamanjoon and we hear her crying, even when you're not here. Look at her! Look at us! We're your family!"

He was shouting now, crying, unafraid, it seemed, pouring out his teenage burdens in undisguised insolence. He stood up and faced his father, posture tense, hands balled in fists. Feeling his rage rise, Rahimi moved towards his son, his own fists ready.

"We're human beings and you treat us like dogs!" Navid screamed, moving away from the table. Then turning quickly, he strode out the front door, slamming it behind him.

Rahimi lowered his arm. He stared at the door, motionless. Soundless. Empty.

Mid-July

Trust is such a fragile thing that it's hard to build. It requires so much investment of the 'self'. The risks can be huge. Its breach is a kick in the teeth that will not willingly suffer a second blow.

And yet, Nikou, exploited by those closest to her, those who should have loved and respected her, had not lost her faith in all people. When she'd married Mehrdad, she'd truly believed in the possibility of a contented life. How could she have known that his impeccable manners, mature speech and handsome features were nothing but a veneer?

She was not inclined to trust again. But her friend Marjan had come through for her. And Fereshteh had rushed to save her, never thinking about consequences.

These two women who had shown her that goodness could be practiced for its own sake, and not just because it was owed or rewarded, had kept ajar her door of hope.

Somewhere in the depths of her heart, lay a sliver of it. And when Sohayla had trusted her with her confidences, Nikou had begun to weave together a tiny net to hold and nurture that fragment.

Sohayla helped Nikou fill in the blanks in her picture of who her Jalili and Azadeh cousins really were. She told Nikou the real-life stories her granddaughter had missed, and with that, dissolved the grotesque caricatures that Aqajoon Reza had fabricated.

Really, what had Nikou actually known about anyone other than Aryana? The other girl cousins — Anisa, Maryam and Sara were all so much older. And the boys? Well, they'd played with her brothers, not her. And as far as Fereshteh, Jamshid, Habib and Taraneh were concerned, all she saw of them was when they were invited to larger family get-togethers. The adults had talked amongst themselves, leaving the kids to their own games. During or after those visits, all Nikou remembered hearing were the barbs and unkind jokes that Aqajoon Reza, Baba, and her uncles made about them all. Sohayla had tried her best to counterbalance all that, but Nikou's mother and aunts had colluded with their men and bit by bit they sowed the seeds that became the weeds that overran reality.

It had taken until now to come to the release of the past. The airing of truth and sharing of sweet memories at last became the gift that Sohayla could give to Nikou. And only to Nikou. It would be completely lost on all the rest.

SOHAYLA NEVER ASKED Nikou about whether she'd ever been able to contact Aryana, but Nikou suspected that her grandmother knew. They had an unspoken agreement not to share this kind of information. For their own protection.

Neither did they discuss Nikou's marriage. Sohayla's eyesight was still sharp and she'd raised her eyebrows at Nikou a few times during family visits earlier in the year. She seemed to know the signs. Nikou wondered what else she knew, but didn't want to ask her, and Sohayla was gracious enough not to ask anything either.

There were barely any external bruises now anyway. Instead, Mehrdad was honing his psychological assault skills.

He had no idea, though, that the harder he worked on her, the more determined she became to keep up her resistance. Not that she showed this. That would have been foolish in the extreme. She played the game. She let him play his tricks and spring his traps. Let him think he was on top. Succeeding in all his efforts. He couldn't guess that she'd found ways to shield herself. And he had no clue as to her acting abilities.

She kept constantly busy. The house, the garden, the cultural events, the museums and galleries. She went to the library to read and frequented cafés that displayed and sold books. She took up painting. Innocuous and womanly as he thought it was, Mehrdad allowed her to attend classes. Still, though, he admonished her: "Just make sure you don't get too chummy with anyone there. Do your lessons, come home and then paint here."

So Nikou did that. And visited family, went shopping, and dined at appealing restaurants. And continued her meetings with her cousin Aryana.

STRICTLY SPEAKING, Aryana would have been better off not knowing much about her cousin. If ever she were detained for questioning, for any reason at all, the less she knew about anyone the better. Particularly since Nikou's husband was, well, as he was. And who he was.

When Nikou had told her about the brutal November beating, Aryana had physically recoiled in her seat, and the café crowd notwithstanding, she hadn't been able to hold back her tears. As difficult as Nikou's side of the family had always been and as hostile as they'd grown over the last few years, Aryana felt certain that none of them had the personality to carry out such savagery.

But Mehrdad was another matter. There was a man who had no compunction, no scruples, and no shred of empathy. She now had no doubt that he'd been at least one of the people behind her mother's imprisonment and she dreaded the possibility that he might carry her punishment to a murderous end. Clearly, her mother was being punished for the crime of helping others. And for her religion. It would all be written in any confessions presented to her to sign. Standard fare for her imprisoned co-religionists.

And what if, she asked herself, *he decides to take out his warped anger on Habib too? And what about all the other BIHE professors still locked up? Was Mehrdad behind that too?*

Her thoughts returned to Nikou. What chance did she stand in that marriage? He'd kill her before he'd ever divorce her. Divorce would look like a failure of some kind. That he'd made a poor choice in his bride. It might be seen as a certain lack of judgment on his part, or perhaps that he didn't have what was required to keep his wife in line. No, he'd never let her go. If Nikou was lucky, she'd be able to continue playing her "dutiful wife" role and make him look great to everyone else. If she did that, she might be safe. But with someone like him, there was always a chance that some switch in his brain would flip and he'd attack her again. Maybe even kill her. *I suppose she knows this,* she thought, *but I wonder if I should bring it up.*

The next time they met she did.

BECAUSE OF THE EXTREME HEAT, they sipped cold water between their usual espressos, and had ordered ice cream.

"Nikou?"

"Yes?" She looked up from her ice cream dish, which she'd been scraping with her spoon. "Mmm, that was so good!" She dabbed her lips with a napkin and asked, "You wanted to say something?"

"Yeah, I did. It's of course none of my business to ask you, so please, just tell me to back off if I'm really out of place, but…"

"Go on."

"Nikou, you know I've been thinking so much about Maman and all her suffering there…" she looked off to the side and blinked a few times.

"Then when I think of her I remember what you went through. You look so well now; so maybe things are fine for you at home. But I keep thinking: what kind of person is it who's capable of doing such things — you know, to you; to Maman; to all those others who are locked up. I — I've been thinking about that. You know, the ones already in prison don't have a choice. They have no escape. Things will continue to happen."

She thought about her Uncle Habib. "Things will continue to happen because nothing's changed. The oppressors are who they are and the victims are who they are."

"Okay. But?"

"Well, I'm just wondering about you. Your plans. You look like you're okay right now and I really hope with all my heart that you stay that way. But… but what if… what if he starts in again? What happens if he just… well, you know… what if that happens? What will you do? You're not in prison but —"

"Oh!" Nikou broke into a hoot. "Am I not? Is my golden cage not a prison? Is being watched 24/7 not a prison? Is the need to fake my life not a prison? Is the necessity to kowtow to a crazy sadistic man not a prison?" Her laugh was bitter.

Aryana was silent for a minute, then leaned across the table and whispered, "Nikoujoon, what will you do?"

Her cousin looked her in the eye, paused, and made a decision. To trust. She whispered back, "I'm done with these tyrants in my life. I'm going to get the hell out, that's what!"

Evin Prison
Early-July

A day after the Jalili woman's unintended beating, Rahimi hauled her in again for interrogation. He started by being reasonable, then gradually ramped it up from simple questioning to outright grilling.

In the stifling heat, Fereshteh sat at the battered wooden table, her hands in her lap. Although he'd made sure that she could see the paper and pen from the space at the bottom of her blindfold, she made no move to use them.

"Give me those names, woman! Write them down! Now!"

"I've told you over and over, I have no names to give! Please, what names are you talking about?"

"Your collaborators! Come on, we know you were involved in subversive activities with other people. With other Baha'is. Give me their names!"

"I've told you — I've been telling everyone who has ever questioned me — for months now — I have not done anything subversive."

"But we know you have been working against the stability of the State. You've been undermining the foundation of our society!"

"Excuse me, *Aqa*, how have I done that? You know that Baha'is do not get involved in such things."

"What I do know about you Baha'is is that you're always talking about pushing women forward. Urging women to disobey their husbands. Disrupting the traditional stability of the family. The family is the foundation of our society! Do you still deny this?"

"I gave medical treatment and counseling to women who had been beaten by their husbands. I'm a doctor. It's the duty of doctors to help the sick and injured."

"You stupid cow, you and your friends pushed them into destroying their families!"

"*Aqa*, please. The only women I treated were ones who came to my office. They had been severely beaten and abused by their husbands. They told me that this had been going on for years and they —"

"Shut up! Don't cover your seditious actions with lies about innocence! You know what you did! Now, give me the names of

Crimson Ink

your collaborators!" He gave her a violent slap on the head with the back of his hand.

AND ON IT WENT. A circle of accusations and denials punctuated by intermittent shouts, shoves, slaps and the banging of his fist.

She lasted nearly four hours before she collapsed.

HE HAULED her in again the day after and hammered her for just over six hours. He sent her back to her cell in a heap.

Day after day he had her dragged in. Literally. Two women guards held her under her arms and pulled her into the interrogation room. She sat hunched over the same sorry table, blindfold securely in place, her hands free to write. If she chose to.

He used every questioning technique imaginable. He played "good cop / bad cop". He badgered. He cajoled. He threatened.

But every day, she stuck to her answers and at the end of every session the papers remained blank. No names were given and no crimes confessed.

THEN HE LEFT her alone in her cell for the better part of a week.

It was mid-July when he called her back in. This time she walked all the way and sat up straight at the table. She seemed calm, he thought.

He began again, his tone benign. In fact, the entire session was civil. He repeated the accusations against her; she refuted them. He asked her a long list of questions; she answered calmly. He asked her again and told her to write her answers this time; she complied. He demanded a confession to her crimes; she refused. He repeated his list of threats; she said nothing.

They repeated this scene for several more days.

Somewhere well into the next session Rahimi started to cough. He pulled a pack of throat lozenges out of his jacket pocket and popped one into his mouth, then continued. Reading his list of questions again, he cleared his throat several times and popped another couple of lozenges. When Fereshteh had finished writing her answers — always the same, he noted — he passed the confession papers to her and stated his demands.

Fereshteh sat still, the pen untouched. Then she asked him about the raspiness of his voice; there was concern in hers.

Taken aback, he said nothing.

"You know, *Aqa*," she said with a small smile, "I'm a doctor. If you don't mind, I suggest that you have that cough seen to. It doesn't sound like an ordinary viral infection."

Nonplussed, he remained speechless.

"I'll bet you have a good wife at home who's worried about you, *Aqa*. Maybe you also have children?"

He found himself murmuring a "yes" and she went on, unimpeded. "One thing this prison has confirmed to me, *Aqa*, is how uncertain life is. And how precious family is." She paused, then said, "I will pray for you."

As she sat back in the sweltering room, her blindfold slid down, carried on rivulets of sweat. Before she managed to catch it, she caught sight of him. For a mere second their eyes locked.

Evin Prison
26 July

Rahimi was under the gun.

Early that morning he'd received an urgent call from the Prosecutor General's Office. He was to report to his superior there immediately. Deciding that a taxi would get him there fastest, he dropped everything and arrived as ordered. And was made to wait for nearly an hour.

The tone of the meeting had been polite, if frosty. His superior was at the end of his patience with Rahimi and his handling of the Jalili woman's case, and this did not bode well for Rahimi's career. In fact, Rahimi was all too well aware of his superior's reputation: to fail him was to cast suspicion on yourself. Your loyalties could be questioned and you, too, could come under some unpleasant scrutiny.

So Rahimi had to get a result. One way or the other, this case had to come to a conclusion this week. He came to a decision. He'd convince the Jalili woman through kindness and temptation.

IN THE INTERROGATION room he played the scene with a new script. As Fereshteh was brought in, he actually greeted her.

"*Salaam, Khanum-doctor* — Greetings, madam doctor. I hope you had a peaceful night and are well-rested this morning. Please, sit down."

Fereshteh hesitated at this unaccustomed courtesy and then responded, "*Salaam, Aqa.* Thank you. I hope you, too, had a comfortable night." Then she sat at the table, her head tilted and brows furrowed.

Rahimi spent some time going through the familiar question drill, just to see if anything had changed in her attitude or answers. When he came to the confession piece of the exercise, however, he told her something new.

"You know, *Khanum*," he began. From her face he saw that Fereshteh still couldn't quite register that he'd replaced the insolence of the simple "Jalili" with the civility of "Madam". *Good*, he thought. *This will keep her off balance.*

"You know, *Khanum*, I appreciated that you said you would pray for me. Really. Thank you. It seems your kind prayers have had an effect. I have been thinking about your case a great deal and reviewing your crimes. I've come to a decision. Instead of the confession that I've been requiring for some time, I believe it will suffice if you write only one simple thing. Just one thing."

He paused to let her absorb this. He began to walk back and forth in front of her. Slowly. Calmly.

"If you do this one small thing, we can allow you to go home. We can end all this questioning. End the unpleasant things that sometimes happen."

When she said nothing, he continued, still walking. Still calm. "Yes, *Khanum*, I'm actually a reasonable man. As you said, I have a family. I'm like you. Like everyone. I love my family. I do my job with all its responsibilities. Like you, *Khanum*. Like you." He stopped.

"Please continue, *Aqa*."

Resuming his walk, he said, "*Khanum*, I know you have family here in Tehran and also in the UK and the United States. You must be proud of them, right?"

"Yes."

"We're all proud of our families and want the best for them, don't we?"

"Yes."

"We want them to be safe, healthy, successful — happy! Don't we, *Khanum*?"

"Yes."

"And think about the grandchildren! I understand that you have a grandchild on the way, isn't that right?"

"Yes."

"And it would be wonderful to be able to see that little child, wouldn't it?"

"Yes."

"It seems all your overseas family live comfortably. Nice homes they have! And good jobs. Excellent prospects for the future! You must be proud."

"Y- y- yes."

"But with them so far away, you must always be slightly worried about them. I would be."

She said nothing.

"And your daughter Aryana. She's back from England now. Working here and doing well, isn't she? Her company really appreciates her work, I understand, and would like to retain her as their employee. I understand she's paid well, too."

When Fereshteh didn't respond, he prompted, "Isn't that so, *Khanum*?" Rahimi noted the new stiffness in her posture.

"Yes."

Crimson Ink

"And Aryana likes to visit you, doesn't she? And you must look forward to her visits?"

"Yes." Her voice wavered slightly.

"Then of course there's the matter of your brother. Habib."

Fereshteh tensed. Her lips were tightly compressed.

"Yes," he drawled. "Habib. Unfortunate. Unfortunate. It seems he was caught up in that nasty business back in May. He's under investigation now, of course. I'm sure this worries you." He stood in front of her. "Doesn't it?"

She cleared her throat and managed a "Yes".

Resuming his calm walk, he continued, "You see, *Khanum*, I know all these things. As I said, I understand the concerns about family members." He paused in his speech but continued to walk for a minute before going on.

"Yes, *Khanum*, I understand how concerned you must be for your children and your brother. Oh! And yes, your sister-in-law, too! I almost forgot about her. Yes. Taraneh, I believe is her name. Yes. Taraneh. Very well educated. Like your brother." Another pause. "I understand she has a reasonable job. But such talent going to waste as an accountant. I'm sure she's better suited to teach. Like your brother. But," he sighed, "such a pity that Baha'is aren't allowed to teach here. Pity, really. And such a shame if they ignore that prohibition. Such a shame." He walked in silence for a minute or two.

Standing in front of her again, he said, "*Khanum*, I really understand your concerns. I do. And as I've said, I am a reasonable man. I'm willing — thanks to your kind prayers, *Khanum* — I'm willing to work with you on these concerns that you must have about your family. I'm willing to help you to get back home to your loved ones and also see how we can keep you all safe in these uncertain times."

He began walking again. "I want to make sure your homes are safe, your jobs are protected, your family close. Yes, *Khanum*, I am reasonable." He stopped in front of her again. "And I have the power to protect you all."

For a minute neither of them moved. Then Rahimi produced a paper and said, "*Khanum*, I want to make this as easy for you as I can. Realizing that your hand might be tired from so much writing these last few days, I've prepared a paper for you myself. Yes, *Khanum*, I wrote it for you. All you need to do is sign it. So easy for you." He pushed the paper close to her so she could see it from the bottom gap in her blindfold, and handed her a pen. So gently. "Please, *Khanum*. Help me to help you."

HUGGING HERSELF, Fereshteh paced in her cell. She had come so close, so close.

She'd picked up the pen. She'd read the interrogator's short text several times. He'd been right. So simple. All the accusations were gone. There were no longer any "crimes" mentioned. Only a simple statement. And all she had to do was sign her name under it.

As she walked around her cell, her heart raced. His "reasonable" statements, now recalled, chilled her. He knew everything. He knew all about every member of her family. Knew where they worked, what they were paid. And turned a blind eye. Allowed them to work. He knew who their landlords were. And allowed their landlords to keep renting to them. He knew all about Habib and BIHE, of course. But she hadn't thought about Taraneh. And now, Aryana. He knew where her other children lived overseas, knew about the baby on the way. Even there. *He knows all about my children. My own precious children!*

She stopped and looked up at the sunlight pouring through the tiny window. She rubbed her arms and took deep breaths. *My children! My very own family!*

That's why she'd picked up the pen. Why she'd bothered to reread the text on that paper. Why her hand had trembled so as she'd brought it down on the sheet. Why her whole body had shuddered.

Two fat teardrops had fallen onto the page. Next to the pen point. It was then that she'd lifted it and moved it to the side. Then, sitting up straight, she'd put it down on the desk.

Her interrogator hadn't insisted. Hadn't even demanded her to speak. All he'd said was, "Why don't you go and think about this for

Crimson Ink

a while, *Khanum*. I can see you're tired." He'd taken the paper and called in the guard. As she'd been leaving he'd said, "*Khanum*, no doubt you'll consider carefully what I've said and see how reasonable my request is. You will get so much for so little."

Resuming her circles around the cell, she tried to banish the words, but they reverberated with her every step. 'So much for so little.' The 'so little' he wanted was a written recantation of her Faith.

AT DINNER TIME the guard arrived with the tray. Through the bars that formed the entrance wall of her cell, Fereshteh had seen her coming. It was the one she called *Gonjeshk* — sparrow. None of them gave their real names. Not in this godforsaken place. They gave the prisoners generic names if they gave any names at all. So the inmates created their own names for the guards. Something that described the person.

Fereshteh rather liked *Gonjeshk*. Her slight build matched her quiet personality. She got on with her duties and said little. She told you what to do but was never vulgar or rude like many of the others. But even sparrows can make a racket if you annoy them. And this little sparrow carried a gun.

Tonight *Gonjeshk* also carried something very enticing.

The plate on the tray held a heaping mound of fragrant basmati rice, yellow with saffron. An egg yolk sat in the middle. To the left of this sat a plump grilled tomato and on the other side lay two strips of *kubideh* — ground lamb kebabs. A separate little bowl held a generous portion of *somagh*, the obligatory condiment to this traditional dish. A cup full of dark gold steaming tea sat in one corner. On its saucer were at least a half-dozen cubes of sugar. Fereshteh, her senses quickened by the flood of aromas, looked up with a mixture of surprise and appreciation. The guard handed her the tray with a brief direct look and a quick nod, and without a word turned and went on her way.

Fereshteh stared at the tray in her hands for a long minute,

383

letting its steam penetrate her nostrils. Her mouth watered. She sat down and continued to gaze at the sumptuous meal. How many of these had she cooked in her life, she wondered. How many had she eaten? And loved every morsel. When was the last time she'd eaten this? Eaten anything of substance? Ah, yes. The evening before she'd been arrested she and Jamshid had enjoyed this together at a small local restaurant after a long workday. She pictured the scene and smiled. Jamshid loved kebab and he'd ordered an extra strip and extra tomatoes that evening. And they'd shared a large portion of *mast-o-khiar* — yoghurt with cucumber and mint. How fresh that had tasted!

She licked her lips and sucked back the saliva that had filled her mouth. She closed her eyes.

Jamshid. Her dearest friend. Her life's partner. Her soul's mate. She smiled at that cheesy phrase. Yet it was true. That's what they'd been to each other. That's what they'd always be.

She leaned back against the wall, the tray still in her lap, her eyes still closed. Jamshid filled her thoughts and she let the memories flow. Whatever the joy and whatever the sorrow, she saw them together. Sharing everything.

Unbidden, Farah flowed into her mind. Fereshteh basked in her mother's smile and in her words of wisdom. She followed Farah over her lifetime. The usual blur that had hidden so many memories now lifted and long-forgotten scenes crystalized in front of her. Decades of them.

She dozed. Farah was talking to her. "I'm so proud of you, Fereshteh. I'm a little afraid for you with the work you do, but I wouldn't have you do otherwise." Fereshteh saw herself and her mother on Farah's comfortable sofa. Farah took her hands, as if in blessing. "Do what you can, *dokhtaram* — my daughter. Help these women. They have no voice. You— you and your friends are giving them a voice. Use wisdom, but help them, *joon-e delam* — dear heart. Speak for them. Help them to heal, my dear Fereshteh."

THE CLANG of the cell door roused her. Gonjeshk was back to collect the tray. Her eyebrows raised, she asked, *"Chera hichchi nakhordi?* - Why haven't you eaten anything? *Heyf-e* — what a pity."

"*Ghorosneh nabudam* — I wasn't hungry."

Gonjeshk cocked her head, looked at her strangely, then shrugged her shoulders. She picked up the tray and left.

Evin Prison
27 July

Rahimi went into the interrogation room early. He had all Dr. Jalili's files and placed them on the desk, where, for the next half hour or so, he'd go through them again to be certain he'd covered everything.

Taking a sip from the paper mug of tea, he read the report of last night's guards. *So she refused the kebab. Damn!* he thought and slammed his fist on the desk. *How could she refuse that?* It had been some of the best kebab in the city. He'd made sure of that. His own mouth was watering just at the thought of it.

This didn't look good. He'd thought he had her. Smart woman! She understood all too well the subtext of everything he'd said. But was she really willing to endanger her family for something so ridiculous as refusing to sign a piece of paper?

He'd seen this many times before, of course, but it always baffled him. His own religion allowed *taghiyeh* — dissimulation in times of danger. Other religions did too. No big thing. But not the Baha'is. Really, they were such a nuisance!

Well, he'd do what he could today. He'd repeat the whole thing from yesterday, adding a few embellishments about just how much they knew about her family, throw in a few more insinuations about consequences, and then appeal to her high sense of loyalty and love. It was perfectly clear she had those.

The guard brought her in a few minutes later and he began.

. . .

Two HOURS later she had still refused to sign. Well, more like 'declined'. She'd been exceptionally polite.

He took a break and came back with a fresh mug of tea. His head still ached, despite the little brown pain relievers.

He was going through her files again, trying to find something more he could use, when the door opened. He caught his breath. In walked his superior from the Prosecutor General's Office, complete with a small entourage of Revolutionary Guards.

The greetings were perfunctory. His superior sat down to the side of and slightly behind Rahimi. His men stood at ease near the door.

Feeling his chest tighten, Rahimi nevertheless addressed Fereshteh again, impressing upon her his power over her life and death. Impressing upon her his ability to 'get to' her family.

The most he was able to extract from her infuriating calmness was "Yes, *Aqa*, I know" and "Yes, *Aqa*, you've made that very clear".

If he couldn't persuade her to sign, he'd have to have her executed. But what did that matter? He'd done that to prisoners countless times. And his superior, well, he could see for himself what a stubborn stupid woman this Jalili was. And *he* certainly didn't care if she was executed.

So why was he here? *What's so special about this case that he comes personally to see what's happening? Is it her he's come for? Or is it me?* he wondered. He exhaled deeply and loosened his collar a bit – *why is it so stuffy in this room today?*

Wiping his hands on his trousers, he looked again at the thick file in front of him, not seeing a word. He raised his hand to his forehead. *Why does this pounding not stop, I can't think straight; no; yes; I can — I must think straight... if only I could breathe; this room is so stuffy.* He cleared his throat, and repeated the formula he'd been using: encouraging, then pushing her into signing the prepared recantation of faith. He reiterated that he had the power to free or execute.

"You have a choice, Jalili. What's it going to be? What's more important to you, eh? Don't you worry about your family anymore? Are you just plain stubborn and selfish? Eh?"

Crimson Ink

He considered those last words, spoken so often to so many: 'you have a choice'. What kind of a choice?

The ventilating system rattled for a moment and poured out a few blasts of especially stale air. The clock ticked. His hands were cold and sticky. He made a mental note about his upcoming appointment with the cardiologist. More tests. *Maybe I really should retire?* His thoughts turned to back to 'choice'. What were *his* choices?

...

He opened his shirt collar wider. *Why is it so hard to breathe in this room?* He looked at his prisoner. She knew exactly what her choice today meant. Would she choose to save her family and get out of these walls?

Walls, walls, walls. Gray, dismal walls. He thought of his drive into the hills of Isfahan that day decades ago when he'd decided that he'd had enough of being a civil servant. He'd left that stuffy, cheerless office and sought the breathing space, the clear green expanses and perspectives of the hills, looking ahead to his future.

A discreet cough from the man behind him snapped him back. "So, Jalili, are you just going to sit there? Sign the paper!" Rahimi barked. He heard her murmur something. "What did you say? Speak up! Talk, you foolish woman!"

But he knew all his bluster was for show. He had to be seen to be tough. But all he felt was tired. A heavy exhaustion weighed down his shoulders. It compressed his back and chest. Especially his chest. Dr. Jalili had told him to look after his health, he remembered.

Looking at his blindfolded prisoner again, he saw that her hands were not about to pick up that pen. They rested loosely on the desk. Why had he never noticed before how fine and delicate they were? They seemed so relaxed. Not tense, not resigned. Relaxed. And then he knew his work with her was finished.

He said, "Since you refuse to comply, you leave me with no choice but —"

"*I* will give you one last chance." Rahimi's superior came forward and stood at the prisoner's desk. Rahimi moved well out of the way.

His superior placed his well-manicured hands on the sheet of paper under Fereshteh's eyes. His ring — a very unusual one, Rahimi had always thought — and his spectacular watch clearly within her range of sight, blindfold notwithstanding.

How odd, thought Rahimi. *What's he doing?* He saw Dr. Jalili sit up straighter. Saw her stiffen. She pulled her hands into her lap, squeezing them into balls; pressed her arms tightly against her body.

"I am directing you to sign this paper. Do it. Do it now."

And for a moment, Rahimi thought she would.

Then it occurred to him that maybe his superior had it out for him as well as her. *Trying to show me how it's done and how useless I am. Probably going to demote me.* His heart was palpitating, his breaths short and rapid.

"My patience has its limits, woman. Are you going to sign this or not?"

She trembled and Rahimi held his breath.

She straightened herself further, relaxing her fists. The lines around her lips softened. Her voice was soft but steady. "No, *Aqa*, I'm not."

THE SENTENCING WAS DONE QUICKLY. Rahimi's superior rattled off a list of crimes, confirmed her unrepentant and informed her that she would be hanged the following morning.

AFTER A SHORT, uncomfortable conversation with his superior, Rahimi returned to his office. He stood at the open window, trying to catch a breeze, but the July air refused to move. He switched on the fan on his desk and sat for a long while, playing with a pencil.

The little white pills he'd taken had helped ease the tightening in his chest, but his stomach was churning, adding heartburn to his ailments. He'd have to ask for something for that. And maybe he'd get that inhaler his doctor had prescribed.

He pulled out his wallet and took from it a dog-eared photo. Five cheerful faces looked at him. They'd grown a lot since this photo, he noted. The girls were almost as tall as Zahra now, but in

Crimson Ink

this photo they were still little kids. And Navid, wow! You could hardly recognize him in this picture. He was just a boy then. Just a boy.

Rahimi stood up and went to the small mirror on the back of the door. There was little similarity between the man he saw there and the man in the photo. That guy looked young. That guy smiled. This one? He had a gray head and a lined face. Sallow. Too thin. One that seemed to have forgotten how to laugh.

He walked again to the window and stared out, not seeing anything.

When it came to him at last, he slapped his hands lightly on his thighs, turned and walked purposefully to his desk.

It didn't take long. He'd always kept his work up to date and his files organized. It was a small matter now to categorize and stack the dossiers for the open cases. He lined up a half-dozen or so stacks along the far end of his desk and put another one in the center of his blotter.

He tidied up the drawers and discarded what he could. He placed his few personal items into a couple of plastic shopping bags. He made one last fastidious check. Satisfied, he went out the door and locked the office behind him.

Evin Prison
28 July

She woke early. Well before dawn. An insistent voice called her from far off. Almost a song, its sweetness beckoned her out of sleep. She lay still on her rough blanket and closed her eyes again. She drifted back down into that special world between sleeping and waking, floating in a kind of benevolent opaqueness. The sweet voice beckoned her gently: "Fereshteh? Fereshtehjoon? Fereshteh, my sweet, beautiful sister!"

A translucent swirling mist gave way to Layla's gentle smiling face.

"I failed you, Layla. You deserved a better sister than I've been."

"You've never failed me."

"But I have. Over and over. I could never be —"

"You never had to be —"

"I couldn't even do the last thing you asked me to do. I could not thank, could not give sweets to — could never forgive — the ones who took you, tortured you and killed you."

"Hush, Fereshtehjoon, hush."

The image was fading,

"Laylajoon! Layla, don't go! Forgive me, Layla! Please, Layla!"

Layla was receding. "There's nothing to forgive, Fereshtehjoon. Nothing. I love you, my sister, I love you".

The mist swirled, claiming the last traces of that lovely face. The last thing Fereshteh saw were Layla's eyes: blue and benevolent.

FERESHTEH SAT UP. She called the guard, who obliged her request for the toilet with surprising swiftness. Fereshteh used the time to wash her face and hands thoroughly. In the cracked mirror she smoothed her hair, shoulder length now, and mostly gray.

Back in her cell, she arranged her blankets neatly on the floor and adjusted her shabby top and loose trousers as best she could. She stood, eyes closed, and let her mind and heart settle. Focusing herself, she began her prayers. With every murmured syllable she felt herself transported up and away until the cell around her no longer existed.

SOMETIME LATER, when the guard returned, Fereshteh greeted her. The guard was confused by her prisoner's smile. Didn't she know where she was taking her? What kind of craziness was this?

She handed Fereshteh the blindfold and put on the handcuffs, then led her out of the cell, leaving the grill door open.

IT WAS JUST after 3:30 a.m. when Rahimi unlocked the door to the little room just above the small courtyard. It was not much more than a large closet, really, but its window provided the view he wanted.

The room was airless. It had probably not been used in years, he thought. Forgotten, most likely. He tried to open the window, but the pane hardly budged. He tried the ventilating system and eventually managed to get the ancient knob to turn. It rattled and wheezed, emitting at first a draft of hot malodorous air. Rahimi coughed and had to open the door to get rid of the reek. He wondered if this vent was connected to the basement interrogation rooms.

When the worst of the smell had gone, he closed the door, and dragged one of the hardback chairs over to the window. Checking it for dirt, he gave it a wipe and sat down. He was soon up again, wiping the window pane, using water from the plastic bottle he'd brought for drinking. There was no activity below yet. He looked around the room and noted the chipped paint and grime. Cobwebs hung from the high ceiling corners. He got up and switched off the light.

He checked his watch. Nearly 4:00. The ventilator rattled, then hesitated and gave a cough. He grabbed the cotton handkerchief from his trouser pocket and covered his nose.

He was about to take a drink from his water bottle when he noticed something below.

A guard switched on additional spotlights. He could see the platforms now. He heard voices. Wiping the sweat from his brow, he leaned forward. Still just guards. But more of them filing in.

"Move, move, move," came an order. "Come on, hurry it up!" Rahimi wondered what the hurry was. They still had a couple of hours before their shift was over.

There were two non-uniformed women below. The guards nudged them across the courtyard. One of the women was resisting and it took two guards to finally drag her over to the platform and force her up its steps. The guards held her there by both arms.

The other woman gently shrugged off her guard. She stood tall and walked steadily toward her designated platform. Her guard followed her. Other guards, rifles in hand, stood sentinel around the quadrangle.

The woman climbed the few wooden stairs and stood under the crossbar that held the noose.

Rahimi ignored the struggling of the first woman. He barely heard her protests as the guards placed the noose around her neck.

He saw only the second woman. The spotlight was on her face. Yes, it was her. She's actually an attractive woman. Has a beautiful, kind face, he thought. He felt his chest tighten and he coughed.

She was talking. What could she possibly have to say at this point? Rahimi opened his shirt collar and wheezed.

She was smiling. Smiling? Smiling and talking to her guard, insisting on something. Refusing the blindfold.

Her guard stepped back. "What about the noose?" Rahimi exclaimed in the dark. Then he saw. The prisoner's delicate hands took the noose and placed it over her own head. She stood tall and smiled once more at her guard before looking up at the dawn sky.

JAMSHIDIYEH PARK, NIYAVARAN DISTRICT – TEHRAN
29 JULY

THE BEST WAY Aryana and Taraneh knew to escape the city's oppressive summer heat without going too far was to walk in Jamshidiyeh Park. At the foot of the mountains in north Tehran's elite Niyavaran district, this park was the go-to place for many city dwellers. One of the few places to breathe fresh air and elude the stresses of metropolitan life, visitors immersed themselves in the quiet of the park's forested hill paths. Young and old, Iranian or foreign, people found themselves drawn to the primordial fall of water on stone and the twitters, hums and chirps of Nature's local creatures. The paths were often steep, but had the benefit of being wide, paved with solid blocks of stone and dotted with benches or large boulders to sit on. And because of its extensive footprint, this park could accommodate many without sacrificing the peacefulness that drew them here.

AUNT AND NIECE enjoyed a vigorous climb. They took a smaller, steeper path and moved up the mountain together in comfortable silence, their thoughts stilled and minds taking in only what Nature offered them. Breathing heavily, they eventually paused and wiped their brows. They took sips from their water bottles and surveyed the scene around them. How far up they'd climbed! But as they gazed upward along the path they'd yet to negotiate, they wondered if they'd have the stamina to go the rest of the distance. Finally, finding a pair of suitable large rocks on the side of the path, they decided to sit.

"Strange how all this physical exertion doesn't bother me," said Taraneh. "It's really less demanding than being at home, even when I'm relaxing."

"You're right. I'm tired just now but it feels so much better than everything else in the city."

"How's the job going, by the way?"

"Fine. No problems. We have a good team. Quite a diverse group, really. A few quirky people too, but actually, they're sometimes the ones with the best ideas."

"You never know what lies underneath," smiled Taraneh.

"Yeah, and I guess that's why our CEO hired such people. You know, he's still young, so he's really switched on about the tech sector. He spent a few years in Silicon Valley, actually, then hopped around a bit, working for some really forward-thinking companies before coming back to Iran. I've heard he has some new kind of start-up going on the side. He's such a hustler that I'll bet he makes that a success too."

"So, you're enjoying it."

"Yup. I've got room to expand at this place. All they care about is the work and the creativity. The CEO pretty much lets us work in any way we want. He knows what creative people need in order to bloom."

"But aren't you working long hours? I mean, you must be tired — especially now during the summer."

"Not really. It's fine. I'm used to long hours, but really, as long as we all get our work done, the boss doesn't mind about how long we work."

"What a perk! I wish my boss thought like that!" Taraneh took a few sips from her water bottle. "But still, you're doing even more now for BIHE —"

"Have to pick up the slack. You're doing it too, so…" Aryana checked her shoes and retied the laces. "You know, I don't think it ends with those other profs arrested in June. I'm guessing we'll lose more. There's something nasty in the air."

"You're probably right. Now that it's clear that Habib and the others won't be free for the next few years, we'll need a new backup plan for dealing with additional losses." She swatted a fly. "How about if I reach out to some of the others? Very discreetly, of course."

"Good idea. Let me know if I can help." Aryana stood up and stretched. Taking one more sip of water, she packed the bottle into her rucksack and said, "Now, where to?"

---

30 July

ARYANA OPENED the apartment door quietly and Taraneh stepped in. Neither spoke.

They sat in stillness on the sofa, leaning on each other, grasping hands. They would hear the condolences and well-meant platitudes from others soon enough. Right now, though, all they wanted was the silence of each other's loving presence.

After all, there was really nothing to say.

IN A CERTAIN SENSE, having expected the worst, they had been grieving for months already. All the frustration and anger they had occasionally succumbed to as they processed the injustice of it all, had expended itself — at least for now — into exhaustion.

Tomorrow they would collect Fereshteh's body. They would, with a friend or two, gently wash her, dress, perfume and shroud her. Place her, sprinkled with rose petals, into a respectable casket, and bury her discreetly.

There would be time enough after that for everything else.

Chapter Nine

2011

AUGUST

2 August

The charcoal gray Peugeot 607 was next in line at the pump. With a small trailer in tow, it nevertheless claimed a large space, no doubt encouraging other drivers coming in to choose the set of pumps on the other side of the station.

When the Peugeot at last pulled up to the pump the driver emerged, his slight frame agitated as he fumbled with the pump handle.

"Hey! Salaam, Aqay-e Rahimi! Let me give you a hand with that." The station's owner gave him a generous smile and Rahimi returned one somewhat less broad.

"Salaam, Aqay-e Firdowsian. Thank you. By the way, I'd like to get a few extra things: a few liters of water, some wiper fluid, a couple of liters of oil… oh, and an extra canister of fuel."

"Sure thing. I'll get those ready for you."

When Firdowsian returned with the items, he found Rahimi filling the tires.

"So, what's up? You've got a trailer, huh? Taking a little vacation with the family?" He nodded briefly and politely to the passengers.

When Rahimi didn't respond immediately, Firdowsian remarked, "Work's been hard, huh? I can see it in your face, *Aqa*. I see it a lot in the summer. You know, people are tired from the heat. The long days. So much stress everywhere, don't you think? It's good to get away." He smiled again and looked at the trailer. "So, a little vacation, eh?"

"Let's just say, it's going to be an extended stay." Rahimi removed the handle and closed the fuel cap, then handed Firdowsian a wad of notes.

He drove south out of Niyavaran along the undeviating stretch of Pasdaran St. and got onto first the Sadr and then the Babaei Expressways, heading east until they came to the connection of the Tehran-Pardis Freeway. Winding up into the cooler foothill towns, they veered off to the north east, taking the zigzagging 77 north, towards Amol and the Caspian Sea.

Window down and relaxing gradually over the hours, Kamran Rahimi drove his family around the twists and turns, and along the rises and dips that made up the long tortuous route up the craggy slopes, then up over the high crest and down the other side into the gentle green slopes beyond.

---

3 August

EARLIER IN THEIR marriage Nikou hadn't been interested in what her husband called his "special guests". He'd entertain them, and Nikou, with assistance from caterers, would act out her expected role and provide the lavish refreshments or meals. But she'd done it with the same indifference as when she'd helped her mother host her father's guests at home. Early on in life Nikou had learned from her father never to ask questions "about matters and people who don't concern you". So she'd set aside her curiosity and performed the tasks assigned to her.

When she was about 9 or 10 years old, her job had been to wash and peel the vegetables and fruits and to set the tables. As she'd gained skill, she'd been entrusted with the chopping and slicing, and preparing the dishes of fresh green herbs. She'd also learned to make simple desserts. By the time she'd reached her mid-teens, she was helping with the actual cooking.

They'd always had a housekeeper, of course, but Nikou's mother had insisted on preparing all the food, knowing well that as Nikou grew into her adult role, she would steadily assume a greater share of the preparation and occasionally create a dish or two of her own. She had to learn, after all.

And there had been plenty of opportunities. Majid entertained guests regularly and his expectations of Samira and Nikou were high.

Nikou's brothers, Atesh and Salman, being older and being boys, had of course been allowed to be present at some of the men's gatherings. All they had to do was dress appropriately, show up, and behave with the courtesy required of observers. This was their introduction to the world of business and its leaders.

Now it was Nikou's year to learn. Now she paid careful attention to everything that Mehrdad did. And when it came to invited guests, she even asked a few innocent questions. If he was in an expansive or self-satisfied mood, he occasionally answered her.

The odd thing about Mehrdad, Nikou thought, was his vanity. He certainly could have every event held at their home catered. And he could hire male waiters. Instead, he chose to have her do the serving. He expected her to do this even if she had caterers helping in the kitchen. It was her job to restock the bowls of nuts, dried fruits or sweets, serve hors d'oeuvres, put the dishes or platters on the table, refill the samovar, the water or other drinks, and serve the dessert. She was to act the part of the charming but unassuming Woman of the House in welcoming guests, serving and seeing to their needs, but speaking only when necessary. And yet, at the same time, he expected her to be modestly but always elegantly dressed, even down to her designer headscarf. Her make-up had to be discreet but also perfectly enhance her natural beauty. And she was to wear her expensive jewelry.

More recently, her husband's "special guests" included names and faces she recognized. Being in the higher echelons of power, these were men that the news media kept in the public eye. For them to accept a home invitation from Mehrdad could only mean that his position in The Judiciary (she still thought of it in capital letters) had risen yet again. He must be very close to the top — although she had no real idea about what that meant. But she knew intuitively that sometimes the most powerful men were the least visible. Mehrdad did not personally get media coverage. So if the visible and invisible were meeting together, then…

But she banished these thoughts. Today she had an agenda and she needed all her focus on that.

Short of putting a GPS collar on her, Mehrdad had used technology against her, keeping her watched and tracked in every way possible. Today she would use it against him.

Her chosen device was dead simple. A friend of a friend of a friend had provided her with a tiny but powerful voice recorder that could pick up speech at a distance of 30 feet.

It was not her primary intention to use it to spy on her husband's high-level meetings with the elite. She wasn't yet sure what she would do with that kind of information, though at some point it might well come in handy.

Today her needs were personal. She wanted information that was potentially going to affect *her*. She wanted to know what neither her husband nor any of the men in her family were telling her. What even Sohayla didn't know. She wanted to know what they were thinking and what information they might have about Fereshteh and Habib and the work they'd been doing before they got arrested. They never answered her questions, no matter how discreetly and innocently formulated. For her own sake, she needed to know "the lay of the land"; what, if anything, might be coming down the road in her direction or might be important for Aryana and Taraneh to know.

This afternoon's meeting was for significant family members only: Rashid, Aqajoon Reza, her father and his two brothers, Farid and Saeed. The fact that her brothers and male cousins were not invited - perhaps still too young? - gave her an odd sense of gratification.

The planning was simple: Tea and refreshments for the meeting. Dinner afterwards.

Since they didn't want to be disturbed during their consultations, she arranged two large samovars and large pots of tea on a convenient sideboard and loaded the coffee table with plates of all their favorite delicacies and fruits. They hardly needed to move to reach anything. They could fully concentrate on their discussion. Perfect.

Later, they'd move to the dining room for dinner and she could clean up in the meeting room, uninterrupted.

HAVING CHOSEN the spot with care, and ever-mindful of the room's cameras, Nikou put the tiny device in place, just before the guests' arrival. Her husband was going to the door to personally welcome them. A last look at the room, a final adjustment to the fresh flowers in the Chinese vase. Nikou was satisfied.

WHILE THE MEN in the dining room were seriously settling down to the main course, Nikou went into the meeting room to clean up.

She brought everything into the kitchen for the housekeeper to sort and wash, then went back to get the flowers to move them to the living room. Before putting the beautiful vase with its mass of large blooms on the coffee table, she removed the recorder and tucked it into her pocket.

4 AUGUST

николи walked deep into Mellat Park. From the usual flowers, ponds and trees, to the areas to eat and play, to the possibilities to sample local artists' works spread on pop-up tables, stroll through a formal art gallery or see films at its huge glass and steel Cineplex, it offered something for everyone, which made it one of the most popular parks in Tehran.

She walked purposefully but at a moderate pace so as not to attract attention. She passed families with their energetic offspring, all anxious to get to the ducks and water birds or to romp in the playgrounds. She glanced at strolling couples and chadored old women resting on benches. She ignored the lines of tables where street artists demonstrated their expertise and sold their wares; neither the calligraphers nor artisans working in paints, tiles or cloth succeeded in distracting her.

She sped up her pace whenever she saw lone walkers, adjusting her large sunglasses and pulling her headscarf more closely around her face. She knew her monitor would be near, and although she thought she knew which one he was, she considered that there might be more than one. She realized she was becoming slightly paranoid, but given what was at stake, she had doubled her precautions.

Selecting at last a small stretch of lawn between a large flower bed and a pond, she spread out a light cotton cloth and sat down. Her earpiece was in place under her scarf and the recorder secure under her summer *manteau*. Looking out onto the water, she pressed "play" and settled in to listen.

As expected, much of the recording contained the usual courtesies and banter that were a part of any get-together in their family. Finally, the men got down to their purpose.

They were ironing out the details, snags and logistics of an intricate business deal. It seemed that the Guard and the government — *Is there a difference anymore?* Nikou wondered — were awarding yet another new contract to the family's now vast construction business.

Rashid (now an ayatollah) also was involved, apparently representing the interests of those even further up the clerical ladder. Saeed, for his part, represented his old cronies from the Guard.

Mehrdad was there, of course, to ensure the legality and furtherance of it all — and perhaps receive a little something for his efforts to smooth the way? Her father? Well, she could almost hear him rubbing his hands together.

The others' comments expressed a level of self-satisfaction that Nikou found disturbing. She'd liked to think that they might at least make an effort to obtain such contracts on merit. But evidently not. There seemed to be some tacit understanding that these were more like favors served up to them as the loyal friends they'd chosen to become. All the expediency and direct dealing as good as anything the corporate corruption of the hated "West" could dish out.

She sighed and listened patiently for what she really wanted to hear. Then, business finally concluded, the talk turned to the clatter and chatter of taking more tea and refreshments. When they finally settled down, laughing at a few jokes, she heard her grandfather's voice. Nikou groaned.

"Well," Reza said, between bites of the tasty morsels Nikou had prepared, "it's done at last. That infernal niece of mine has finally gotten what she's always deserved. Had you heard yet?" He was apparently asking his sons, who mumbled their ignorance of the matter.

"Thanks to Mehrdad, that troublesome Fereshteh is no more."

Nikou stopped and backed up the recording to listen to it again. So. Eyes filled to overflowing, she stared out at the water, the dreaded news blurring the view of the preening ducks.

Fereshteh had been executed. Mehrdad had arranged it. She let the tears fall a while, then blew her nose and pressed "play" again.

"Anyway, you know how much I loved my sister and because of that, I always tried to help her and her ungrateful children to return to the True Faith." Nikou could imagine him looking pointedly at his friend Rashid.

"But no. They remained stuck in their religion. As Baha'is who refuse to change, they should die," he pontificated. "I'm glad that was the verdict of the good judge." He was chewing again, but swallowed quickly and went on.

"I even helped them materially for a while," he boasted. I spoke to Farah but she wouldn't listen. She spoiled those kids. Habib was away, of course, but I spoke to the two girls, hoping they'd see what danger they were playing with. Well, Layla got herself killed early. She turned out to be a wild uncontrollable thing too. Very unwise right from the start of the blessed Revolution. Habib, well, actually he's a good man. Decent. Polite. Always tried to smooth things over in the family, didn't he, Majid? Eh, Farid? Took you under his wing, he did, and when you were very young, too. Yes, yes. And nice to you, too, right, Saeed?" More murmurings of agreement.

"But he had this thing about education." Another grunt. "And what was really unpardonable was his getting involved in that Baha'i education thing. You know — what's it called, Saeed?"

"Baha'i Institute for Higher Education."

"Right. Right. Well, of course I had to say something to you, Mehrdad. I mean I hadn't realized he'd been involved for some time already, but — . Anyway, it's done and maybe after a few years in Evin he'll figure out what side he needs to be on, eh, Mehrdad?"

Her husband agreed.

There was sipping of tea. Some chewing.

Aqajoon Reza had the floor now and although no one said a thing, Nikou knew well that everyone would bite their tongues and tolerate the rest of the rant. They understood it was best to just let him talk himself out.

But as she listened, Nikou had all she could do to hold her stomach in check. He went on and on. His old gripes about the role of women, his views on education, marriage, activism…

Although Nikou had heard this since she could remember, it was only now that she truly registered the degree of his hatred and felt the sting of its venom. Only now saw with crystal clarity the source of the poison in her family. Only now realized that her own grandfather had been the originator of all that she'd endured for the entire 23 years of her life.

She stopped the recording again and reflected on the contrast between him and his family, and Farah and hers. How could it have taken her this long to see the difference for what it was?

She let her thoughts go to the women in her family. Picturing her grandmother Sohayla, her anger softened for a moment. How she loved that gentle soul! She must be a saint to have lived with that odious patriarch all her life!

She thought about her aunts, Mitra and Gita. They'd always parroted their father's opinions and conformed to his ideals. But as she looked back, she saw how they'd actually been pushed into a corner and had stayed there because it had just been easier. As little vignettes of their lives came into Nikou's mind, she began to recognize the patronizing remarks, the unreasonable expectations and the loaded admonitions. And the greatest of all hypocrisies was that none of what any of them had suffered had actually had anything to do with "religion" at all. It was a warped sense of gender roles and a matter of power and control.

She restarted the recording. "…Yes, and Fereshteh got involved with all those activists — those, those, protesters. Well I'm glad she's dead!"

"Yes, Baba, I think we all agree with that," Saeed interjected, obviously anxious to move the conversation on to other topics. "After the elections it was very difficult to bring order back. But we did. That was never in question. But it did waste a lot of time and resources. Then there was the video of that girl Neda getting shot that went viral. We've been working on ways to prevent such things in the future."

"Oh yes? Such as?" Farid wanted to know.

"Well, we've been discussing limiting Internet access. You know, creating a kind of "Intranet" for Iran. Something we'd have control over. There's some other legislation in the pipeline. I don't know how long it will take, mind you. The Majlis has so much to do and there's a backlog of proposals. But anyway, among other things, we're looking at the problem of too much university access for women — just what you like to hear, Baba, isn't it?" They all laughed.

"We're planning to restrict the number and type of courses that women can take. Some statistics indicate that more women than men are at university and we need to rectify that." Murmurs of approval.

Crimson Ink

"And then there are family issues that we're looking at. For example, there's a proposal to make it possible for men to marry their adopted or step-daughters. You know, there's been some difficulty because of so-called "blended families". Unfortunately, the divorce rate is climbing and men are now marrying divorced women or widows with children. It's awkward with the hijab at home, since the men are not the girls' fathers. A marriage would eliminate that problem. But, we'll see. There is resistance to this, so it may not be passed."

"Well," Mehrdad joined in, "you and I can talk more about that. I know a number of people who might be interested in these matters. Perhaps we can have a separate meeting with the relevant committee? I can arrange it, if you like."

"Certainly. I'll leave it to you."

The men had started to stir. Mehrdad announced that dinner would be served shortly, but in the meantime how about a walk in the garden to stretch their legs?

When Nikou was sure that the recording was over she stopped the device. She shifted her position and sat hugging her knees, digesting what she'd heard. She thought of Habib and imagined him languishing in prison, and how that affected his family; of Fereshteh, and of how she — Nikou — had contributed to that tragedy. Poor Fereshteh, whose only "crime" – besides her religion – had been to minister to the needs of the sick and injured, to help the oppressed and abused!

Nikou's tears ran freely and her shoulders shook. It had all been for nothing! Nothing! Fereshteh had been executed for nothing and if it wasn't bad enough already, it was going to get worse for women.

Nikou rewound the thought: Fereshteh had been executed. Mehrdad had arranged it. It was only going to get worse for women. For her. A man with his power will use it.

Anger washed away the sadness. A sense of justice replaced her remorse. *No. My cousin will not have died for nothing. It's time. My time. I'm leaving.* If ever she'd had reservations about this, they'd been obliterated by what she'd just heard. She knew her path now. Thanks to that telephone number Fereshteh had managed to burn into her brain and the first woman she'd called and met secretly in the café, she now had the contacts she needed. She had money. She had phones. And even a computer. She'd get out. And get working for justice.

With a resolve she hardly recognized, she pulled out her "burn phone" and punched in the number.

Glossary

Apostate = a person who renounces a religious or political belief or principle. In the Islamic Republic, a crime against God.

Ayatollah = a high-ranking title given to Usuli Twelver Shī'ah clerics. Those who carry the title are experts in Islamic studies such as jurisprudence, Quran reading, and philosophy and usually teach in Islamic seminaries. The next lower clerical rank is Hujjat al-Islam {see below} (Wikipedia).

Basij = the force consists of young Iranians who volunteer, often in exchange for official benefits. Basij serve as an auxiliary force engaged in activities such as internal security, law enforcement auxiliary, providing social services, organizing public religious ceremonies, policing morals, and suppression of dissident gatherings. The force is named Basij; an individual member is called a basiji. The Basij are subordinate to and receive their orders from the Iranian Revolutionary Guards and the Supreme Leader of Iran to whom they are known for their loyalty. They have a local organization in almost every city in Iran. (Wikipedia)

Chador = the head-to-toe covering (often black) prescribed historically in Islam to preserve women's modesty when outdoors or in the presence of non-family men. For a period of time, its use was

Glossary

discouraged and even banned under the Pahlavi shahs of the 20th century. Its use became obligatory again during the Iranian Revolution of 1979.

Hujjat-al-Islam = is an honorific title meaning "authority on Islam" or "proof of Islam" (Wikipedia). In Shi'a Islam it has historically been applied to recognized scholars of Islam.

Imams = **1:** the prayer leader of a mosque; **2:** *a Muslim leader of the line of Ali held by Shiites to be the divinely appointed, sinless, infallible successors of Muhammad;* **3:** any of various rulers that claim descent from Muhammad and exercise spiritual and temporal leadership over a Muslim region (Merriam-Webster Dictionary).

Islamic Revolutionary Guard Corps (IRGC) = (The Army of Guardians of the Islamic Revolution) is a branch of Iran's Armed Forces founded after the 1979 Revolution [22 April 1979] by order of Ayatollah Khomeini. Whereas the regular military defends Iran's borders and maintains internal order, according to the Iranian constitution, the Revolutionary Guard is intended to protect the country's Islamic Republic System. The Revolutionary Guards state that their role in protecting the Islamic system is preventing foreign interference as well as coups by the military or "deviant movements". (Wikipedia)

Manteau = a coat; often worn instead of the chador to preserve modest dress prescribed for women in Iran since the Revolution.

Mehdi = (Mahdi, meaning "the guided one") is an eschatological redeemer of Islam who, according to some Islamic traditions, will appear and rule for five, seven, nine, or nineteen years (according to differing interpretations) before the Day of Judgment, and rid the world of evil. There is no direct reference to the Mahdi in the Quran, only in the *hadith* (the reports and traditions of Muhammad's teachings collected after his death). (Wikipedia)

Mofsed fel-arz = the crime of "sowing corruption on earth", for which the penalty is death, includes enmity against God... Pursuant to the old code, prosecutors for the most part limited the charges of enmity against God and sowing corruption to individuals suspected of engaging in terrorist-related activities (or being "affiliated with"

Glossary

terrorist organizations)... [In 2012] Legislators... greatly expanded the definition of this crime, which was previously largely limited to prosecuting individuals alleged to be involved in armed resistance or terrorism against the state, to include an even broader set of ill-defined activities, such as "publish[ing] lies," "operat[ing] or manag[ing] centers of corruption or prostitution," or "damag[ing] the economy of the country" if these actions are deemed to "seriously disturb the public order and security of the nation." Furthermore, because this crime is considered a "crime against God" for which shari'a law assigns fixed and specific punishments... Judges (and even the Supreme Leader of the Islamic Republic) are, in contravention of international law, generally precluded from granting convicts pardons or commuting their sentences. (Excerpted from Human Rights Watch - hrw.org - 29 August 2012.)

Mujahedin-e-Khalq = The People's Mojahedin Organization of Iran, or the Mojahedin-e Khalq, abbreviated MEK, PMOI or MKO, is an Iranian political-militant organization based on Islamic and socialist ideology. It advocates overthrowing the Islamic Republic of Iran leadership and installing its own government. It was the "first Iranian organization to develop systematically a modern revolutionary interpretation of Islam – an interpretation that differed sharply from both the old conservative Islam of the traditional clergy and the new populist version formulated in the 1970s by Ayatollah Khomeini and his government". The MEK is considered the Islamic Republic of Iran's biggest and most active political opposition group. (Wikipedia)

Mullah = The term is most often applied to Shi'ite clerics and is the name commonly given to local Islamic clerics or mosque leaders.

Najjess = Things or persons regarded as ritually unclean.

Naw-Ruz = Traditional Persian New Year, which starts with the Spring Equinox (20 – 21 March, according to the Gregorian calendar). Celebrated by all Iranians, regardless of religious background, festivities last 13 days.

Nonahalan Company = Established by the Baha'is in the early 20th Century, they would invest their savings in this bank and buy

Glossary

shares, as in a cooperative. If an investor needed assistance he could get help, or could get a loan to buy a house. Right after the Revolution, the Nonahalan Company was confiscated and anyone who had bought a house using a loan from the company had their home confiscated and loan recalled.

Ramadan = the Muslim month of fasting. No food or drink is taken between dawn and sunset. Following the Lunar calendar, its dates change each year.

SAVAK = the secret police, domestic security and intelligence service in Iran during the reign of the Pahlavi dynasty. It was established by Mohammad Reza Shah with the help of the U.S. Central Intelligence Agency and the Israeli MOSSAD. (Wikipedia)

Shahnameh = "The Book of Kings"), is a long epic poem written by the Persian poet Ferdowsi between c. 977 and 1010 CE and is the national epic of Greater Iran… the Shahnameh is the world's longest epic poem written by a single poet. It tells mainly the mythical and to some extent the historical past of the Persian Empire from the creation of the world until the Islamic conquest of Persia in the 7th century. Modern Iran, Azerbaijan, Afghanistan and the greater region influenced by the Persian culture celebrate this national epic.

The work is of central importance in Persian culture, regarded as a literary masterpiece, and definitive of the ethno-national cultural identity of modern-day Iran, Afghanistan and Tajikistan. (Wikipedia)

Shi'a Islam = the branch of Islam that believes that Ali is designated as the Heir, Imam and caliph of Muhammad and also that Ali's authority continues through his descendants (the *Imams* - see above). For the Shia, this conviction is implicit in the Quran and history of Islam. Shia scholars emphasize that the notion of authority is linked to the family of the prophets. The vast majority of Muslims in Iran are Shi'as and the Islamic Republic is based on Shi'a doctrine. (See Wikipedia.)

Sunni Islam = the branch of Islam that believes that Muhammad did not appoint a successor and consider Abu Bakr (who was appointed Caliph through a Shura, i.e. community

Glossary

consensus) to be the correct first Caliph (ruler regarded as the successor of Muhammad). (Wikipedia). Sunnis are a minority in Iran but constitute the vast majority of Muslims in the world.

Sigheh = a "temporary marriage" allowed under Islamic law. No divorce is necessary; instead, the marriage is done by a time-specified contract that sets out conditions e.g. whether a sexual relationship is part of this arrangement or not; and a specific duration. Any children of the relationship must be supported by the father. The mother does not get support. The woman is free to marry again after 3 months if there has been a sexual relationship.

Supreme Leader = In its history, the Islamic Republic has had two Supreme Leaders: Ruhollah Khomeini, who held the position from 1979 until his death in 1989, and Ali Khamenei, who has held the position since Khomeini's death. In theory, the Supreme Leader is appointed and supervised by the Assembly of Experts. (Wikipedia)

Ta'arof = refers to "an Iranian form of civility emphasizing both deference and social rank. It encompasses a range of social behaviors... The prevalence of ta'arof often gives rise to distinctly Iranian styles of negotiation... Ta'arof also governs the rules of hospitality: a host is obliged to offer anything a guest might want, and a guest is equally obliged to refuse it. This ritual may repeat itself several times (three times) before the host and guest finally determine whether the host's offer and the guest's refusal are real or simply polite.

Ta'arof plays a large role in the etiquette of food. If you go to any meal, are invited to any house for food, then you will be expected to eat seconds and thirds. You must eat to please the host but at the same time ta'arof demands that you can't just go ahead and dig into the food once you are done with your first round. Good manners dictate that you have to pretend you are full, the food was excellent and that it would be impossible to fit anything else in. Your host will then demand you do not do ta'arof ("ta'arof nakon") – you say 'no' 2 or 3 times and then you pretend you have caved into their insistence and pile on the food. If you do it any other way, you can come across as either starving or simply a bit uncouth." (Wikipedia)

Velayat-e faqih = The intellectual and theoretical foundation of the Islamic Republic is based on the views and theories of Ayatollah Khomeini and the constitution, as the legal and administrative structure founded on those views and theories. In other words, intellectually and theoretically speaking, Velayat-e Faqih is an absolute power, and politically speaking, it encompasses the constitution. The constitution is composed within a legal framework born out of the Shari'a, which according to qualified Islamic jurists, is obtained from the Book (Koran) and Sunna (tradition). The Velayat-e Faqih, then, is the symbol of Islamic jurisprudence. In this light, Shari'a laws are considered as the foundation, and the constitution built on that foundation. (From Hamid Hamidi in Iran Human Rights Review, October 2010.)

Yaran = literally, Friends in Iran: Seven members of the Iranian Baha'i community whose purpose was to tend to the spiritual and social needs of the 300,000-member community. This group was formed specifically for these purposes only because all the regular structures for the administrative, social and spiritual needs of the community had been banned by the Islamic Republic. The 9 members of their national administration were "disappeared" in 1979 and the 9 who replaced them were executed by firing squad in December of 1981. The Yaran were arrested and imprisoned in 2008 with sentences of 20 years. For the first year they were denied access to any legal counsel. Subsequently, their sentences were reduced to 10 years, in line with the new 2013 Penal Code. Refer to https://www.bic.org/focus-areas/situation-iranian-bahais/current-situation

Persian Words and Phrases

Family relations:
    Aqa - Mr. / Sir
    Khanum - Mrs. / Madam
    Maman - Mama / Mom
    Baba - Papa / Dad / Daddy
    Pedarbozorg — grandfather
    Aqajan / Aqajoon - used in some families to say "Grandpa"
    Khanumjan / Khanumjoon - used in some families to say "Grandma"
    Dayi - maternal uncle
    —Jan or *—joon*, meaning "dear", is very often appended to family names, and names of friends: e.g. Mamanjan or Mamanjoon, Aqajan or Aqajoon, Laylajan or Laylajoon, Habibjan or Habibjoon etc.

Words of endearment:
    Azizam - dear, darling, sweetheart
    Janam / Joonam - "my dear"
    Asalam - "my sweet one" / "honey"

Persian Words and Phrases

Food and Drink:

Estekan - tiny glassware used for drinking tea

Samovar - a large tea urn; used to boil water, which pours from a spout at the bottom. A teapot sits on the top, kept warm by the steam. The tea is very strong and is meant to be diluted to taste with the boiling water.

Ash-e-rishte — a thick noodle soup

Bademjan — eggplant

Chelow-kebab — more or less a national dish: fragrant long-grain plain rice served with either beef, lamb or chicken kebabs. The kebabs are either in cubes of meat or strips of ground meat. Garnished with grilled tomatoes and sometimes a raw egg in the center of the rice; seasoned with somagh, a purplish, pungent coarsely ground spice.

Ghormeh-sabzie — a khoresh made of green herbs and vegetables, with kidney beans and cubes of meat

Kafgir — a serving spatula for rice.

Khoresh — a stew made with vegetables and meat and / or split peas or beans; Khoresh is served over long-grain steamed rice and is typical Iranian fare.

Kubideh — a type of kebab made with ground beef or lamb

Kuku-Sabzie — a firm green omelet of herbs

Polo / polo khoresh — long-grain rice steamed in the typical Persian style and served with a stew

Sabzijat — plated fresh green herbs to accompany a meal

Sharbat — juice

Shirini — sweets

Tahdigh — literally, 'bottom of the pot'; rice or thinly sliced potatoes crisped in oil at the bottom of a pot of rice; typically much-appreciated and often served on a separate serving dish.

Note:

"Daste-shoma dard na-koneh" — (literally, "may your hand not give you pain") is used where one might say, "Thank you so much for all the trouble you went to." There is no exact English equivalent. This and many other self-deprecating expressions, such as *"Ghorban-e-*

shoma" / *"Ghorbanet beram"* (literally, "May I be sacrificed for you") are used to express thanks, appreciation, or even humility after being complimented or thanked). Although sounding hyperbolic to westerners, such expressions are used all the time and in various circumstances as part of maintaining good relationships with others.

Select References for further reading

There are innumerable books, websites, articles, and YouTube videos concerning Iran, ranging from Wikipedia-based information on every aspect of the country, its history and culture, to mainstream as well as controversial political and religious sites. Of particular interest to the reader of this book might be the following:

A reference explaining the festival of Naw Ruz. Very readable and entertaining, complete with photographs:

https://www.vox.com/culture/2018/3/19/17138516/persian-new-year-nowruz-explained

References to persecution and torture:
The Seven Martyrs of Hurmuzak, by Muhammad Habib, translated by Dr. Moojan Momen. George Ronald Publishing, Ltd, 1982

https://www.youtube.com/watch?v=MIj0OJvVW9k
This one gives a brief overview of tribunals held in Europe to review what transpired in the "Bloody Decade" of the 1980s:
https://www.youtube.com/watch?v=jJwrCL-kqzs
The Chapter 17 interview of "Rana" is closely based on an

Select References for further reading

actual YouTube video. The young woman in that video remains anonymous. She states that she consented to her interview for precisely the same reasons as "Rana". Here are the links:
https://www.iranhumanrights.org/2011/06/rape-and-torture-video-testimony/

https://www.youtube.com/watch?v=2dpQgBH37HM
https://www.youtube.com/watch?v=aMFVt2l9pto

Documentaries on the Iran-Iraq war: This example is in 3 parts:
https://www.youtube.com/watch?v=bdO9h_5Nupk

Information on BIHE (Baha'i Institute for Higher Education):
www.bihe.org
www.educationunderfire.com

General information relating to the Baha'i Faith and its beliefs:
The official Baha'i website provides these:www.bahai.org

Other useful links:
https://www.bic.org/focus-areas/situation-iranian-bahais/current-situation
http://iranpresswatch.org/post/category/yaran/

A useful and informative interview with Human Rights lawyer Shirin Ebadi and statements by Ayatollah Hossein Ali Montazeri regarding the Baha'is and how they should be treated. Montazeri defends their rights. Neither person is a Baha'i.
https://www.youtube.com/watch?v=jqkzJOy_1WE

Organizations:
Iran Human Rights Documentation Center Iranhrdc.org
Justice for Iran https://justice4iran.org
Human Rights Watch Hrw.org
Amnesty International Amnesty.org
Baha'i International Community Bic.org

Acknowledgments

This book is a work of fiction, but it is closely based on actual events that took place in Iran over many decades.

The incident described in the hamlet of Hurmuzak actually occurred as described, although Munirih and Esfandiar are my own fictitious observers. Many thanks to Muhammad Labib (and Dr. Moojan Momen, translator) for this moving account in "The Seven Martyrs of Hurmuzak".

The clergy's incitement of the general population in Iran in 1955 against the Baha'i community is well-documented by both Muslim and Baha'i sources and media. The Hujjat-al-Islam Falsafi was a real cleric whose vitriolic speeches were broadcasted during Ramadan 1955.

The street protests, the Islamic Revolution, Black Friday, the American hostage-taking, the establishment of the Revolutionary Guard, Basij militia, and local "*Komitehs*", are all real events and institutions.

Ayatollah Khomeini was the first Supreme Leader of the Islamic

Revolution and his image is still found on huge building murals, posters and pictures in Iran.

The 2009 election protests and violent repression afterwards, including the videoed death of Neda Agha-Soltan were real events. Descriptions of the types of torture, detention centers and prisons are based on testimony from survivors of these. The recorded interview of "Rana", the young woman detained, repeatedly raped and abused, is closely based on the words of a real-life victim of those circumstances who posted her interview on YouTube.

The U.N. Special Rapporteur for Iran in 1993 was real and his report on the plan to systematically destroy the Baha'i community in Iran and elsewhere is available in the public domain.

Descriptions of the social and economic restrictions on Baha'is, harassment, persecution, imprisonment, torture, and execution of them in Iran are all based on facts and data in the public domain.

The BIHE (Baha'i Institute for Higher Education) still exists and the story of its members' arrests is based on actual events.

Shirin Ebadi is one of a number of real Iranian women who are or have been Human Rights lawyers. None of these are Baha'is. Ms. Ebadi lives in exile and remains active in her work on behalf of many clients. She was awarded the Nobel Peace Prize in 2003 for her work in helping women and children.

In the Reference section I've included some links, but there are hundreds of articles on the Internet that document all of the above.

The remaining characters are fictional, but some are composites of actual people. The story of Layla's imprisonment and execution, for example, is based on actual events involving 10 young Baha'i women at that time.

As I have taken some small liberties and "literary license" with facts, locations and events, any errors or inaccuracies in that regard are my own.

I owe an enormous debt of gratitude to the journalists, authors and videographers whose research and works enabled me to flesh out the storyline I had in mind. And most especially, I honor those individuals whose stories of suffering, resilience and survival, and of ultimate sacrifice were the motivating force for writing this book. This book is theirs.

— Gail Madjzoub
October, 2019

Made in the USA
Lexington, KY
19 November 2019